The English Assassin

Daniel Silva

The English Assassin

WHEELER
PUBLISHING, INC.
ROCKLAND, MA

★ AN AMERICAN COMPANY ★

Published in large print by arrangement with G. P. Putnam's Sons, a member of Penguin Putnam Inc., in the United States and Canada.

Wheeler Large Print Book Series.

Set in 16 pt Plantin.

Library of Congress Cataloging-in-Publication Data

Silva, Daniel, 1960-
   The English assassin / Daniel Silva.
      p. (large print) cm. (Wheeler large print book series)
   ISBN 1-58724-185-4 (hardcover)
   1. Intelligence officers—Fiction. 2. Israelis—Switzerland—Fiction.
3. Art—Collectors and collecting—Fiction. 4. Zèrich (Switzerland)—
Fiction. 5. Art thefts—Fiction. 6. Assassins—Fiction. 7. Large type
books. I. Title. II. Series.

[PR6069.I362 E54   2002]
823'.914—dc21   2002016783
                                                                        CIP

To Phyllis Grann, finally,
and as always, for my wife, Jamie,
and my children, Lily and Nicholas.

gnome[1] (nōm) *n. Folklore* any of a race of small, misshapen, dwarflike beings, supposed to dwell in the earth and guard its treasures

WEBSTER'S NEW WORLD DICTIONARY

"Suppressing the past is a tradition in Switzerland."

JEAN ZIEGLER
THE SWISS, THE GOLD, AND THE DEAD

Prologue

SWITZERLAND
1975

*M*ARGUERITE ROLFE WAS DIGGING IN HER *garden because of the secrets she'd found hidden in her husband's study. It was late to be working in the garden, well past midnight by now. The spring thaw had left the earth soft and moist, and her spade split the soil with little effort, allowing her to progress with minimal noise. For this she was grateful. Her husband and daughter were asleep in the villa, and she didn't want to wake them.*

Why couldn't it have been something simple, like love letters from another woman? There would have been a good row, Marguerite would have confessed her own affair. Lovers would have been relinquished, and soon their home would return to normal. But she hadn't found love letters—she'd found something much worse.

For a moment she blamed herself. If she hadn't been searching his study, she never would have found the photographs. She could have spent the rest of her life in blissful oblivion, believing her husband was the man he appeared to be. But now she knew. Her husband was a monster, his life a lie—a complete and meticulously maintained lie. Therefore she too was a lie.

Marguerite Rolfe concentrated on her work, making slow and steady progress. After an hour it was done. A good hole, she decided: about six feet in length and two feet across. Six inches below the surface she had encountered a dense layer of clay. As a result it was a bit shallower than she would have preferred. It didn't matter. She knew it wasn't permanent.

She picked up the gun. It was her husband's

3

favorite weapon, a beautiful shotgun, hand-crafted for him by a master gunsmith in Milan. He would never be able to use it again. This pleased her. She thought of Anna. Please don't wake up, Anna. Sleep, my love.

Then she stepped into the ditch, lay down on her back, placed the end of the barrel in her mouth, pulled the trigger.

THE GIRL WAS AWAKENED BY MUSIC. SHE DID NOT recognize the piece and wondered how it had found its way into her head. It lingered a moment, a descending series of notes, a serene diminishment. She reached out, eyes still closed, and searched the folds of the bedding until her palm found the body which lay a few inches away. Her fingers slipped over the narrow waist, up the slender, elegant neck, toward the graceful curved features of the scroll. Last night they had quarreled. Now it was time to set aside their differences and make peace.

She eased from the bed, pulled on a dressing gown. Five hours of practice stretched before her. Thirteen years old, a sun-drenched June morning, and this was how she would spend her day—and every other day that summer.

Stretching the muscles of her neck, she gazed out the window at the flowering garden. It was a melee of spring color. Beyond the garden rose the steep slope of the valley wall. High above it all loomed the snow-capped mountain peaks, glittering in the bright summer sun. She pressed her violin to her neck and prepared to play the first étude.

Then she noticed something in the garden: a mound of dirt, a long shallow hole. From her vantage point in the window she could see a swath of white fabric stretched across the bottom and pale hands wrapped around the barrel of a gun.

"Mama!" she screamed, and the violin crashed to the floor.

SHE THREW OPEN THE DOOR TO HER FATHER'S study without knocking. She had expected to find him at his desk, hunched over his ledgers, but instead he was perched on the edge of a high-backed wing chair, next to the fireplace. A tiny, elfin figure, he wore his habitual blue blazer and striped tie. He was not alone. The second man wore sunglasses in spite of the masculine gloom of the study.

"What on earth do you think you're doing?" snapped her father. "How many times have I asked you to respect my closed door? Can't you see I'm in the middle of an important discussion?"

"But Papa—"

"And put on some proper clothing! Ten o'clock in the morning and you're still wearing only a housecoat."

"Papa, I must—"

"It can wait until I've finished."

"No, it can't, Papa!"

She screamed this so loudly the man in sunglasses flinched.

"I apologize, Otto, but I'm afraid my daughter's manners have suffered from spending too many hours alone with her instrument. Will you excuse me? I won't be but a moment."

5

♦ ♦ ♦

ANNA ROLFE'S FATHER HANDLED IMPORTANT *documents with care, and the note he removed from the grave was no exception. When he finished reading it, he looked up sharply, his gaze flickering from side to side, as if he feared someone was reading over his shoulder. This Anna saw from her bedroom window.*

As he turned and started back toward the villa, he glanced up at the window and his eyes met Anna's. He paused, holding her gaze for a moment. It was not a gaze of sympathy. Or remorse. It was a gaze of suspicion.

She turned from the window. The Stradivarius lay where she had dropped it. She picked it up. Downstairs she heard her father calmly telling his guest of his wife's suicide. She lifted the violin to her neck, laid the bow upon the strings, closed her eyes. G minor. Various patterns of ascent and descent. Arpeggios. Broken thirds.

"HOW CAN SHE PLAY AT A TIME LIKE THIS?"

"I'm afraid she knows little else."

Late afternoon. The two men alone in the study again. The police had completed their initial investigation, and the body had been removed. The note lay on the drop-leaf table between them.

"A doctor could give her a sedative."

"She doesn't want a doctor. I'm afraid she has her mother's temper and her mother's stubborn nature."

"Did the police ask whether there was a note?"

"I see no need to involve the police in the personal matters of this family, especially when it concerns the suicide of my wife."

"And your daughter?"

"What about my daughter?"

"She was watching you from the window."

"My daughter is my business. I'll deal with her as I see fit."

"I certainly hope so. But do me one small favor."

"What's that, Otto?"

His pale hand patted the top of the table until it came to rest on the note.

"Burn this damned thing, along with everything else. Make sure no one else stumbles on any unpleasant reminders of the past. This is Switzerland. There is no past."

Part One

THE PRESENT

1

*T*HE SOMETIMES-SOLVENT FIRM OF Isherwood Fine Arts had once occupied a piece of fine commercial property on stylish New Bond Street in Mayfair. Then came London's retail renaissance, and New Bond Street—or New Bondstrasse, as it was derisively known in the trade—was overrun by the likes of Tiffany and Gucci and Versace and Mikimoto. Julian Isherwood and other dealers specializing in museum-quality Old Masters were driven into St. Jamesian exile—the Bond Street Diaspora, as Isherwood was fond of calling it. He eventually settled in a sagging Victorian warehouse in a quiet quadrangle known as Mason's Yard, next to the London offices of a minor Greek shipping company and a pub that catered to pretty office girls who rode motor scooters.

Among the incestuous, backbiting villagers of St. James's, Isherwood Fine Arts was considered rather good theater. Isherwood Fine Arts had drama and tension, comedy and tragedy, stunning highs and seemingly bottomless lows. This was, in large measure, a consequence of its owner's personality. He was cursed with a near-fatal flaw for an art dealer: He liked to possess art more than to sell it. Each time a painting left the wall of his exquisite

11

exposition room, Isherwood fell into a raging blue funk. As a result of this affliction he was now burdened by an apocalyptic inventory of what is affectionately known in the trade as dead stock—paintings for which no buyer would ever pay a fair price. Unsellable paintings. Burned, as they liked to say in Duke Street. Toast. If Isherwood had been asked to explain this seemingly inexplicable failure of business acumen, he might have raised the issue of his father, though he made a point of never— *And I mean never, petal*—talking about his father.

He was up now. Afloat. Flush with funds. A million pounds, to be precise, tucked nicely into his account at Barclays Bank, thanks to a Venetian painter named Francesco Vecellio and the morose-looking art restorer now making his way across the wet bricks of Mason's Yard.

Isherwood pulled on a macintosh. His English scale and devoutly English wardrobe concealed the fact that he was not—at least not technically speaking—English at all. English by nationality and passport, yes, but German by birth, French by upbringing, and Jewish by religion. Few people knew that his last name was merely a phonetic perversion of its original. Fewer still knew that he'd done favors over the years for a certain bullet-headed gentleman from a certain clandestine agency based in Tel Aviv. Rudolf Heller was the name the gentleman used when calling on Isherwood at the gallery. It was a borrowed name, borrowed like the gentleman's blue suit and gentleman's manners. His real name was Ari Shamron.

"One makes choices in life, doesn't one?" Shamron had said at the time of Isherwood's recruitment. "One doesn't betray one's adopted country, one's college, or one's regiment, but one looks out for one's flesh and blood, one's tribe, lest another Austrian madman, or the Butcher of Baghdad, try to turn us all into soap again, eh, Julian?"

"Hear, hear, Herr Heller."

"We won't pay you a pound. Your name will never appear in our files. You'll do favors for me from time to time. Very specific favors for a very special agent."

"Super. Marvelous. Where do I sign up? What sort of favors? Nothing shady, I take it?"

"Say I need to send him to Prague. Or Oslo. Or Berlin, God forbid. I'd like you to find legitimate work for him there. A restoration. An authentication. A consultation. Something appropriate for the amount of time he'll be staying."

"Not a problem, Herr Heller. By the way, does this agent of yours have a name?"

The agent had many names, thought Isherwood now, watching the man make his way across the quadrangle. His real name was Gabriel Allon, and the nature of his secret work for Shamron was betrayed by subtle things he did now. The way he glanced over his shoulder as he slipped through the passageway from Duke Street. The way that, in spite of a steady rain, he made not one but two complete circuits of the old yard before approaching the gallery's secure door and ringing Isherwood's bell. *Poor Gabriel. One of the three or four best in the world at what he does, but he can't walk a straight line.* And why not? After what happened to his wife and child in Vienna...no man would be the same after that.

He was unexpectedly average in height, and his smooth gait seemed to propel him effortlessly across Duke Street to Green's Restaurant, where Isherwood had booked a table for lunch. As they sat down, Gabriel's eyes flickered about the room like search-lights. They were almond-shaped, unnaturally green, and very quick. The cheekbones were broad and square, the lips dark, and the sharp-edged nose looked as though it had been carved from wood. It was a timeless face, thought Isherwood. It could be a face on the cover of a glossy men's fashion magazine or a face from a dour Rembrandt portrait. It was also a face of many possible origins. It had been a superb professional asset.

Isherwood ordered stuffed sole and Sancerre, Gabriel black tea and a bowl of consommé. He reminded Isherwood of an Orthodox hermit who subsisted on rancid feta and concrete flatbread, only Gabriel lived in a pleasant cottage on a remote tidal creek in Cornwall instead of a monastery. Isherwood had never seen him eat a rich meal, had never seen him smile or admire an attractive pair of hips. He never lusted after material objects. He had only two toys, an old MG motorcar and a wooden ketch, both of which he had restored himself. He listened to his opera on a dreadful little portable CD player stained with paint and varnish. He spent money only on his supplies. He had more high-tech toys in his little Cornish studio than there were in the conservation department of the Tate.

How little Gabriel had changed in the twenty-five years since they had first met. A few more wrinkles around those watchful eyes, a few more pounds on his spare frame. He'd been little more than a boy that day, quiet as a church mouse. Even then, his hair was streaked with gray, the stain of a boy who'd done a man's job. "Julian Isherwood, meet Gabriel," Shamron had said. "Gabriel is a man of enormous talent, I assure you."

Enormous talent, indeed, but there had been gaps in the young man's provenance— like the missing three years between his graduation from the prestigious Betsal'el School of Art in Jerusalem and his apprenticeship in Venice with the master restorer Umberto Conti. "Gabriel spent time traveling in Europe," Shamron had said curtly. That was the last time the subject of Gabriel's European adventures was ever raised. Julian Isherwood didn't talk about what had happened to his father, and Gabriel didn't talk about the things he had done for Ari Shamron, alias Rudolf Heller, from approximately 1972 to 1975. Secretly, Isherwood referred to them as the Lost Years.

Isherwood reached into the breast pocket of his jacket and withdrew a check. "Your share from the sale of the Vecellio. One hundred thousand pounds."

Gabriel scooped up the check and pocketed it with a smooth movement of his hand. He had magician's hands and a magician's sense of misdirection. The check was there, the check was gone.

"How much was your share?"

"I'll tell you, but you must first promise me that you won't divulge the figure to any of these vultures," Isherwood said, sweeping his hand across the dining room of Green's.

Gabriel said nothing, which Isherwood interpreted as a blood oath of everlasting silence.

"One million."

"Dollars?"

"Pounds, petal. Pounds."

"Who bought it?"

"A very nice gallery in the American Midwest. Tastefully displayed, I assure you. Can you imagine? I picked it up for sixteen thousand from a dusty sale room in Hull on the hunch—the wild bloody hunch—that it was the missing altarpiece from the church of San Salvatore in Venice. And I was right! A coup like this comes along once in a career, twice if you're lucky. Cheers."

They toasted each other, stemmed wineglass to bone-china teacup. Just then a tubby man with a pink shirt and pink cheeks to match presented himself breathlessly at their table.

16

"Julie!" he sang.

"Hullo, Oliver."

"Word on Duke Street is you picked up a cool million for your Vecellio."

"Where the bloody hell did you hear that?"

"There are no secrets down here, love. Just tell me if it's the truth or a dirty, seditious lie." He turned to Gabriel, as if noticing him for the first time, and thrust out a fleshy paw with a gold-embossed business card wedged between the thick fingers. "Oliver Dimbleby. Dimbleby Fine Arts."

Gabriel took the card silently.

"Why don't you join us for a drink, Oliver?" said Isherwood.

Beneath the table Gabriel put his foot on Isherwood's toe and pressed hard.

"Can't now, love. That leggy creature in the booth over there has promised to whisper filth into my ear if I buy her another glass of champagne."

"Thank God!" blurted Isherwood through clenched teeth.

Oliver Dimbleby waddled off. Gabriel released the pressure on Isherwood's foot.

"So much for your secrets."

"Vultures," Isherwood repeated. "I'm up now, but the moment I stumble they'll be hovering again, waiting for me to die so they can pick over the bones."

"Maybe this time you should watch your money a little more carefully."

"I'm afraid I'm a hopeless case. In fact—"

"Oh, God."

"—I'm traveling to Amsterdam to have a look at a painting next week. It's the centerpiece of a triptych, classified as artist unknown, but I have another one of my hunches. I think it may have come from the workshop of Rogier van der Weyden. In fact, I may be willing to bet a great deal of money on it."

"Van der Weydens are notoriously difficult to authenticate. There are only a handful of works firmly attributed to him, and he never signed or dated any of them."

"If it came from his workshop, his fingerprints will be on it. And if there's anyone who can find them, it's you."

"I'll be happy to take a look at it for you."

"Are you working on anything now?"

"I just finished a Modigliani."

"I have a job for you."

"What kind of job?"

"I received a call from a lawyer a few days ago. Said his client has a painting that requires cleaning. Said his client wanted you to handle the job and would pay handsomely."

"What's the client's name?"

"Didn't say."

"What's the painting?"

"Didn't say."

"So how is it supposed to work?"

"You go to the villa, you work on the painting. The owner pays for your hotel and expenses."

"Where?"

"Zürich."

Something flashed behind Gabriel's green eyes, a vision, a memory. Isherwood frantically rifled through the file drawers of his own less reliable memory. *Have I ever sent him to Zürich for Herr Heller?*

"Is Zürich a problem?"

"No, Zürich is fine. How much would I be paid?"

"Twice what I've just given you—if you start right away."

"Give me the address."

GABRIEL DID NOT HAVE TIME TO RETURN TO Cornwall to pick up his things, so after lunch he went shopping. In Oxford Street he purchased two changes of clothing and a small leather bag. Then he walked over to Great Russell Street and visited the venerable art-supply store of L. Cornelissen & Son. A flaxenhaired angel called Penelope helped him assemble a traveling kit of pigments, brushes, and solvents. She knew him by his work name, and he flirted with her shamelessly in the faded accent of an Italian expatriate. She wrapped his things in brown paper and bound them with a string. He kissed her cheek. Her hair smelled of cocoa and incense.

Gabriel knew too much about terrorism and security to enjoy traveling by airplane, so he rode the Underground to Waterloo Station and caught a late-afternoon Eurostar to Paris. In the Gare de l'Est he boarded a night train for Zürich, and by nine o'clock the next morning he was strolling down the gentle sweep of the Bahnhofstrasse.

How gracefully Zürich conceals her riches, he thought. Much of the world's gold and silver lay in the bank vaults beneath his feet, but there were no hideous office towers to mark the boundaries of the financial district and no monuments to moneymaking. Just understatement, discretion, and deception. A scorned woman who looks away to hide her shame. Switzerland.

He came upon the Paradeplatz. On one side of the square stood the headquarters of Credit Suisse, on the other the Union Bank of Switzerland. A burst of pigeons shattered the calm. He crossed the street.

Opposite the Savoy hotel was a taxi stand. He climbed into a waiting car after first glancing at the registration number and committing it to memory. He gave the driver the address of the villa, doing his best to conceal the Berlin accent he had acquired from his mother.

Crossing the river, the driver switched on the radio. An announcer was reading the overnight news. Gabriel struggled to comprehend his *Züridütsch*. He tuned out the radio and focused on the task ahead. There were some in the art world who thought of restoration as tedious work, but Gabriel viewed each assignment as an adventure waiting to unfold; an opportunity to step through a looking glass into another time and place. A place where success or failure was determined by his own skills and nerve and nothing else.

He wondered what awaited him. The very fact that the owner had specifically requested him meant that the work was almost certainly an Old Master. He could also assume that the painting was quite dirty and damaged. The owner wouldn't have gone to the trouble and expense of bringing him to Zürich if it required only a fresh coat of varnish.

So how long would he be here? Six weeks? Six months? Difficult to say. No two restorations were the same; much would depend on the condition of the painting. Isherwood's Vecellio had required a year to restore, though he had taken a brief sabbatical in the middle of the job, courtesy of Ari Shamron.

THE ROSENBÜHLWEG WAS A NARROW STREET, just wide enough to accommodate two cars at once, and it rose sharply up the slope of the Zürichberg. The villas were old and big and huddled closely together. Stucco walls, tile roofs, small tangled gardens. All except the one where the taxi driver pulled to a stop.

It stood atop its own promontory and unlike its neighbors was set several meters back from the street. A high metal fence, like the bars of a jail cell, ran round the perimeter. At the level of the pavement there was a security gate, complete with a small surveillance camera. Beyond the gate rose a flight of stone steps. Then came the villa, a melancholy graystone structure with turrets and a towering front portico.

The taxi drove off. Below lay central Zürich and the lake. Cloud veiled the far shore. Gabriel remembered that it was possible to see the Alps on a clear day, but now they too were shrouded.

Mounted next to the gate on a stone wall was a telephone. Gabriel picked up the receiver, heard ringing at the other end of the line, waited. Nothing. He replaced the receiver, picked it up again. Still no answer.

He pulled out the lawyer's fax that Julian Isherwood had given him in London. *You are to arrive at precisely 9 A.M. Ring the bell and you'll be escorted inside.* Gabriel looked at his watch. Three minutes after nine.

As he slipped the papers back into his pocket it began to rain. He looked around: no cafés where he might sit in comfort, no parks or squares where he might find some shelter from the weather. Just a desert of inherited residential wealth. If he stood on the pavement too long, he'd probably be arrested for loitering.

He pulled out his mobile phone and dialed Isherwood's number. He was probably still on his way to the gallery. As Gabriel waited for the connection to go through, he had a mental image of Isherwood, hunched over the wheel of his shining new Jaguar motorcar, crawling along Piccadilly as if he were piloting an oil tanker through treacherous waters.

"Sorry, but I'm afraid there's been a change in plan. The fellow who was supposed to meet you was apparently called out of town suddenly. An emergency of some sort. He

22

was vague about it. You know how the Swiss can be, petal."

"What am I supposed to do?"

"He sent me the security codes for the gate and the front door. You're to let yourself in. There's supposed to be a note for you on the table in the entrance hall explaining where you can find the painting and your accommodations."

"Rather unorthodox, don't you think?"

"Consider yourself fortunate. It sounds as if you're going to have the run of the place for a few days, and you won't have anyone watching over your shoulder while you work."

"I suppose you're right."

"Let me give you the security codes. Do you have paper and pen by any chance? They're rather long."

"Just tell me the numbers, Julian. It's pouring rain, and I'm getting soaked out here."

"Ah, yes. You and your little parlor tricks. I used to have a girl at the gallery who could do the same thing."

Isherwood rattled off two series of numbers, each eight digits in length, and severed the connection. Gabriel lifted the receiver of the security phone and punched in the numbers. A buzzer sounded; he turned the latch and stepped through the gate. At the front entrance of the house he repeated the routine, and a moment later he was standing in the darkened front hall, groping for a light switch.

The envelope lay in a large glass bowl on a carved antique table at the foot of the staircase. It was addressed to Signore Delvecchio,

23

Gabriel's work name. He picked up the envelope and sliced it open with his forefinger. Plain dove-gray paper, heavy bond, no letterhead. Precise careful handwriting, unsigned. He lifted it to his nose. No scent.

Gabriel began to read. The painting hung in the drawing room, a Raphael, *Portrait of a Young Man*. A reservation had been made for him at the Dolder Grand Hotel, about a mile away on the other side of the Zürichberg. There was food in the refrigerator. The owner would return to Zürich the following day. He would appreciate it greatly if Signore Delvecchio could begin work without delay.

Gabriel slipped the note into his pocket. So, a Raphael. It would be his second. Five years ago he had restored a small devotional piece, a Madonna and Child, based on the renowned composition of Leonardo. Gabriel could feel a tingling sensation spreading over the tips of his fingers. It was a marvelous opportunity. He was glad he had taken the job, regardless of the unorthodox arrangements.

He stepped through a passageway into a large room. It was dark, no lights burning, the heavy curtains tightly drawn. Despite the gloom he had the sensation of Middle European aristocratic clutter.

He took a few steps forward. Beneath his feet the carpet was damp. The air tasted of salt and rust. It was an odor Gabriel had smelled before. He reached down, touched his fingers to the carpet, and brought them to his face.

He was standing in blood.

THE ORIENTAL CARPET WAS FADED AND VERY old, and so was the dead man sprawled in the center of it. He lay face-down, and in death he was reaching forward with his right hand. He wore a double-vented blue blazer, shiny with wear in the back, and gray flannel trousers. His shoes were brown suede. One shoe, the right, had a thickened heel and sole. The trousers had ridden up along his lower leg. The skin was shockingly white, like exposed bone. The socks were mismatched.

Gabriel squatted on his haunches with the casualness of someone who was at ease around the dead. The corpse had been a tiny man; five feet in height, no more. He lay in profile, the left side of the face exposed. Through the blood, Gabriel could see a square jaw and a delicate cheekbone. The hair was thick and snowy white. It appeared that the man had been shot once, through the left eye, and that the slug had exited the back of the skull. Judging from the size of the exit wound, the weapon was a rather large-caliber handgun. Gabriel looked up and saw that the slug had shattered the mirror above the large fireplace. He suspected the old man had been dead a few hours.

He supposed he should telephone the police, but then he imagined the situation from their point of view. A foreigner in an expensive home, a corpse shot through the eye. At the very least, he would be detained for questioning. Gabriel couldn't allow that to happen.

He rose and turned his gaze from the dead man to the Raphael. A striking image: a beautiful young man in semi-profile, sensuously lit. Gabriel guessed it had been painted while Raphael was living and working in Florence, probably between 1504 and 1508. Too bad about the old man; it would have been a pleasure to restore such a painting.

He walked back to the entrance hall, stopped and looked down. He had tracked blood across the marble floor. There was nothing to be done about it. In circumstances like these he had been trained to leave quickly without worrying about making a bit of a mess or noise.

He collected his cases, opened the door, and stepped outside. It was raining harder now, and by the time he reached the gate at the end of the flagstone walk he was no longer leaving bloody footprints.

He walked quickly until he came to a thoroughfare: the Krähbühlstrasse. The Number 6 tram slithered down the slope of the hill. He raced it to the next stop, walking quickly but not running, and hopped on without a ticket.

The streetcar jerked forward. Gabriel sat down and looked to his right. Scrawled on the carriage wall, in black indelible marker, was a swastika superimposed over a Star of David. Beneath it were two words: *JUDEN SCHEISS*.

◆ ◆ ◆

THE TRAM TOOK HIM DIRECTLY TO HAUPT-bahnhof. Inside the terminal, in an underground shopping arcade, he purchased an exorbitantly priced pair of Bally leather boots. Upstairs in the main hall he checked the departure board. A train was leaving for München in fifteen minutes. From München he could make an evening flight back to London, where he would go directly to Isherwood's house in South Kensington and strangle him.

He purchased a first-class ticket and walked to the toilet. In a stall he changed from his loafers into the new boots. On the way out he dropped the loafers into a rubbish bin and covered them with paper towels.

By the time he reached the platform, the train was boarding. He stepped onto the second carriage and picked his way along the corridor until he came to his compartment. It was empty. A moment later, as the train eased forward, Gabriel closed his eyes, but all he could see was the dead man lying at the foot of the Raphael, and the two words scrawled on a streetcar: *JUDEN SCHEISS*.

The train slowed to a stop. They were still on the platform. Outside, in the corridor, Gabriel heard footfalls. Then the door to his compartment flew back as though blown open by a bomb, and two police officers burst inside.

2

$\mathcal{S}$IX HUNDRED MILES TO THE WEST, IN THE Basque town of Vitoria, an Englishman sat amid the cool shadows of the Plaza de España, sipping coffee at a café beneath the graceful arcade. Though he was unaware of the events taking place in Zürich, they would soon alter the course of his well-ordered life. For now, his attention was focused on the bank entrance across the square.

He ordered another *café con leche* and lit a cigarette. He wore a brimmed hat and sunglasses. His hair had the healthy silver sheen of a man gone prematurely gray. His sandstone-colored poplin suit matched the prevailing architecture of Vitoria, allowing him to blend, chameleon-like, into his surroundings. He appeared to be entranced by that morning's editions of *El País* and *El Mundo*. He was not.

On the pale yellow stonework a graffiti artist had scrawled a warning: TOURISTS BEWARE! YOU ARE NOT IN SPAIN ANY LONGER! THIS IS BASQUE COUNTRY! The Englishman did not feel any sense of unease. If for some reason he was targeted by the separatists, he was quite certain he would be able to look after himself.

His gaze settled on the door of the bank. In a few minutes, a teller called Felipe Navarra would be leaving for his midday break. His colleagues believed he went home for lunch and siesta with his wife. His wife believed he was meeting secretly with his Basque political associates. In reality, Felipe Navarra would be heading to an apartment house in the old town, just off the Plaza de la Virgen Blanca, where he would spend the afternoon with his mistress, a beautiful black-haired girl called Amaia. The Englishman knew this because he had been watching Navarra for nearly a week.

At one-fifteen Navarra emerged from the bank and headed toward the old town. The Englishman left a handful of pesetas on the table, enough to cover his tab along with a generous tip for the waiter, and trailed softly after him. Entering a crowded market street, he kept to a safe distance. There was no need to get too close. He knew where his quarry was going.

Felipe Navarra was no ordinary bank teller. He was an active service agent of the Euzkadi Ta Askatasuna (Basque Fatherland and Liberty) better known as ETA. In the lexicon of ETA, Navarra was a sleeping commando. He lived a normal life with a normal job and received his orders from an anonymous commander. A year ago he had been directed to assassinate a young officer of the Guardia Civil. Unfortunately for Navarra, the officer's father was a successful wine maker, a man with plenty of money to finance an extensive search for his son's killer. Some of that money now resided in the Englishman's numbered Swiss bank account.

Among the terror experts of Europe, ETA had a reputation for training and operational discipline that rivaled that of the Irish Republican Army, a group with which the Englishman had dealt in the past. But based on the Englishman's observations thus far, Felipe Navarra seemed a rather free-spirited agent. He walked directly toward the girl's flat, taking no security precautions or counter-surveillance measures. It was a miracle he'd managed to kill the Guardia Civil officer and escape. The Englishman thought he was probably doing ETA a favor by eliminating such an incompetent agent.

Navarra entered an apartment building. The Englishman walked across the street to a bakery, where he consumed two sugared pastries and drank another *café con leche*. He didn't like to work on an empty stomach. He looked at his watch. Navarra had been inside for twenty minutes, plenty of time for the preliminaries of a sexual liaison.

Crossing the quiet street, he had an amusing thought. If he telephoned Navarra's wife, a redhead with a fiery Basque temper, she would probably do the job for him. But, strictly speaking, that would be a breach of contract. Besides, he wanted to do it himself. The Englishman was happy in his work.

He entered the cool, dark foyer. Directly in front of him was the entrance to a shaded courtyard. To his right was a row of post boxes. He mounted the stairs quickly to the door of the girl's flat on the fourth floor.

A television was playing; a senseless game show on Antena 3. It helped to cover the minimal sound the Englishman made while picking the lock. He entered the flat, closed the door, and locked it again. Then he padded into the bedroom.

Navarra was seated at the end of the bed. The woman was kneeling on the floor, her head moving rhythmically between his legs. Navarra's fingers were entwined in her hair, and his eyes were closed, so he was unaware of the new presence in the room. The Englishman wondered why they were making love to a game show. *To each his own,* he thought.

The Englishman crossed the room quickly in three powerful strides, his footfalls covered by the sound of the television. A knife slipped from a sheath on his right forearm and fell into his palm. It was the weapon of a soldier, a heavy serrated blade, with a thick leather-bound grip. He held it the way he had been trained at the headquarters of his old regiment on a windswept moorland in the Midlands of England.

The natural inclination when stabbing a man is to do it from behind, so that the killer and victim are never face to face, but the Englishman had been trained to kill with a knife from the front. In this case it meant the element of surprise was lost, but the Englishman was a creature of habit and believed in doing things by the book.

He moved a few feet forward, so that he was standing behind the girl. Her hair spilled down a long, V-shaped back. His eye followed the line of her spinal column to the slender waist, to the rounded child-bearing hips and curved buttocks.

Navarra opened his eyes. Frantically he tried to push the girl out of the way. The assassin did it for him, taking a handful of her hair and tossing her across the room, so that she skidded along the hardwood floor on her backside and toppled a standing lamp.

Navarra, without taking his eyes from the intruder, reached backward across the rumpled sheets and beat his palm against a twisted pile of clothing. So, he had a gun. The Englishman stepped forward and took hold of the Basque's throat with his left hand, squeezing his larynx to the breaking point. Then he pushed the man down onto the bed, settling atop him with one knee on his abdomen. Navarra writhed, struggling for air, the look on his face a combination of panic and utter resignation.

The Englishman thrust the knife into the soft tissue beneath the Basque's ribcage, angling upward toward the heart. The man's eyes bulged and his body stiffened, then relaxed. Blood pumped over the blade of the knife.

The Englishman removed the knife from the dead man's chest and stood up. The girl scrambled to her feet. Then she stepped forward and slapped him hard across the face.

"Who the hell do you think you are?"

The Englishman didn't know quite what to make of this woman. She had just watched him stab her lover to death, but she was acting as if he had tracked mud across her clean floor.

She hit him a second time. "I work for Aragón, you idiot! I've been seeing Navarra for a month. We were about to arrest him and take down the rest of his cell. Who sent you here? It wasn't Aragón. He would have told me."

She stood there, awaiting his reply, seemingly unashamed of her nudity.

"I work for Castillo." He spoke calmly and in fluent Spanish. He didn't know anyone called Castillo—it was just the first name that popped into his head. Where had he seen it? The bakery? Yes, that was it. The bakery across the street.

She asked, "Who's Castillo?"

"The man I work for."

"Does Castillo work for Aragón?"

"How should I know? Why don't you call Aragón? He'll call Castillo, and we'll straighten this mess out."

"Fine."

"Call him on that telephone over there."

"I will, you fucking idiot!"

"Just do it quietly, before you alert every tenant in the building that we've just killed a man."

She folded her arms across her breasts, as if she was aware of her nakedness for the first time. "What's your name?"

"I'm not telling you my name."

"Why not?"

"How do I know you really work for Aragón? Maybe you work with lover boy here. Maybe you're a member of his cell. Maybe you're going to call some of his friends, and they'll come here and kill me."

He raised the bloody knife and ran his thumb across the blade. The girl scowled. "Don't even think about trying it! Fucking idiot!"

"Get Aragón on the line. Then I'll tell you my name."

"You're going to be in big trouble."

"Just get Aragón on the phone, and I'll explain everything."

She sat down on the edge of the bed, snatched up the receiver, and violently punched in the number. The Englishman moved a step closer and placed his finger on the cradle, severing the connection.

"What do you think you're doing? What's your name?"

The assassin brought the blade across her throat in a slashing movement. He stepped back to avoid the initial geyserlike burst of blood; then he knelt before her and watched the life draining out of her eyes. As she slipped away he leaned forward and whispered his name into her ear.

THE ENGLISHMAN SPENT THE REST OF THE DAY driving: the fast road from Vitoria to Barcelona, then the coast highway from Barcelona across the border to Marseilles. Late that evening he boarded a passenger ferry for the night crossing to Corsica.

He was dressed like a typical Corsican man: loose-fitting cotton trousers, dusty leather sandals, a heavy sweater against the autumn chill. His dark brown hair was cropped short. The poplin suit and brimmed hat he'd worn in Vitoria were resting in the rubbish bin of a roadside café in Bordeaux. The silver wig had been tossed out the car window into a mountain gorge. The car itself, registered to a David Mandelson, one of his many false identities, had been returned to the rental agent in town.

He went below deck to his cabin. It was private, with its own shower and toilet. He left his small leather grip on the berth and went up to the passenger deck. The ferry was nearly empty, a few people gathering in the bar for a drink and a bite to eat. He was tired after the long drive, but his strict sense of internal discipline would not permit him to sleep until he had scanned the faces of the passengers.

He toured the deck, saw nothing alarming, then went into the bar, where he ordered a half-liter of red wine and fell into conversation with a Corsican named Matteo. Matteo lived in the northwest part of the island, like the Englishman, but two valleys to the south in the shadow of Monte d'Oro. It had been twenty years since he had been to the Englishman's valley. Such was the rhythm of life on the island.

The conversation turned to the arson fire that had ravaged the Englishman's valley the previous dry season. "Did they ever find out who did it?" Matteo asked, helping himself to some of the Englishman's wine. When the Englishman told him the authorities suspected the separatists from the FLNC, the Corsican lit a cigarette and spit smoke at the ceiling. "Young hotheads!" he growled, and the Englishman nodded slowly in agreement.

After an hour he bid Matteo goodnight and returned to his cabin. In his suitcase was a small radio. He listened to the midnight newscast on a Marseilles station. After a few minutes of local news, there was a roundup of foreign stories. In the West Bank, there had been another day of fighting between Palestinian and Israeli forces. In Spain, two members of the Basque terror group ETA had been murdered in the town of Vitoria. And in Switzerland, a prominent banker named Augustus Rolfe had been found murdered in his home in an exclusive Zürich neighborhood. An unidentified man was in custody. The Englishman switched off the radio, closed his eyes, and was immediately asleep.

3

◆ *ZÜRICH*

*T*HE HEADQUARTERS OF THE STADTPOLIZEI Zürich was located only a few hundred meters from the train station on the Zeughausstrasse, wedged between the smoke-colored Sihl River and a sprawling rail yard. Gabriel had been led across a stone central courtyard into the aluminum-and-glass annex which housed the murder squad. There he was placed in a windowless interrogation room furnished with a table of blond wood and a trio of mismatched chairs. His luggage had been seized, along with his paints, brushes, and chemicals. So had his wallet, his passport, and his mobile telephone. They had even taken his wristwatch. He supposed they were hoping he would become disoriented and confused. He was confident that he knew more about the techniques of interrogation than the Zürich police did.

He had been questioned three times by three different officers: once briefly at the train station, before being taken into custody, and twice more in this room. Judging by clothing and age, the importance of his interrogators was getting progressively greater.

The door opened and a single officer entered the room. He wore a tweed coat and no tie. He called himself Sergeant-Major Baer. He sat down opposite Gabriel, placed a file on the table, and stared at it as if it was a chessboard and he was contemplating his next move.

"Tell me your name," he blurted in English.

"It hasn't changed since the last time I was asked."

"Tell me your name."

"My name is Mario Delvecchio."

"Where do you reside?"

"Port Navas, Cornwall."

"England?"

"Yes."

"You are an Italian, but you live in England?"

"That's not a crime the last time I checked."

"I didn't say it was, but it is interesting, though. What do you do in Port Navas, England?"

"I told the first three officers who questioned me."

"Yes, I know."

"I'm an art restorer."

"Why are you in Zürich?"

"I was hired to clean a painting."

"At the villa on the Zürichberg?"

"Yes."

"Who hired you to clean this painting? *Clean?* Is that the word you used? Peculiar word: clean. One thinks of cleaning floors, cleaning cars or clothing. But not paintings. Is that a common expression in your line of work?"

"Yes," said Gabriel and the inspector seemed disappointed he did not elaborate.

"Who hired you?"

"I don't know."

"What do you mean?"

"I mean it was never made clear to me. The arrangements were made by a lawyer in Zürich and an art dealer in London."

"Ah, yes—Julius Isherwood."

"Julian."

With a Germanic reverence for paperwork, the detective made a vast show of expunging the offending word and carefully penciling in the correction. When he had finished, he looked up triumphantly, as if awaiting applause. "Go on."

"I was simply told to go to the villa. I would be met there and shown inside."

"Met by whom?"

"That was never made clear to me."

Isherwood's fax was in the file. The detective slipped on a pair of half-moon glasses and held the fax up to the light. His lips moved as he read. "When did you arrive in Zürich?"

"You have the stub of my train ticket. You know that I arrived this morning."

The detective pulled a frown that said he did not like suspects telling him what he did and didn't know.

"Where did you go after you arrived?"

"Straight to the villa."

"You didn't check into your hotel first?"

"No, I didn't know where I was staying yet."

"Where *were* you planning to stay?"

"As you can see from the note that was left for me at the villa, arrangements had been made for me to stay at the Dolder Grand Hotel."

Baer overlooked this seeming misstep and carried on.

"How did you get from Hauptbahnhof to the villa?"

"By taxi."

"How much was the fare?"

"About fifteen francs."

"What time did you arrive at the villa?"

"Two minutes after nine o'clock."

"How can you be so certain of the time?"

"Look at the fax from Julian Isherwood. I was told to arrive at precisely nine o'clock. I don't make a habit of being late for appointments, Sergeant-Major Baer."

The detective smiled in admiration. He was a prompt man, and he appreciated punctuality and attention to detail in others, even if he suspected them of murder.

"And when you arrived at the villa?"

"I used the security phone, but no one answered. So I called Mr. Isherwood in London. He told me that the person who was supposed to meet me had been called out of town suddenly."

"Is that what he said? 'Called out of town'?"

"Something like that."

"And this Mr. Isherwood gave you the codes?"

"Yes."

"Who gave Mr. Isherwood the codes?"

"I don't know. The man's lawyer, I suppose."

"Did you write the codes down?"

"No."

"Why not?"

"It wasn't necessary."

"Why not?"

"Because I memorized the codes."

"Really? You must have a very good memory, Signore Delvecchio."

THE DETECTIVE LEFT THE ROOM FOR FIFTEEN minutes. When he returned, he had a cup of coffee for himself and nothing for Gabriel. He sat down and resumed where he had left off.

"These arrangements seem peculiar to me, Signore Delvecchio. Is it customary that you are kept unaware of the artist until you arrive to begin work on restoration?"

"No, it isn't customary. In fact, it's unusual."

"Indeed." He sat back and folded his arms, as though this admission were tantamount to a signed confession. "Is it also customary that you are not given the name of the owner of a painting you are restoring?"

"It's not unheard of."

"Rolfe." He looked at Gabriel to see if the name produced any reaction, which it did not. "The person who owns the painting is named Augustus Rolfe. He is also the man you murdered in the villa."

"I didn't murder anyone, and you know it. He was killed long before I arrived in Zürich. I was still on the train when he was murdered. A hundred people can place me on that train."

The detective seemed unmoved by Gabriel's argument. He sipped his coffee and said calmly: "Tell me what happened after you entered the villa."

Gabriel recounted the chain of events in a dull monotone: the dark entrance hall, groping for the light switch, the unsigned letter in the bowl on the table, the strange odor on the air as he entered the drawing room, the discovery of the body.

"Did you see the painting?"

"Yes."

"Before you saw the body or after?"

"After."

"And how long did you look at it?"

41

"I don't know. A minute or so."

"You've just discovered a dead body, but you stop to look at a painting." The detective didn't seem to know what to make of this piece of information. "Tell me about this painter"—He looked down at his notes—"Raphael. I'm afraid I know little of art."

Gabriel could tell he was lying but decided to play along. For the next fifteen minutes, he delivered a detailed lecture on the life and work of Raphael: his training and his influences, the innovations of his technique, the lasting relevance of his major works. By the time he had finished, the policeman was staring into the remains of his coffee, a beaten man.

"Would you like me to go on?"

"No, thank you. That was very helpful. If you did not kill Augustus Rolfe, why did you leave the villa without telephoning the police? Why did you try to flee Zürich?"

"I knew the circumstances would appear suspicious, so I panicked."

The detective looked him over skeptically, as if he did not quite believe Mario Delvecchio was a man given to panic. "How did you get from the Zürichberg to the Hauptbahnhof?"

"I took the tram."

Baer made a careful inspection of Gabriel's seized possessions. "I don't see a tram ticket among your things. Surely, you purchased a ticket before you boarded the streetcar?"

Gabriel shook his head: guilty as charged. Baer's eyebrows shot up. The notion that Gabriel had boarded a tram ticketless seemed more horrifying to him than the possibility that he had shot an old man in the head.

"That's a very serious offense, Signore Delvecchio! I'm afraid you're going to be fined fifty francs!"

"I'm deeply sorry."

"Have you been to Zürich before?"

"No, never."

"Then how did you know which tram would take you to the Hauptbahnhof?"

"It was a lucky guess, I suppose. It was heading in the right direction, so I got on."

"Tell me one more thing, Signore Delvecchio. Did you make any purchases while you were in Zürich?"

"Purchases?"

"Did you buy anything? Did you do any shopping?"

"I bought a pair of shoes."

"Why?"

"Because while I was waiting to get into the villa, my shoes became soaked in the rain."

"You were panicked. You were afraid to go to the police, desperate to get out of Zürich, but you took time to get new shoes because your feet were wet?"

"Yes."

He leaned back in his chair and knocked on the door. It opened, and an arm appeared, holding an evidence bag containing Gabriel's shoes.

"We found these in a toilet at the Hauptbanhof, buried in a rubbish bin. I suspect they're yours. I also suspect that they will match the set of bloody footprints we found in the entrance hall and the walkway of the villa."

"I've already told you I was there. The footprints, if they do match those shoes, prove nothing."

"Rather nice shoes to simply toss away in the toilet of a rail station. And they don't look that wet to me." He looked up at Gabriel and smiled briefly. "But then, I've heard it said that people who panic easily often have sensitive feet."

IT WAS THREE HOURS BEFORE BAER ENTERED the room again. For the first time he was not alone. It was obvious to Gabriel that the new man represented higher authority. It was also obvious that he was not an ordinary detective from the Zürich murder squad. Gabriel could see it in the small ways that Baer deferred to him physically; the way his heels clicked together when, like a headwaiter, he seated the new man at the interrogation table and moved unobtrusively into the background.

The man called himself Peterson. He provided no first name and no professional information. He wore an immaculately pressed suit of charcoal gray and a banker's tie. His hair was nearly white and neatly trimmed. His hands, folded on the table in front of him, were the hands of a pianist. On his left wrist was a thick silver watch, Swiss-made of course, with a dark-blue face, an instrument that could withstand the pressure of great depths. He studied Gabriel for a moment with slow, humorless eyes. He had the natural arrogance of a man who knows secrets and keeps files.

"The security codes." Like Baer, he spoke to Gabriel in English, though almost without a trace of an accent. "Where did you write them down?"

"I didn't write them down. As I told Sergeant-Major Baer—"

"I know what you told Sergeant-Major Baer." His eyes suddenly came to life. "I'm asking you for myself. Where did you write them down?"

"I received the codes over the telephone from Mr. Isherwood in London, and I used them to open the security gate and the front door of the villa."

"You committed the numbers to memory?"

"Yes."

"Give them to me now."

Gabriel recited the numbers calmly. Peterson looked at Baer, who nodded once.

"You have a very good memory, Signore Delvecchio."

He had switched from English to German. Gabriel stared back at him blankly, as if he did not understand. The interrogator resumed in English.

"You don't speak German, Signore Delvecchio?"

"No."

"According to the taxi driver, the one who took you from the Bahnhofstrasse to the villa on the Zürichberg, you speak German quite well."

"Speaking a few words of German and actually *speaking* German are two very different things."

"The driver told us that you gave him the address in rapid and confident German with the pronounced accent of a Berliner. Tell me something, Signore Delvecchio. How is it that you speak German with the accent of a Berliner?"

"I told you—I don't speak German. I speak a few words of German. I spent a few weeks in Berlin restoring a painting. I suppose I acquired the accent while I was there."

"How long ago was that?"

"About four years ago?"

"*About* four years?"

"Yes."

"Which painting?"

"I'm sorry?"

"The painting you restored in Berlin. Who was the artist? What was it called?"

"I'm afraid that's confidential."

"Nothing is confidential at this point, Signore Delvecchio. I'd like the name of the painting and the name of the owner."

"It was a Caravaggio in private hands. I'm sorry, but I cannot divulge the name of the owner."

Peterson held out his hand toward Baer without looking at him. Baer reached into his file folder and handed him a single sheet of paper. He reviewed it sadly, as if the patient did not have long to live.

"We ran your name through our computer database to see if there happened to be any outstanding arrest warrants for you in Switzerland. I'm pleased to announce there was nothing—not even a traffic citation. We asked our friends across the border in Italy to do the same thing. Once again, there was nothing recorded against you. But our Italian friends told us something more interesting. It seems that a Mario Delvecchio, born 23 September 1951, died in Turin twenty-three years ago of lymphatic cancer." He looked up from the paper and fixed his gaze on Gabriel. "What do you think are the odds of two men having precisely the same name and the same date of birth?"

"How should I know?"

"I think they're very long, indeed. I think there is only one Mario Delvecchio, and you stole his identity in order to obtain an Italian passport. I don't believe your name is Mario Delvecchio. In fact, I'm quite certain it isn't. I believe your name is Gabriel Allon, and that you work for the Israeli secret service."

Peterson smiled for the first time, not a pleasant smile, more like a tear in a scrap of paper. Then he carried on:

"Twenty-five years ago, you murdered a Palestinian playwright living in Zürich named Ali Abdel Hamidi. You slipped out of the country an hour after the killing and were probably back home in your bed in Tel Aviv before midnight. This time, I'm afraid you're not going anywhere."

47

4

$\mathcal{S}$OMETIME AFTER MIDNIGHT GABRIEL WAS moved from the interrogation room to a holding cell in an adjacent wing of the building. It was small and institutional gray, with a bare mattress mounted on a steel frame and a rust-stained toilet that never stopped running. Overhead, a single light bulb buzzed behind a mesh cage. His untouched dinner—a fatty pork sausage, some wilted greens, and a pile of greasy potatoes—sat on the ground next to the door like room service waiting to be collected. Gabriel supposed the pork sausage had been Peterson's idea of a joke.

He tried to picture the events he knew were taking place outside these walls. Peterson had contacted his superior, his superior had contacted the Foreign Ministry. By now word had probably reached Tel Aviv. The prime minister would be livid. He had enough problems: the West Bank in flames, the peace process in tatters, his brittle coalition crumbling. The last thing he needed was a *kidon*, even a former *kidon*, behind bars in Switzerland—yet another Office scandal waiting to explode across the front pages of the world's newspapers.

And so the lights were certainly burning with urgency tonight in the anonymous office block on Tel Aviv's King Saul Boulevard.

And Shamron? Had the call gone out to his lake-side fortress in Tiberias? Was he in or out these days? It was always hard to tell with Shamron. He'd been dug out of his precarious retirement three or four times, called back to deal with this crisis or that, tapped to serve on some dubious advisory panel or to sit in wizened judgment on a supposedly independent fact-finding committee. Not long ago he'd been appointed interim chief of the service, the position he'd held the first time he was sent into the Judean wilderness of retirement. Gabriel wondered whether that term had ended. With Shamron the word *interim* could mean a hundred days or a hundred years. He was Polish by birth but had a Bedouin's elastic sense of time. Gabriel was Shamron's *kidon*. Shamron would handle it, retired or not.

The old man... He'd always been "the old man," even during his brief fling with middle age. *Where's the old man? Anyone seen the old man? Run for the hills! The old man is coming this way!* Now he *was* an old man, but in Gabriel's mind's eye he always appeared as the menacing little figure who'd come to see him one afternoon in September 1972 between classes at Betsal'el. An iron bar of a man. You could almost hear him clanking as he walked. He had known everything about Gabriel. That he had been raised on an agricultural kibbutz in the Jezreel Valley and that he had a passionate hatred of farming. That he was something of a lone wolf, even though he was already married at the time to a fellow art student named Leah

Savir. That his mother had found the strength to survive Auschwitz but was no match for the cancer that ravaged her body; that his father had survived Auschwitz too but was no match for the Egyptian artillery shell that blew him to bits in the Sinai. Shamron knew from Gabriel's military service that he was nearly as good with a gun as he was with a paintbrush.

"You watch the news?"

"I paint."

"You know about Münich? You know what happened to our boys there?"

"Yeah, I heard."

"You're not upset by it?"

"Of course, but I'm not more upset because they're athletes or because it's the Olympics."

"You can still be angry."

"At who?"

"At the Palestinians. At the Black September terrorists who walk around with the blood of your people on their hands."

"I never get angry."

And though Gabriel did not realize it at the time, those words had sealed Shamron's commitment to him, and the seduction was begun.

"You speak languages, yes."

"A few."

"A few?"

"My parents didn't like Hebrew, so they spoke the languages from Europe."

"Which ones?"

"You know already. You know all about me. Don't play games with me."

And so Shamron decided to play his pickup line. Golda had ordered Shamron to "send forth the boys" to take down the Black September bastards who had carried out this bloodbath. The operation was to be called Wrath of God. It was not about justice, Shamron had said. It was about taking an eye for an eye. It was about revenge, pure and simple.

"Sorry, not interested."

"Not interested? Do you know how many boys in this country would give anything to be part of this team?"

"Go ask them."

"I don't want them. I want you."

"Why me?"

"Because you have gifts. You have languages. You have a clear head. You don't drink, and you don't smoke hash. You're not a crazy who's going to go off half-cocked."

And because you have the emotional coldness of a killer, Shamron thought, although he didn't say these words to Gabriel then. Instead, he told him a story, the story of a young intelligence officer who had been chosen for a special mission because he had a gift, an unusually powerful grip for so small a man. The story of a night in a Buenos Aires suburb, when this young intelligence officer had seen a man waiting at a bus stop. *Waiting like an ordinary man, Gabriel. An ordinary pathetic little man.* And how this young intelligence officer had leapt from a car and grabbed the man by the throat and how he had sat on him as the car drove away and how he had smelled

51

the stink of fear on his breath. The same stink the Jews had emitted as this pathetic little man sent them off to the gas chambers. And the story worked, as Shamron had known it would. Because Gabriel was the only son of two Auschwitz survivors, and their scars were his.

He was suddenly very tired. Imagine, all those years, all those killings, and now he was behind bars for the first time, for a murder he did not commit. *Thou shalt not get caught!* Shamron's Eleventh Commandment. *Thou shalt do anything to avoid being arrested. Thou shalt shed the blood of innocents if necessary.* No, thought Gabriel. Thou shalt not shed innocent blood.

He squeezed his eyes shut and tried to sleep but it was no good: Peterson's incessant light. The lights were surely burning on King Saul Boulevard too. And a call would go out. Don't wake him, thought Gabriel, because I don't ever want to see his lying face again. Let him sleep. Let the old man sleep.

IT WAS A FEW MINUTES AFTER 8:00 A.M. WHEN Peterson entered Gabriel's cell. Gabriel knew this not because Peterson bothered to tell him but because he managed a glance at the face of Peterson's big diver's watch as Peterson tipped coffee into his mouth.

"I've spoken to your chief."

He paused to see if his words provoked any response, but Gabriel remained silent. His position was that he was an art restorer, nothing more, and that Herr Peterson was suffering from a case of temporary insanity.

"He did me the professional courtesy of not trying to lie his way out of this situation. I appreciate the way he handled things. But it seems Bern has no appetite to pursue this matter further."

"Which matter is that?"

"The matter of your involvement in the murder of Ali Hamidi," Peterson said coldly. Gabriel had the impression he was struggling to control violent thoughts. "Since prosecuting you for your role in the Rolfe affair would inevitably reveal your sordid past, we have no choice but to drop charges against you in that matter as well."

Peterson clearly disagreed with the decision of his masters in Bern.

"Your government has assured us that you are no longer a member of any branch of Israeli intelligence and that you did not come to Zürich in any *official* capacity. My government has chosen to accept these assurances at face value. It has no stomach for allowing Switzerland to become a stage for the Israelis and the Palestinians to relive the horrors of the past."

"When do I get to leave?"

"A representative of your government will collect you."

"I'd like to change my clothes. May I have my suitcase?"

"No."

Peterson stood up, straightened his tie, and smoothed his hair. Gabriel thought it was an oddly intimate thing for one man to do in front of another. Then he walked to the door, knocked once, and waited for the guard to unlock it.

"I don't like murderers, Mr. Allon. Especially when they kill for a government. One of the conditions of your release is that you never set foot in Switzerland again. If you come back here, I'll see to it that you never leave."

The door opened. Peterson started to leave, then turned and faced Gabriel.

"It's a shame about what happened to your wife and son in Vienna. It must be very hard living with a memory like that. I suppose sometimes you wish it had been you in the car instead of them. Good day, Mr. Allon."

It was late afternoon by the time Peterson finally saw fit to release him. Sergeant-Major Baer escorted Gabriel from his holding cell, performing this task silently, as though Gabriel was bound for the gallows instead of freedom. Baer surrendered Gabriel's suitcase, his restoration supplies, and a thick honey-colored envelope containing his personal effects. Gabriel spent a long moment taking careful inventory of his things. Baer looked at his watch as if pressing matters were tugging at him. The clothing in Gabriel's suitcase had been dumped, searched, and stuffed haphazardly back into place. Someone had spilled a flask of arcosolve in his case. Baer tilted his

54

head—*Sorry, dear man, but these things happen when one bumps up against police officers.*

Outside, in the misty courtyard, stood a black Mercedes sedan surrounded by a half-dozen uniformed officers. In the windows of the surrounding buildings stood policemen and secretaries come to see the Israeli assassin led away. As Gabriel approached the car, the rear door opened and a cloud of cigarette smoke billowed forth. A glimpse into the shadowed back seat established the source.

He stopped in his tracks, a move that seemed to take Baer completely by surprise. Then, reluctantly, he started walking again and climbed into the back seat. Baer closed the door, and the car immediately pulled away, the tires slipping over the wet cobblestones. Shamron didn't look at him. Shamron was gazing out the window, his eyes on the next battlefield, his thoughts on the next campaign.

5

♦ *ZÜRICH*

*T*O GET TO KLOTEN AIRPORT IT WAS necessary to make the ascent up the Zürichberg one more time. As they breasted the summit, the graceful villas receded and they entered a river flatland scarred by ugly modular strip malls. They moved slowly along a clogged two-lane commuter road as the afternoon sun tried to fight its way out of the clouds. A car was following them. The man on the passenger side could have been Peterson.

Ari Shamron had come to Zürich in an official capacity, but in dress and manner he had assumed the identity of Herr Heller, the cover he used for his frequent European travels. Herr Rudolf Heller of Heller Enterprises, Ltd., an international venture capital firm with offices in London, Paris, Berlin, Bern, and Nassau. His multitude of critics might have said that Heller Enterprises specialized in murder and mayhem, blackmail and betrayal. Heller Enterprises was an Old Economy firm, the critics said. What King Saul Boulevard needed to shake off its long winter of despair was a New Economy chief for the New Economy world. But Herr Heller clung to the keys of the executive suite with one of his patented vise grips, and few in Israel, prime ministers included, could muster the courage to wrest them away from him.

To his brotherhood of devoted acolytes, Shamron was a legend. Once Gabriel had been among them. But Shamron was also a liar, an unrepentant, unreconstructed liar. He lied as a matter of course, lied because he knew no other way, and he had lied to Gabriel time and time again. For a time their relationship had been like that of a father and a son. But the father became like a man who gambles or drinks or sleeps with many women and is forced to lie to his children, and now Gabriel hated him the way only a son can hate his father.

56

"What are you doing here? Why didn't you just send someone from Bern station to pick me up?"

"Because you're too important to entrust to someone from the station." Shamron lit another one of his vile Turkish cigarettes and violently snapped the lighter closed. "Besides, Herr Peterson and his friends from the Foreign Ministry made my appearance here a condition of your release. The Swiss love to yell at me when one of our agents gets in trouble. I'm not sure why. I suppose it reinforces their superiority complex—makes them feel better for their past sins."

"Who's Peterson?"

"*Gerhardt* Peterson works for the Division of Analysis and Protection."

"What the hell is that?"

"The new name for Switzerland's internal security service. It has responsibility for national security matters, counterintelligence, and investigating Swiss citizens suspected of treason. Peterson is the number-two man in the division. He oversees all operations."

"How did you convince him to let me go?"

"I played the subservient Jew. I gave them the usual promises that we would not operate on Swiss soil without first consulting Herr Peterson and his superiors in the Swiss security service. I also told them about a certain Swiss arms-maker who's flogging bomb triggers to terrorists on the open market. I suggested that they see to the situation themselves before someone takes matters into their own hands."

"You always have an ace in the hole."

"It's been my experience that one can never be too prepared."

"I thought your term was over."

"It was supposed to end six months ago, but the prime minister asked me to stay on. Given the current situation in the territories, we both agreed that now was not the time for a change of leadership at King Saul Boulevard."

Shamron had probably engineered the uprising himself, thought Gabriel. What better way to make himself indispensable? No, that was beyond even Shamron.

"My offer still stands."

"Which offer is that?"

"Deputy director for operations."

"No, thank you."

Shamron shrugged. "Tell me what happened. I want to hear it all, from beginning to end."

Gabriel so mistrusted Shamron that he considered giving him an abridged account of the affair, based on the theory that the less Shamron knew about anything, the better. But at least it would give them something new to talk about instead of refighting old wars, so Gabriel told him everything, starting with his arrival on the overnight train from Paris and ending with his arrest and interrogation. Shamron looked out the window as Gabriel spoke, turning over his lighter in his fingers: clockwise, counterclockwise, clockwise, counterclockwise...

"Did you see the body?"

"Very professional, one shot through the eye. He was probably dead before he hit the ground. A *coup de grâce* wasn't necessary."

"Did the police ever hit you?"

"No."

Shamron seemed disappointed by this.

Gabriel said, "Peterson told me the case was dropped because of pressure from Bern."

"Perhaps, but there was no way Peterson was ever going to hang the Ali Hamidi job on you. Prosecuting anyone on a twenty-five-year-old murder is hard enough. Prosecuting a professional—" He shrugged his shoulders, as if to say such things are just not done. "The Hamidi job was a work of art. No witnesses, no evidence."

The movie-star-handsome face of Ali Abdel Hamidi flashed in Gabriel's memory. Within the corridors of King Saul Boulevard, the amorous Palestinian has been known as the Swordsman of Allah. Writer of plays that graced no stage, seducer and manipulator of foolish young women. *Would you mind delivering this package to this address for me? You're flying to Tel Aviv? Would you mind taking a package to a friend?* The packages would inevitably be filled with explosives, and his lovers would be blown to bits along with anyone else who happened to be nearby. One night in Zürich, Hamidi met a university student named Trude in a bar in the Niederdorf section. When the girl suggested they go back to her flat, Hamidi agreed. Five minutes later, she led him into the narrow alley where Gabriel was waiting with a .22-caliber Beretta. Even now, Gabriel could hear the sound of bullets tearing into Hamidi's body.

"I suppose I should thank you for getting me out."

"A show of gratitude isn't necessary. In fact, I'm afraid I owe you an apology."

"An apology? Whatever for?"

"Because if it wasn't for me, you would have never been at Augustus Rolfe's villa in the first place."

RAMI, SHAMRON'S EVER-PRESENT PERSONAL bodyguard, was behind the wheel of the car. Shamron told him to drive in circles at Kloten. For twenty minutes Gabriel watched the same parade of airline signs and departure gates marching past his window. In his mind he was seeing something else: flash frames of past operations, old colleagues and old enemies. His palms were damp, his heart was beating faster. *Shamron*. He had done it again.

"Rolfe sent a message to us through our embassy," Shamron began. "He wanted to meet with someone from the Office. He didn't say why, but when a man like Augustus Rolfe wants to talk, we usually try to accommodate him. He wanted the meeting to be handled with discretion. I looked into Rolfe's background and discovered he was an art collector. Naturally, I thought you were the perfect man for the job, so I arranged for you to be hired to clean one of his paintings. A Rubens, if I'm not mistaken."

"It was a Raphael."

Shamron pulled a face, as if to say such distinctions were of no interest to him. Art, music, literature, the theater—these things bored him. He was a man of the real world.

"Did Isherwood know it was all a game?"

"Julian? No, I'm afraid I deceived him as well."

"Why do it like this? Why didn't you just tell me the truth?"

"Would you have done it?

"No."

A tilt of his bald head, another long pull from his Turkish cigarette—*I rest my case.* "I'm afraid the truth and I are somewhat estranged. I'm an old man, Gabriel. I've spent my entire life telling lies. To me, lies are more comfortable than the truth."

"Let me out of the car! I don't want to hear anymore!"

"Let me finish."

"Shut up! I don't want to hear your voice."

"Listen to me, Gabriel!" Shamron slammed his fist onto the console. "Augustus Rolfe, a Swiss banker, wanted to speak to us and for that he was murdered. I want to know what Rolfe was going to tell us, and I want to know who killed him for it!"

"Find someone else, Ari. Investigating murder cases was never my specialty. Actually, thanks to you, I excelled at quite the other thing."

"Please, Gabriel, let's not have this argument again."

"You and Peterson seem to be very tight. If you play the subservient Jew again, I'm sure he'd be willing to keep you abreast of all the developments in his investigation."

"Augustus Rolfe was killed because someone knew you were coming to Zürich—someone who didn't want you to hear what Augustus Rolfe had to say. Someone who was willing to make it appear as though *you* were the killer."

"If that was their intention, they did a damned lousy job of it. I was on the train from Paris at the time Rolfe was killed." Gabriel was calmer now. He was furious with Shamron for deceiving him, but at the same time he was intrigued. "What do you know about Augustus Rolfe?"

"The Rolfe family has been stashing money beneath the Bahnhofstrasse for a couple of hundred years. They're one of the most prominent banking families in Switzerland."

"Who would want him dead?"

"A lot of dirty money has flowed through the numbered accounts of Rolfe's bank. It's safe to assume he'd made his fair share of enemies."

"What else?"

"The family suffers from a legendary curse. Twenty-five years ago, Rolfe's wife committed suicide. She dug her own grave in the garden of Rolfe's country chalet, climbed in, and shot herself. A few years after that, Rolfe's only son, Maximilian, died in a cycling accident in the Alps."

"Is there any family that's *alive?*"

"His daughter, at least she was the last time anyone heard from her. Her name is Anna."

"His daughter is *Anna* Rolfe?"

"So you know her? I'm impressed."

"She's only one of the most famous musicians in the world."

"Do you still want to get out of the car?"

GABRIEL HAD BEEN GIVEN TWO GIFTS THAT made him a great art restorer: a meticulous attention to detail and an unflagging desire to see every task, no matter how mundane, through to its conclusion. He never left his studio until his work space and supplies were spotless, never went to bed with dirty dishes in the sink. And he never left a painting unfinished, even when it was a cover job for Shamron. To Gabriel, a half-restored painting was no longer a work of art, just a bit of oil and pigment smeared on a canvas or a wood panel. The dead body of Augustus Rolfe, lying at the foot of the Raphael, was like a painting that had only been half-restored. It would not be whole again until Gabriel knew who had killed him and why.

"What do you want me to do?"

"Talk to her."

"Why me?"

"Apparently, she has something of an artistic temperament."

"From what I've read, that's an understatement."

"You're an artist. You speak her language. Perhaps she'll trust you enough to tell you what she knows about her father's affairs. If you come up empty, you can go back to your studio, and I'll never darken your door again."

"Promises, promises."

"There's no need to be hurtful, Gabriel."

"Last time you came into my life, I nearly got myself killed."

"True, but at least it wasn't boring."

"Peterson says I can't come back to Switzerland. How am I supposed to talk to Anna Rolfe?"

"Apparently she refuses to live in Switzerland." Shamron handed him a slip of paper. "This is her management company in London. Give her a few days to bury her father. So you'll do it?"

"Not for you. I want to know who tried to pin Rolfe's murder on me. Who shall I be when I talk to Anna Rolfe?"

"I always prefer the subtle approach, but I'll leave it to your discretion. Play it as you see fit."

Gabriel slipped the address into his pocket. A thin smile appeared briefly on Shamron's face. He had learned long ago that professional victories, even small ones, were to be savored.

The car pulled to the curb beneath a British Airways sign. Gabriel climbed out, collected his things from the trunk, then looked into Shamron's window.

Shamron said, "We didn't discuss your fee."

"Don't worry. It will be substantial."

"You're on expense account as of now, but remember, throwing money around never solved a case."

"I'll consider that pearl of wisdom while I'm flying first-class back to London tonight."

Shamron grimaced. "Stay in touch. Usual channels and methods. Do you remember?"

"How could I ever forget?"

"It was quite an accomplishment, don't you think?"

"What was that?"

"Finding a man thirty minutes after he leaves the scene of a murder. I wonder how Herr Peterson managed to do that. He must be very good."

6

NIDWALDEN, ♦ SWITZERLAND

ITHIN THE DIVISION OF ANALYSIS and Protection, Gerhardt Peterson was regarded as a man on the rise. Superiors handled him with care. Subordinates withered under his cold stare. His colleagues looked on in wonder and jealousy. How had the schoolteacher's boy from Erstfeld risen to such heights? *Look at him! Never a hair out of place! Never a loose tie! He wears power and success like his expensive aftershave.* Peterson never made a move that wasn't calculated to advance his career. His family life was as neat and orderly as his office. His sexual affairs were discreet and appropriate. Anyone foolish enough to stand in his way quickly discovered that Gerhardt Peterson was a man with powerful friends. Friends in Bern. Friends in the banks. He would be the chief soon—everyone agreed on that. Then a senior posting in the Federal Office for Police. Someday, perhaps, control of the entire Department of Justice and Police.

Peterson *did* have friends in the banks. And they *did* do favors for him. The Swiss financial oligarchy had been like an invisible hand on his back, nudging him up each rung of the ladder of power. But it was not a one-way street. Peterson did favors for them, too, which is why he was behind the wheel of his Mercedes sedan, racing through the gloomy forest of the Kernwald.

At the base of the mountains, he came to a road marked private. He followed the road until he came to an imposing black iron gate. Peterson knew the routine. As he slipped the Mercedes into park and lowered his window, a guard stepped out of a small hut. He had the smooth, precise walk of a man with a military background. Peterson could see the bulge of a weapon beneath his blue ski jacket.

Peterson poked his head out the window. "My name is Herr Köhler."

"Are you here for the conference, Herr Köhler?"

"Actually, I'm the entertainment."

"Follow the road to the house. Another man will meet you there."

IT WAS A TRADITIONAL SWISS CHALET IN CONception but grotesque in its massive scale. Anchored to the side of the mountain, it stared out across the valley below with a look of deep satisfaction. Peterson was the last to arrive. The others were already there. They had come from Zürich and Zug, from Lucerne and Bern, and from Geneva and Basel. As was their custom, they had traveled separately and arrived at unevenly spaced intervals so as not to attract attention. They were all Swiss. Foreigners were not permitted. Foreigners were the reason the group existed.

As usual, the meeting would take place in the sprawling, glass-walled living room on the second level of the house. Had any of them bothered to stand in the windows, they would have been treated to a truly remarkable view: a carpet of wet lights on the valley floor, shrouded by a bridal veil of drifting snow. Instead, they huddled together in small groups, smoking, chatting quietly, sipping coffee or tea. Alcoholic beverages were never served at the house. The host, Herr Gessler, drank only tea and mineral water and was a vegetarian. He credited his strict diet for his remarkable longevity.

Despite the informal surroundings, Herr Gessler insisted on a boardroom approach to the meetings. The guests did not sit on the comfortable sofas and armchairs but at a long conference table. At precisely 6:00 P.M., each man went to his assigned chair and stood behind it.

A moment later, a door opened and a man appeared. Thin and frail, with dark glasses and a gossamer layer of gray hair, he leaned on the arm of a young security man. When he had taken his seat at the head of the table, the others sat down too.

There was one empty chair, an unfortunate oversight. After a moment of embarrassed silence, the security guard lifted it by the back and carried it out.

IN THE NEXT ROOM, GERHARDT PETERSON stared directly into the lens of a video camera like a talk-show guest waiting to appear on a program by remote. It was always this way. Whenever Peterson had business before the Council, he spoke to them electronically from a distance. He had never seen Herr Gessler or any of the other men in the room—at least not in connection with the Council. Herr Gessler said the peculiar arrangement was for their protection—and, perhaps more importantly, his.

"Gerhardt, are you ready?"

It was the reedy voice of Herr Gessler, made even thinner by the tiny earpiece.

"Yes, I'm ready."

"I hope we haven't taken you away from any pressing state business, Gerhardt."

"Not at all, Herr Gessler. Just an interdepartmental meeting on drug trafficking."

"Such a waste of time, this silly war on narcotics."

Gessler was infamous for his sudden digressions. Peterson folded his hands and bided his time.

"Personally, I've never seen the attraction of drugs, but then I've never seen the harm either. What someone puts in their body is none of my business. If they wish to destroy their life and their health with these chemicals, why should I care? Why should governments care? Why should governments spend untold resources combating a problem that is as old as human nature itself? After all, one could argue that Adam was the first substance abuser. God forbade young Adam the fruit, and he consumed it the first chance he got."

"You make an interesting point, Herr Gessler."

"Our detractors say that the drug trade has been very good to Switzerland. I'm afraid I would have to concur. I'm certain my own bank contains accounts of the so-called drug kingpins. But what is the harm? At least if the money is deposited in Switzerland it is put to good use. It is loaned to legitimate enterprises that produce goods and services and employment for millions of people."

"So they can go out and buy more drugs?"

"If that's what they wish. You see, there is a circular quality to life on earth. Nature is in harmony. So is the global financial system. But just as nature can be thrown out of balance by a seemingly small occurrence, so can business. Imagine the destructive consequences if the profits of the drug trade were not recirculated back into the world economy. The bankers of Switzerland are performing a valuable service."

Gessler sipped his tea. Peterson could not see this but could hear it in the sensitive microphone used to amplify the old man's weak voice.

"But I digress," Gessler said, as his teacup rattled back into the saucer. "Back to the business at hand. It seems we have another complication concerning the Rolfe matter."

"DOES THIS FELLOW STRIKE YOU AS THE KIND of man who will let the matter drop?" Gessler said when Peterson was finished with his briefing.

"No, Herr Gessler."

"Then what do you suggest?"

"That we clean up the mess as quickly as possible and make certain there's nothing for him to find."

Gessler sighed. "It was never the purpose of this body to engage in violence—only to combat the violence that is being done to us."

"In war there are casualties."

"Surveillance and intimidation is one thing—killing is quite another. It's critical we use someone who can't be linked to the Council

70

in any way. Surely, in your other line of work, you've come across people like this."

"I have."

The old man sighed.

Gerhardt Peterson pulled out the earpiece and headed back to Zürich.

7

*T*HERE WAS AN OLD JOKE ON CORSICA that the island's notoriously treacherous roads had been designed jointly by Machiavelli and the Marquis de Sade. Yet the Englishman had never minded driving there. Indeed, he tore around the island with a certain fatalistic abandon that had earned him the reputation of being something of a madman. At the moment he was racing along a windswept highway on the western edge of the island through a thick blanket of marine fog. Five miles on, he turned inland. As he climbed into the hills, the fog gave way to a clear blue afternoon sky. The autumn sunlight brought out the contrasting shades of green in the olive trees and Laricio pine. In the shadow of the trees were dense patches of gorse and brier and rockrose, the legendary Corsican undergrowth known as the *macchia* that had concealed bandits and murderers for centuries. The

Englishman lowered his window. The warm scent of rosemary washed over his face.

Ahead of him stood a hill town, a cluster of sand-colored houses with red-tile roofs huddled around a bell tower, half in shadow, half in brilliant sunlight. In the background rose the mountains, ice-blue snow on the highest peaks. Ten years ago, when he had first settled here, the children would point at him with their index fingers and pinkies, the Corsican way of warding off the evil eye of a stranger. Now they smiled and waved as he sped through the town and headed up the cul-de-sac valley toward his villa.

Along the way he passed a *paesanu* working a small patch of vegetables at the roadside. The man peered at the Englishman, black eyes smoldering beneath the brim of his broad hat, and signaled his recognition with an almost imperceptible wave of his first two fingers. The old *paesanu* was one of the Englishman's adopted clansmen. Farther up the road, a young boy called Giancomo stepped into his path and waved his arms for the Englishman to stop.

"Welcome home. Was your trip good?"

"Very good."

"What did you bring me?"

"That depends."

"On what?"

"On whether you watched my villa for me while I was away."

"Of course I did, just as I promised."

"Did anyone come?"

"No, I saw no one."

"You're quite sure?"

The boy nodded. From his suitcase the Englishman removed a beautiful satchel, handmade of fine Spanish leather, and handed it to the boy. "For your books—so you won't lose them on the way home from school anymore."

The boy pulled the satchel to his nose and smelled the new leather. Then he said: "Do you have any cigarettes?"

"You won't tell your mother?"

"Of course not!"

The men pretended to rule Corsica, but the real power lay in the hands of the mothers. The Englishman handed the boy a half-empty packet.

He slipped the cigarettes into his satchel. "One more thing."

"What's that?"

"Don Orsati wishes to speak with you."

"When did you see him?"

"This morning."

"Where?"

"At the café in the village."

"Where is he now?"

"At the café in the village."

Orsati lives a stressful life, thought the Englishman.

"Invite the don to my villa for lunch. But tell him that if he expects to eat, he should bring along some food."

The boy smiled and scampered off, the leather satchel flailing behind him like a banner. The Englishman slipped the jeep into gear and continued up the road. About a half-mile from his villa, he slammed on his brakes, and the jeep skidded to a stop amid a cloud of red dust.

Standing in the center of the narrow track was a large male goat. He had the markings of a palomino and a red beard. Like the Englishman, he was scarred from old battles. The goat detested the Englishman and blocked the road to his villa whenever it pleased him. The Englishman had dreamed many times of ending the conflict once and for all with the Glock pistol he kept in his glove box. But the beast belonged to Don Casabianca, and if he were ever harmed there would be a feud.

The Englishman honked his horn. Don Casabianca's goat threw back his head and glared at him defiantly. The Englishman had two choices, both unpleasant. He could wait out the goat, or he could try to move him.

He took a long look over his shoulder to make sure no one was watching. Then he threw open his door and charged the goat, waving his hands and screaming like a lunatic, until the beast gave ground and darted into the shelter of the *macchia*. A fitting place for him, thought the Englishman—the *macchia*, the place where all thieves and bandits eventually reside.

He got back into his jeep and headed up the road to his villa, thinking about the terrible shame of it. A highly accomplished assassin, yet he couldn't get to his own home without first suffering a humiliation at the hands of Don Casabianca's wretched goat.

IT HAD NEVER TAKEN MUCH TO SPARK A FEUD on Corsica. An insult. An accusation of cheating in the marketplace. Dissolution of an engagement. The pregnancy of an unmarried woman. Once, in the Englishman's village, there had been a forty-year feud over the keys to the church. After the initial spark, unrest quickly followed. An ox would be killed. The owner of the ox would retaliate by killing a mule or a flock of sheep. A prized olive tree would be chopped down. A fence toppled. A house would burn. Then the murders would start. And on it would go, sometimes for a generation or more, until the aggrieved parties had settled their differences or given up the fight in exhaustion.

On Corsica most men were all too willing to do their killing themselves. But there were always some who needed others to do the blood work for them: notables who were too squeamish to get their hands dirty or unwilling to risk arrest or exile; women who could not kill for themselves or had no male kin to do the deed on their behalf. People like these relied on professionals: the *taddunaghiu*. Usually they turned to the Orsati clan.

The Orsatis had fine land with many olive trees, and their oil was regarded as the sweetest in all of Corsica. But they did more than produce fine olive oil. No one knew how many Corsicans had died at the hands of Orsati assassins over the ages—least of all the Orsatis themselves—but local lore placed the number in the thousands. It might have been significantly higher if not for the clan's rigorous vetting process. In the old days, the Orsatis operated by a strict code. They refused to carry out a killing unless satisfied that the party before them had indeed been wronged and blood vengeance was required.

Anton Orsati had taken over the helm of the family business in troubled times. The French authorities had managed to eradicate feuding and the vendetta in all but the most isolated pockets of the island. Few Corsicans required the services of the *taddunaghiu* any longer. But Anton Orsati was a shrewd businessman. He knew he could either fold his tent and become a mere producer of excellent olive oil or expand his base of operations and look for opportunities elsewhere. He decided on the second course and took his business across the water. Now, his band of assassins was regarded as the most reliable and professional in Europe. They roamed the continent, killing on behalf of wealthy men, criminals, insurance cheats, and sometimes even governments. Most of the men they killed deserved to die, but competition and the exigencies of the modern age had required Anton Orsati to forsake the old code of his ancestors. Every job offer that crossed his desk was accepted, no matter how distasteful, as long as it did not place the life of one of his assassins in unreasonable danger.

Orsati always found it slightly amusing that his most skilled employee was not a Corsican but an Englishman from Highgate in North London. Only Orsati knew the truth about him. That he had served in the famed Special Air Service. That he had killed men in Northern Ireland and Iraq. That his former masters believed him to be dead. Once, the Englishman showed Orsati a clipping from a London newspaper. His obituary. A very useful thing in this line of work, thought Orsati. People don't often look for a dead man.

He may have been born an Englishman, but Orsati always thought he had been given the restless soul of a Corsican. He spoke the dialect as well as Orsati, mistrusted outsiders, and despised all authority. At night he would sit in the village square with the old men, scowling at the boys on their skateboards and grumbling about how the young had no respect for the old ways. He was a man of honor—sometimes too much honor for Orsati's taste. Still, he was a superb assassin, the finest Orsati had ever known. He had been trained by the most efficient killers on the planet, and Orsati had learned much from him. He was also perfectly suited to certain assignments on the continent, which is why Anton Orsati came calling on the Englishman's villa that afternoon with an armful of groceries.

ORSATI WAS A DESCENDANT OF A FAMILY OF notables, but in dress and appetite he was not much different than the *paesanu* working his patch down the valley road. He wore a

77

bleached white shirt, unbuttoned to the center of his barrel chest, and dusty leather sandals. The "lunch" that he brought with him consisted of a loaf of coarse bread, a flask of olive oil, a chunk of aromatic Corsican ham, and a lump of strong cheese. The Englishman provided the wine. The afternoon was warm, so they ate outside on the terrace overlooking the cul-de-sac valley, in the dappled shade of a pair of towering Corsican pines.

Orsati handed the Englishman a check bearing the imprint of Orsati Olive Oil. All of Orsati's assassins were officially employees of the company. The Englishman was a vice president for marketing, whatever that meant. "Your share of the fee for the Spain assignment." Orsati swirled a piece of the bread in oil and shoved it into his mouth. "Any problems?"

"The girl was working for the Spanish security service."

"Which girl?"

"The girl Navarra was seeing."

"Oh, shit. What did you do?"

"She saw my face."

Orsati contemplated this news while he sawed off a slice of the ham and placed it on the Englishman's plate. Neither man liked collateral casualties. They were usually bad for business.

"How are you feeling?"

"I'm tired."

"Still not sleeping well?"

"Not while I'm in a foreign country killing a man."

"And here?"

"Better."

"You should try to get some rest tonight instead of sitting up all hours with the old ones in the village."

"Why?"

"Because I have another job for you."

"I just finished a job. Give it to one of the others."

"It's too sensitive."

"You have a dossier?"

Orsati finished his lunch and swam lazy laps in the pool while the Englishman read. When he finished, he looked up. "What has this man done to deserve to die?"

"Apparently, he stole something quite valuable."

The Englishman closed the file. He had no compunction about killing someone who stole for a living. In the Englishman's opinion, a thief was earth's lowest life form.

"So why does this job require me?"

"Because the contractors would like the target dead and his business destroyed. The men who trained you at Hereford taught you how to use explosives. My men are comfortable with more conventional weapons."

"Where am I going to get a bomb?"

Orsati climbed out of the pool and vigorously toweled his thick silver hair. "Do you know Pascal Debré?"

Unfortunately, the Englishman did know Pascal Debré. He was an arsonist who did jobs for a Marseilles-based criminal enterprise. Debré would have to be handled carefully.

79

"Debré knows to expect you. He'll give you whatever you need for the job."

"When do I leave?"

8

*B*Y ALL APPEARANCES THE WOMAN WHO HAD settled in the refurbished old monastery on the steep hill overlooking the sea had taken a vow to live the sequestered existence of an ascetic. For a long time no one in the village knew even her name. Senhora Rosa, the scandalmonger checkout clerk at the market, decided she was a woman scorned, and she inflicted her dubious theory on anyone unfortunate enough to pass by her register. It was Rosa who christened the woman Our Lady of the Hillside. The moniker clung to her, even after her real name became known.

She came to the village each morning to do her marketing, sweeping down the hill on her bright-red motor scooter, her blond ponytail flying behind her like a banner. In wet weather she wore a hooded anorak the color of mushrooms. There was a great deal of speculation about her country of origin. Her limited Portuguese was heavily accented. Carlos, the man who cared for the villa's grounds and small vineyard, thought she had the accent of a German and the dark soul of a Viennese Jew. María, the pious woman who cleaned her home, decided she was Dutch. José from the fish market thought Danish. But Manuel, the owner of the café on the village square and the town's unofficial mayor, settled the question, as he usually did. "Our Lady is not German, or Austrian, or Dutch, or Danish." Then he rubbed his first two fingers against his thumb, the international symbol for money. "Our Lady of the Hillside is Swiss."

Her days had a predictable rhythm. After her morning visit to the village, she could be seen swimming laps in her dark-blue pool, her hair tucked beneath a black rubber cap. Then she would walk, usually among the jagged granite outcroppings on the ridge of the hill or up the dusty track to the Moorish ruins. Beginning in the late afternoon, she would play the violin—exceptionally well, according to those who had heard her—in a bare room on the second floor of the villa. Once, María stole a glance inside and found Our Lady in a feverish state, her body rocking and pitching about, her hair damp, her eyes tightly closed. "Our Lady plays like she's possessed by demons," María said to Carlos. "And no sheet music. She plays from memory."

Only once, during the festival of Santo António, did she take part in the social life of the village. Shortly after dark, as the men set fire to the charcoal grills and uncorked the wine, she traipsed down the hill in a sleeveless white dress and sandals. For the first time she was not alone. There were fourteen in all: an Italian opera singer, a French fashion model, a British film actor, a German painter— along with wives, girlfriends, mistresses, and lovers. The opera singer and the film actor had a contest to see who could consume the most grilled sardines, the traditional fare of the festival. The opera singer easily dispatched the actor, who then tried to console himself by making a clumsy pass at the fashion model. The actor's wife slapped him silly in the center of the square. The Portuguese vil- lagers, who had never seen a woman slap- ping a man, applauded wildly, and the dancing resumed. Afterward, all agreed that the band of gypsies from the villa on the hillside had made the festival the most enjoyable in memory.

Only Our Lady seemed to take no joy from it. To Carlos, she seemed an island of melan- cholia in a sea of wild debauchery. She picked at her food; she drank her wine as though it was something that was expected of her. When the handsome German painter planted himself at her side and showered her with attention, Our Lady was polite but clearly indifferent. The painter finally gave up and went in search of other prey.

At midnight, just as the festival reached fever pitch, Our Lady slipped away from the party and headed up the track alone to her villa on the hillside. Twenty minutes later, Carlos saw a light flare briefly in the room on the second floor. It was the room where Our Lady played her violin.

♦ ♦ ♦

WITH LITTLE ELSE TO DO THAT SUMMER, THE villagers set out to finally learn the name and occupation of the mysterious woman from the hillside. Carlos and María, the two people closest to her, were carefully interrogated but could offer little help. Once a month they received a check, sent by certified mail, from a company in London called European Artistic Management. Because of the barriers of language and class, their communication with the woman was restricted to the simplest of greetings. They *were* able to supply one piece of critical information: Our Lady was prone to sudden unexplained absences. Rosa of the market read much into this. She decided Our Lady was a spy and that European Artistic Management was nothing but a front. What else would explain her secretive nature? Her sudden disappearances and even more sudden returns? But once again, it was Manuel who settled this question. One evening, while the debate raged in his café, he reached beneath the bar and produced a compact-disc recording of several Brahms violin sonatas. On the cover was a photograph of Our Lady. "Her name is Anna Rolfe," Manuel said in triumph. "Our Lady of the Hillside is a very famous woman."

She was also a woman prone to accidents. There was the afternoon she lost control of her motor scooter and Carlos found her by the roadside with a pair of broken ribs. A month later she slipped on the edge of the pool and cracked her head. Just two weeks after that, she lost her balance at the top of the stairs and tumbled down to the landing, coming to rest in María's dustpan.

Carlos concluded that, for some reason, Our Lady simply lacked the ability to look after herself. She was not a reckless woman, just careless, and she seemed to learn nothing from her previous mistakes. "It will be very bad for the reputation of the village if something happened to so famous a woman," Manuel concluded gravely. "She needs to be protected from herself."

And so quietly, carefully, Carlos began to watch her. In the mornings, when she swam laps in her pool, he would find work to do close by so he could monitor her progress. He conducted regular clandestine inspections of her motor scooter to make certain it was in good working order. In the tiny hamlets along the top of the ridge, he created a network of watchers, so that whenever Our Lady went for her afternoon expeditions, she was under constant surveillance.

His diligence paid off. It was Carlos who discovered that Our Lady was hiking on the ridge the afternoon a powerful gale swept in from the sea. He found her amid the wreckage of a rock slide with her hand pinned beneath a hundred-pound boulder, and carried her unconscious down to the village. Had it not been for Carlos, the doctors in Lisbon said, Anna Rolfe would surely have lost her famous left hand.

◆ ◆ ◆

HER REHABILITATION WAS LONG AND PAINFUL— for everyone. For several weeks, her left arm was immobilized by a heavy fiberglass cast. Since she was no longer able to ride her motor scooter, Carlos was pressed into service as her driver. Each morning they climbed into her white Land Rover and rattled down the hill into the village. Our Lady remained silent during these trips, staring out the window, her bandaged hand in her lap. Once, Carlos tried to brighten her mood with Mozart. She removed the disc and hurled it into the passing trees. Carlos never again made the mistake of trying to play music for her.

The bandages became progressively smaller, until finally she required none at all. The severe swelling receded, and the shape of her hand returned to normal. Only the scars remained. Our Lady did her best to conceal them. She wore long-sleeved blouses with lacy cuffs. As she moved round the village doing her marketing, she tucked her hand beneath her right arm.

Her mood darkened further when she tried to play the violin again. Each afternoon for five consecutive days, she walked up to her practice room on the second floor of the villa. Each day she would attempt something elementary—a minor scale over two octaves, an arpeggio—but even that would be too much for her ruined hand. Before long there would be a scream of anguish, followed by shouting in German. On the fifth day, Carlos watched from the vineyard as Our Lady lifted her priceless Guarneri violin over her head and prepared to hurl it to the floor. Instead, she lowered it to her breast and hugged it as she wept. That evening, in the café, Carlos told Manuel about the scene he had witnessed. Manuel reached for the telephone and asked the operator for the number of a company called European Artistic Management in London.

Forty-eight hours later, a small delegation arrived. There was an Englishwoman named Fiona, an American called Gregory, and a dour German called Herr Lang. Each morning, Gregory forced Our Lady to do several hours of punishing exercises to regain the strength and mobility in her hand. In the afternoon, Herr Lang stood over her in her practice room, teaching her how to play her instrument again. Slowly her skills returned, though even Carlos the vineyard keeper could tell that she was not the same musician she had been before the accident.

By October the delegation was gone, and Our Lady was alone again. Her days assumed the predictable rhythm they'd had before the accident, though she took more care when riding her red motor scooter and never set out for the ridge without first checking the weather forecast.

Then, on All Souls Day, she vanished. Carlos took note of the fact that, as she climbed into her Range Rover and headed toward Lisbon, she carried only a black-leather garment bag and no violin. The next day he went to the café and told Manuel what he had seen. Manuel showed him a story in the *International Herald-Tribune*. The vineyard keeper could not read English, so Manuel handled the translation.

"The death of a father is a terrible thing," Carlos said. "But murder...this is much worse."

"Indeed," said Manuel, folding the newspaper. "But you should hear what happened to that poor woman's mother."

CARLOS WAS WORKING IN THE VINEYARD, preparing the vines for the onset of winter, when Our Lady returned from Zürich. She paused briefly in the drive to unclasp her hair and shake it loose in the sea wind, then disappeared into the villa. A moment later Carlos saw her flash past the window of her practice room. No lights. Our Lady always practiced in the dark.

As she began to play, Carlos lowered his head and resumed his work, his pruning shears snapping rhythmically, keeping time with the beating of the waves on the beach below. It was a piece she had played often—a mystical, haunting sonata, supposedly inspired by the Devil himself—but since the accident it had eluded her. He braced himself for the inevitable explosion, but after five minutes his shears fell silent, and he looked up the terraced hillside toward the villa. So skillful was her playing tonight that it seemed there were two violinists in the villa instead of one.

The air had turned colder, and a gauzy sea haze was creeping up the slope of the hill. Carlos set his pile of rubbish alight and squatted next to the flames. She was approaching a difficult section of the piece, a treacherous run of descending notes—a *devilish* passage, he thought, smiling. Once again he braced himself, but tonight only music exploded, a blistering descent that ended in the quiet resolution of the first movement.

She paused a few seconds, then began the second movement. Carlos turned and looked up the hillside. The villa was bathed in the orange light of sunset. María the housekeeper was outside on the terrace, sweeping. Carlos removed his hat and held it aloft, waiting for María to see him—shouting or noise of any kind was forbidden while Our Lady was practicing. After a moment María lifted her head, and her broom paused in midstroke. Carlos held out his hands. *What do you think, María? Will it be all right this time?* The housekeeper pressed her palms together and gazed up toward the heavens. *Thank you, God.*

Indeed, thought Carlos as he watched the smoke of his fire dancing on the evening wind. Thank you, God. Tonight, things are good. The weather is fine, the vineyards are ready for winter, and Our Lady of the Hillside is playing her sonata again.

FOUR HOURS LATER, ANNA ROLFE LOWERED HER violin and placed it in its case. Immediately she was overcome by the unique combination of exhaustion and restlessness she felt at the end of every practice session. She walked into her bedroom and lay atop the cool duvet, her arms spread wide, listening to the sound of her own breathing and to the night wind rustling in the eaves. She felt something else besides fatigue and restlessness; something she had not felt in a very long time. She supposed it was satisfaction. The Tartini sonata had always been her signature piece, but since the accident the wicked string crossings and demanding double-stops had been too much for her hand. Tonight she had played it exceptionally well for the first time since her recovery. She had always found that her mood was reflected in her playing. Anger, sadness, anxiety—all these emotions revealed themselves when she placed a bow against the strings of a violin. She wondered why the emotions unleashed by the death of her father would allow her to again play Tartini's sonata.

Suddenly she required activity. She sat upright, pulled off her damp T-shirt, and slipped into a cotton sweater. For several minutes she wandered aimlessly through the rooms of her villa, here switching on a lamp, here closing a shutter. The smooth terra-cotta floors were cold against her bare feet. How she loved this place, with its whitewashed walls and comfortable sailcloth-covered furniture. It was so unlike the house on the Zürichberg where she was raised. The rooms were big and open instead of small and dark, the furnishings unpretentious and simple. This was an honest house, a house with no secrets. It was *her* house.

In the kitchen she poured herself a large glass of red wine. It was from a local vintner; indeed, some of her own grapes had been used in the blend. After a moment, the wine took the edge off her mood. It was a dirty little secret of the classical music world: the drinking. She had worked with orchestras that had come back from lunch breaks so medicated with alcohol it was a wonder anyone could play at all. She peered into the refrigerator. She had hardly eaten in Zürich and was famished. She sautéed mushrooms and tomatoes in olive oil and fresh local herbs, then stirred in three beaten eggs and added some grated cheese. After the nightmare of Zürich, this simple domestic task gave her an inordinate amount of pleasure. When the omelet was finished, she sat on a tall stool at the kitchen counter and ate it with the last of her wine.

It was then she noticed the light winking on her answering machine. There were four messages. Long ago she had switched off all the ringers on the telephones to avoid being disturbed while she was practicing. She forked a bite of the omelet into her mouth and pressed the play button on the machine.

The first message was from her father's lawyer in Zürich. It seemed he had some more papers for her to sign. "Would it be convenient to send them by overnight parcel to the villa?"

Yes, it would be, she thought. She'd telephone him in the morning.

The second call was Marco. A long time ago they had been engaged to be married. Like Anna, Marco was a gifted soloist, but he was little known outside Italy. He could never get over the fact that Anna was a star and he was not, and he had punished her by sleeping with half the women in Rome. After Marco she had taken a vow never to never again fall in love with a musician.

"I read about your father in the papers, Anna darling. I'm so sorry, my love. What can I do? Do you need anything from me? I'll get on the next plane."

No, you won't, she thought. She'd call Marco in the morning, after she finished with the lawyer. With a bit of luck, she'd get his machine and be spared the indignity of having to hear his voice in real time.

The third message was from Fiona Richardson. Fiona was the only person in the world Anna trusted completely. Each time she had stumbled, Fiona had been there to pull her back onto her feet. "Are you home yet, Anna? How was the funeral? Perfectly awful, I'm sure. They always are. I've been thinking about Venice. Perhaps we should postpone it. Zaccaria will understand, and so will your fans. No one can be expected to perform so soon after something like this. You need time to grieve, Anna—even if you did despise the old bastard. Call me."

She would not be postponing her recital in Venice. She was surprised Fiona would even suggest it. She had canceled two coming-out appearances already. There had been rumblings in the press and among orchestra masters and concert promoters. If she canceled a third, the damage could be irreparable. She'd call Fiona in the morning and tell her she was going to Venice in two weeks.

The final message: Fiona again.

"One more thing, Anna. A very nice gentlemen from the Israeli embassy stopped by the office two days ago. Said he wanted to contact you. Said he had information about your father's death. He seemed perfectly harmless. You might want to hear what he has to say. He left a number. Have a pen?"

Fiona recited the number.

CARLOS HAD LAID A BED OF OLIVE WOOD IN THE fireplace. Anna set the kindling alight and stretched out on the couch, watched the flames spreading over the wood. In the firelight she studied her hand. The flickering shadows set her scars in motion.

She had always assumed the death of her father would bring some sort of inner peace— closure, as the Americans were so fond of saying. To be orphaned seemed more tolerable

92

to Anna than did the alienation of estrangement. She might have been able to find that peace tonight if her father had died the usual death of an old man. Instead, he had been shot to death in his home.

She closed her eyes and saw his funeral. It had been held in the ancient Fraumünster church on the banks of the Limmat. The mourners looked like spectators at a shareholders conference. It seemed that all of the Zürich financial world was there: the young stars and financial sharps from the big banks and trading houses, along with the last of her father's contemporaries—the old guard of the Zürich financial oligarchy. Some of them had been there twenty-five years earlier for her mother's funeral.

As she had listened to the eulogies, Anna found herself hating her father for being murdered. It was as if he had conspired to commit one final act to make her life more painful. The press had dredged up stories of the Rolfe family tragedies: the suicide of her mother, the death of her brother in the Tour of Switzerland, the injury to her hand. "A Family Cursed" was the headline in the *Neue Züricher Zeitung.*

Anna Rolfe did not believe in curses. Things happened for a reason. She had injured her hand because she had been foolish enough to stay on the ridge when the sky turned black with storm clouds. Her brother had been killed because he had deliberately chosen a dangerous profession to spite his father. *And her mother...* Anna did not know exactly why her mother had killed herself. Only her father knew the answer to that question. Anna was certain of one thing. She had killed herself for a reason. It was not the result of a family curse.

Neither was her father's murder.

But why was he murdered? The day before the funeral she had endured a long interview by the Zürich police and by an officer from the Swiss security service named Gerhardt Peterson. *Did your father have enemies, Miss Rolfe? Do you know anyone who might have wanted to harm your father? If you know any information that might assist us in our investigation, please tell us now, Miss Rolfe.* She did know things, but they were not the kind of things one tells the Swiss police. Anna Rolfe had always believed that they were part of the problem.

But who could she trust?

"A very nice gentlemen from the Israeli embassy stopped by the office two days ago. Said he wanted to contact you."

She looked at the telephone number Fiona had given her.

"Said he had information about your father's death."

Why would a man from Israel claim to know anything about the murder of her father? And did she really want to hear what he had to say? Perhaps it would be better to leave things as they were. She could concentrate on her playing and get ready for Venice. She looked at the number one last time, committed it to

94

memory, and dropped the paper onto the fire.

Then she looked at the scars on her hand. *There is no Rolfe family curse*, she thought. *Things happen for a reason.* Her mother killed herself. Twenty-five years later, her father was murdered. *Why? Who could she trust?*

"He seemed perfectly harmless. You might want to hear what he has to say."

She lay there for a few minutes, thinking it through. Then she walked into the kitchen, picked up the receiver of the telephone, and dialed the number.

9

COSTA DE PRATA, ♦ PORTUGAL

*T*HE ROAD TO ANNA ROLFE'S VILLA WOUND along the shoulder of a hill overlooking the Atlantic. Sometimes the view was hidden by a stand of fir or an outcropping of smoke-colored granite. Then Gabriel would round another bend, the trees would thin, and the sea would appear again. It was late afternoon, the sun was nearly touching the horizon, the water was the color of apricot and gold leaf. Giant rollers pummeled a small beach. He lowered the window and rested his arm on the sill. Cold air filled the car, heavy with the scent of the sea.

He turned toward the village, following the instructions she had given him. Left after the Moorish ruins, down the hill past the old winery, follow the track along the edge of the vineyard into the wood. The road turned to gravel, then to dirt and matted pine needles.

The track ended at a wooden gate. Gabriel got out and pulled it open wide enough to allow the car to pass, then drove onto the grounds. The villa rose before him, shaped like an L, with a terra-cotta roof and pale stone walls. When Gabriel killed the engine, he could hear the sound of Anna Rolfe practicing. He listened for a moment, trying to place the piece, but could not.

As he climbed out of the car, a man ambled up the hillside: broad-brimmed hat, leather work gloves, the stub of a hand-rolled cigarette hanging from the corner of his mouth. He patted the dirt from his gloves, then removed them as he inspected the visitor.

"You are the man from Israel, yes?"

Gabriel gave a small, reluctant nod.

The vineyard keeper smiled. "Come with me."

THE VIEW FROM THE TERRACE WAS REMARKable: the hillside and the vineyard, the sea beyond. From an open window above Gabriel's head came the sound of Anna Rolfe's playing. A housekeeper materialized; she left coffee and a stack of week-old German-language newspapers, then silently disappeared into villa. In the *Neue Züricher Zeitung* he found an article on the investigation into Rolfe's murder. Next to it was a long feature piece on the career of Anna Rolfe. He read it quickly, then set it aside. It told him nothing he did not already know.

Before Gabriel touched a painting, he first read everything he could about the artist. He had used the same approach for Anna Rolfe. She had begun playing the violin at the age of four and immediately showed uncommon promise. The Swiss master Karl Wehrli agreed to take her on as a pupil, and the two began a relationship that remained intact until his death. When Anna was ten, Wehrli requested that she be removed from school so she would have more time to devote to her music. Anna's father reluctantly agreed. A private tutor came to the villa in Zürich two hours each day, and the rest of the time Anna played the violin.

At fifteen she made an appearance at the Lucerne International Music Festival that electrified the European music scene, and she was then invited to give a series of recitals in Germany and the Netherlands. The following year, she won the prestigious Jean Sibelius Violin Competition in Helsinki. She was awarded a large cash prize, along with a Guarneri violin, a string of concert appearances, and a recording contract.

Soon after the Sibelius competition, Anna Rolfe's career took flight. She embarked on a grinding schedule of concert dates and recording sessions. Her physical beauty made her a cross-cultural phenomenon. Her photograph appeared on the covers of European fashion magazines. In America she performed on a holiday television special.

Then, after twenty years of relentless touring and recording, Anna Rolfe had suffered the accident that nearly destroyed her hand. Gabriel tried to imagine how he would feel if his ability to restore paintings was suddenly taken from him. He did not expect to find her in a good mood.

One hour after Gabriel arrived, she stopped playing. All that remained was the steady beat of a metronome. Then it too fell silent. Five minutes later she appeared on the terrace, dressed in a pair of faded blue jeans and a pearl-gray cotton pullover. Her hair was damp.

She held out her hand. "I'm Anna Rolfe."

"It's an honor to meet you, Miss Rolfe."

"Please, sit down."

IF GABRIEL HAD BEEN A PORTRAIT PAINTER, HE might have enjoyed a subject like Anna Rolfe. Her face displayed a technical brilliance: the wide even cheekbones, the catlike green eyes, the ample mouth and teardrop chin. But it was also a face of many layers. Sensuous and vulnerable, contemptuous and iron-willed. Somewhere a trace of sadness. But it was her energy—her restless, reckless energy—that intrigued him the most and would have been most difficult to capture on canvas. Her eyes flashed about him. Even after the long rehearsal session, her hands could not remain quiet. They set out on private journeys: toyed with a cigarette lighter, drummed on the glass tabletop, made repeated trips to her face to chase away the stray lock of hair which fell across her cheek. She wore no jewelry; no bracelets on her wrist or rings on her fingers, nothing around her neck.

"I hope you didn't have to wait long. I'm afraid I've left strict instructions with Carlos and María not to interrupt me during my practice sessions."

"It was my pleasure. Your playing was extraordinary."

"Actually, it wasn't, but that's very kind of you to say."

"I saw you perform once. It was in Brussels a few years ago. An evening of Tchaikovsky, if I'm not mistaken. You were amazing that night."

"I couldn't touch those pieces now." She rubbed at the scars on her left hand. It seemed an involuntary gesture. She placed the hand in her lap and looked at the newspaper. "I see you've been reading about my father. The Zürich police don't seem to know much about his murder, do they?"

"That's hard to say."

"Do you know something the Zürich police don't know?"

"That's also hard to say."

"Before you tell me what it is you *do* know,

I hope you don't mind if I ask you a question first."

"No, of course not."

"Just who are you?"

"In this matter, I'm a representative of the government of Israel."

"And which matter is that?"

"The death of your father."

"And why is the death of my father of interest to the government of Israel?"

"Because I was the one to discover your father's body."

"The detectives in Zürich said my father's body was discovered by the art restorer who came to clean the Raphael."

"That's true."

"*You're* the art restorer?"

"Yes."

"And you work for the government of Israel?"

"In this matter."

He could see her mind struggling to make the connections.

"Forgive me, Mr. Allon, but I've just finished an eight-hour practice session. Maybe my mind isn't what it should be. Perhaps you should start from the beginning."

GABRIEL TOLD HER THE STORY SHAMRON HAD relayed to him in Zürich. That her father had contacted the Israeli government and requested a secret meeting. That he had given no details of why he wanted to meet. That Gabriel had

100

been sent to Zürich to see him and that her father was dead by the time he arrived. Anna Rolfe listened to this account impassively, her hands toying with her hair.

"And what do you want from me, Mr. Allon?" she asked when Gabriel had finished.

"I want to know whether you have any idea why your father would want to meet with us."

"My father was a banker, Mr. Allon. A *Swiss* banker. There were many things about his life, personal and professional, that he did not share with me. If you've read that newspaper account, then you know we were not particularly close, and that he never spoke to me about his work."

"Nothing at all?"

She ignored this and asked: "Who's *us?*"

"What do you mean?"

"You said my father wanted to meet with 'us.' Who's *us?* Who do you work for?"

"I work for a small agency connected to the Ministry of Defense."

"The Ministry of Defense?"

"Yes."

"So you're a spy?"

"No, I'm not a spy."

"Did you murder my father?"

"Miss Rolfe, please. I came here looking for your help, not to play games."

"Let the record show that the defendant failed to answer the question."

"I didn't murder your father, but I'd like to know who did. And if I knew why he wanted to meet with us in the first place, it might provide some answers."

She turned her face toward the sea. "So you think he was killed because of what he might have said to you?"

"That would seem to be the case." Gabriel allowed a silence to settle between them. Then he asked: "Do you know why your father wished to speak with us?"

"I think I can guess."

"Will you tell me?"

"That depends."

"On what?"

"On whether I decide to involve you and the government of Israel in the private affairs of my family."

"I can assure you that we will handle the matter with utmost discretion."

"You sound very much like a Swiss banker, Mr. Allon—but then I suppose you're not so very different." Her green eyes settled on him but betrayed nothing of her intentions. "I need some time to think about your offer."

"I understand."

"There's a café in the village square. It's owned by a man named Manuel. He has a guest room upstairs. It's not much, but you'll be comfortable there for a night. I'll give you my decision in the morning."

10

*T*HEY DROVE TO LISBON AIRPORT EARLY the following afternoon. Anna Rolfe insisted on first class. Gabriel, traveling on Shamron's parsimonious account, was relegated to economy. He trailed her through the Lisbon airport to make certain no one was following. As she neared the gate, a woman breathlessly thrust out a scrap of paper for an autograph. Anna obliged, smiled, and boarded the flight. Five minutes later, Gabriel followed. As he passed her seat she was sipping champagne. Gabriel trudged back to a middle seat in the twenty-third row. His back still ached from a sleepless night on Senhor Manuel's beastly bed.

Gerhardt Peterson's warning about not setting foot on Swiss soil still echoed in Gabriel's ears, so instead of going directly to Zürich they went first to Stuttgart. There they engaged in a similar routine: Anna leaving the plane first, Gabriel following her through the terminal to a rental-car counter. She collected the keys and the paperwork for a small Mercedes sedan and rode a shuttle bus to the parking lot. Gabriel took a taxi to a nearby hotel and waited in the lobby bar. Twenty minutes later, he went outside and found Anna parked in the drive. She drove a short distance through the darkened streets, then pulled over and traded places with him. Gabriel turned onto the expressway and headed south. One hundred miles to Zürich. Anna reclined the front passenger seat, rolled her coat into the shape of a pillow, and tucked it beneath her head.

Gabriel said, "I enjoyed the piece that you were practicing yesterday."

"It's called 'The Devil's Trill.' It was composed by Giuseppe Tartini. He said it was inspired by a dream. In the dream, he handed his violin to the Devil, and the Devil played a sonata that was more beautiful than anything he'd ever heard. Tartini claimed to have awoken in a feverish state. He had to possess the sonata, so he wrote down as much as he could remember."

"Do you believe the story?"

"I don't believe in the Devil, but I certainly understand the need to possess the piece. I spent three years learning how to play it properly. It was the piece that I played when I won the Sibelius competition. After that it became my signature piece. But technically, it's very demanding. I've just started to play it again."

"It sounded beautiful."

"Not to me. I hear only the mistakes and the imperfections."

"Is that why you canceled the two concert dates?"

"I didn't *cancel* them—I postponed them." Gabriel could feel her eyes on him. "I see you've done your homework."

"Are you planning to play any time soon?"

"I am, actually. A recital in Venice ten days from now. The Venetians have always been very kind to me. I feel comfortable there. Do you know Venice?"

"I lived in Venice for two years."

"Really? Why?"

"It's where I learned how to restore paintings. I served an apprenticeship with an Italian restorer named Umberto Conti. It's still one of my favorite cities in the world."

"Ah, mine too. Once Venice is in your blood, it's hard to live without her. I'm hoping Venice will work its magic for me."

"Why *did* you postpone the other recitals?"

"Because my ability to play my instrument was still diminished by the injury to my hand. Because I didn't want to become something of a freak show. I didn't want to hear people say, 'There's Anna Rolfe. She plays the violin quite well for someone who nearly lost her hand.' I want to stand on the stage as a musician and nothing more."

"Are you ready?"

"We'll find out in ten days. I only know one thing for certain: This time I'm not backing down." She lit a cigarette. "So why did you try to leave Zürich without telling the police about my father's murder?"

"Because I was afraid they wouldn't believe that I had nothing to do with it," Gabriel said.

"Is that the only reason?"

"I told you that I was there in an official capacity."

"What sort of official capacity? What's the name of this obscure agency that you work for? This agency connected to the Ministry of Defense."

"I don't work for them. I'm just performing a service for them."

"Do they have a name?"

"It's called the Institute for Coordination, but most of the people who work there call it the Office."

"You're a spy, aren't you?"

"I'm not a spy."

"Why do I know that you're lying to me?"

"I'm an art restorer."

"So why did we travel separately to Zürich? Why did we go to so much trouble at the airport in Stuttgart to avoid being seen together?"

"It was a precautionary measure. The Swiss police made it clear to me I'm no longer welcome."

"Why would they take a step like that?"

"Because they were a little miffed that I'd fled the scene of a crime."

"Why *did* you flee my father's house?"

"I've told you that already."

"You fled my father's house because you're a spy, and you were afraid of going to the police. I was watching you at the airport. You're very good."

"I'm not a spy."

"Then what are you? And don't tell me you're just an art restorer who's doing a favor for someone in some obscure agency called the Office, because I don't believe you. And if you don't tell me the truth right now, you might as well turn around and drive back to Stuttgart, because I'm not going to tell you a fucking thing."

She tossed her cigarette out the window and waited for his answer. The legendary temper of Anna Rolfe.

IT WAS AFTER MIDNIGHT WHEN THEY ARRIVED in Zürich. An air of abandonment hung over the city center: the Bahnhofstrasse dark and still, pavements deserted, ice falling through the lights. They crossed the river; Gabriel drove carefully up the slick roads of the Zürichberg. The last thing he wanted was to get stopped for a traffic violation.

They parked on the street outside the villa. Anna dealt with the keyless locks at the gate and the front entrance. Gabriel saw enough to tell him that the codes had been changed since the murder.

The foyer was in darkness. Anna closed the door before switching on the lights. Without speaking she led him inside, passing the entrance to the large drawing room where Gabriel had discovered the body of her father. He glanced inside. The air was drenched with the scent of cleaning fluid. The Oriental carpet was gone, but the Raphael still hung on the wall.

The deep silence of the house was emphasized by the clatter of Anna's heels over the bare floor. They passed through a large, formal dining room with an imposing table of polished dark wood and high-backed chairs; then a pantry; then a large kitchen.

Finally, they came to a flight of stairs. This time Anna turned on no lights. Gabriel followed her downward into the gloom. At the bottom was a wine cellar, alcoves filled with dusty bottles. Next to the wine cellar was a cutting room with a stone sink. Rusted gardening tools hung from hooks on the walls.

They passed through another doorway and followed a dark corridor. It ended at a door, which Anna pulled aside, revealing a small lift. It was barely big enough for one person, but they crowded in together. As the lift slowly descended, Gabriel could feel the heat of her body pressing against his, smell the scent of her shampoo, the French tobacco on her breath. She seemed perfectly at ease with the situation. Gabriel tried to look away, but Anna gazed directly into his eyes with an unnerving animal intensity.

The lift came to a stop. Anna opened the door and they stepped into a small foyer of black and white marble. A heavy steel door stood opposite the lift. On the wall next to the door was a keypad, and next to the keypad was a device that looked something like the magnifying visors in his studio. Gabriel had seen a device like this before; it was a biometric security mechanism used to scan the retina of anyone trying to enter the room. If the retina matched any of those recorded in the database, the person would be permitted to enter. If not, all hell would break loose.

Anna punched in the security code and placed her eyes against the scanning device. A few seconds later, a bolt snapped back and the great door slowly fell open. As they entered the room, lights automatically flickered to life.

A LARGE SPACE, ABOUT FIFTY FEET BY THIRTY, polished wood floor, cream-colored walls. In the center were two ornate swivel chairs. Anna stood next to one and folded her arms. Gabriel scanned the blank walls.

"What is this?"

"My father had two collections. One that he allowed the world to see and one that used to hang here. It was for private viewing only."

"What kind of paintings were they?"

"Nineteenth- and twentieth-century French—Impressionist, mainly."

"Do you have a list of them?"

She nodded.

"Who else knew about this?"

"My mother and my brother, of course, but they're both dead."

"That's all?"

"No, there was Werner Müller."

"Who's Werner Müller?"

"He's an art dealer and my father's chief adviser. He oversaw the design and construction of this place."

"Is he Swiss?"

She nodded. "He has two galleries. One in Lucerne and the other in Paris near the rue de Rivoli. He spends most of his time there. Seen enough?"

"For now."

"There's something else I want to show you."

Back up the elevator, another walk through the darkened villa to a windowless chamber of winking electronics and video monitors. Gabriel could see the villa from every angle: the street, the entrance, the gardens front and back.

"In addition to the security cameras, every inch of the property is covered by motion detectors," Anna said. "The windows and doors all have trip wires and alarms. My father didn't employ a full-time security guard, but the house was impenetrable and he could summon the police in a matter of seconds in the event of an intruder."

"So what happened on the night of the murder?"

"The system failed inexplicably."

"How convenient."

She sat down in front of a computer terminal. "There's a separate system for the room downstairs. It's activated when the outer door opens. The time of entry is automatically logged, and inside the room two digital cameras begin recording still images every three seconds."

She typed in a few characters on the keyboard, moved the mouse, clicked. "This is when we entered the room, twelve forty-nine A.M., and here we are inside."

Gabriel leaned over her shoulder and peered into the computer monitor. A grainy color image of their visit appeared on the screen and then dissolved, only to be replaced by another. Anna worked the mouse again. A directory appeared.

"This is the master list of visits to that room for the past three months. As you can see, my father spent a great deal of time with the collection. He came down at least once a day, sometimes twice." She touched the screen with her forefinger. "Here's his last visit, shortly after midnight, the morning he was murdered. The security system shows no other entries after that."

"Did the police give you an estimate of when they thought he was killed?"

"They said around three A.M."

"So it stands to reason that the same people who killed your father also took the paintings and that it probably happened around three o'clock in the morning, six hours before I arrived at the villa."

"Yes, that's right."

Gabriel pointed to the last entry on the screen. "Let me see that one."

A MOMENT LATER, THE IMAGES FLICKERED onto the monitor. The camera angles did not reveal all the paintings, but Gabriel could see enough to realize that it was a remarkable collection. Manet, Bonnard, Toulouse-Lautrec, Cézanne, Pissarro, Degas, a nude by Renoir, a canal landscape by van Gogh, two street scenes by Monet, a large portrait of a woman painted by Picasso during his blue period. And seated in the center of the room, in a straight-backed wing chair, was an old man, gazing at his collection one last time before his death.

11

*F*OUR HOURS LATER, GERHARDT PETERSON was sitting alone in his office, a grotto of pale Scandinavian wood overlooking the grimy inner courtyard of blackened brick. His computer screen was blank, his morning correspondence unopened, his morning coffee untouched, his outer door uncustomarily locked. A cigarette slowly turned to dust in his ashtray. Peterson did not notice. His gaze was downward, toward the three photographs that lay side by side on his leather blotter. Allon and Anna Rolfe, leaving the villa. Allon and Anna Rolfe, getting into a Mercedes sedan. Allon and Anna Rolfe, driving away. Finally he stirred, as if awakened from an unpleasant daydream, and fed the photographs into his shredder, one by one, watching with particular satisfaction as they turned to confetti. Then he picked up the telephone, dialed a number from memory, and waited for an answer.

112

Twenty minutes later, his appointments for the rest of the day canceled, he climbed into his Mercedes sedan and raced down the shore of the Zürichsee toward Herr Gessler's mountain chalet.

12

*T*HE OLD *SIGNADORA* LIVED IN A CROOKED house in the village, not far from the church. She greeted the Englishman as always, with a worried smile and a hand on his cheek. She wore a heavy black dress with an embroidered neck. Her skin was the color of flour, her white hair was pulled back and held in place by metal pins. Funny how the marks of ethnicity and national origin are diminished by time, thought the Englishman. If it wasn't for her Corsican language and mystical Catholic ways she might have been his old Auntie Beatrice from Ipswich. "The evil has returned, my son," she whispered, stroking his cheek. "I can see it in your eyes. Sit down. Let me help you."

The old woman lit a candle as the Englishman sat down at the small, wooden table. In front of him she placed a china plate filled with water and a small bowl of oil. "Three drops," she said. "Then we will see if my fears are correct."

113

The Englishman dipped his forefinger in the oil; then he held it over the plate and allowed three drops to fall onto the water. By the laws of physics the oil should have gathered into a single globule, but instead it shattered into a thousand droplets, and soon there was no trace of it. The old woman sighed heavily and made the sign of the cross. There it was, undeniable proof that the *occhju*, the Evil Eye, had invaded the Englishman's soul.

She took hold of the Englishman's hand and prayed. After a moment she began to cry, a sign the *occhju* had passed from his body into hers. Then she closed her eyes and appeared to be sleeping. She opened her eyes a moment later and instructed him to repeat the trial of the oil and the water. This time, the oil coalesced into a single drop. The evil had been exorcised.

"Thank you," he said, taking the old woman's hand. She held it for a moment, then drew away, as if he had fever. The Englishman asked: "What's wrong?"

"Are you going to remain in the valley for a time, or are you going away again?"

"I'm afraid I have to go away."

"In the service of Don Orsati?"

The Englishman nodded. He kept no secrets from the old *signadora*.

"Do you have your charm?"

He opened his shirt. A piece of coral, shaped like a hand, hung by a leather cord from his neck. She took it in her fingers and stroked it, as if to ascertain whether it still contained the

114

mystical power to ward off the *occhju*. She seemed satisfied but still concerned.

The Englishman asked, "Do you see something?"

"I see a man."

"What's this man like?"

"He's like you, only a heretic. You should avoid him. You will do as I have instructed?"

"I always do."

The Englishman kissed her hand, then slipped a roll of francs into her palm.

"It's too much," she said.

"You always say that."

"That's because you always give me too much."

Part Two

13

*A*N HOUR AFTER DAWN THEY CROSSED the Italian border. It had been a long time since Gabriel had been so glad to leave a place. He drove toward Milan while Anna slept. She was troubled by nightmares, tossing her head, waging private battles. When the dream finally released her, she woke and stared wide-eyed at Gabriel, as if startled by his presence. She closed her eyes and soon the struggle began again.

In a roadside café they ate silently, like famished lovers: omelets and bread, bowls of milky coffee. During the last miles before Milan, they talked through the plans one last time. Anna would fly to Lisbon; Gabriel would keep the Mercedes and drive on to Rome. At the airport, he pulled to the curb on the departure level and slid the car into park. "Before we continue, there's one thing I have to know," he said.

"You want to know why I didn't tell the Zürich police about the missing paintings."

"That's right."

"The answer is quite simple: I don't trust them. It's why I returned your phone call and why I showed you the missing collection in the first place." She took his hand. "I don't trust the Swiss police, Mr. Allon, and neither

119

should you. Does that answer your question?"

"For now."

She climbed out and disappeared into the terminal. Her scent lingered in the car for the remainder of the morning, like the simple question which ran ceaselessly round his head. Why would a band of professional art thieves go to the trouble of stealing Rolfe's private collection but leave a Raphael hanging on the parlor wall?

ROME SMELLED OF AUTUMN: BITTER COFFEE, garlic frying in olive oil, woodsmoke and dead leaves. Gabriel checked into a small hotel on the Corso d'Italia, opposite the Villa Borghese. His room overlooked a tiny courtyard with a still fountain and parasols bound for winter. He climbed into bed and immediately was asleep.

It had been a long time since he had dreamed of Vienna, but something he had seen in Zürich had set his subconscious aflame, and he dreamed of it again now. The dream began as it always did, with Gabriel buckling his son into the backseat of the car, unaware he is strapping him to a bomb planted by a Palestinian who has sworn to destroy him. He kisses his wife, says goodnight to her for the last time, walks away. Then the car explodes. He turns and begins to run. In his dream it takes several minutes for him to reach the car, even though it is only a few yards away. He finds his son, torn to pieces by the bomb. In the front seat is a woman, blackened by fire. Now, instead of Leah, the woman is Anna Rolfe.

Finally he forced the dream to end. He awoke in damp sheets, looked at his wristwatch. He had slept twelve hours.

He showered and dressed. Outside it was midmorning, puffy white clouds scudding across an azure sky, wind prowling the Corso d'Italia. Overnight it had stormed, and the gusts were making tiny whitecaps in large puddles on the pavement. He walked to the Via Veneto, bought the papers, and read them over breakfast in a café.

After an hour he left the café, walked to a telephone booth, and dialed a number from memory. *Click...hum...click...* Finally a voice, slightly distant, a bit of an echo. "Yes?"

Gabriel identified himself as Stevens, one of his old work names, and said he wished to have lunch with Mr. Baker at Il Drappo. A pause, another click, more humming, something that sounded like shattering china. Then the voice returned.

"Mr. Baker says lunch at Il Drappo is suitable."

After that the line went dead.

FOR TWO DAYS GABRIEL WAITED. HE ROSE early each morning and jogged the quiet footpaths of the Villa Borghese. Then he would walk to the Via Veneto for coffee at a counter tended by a pretty girl with auburn hair. On

121

the second day, he noticed a priest in a black cassock whose face looked familiar to him. Gabriel searched his memory for the face but could not find it. When he asked the girl for his check, her telephone number was written on the back of it. He smiled apologetically and dropped it on the bar when he left. The priest stayed in the café.

That afternoon, Gabriel spent a long time checking his tail. He wandered through churches, studying frescoes and altarpieces until his neck ached. He could almost feel the presence of Umberto Conti at his side. Conti, like Ari Shamron, believed Gabriel was a man of special gifts, and he doted on Gabriel, just as Shamron had done. Sometimes he would come to Gabriel's sagging pensione and drag him into the Venetian night to look at art. He spoke of paintings the way some men speak of women. "Look at the light, Gabriel. Look at the technique, the hands, my God, the hands."

Gabriel's neighbor in Venice had been a Palestinian called Saeb, a skinny intellectual who wrote violent poetry and incendiary tracts comparing the Israelis to the Nazis. He reminded Gabriel too much of a man named Wadal Adel Zwaiter, the Black September chief in Italy, whom Gabriel had assassinated in the stairwell of an apartment building in Rome's Piazza Annabaliano.

"I was part of a special unit, Miss Rolfe."

"What kind of special unit?"

"A counterterrorism unit that tracked down people who committed acts of violence against Israel."

"*Palestinians?*"

"*For the most part, yes.*"

"*And what did you do to these terrorists when you found them?*"

Silence...

"*Tell me, Mr. Allon. What did you do when you found them?*"

Late at night, Saeb would come to Gabriel's room like Zwaiter's ghost, always with a bottle of cheap red wine and French cigarettes, and he would sit cross-legged on the floor and lecture Gabriel on the injustices heaped upon the Palestinian people. *The Jews! The West! The corrupt Arab regimes! All of them have Palestinian blood on their hands!* Gabriel would nod and help himself to Saeb's wine and another of his cigarettes. Occasionally he would contribute his own condemnation of Israel. The State could not last, Gabriel had said in one of his more memorable speeches. Eventually, it would collapse, like capitalism, beneath the weight of its inherent contradictions. Saeb was so moved he included a variation of the line in his next article.

During Gabriel's apprenticeship Shamron had permitted Leah to visit him once each month. They would make love frantically, and afterward she would lie next to him on the single bed and beg him to come home to Tel Aviv. She posed as a German sociology student from Hamburg named Eva. When Saeb came to the room with his wine and cigarettes, she spoke in glowing terms of the Baader-Meinhof Gang and the PLO. Saeb declared her an enchantress. "Someday, you must come to Palestine and see the land," he said. *Yes*, Leah had agreed. *Someday.*

GABRIEL ATE EACH NIGHT IN A SMALL TRATtoria near his hotel. On the second night the owner treated him as though he was a regular who had been coming once a week for twenty years. Placed him at a special table near the kitchen and plied him with *antipasti* until Gabriel begged for mercy. Then pasta, then fish, then an assortment of *dolci*. Over coffee he handed Gabriel a note.

"Who left this?" said Gabriel.

He lifted his hands in a Roman gesture of befuddlement. "A man."

Gabriel looked at the note: plain paper, anonymous script, no signature.

Church of Santa Maria della Pace. One hour.

THE NIGHT HAD TURNED COLDER, A GUSTY WIND moving in the trees of the Villa Borghese. Gabriel walked for a time—along the Corso d'Italia, down the Via Veneto—then stopped a taxi and took it to the edge of the Centro Storico.

For twenty minutes he wandered through the narrow streets and quiet squares until confident he was not being followed. Then he walked to the Piazza Navona. The square was crowded in spite of the chill, cafés filled, street artists hawking cheap paintings.

Gabriel slowly circled the piazza, now pausing to gaze at an ornate fountain, now stopping to drop a few coins into the basket of a blind man strumming a guitar with just four strings. Someone was following him; he could feel it.

He started toward the church, then doubled back suddenly. His pursuer was now standing among a small group of people listening to the guitarist. Gabriel walked over and stood next to him.

"You're clean," the man said. "Go inside."

THE CHURCH WAS EMPTY, THE SMELL OF burning wax and incense heavy on the air. Gabriel moved forward through the nave and stood before the altar. Behind him the door opened and the sounds of the busy square filled the church. He turned to look, but it was only an old woman come to pray.

A moment later the doors opened again. A man this time, leather jacket, quick dark eyes—Rami, the old man's personal bodyguard. He knelt in a pew and made the sign of the cross.

Gabriel suppressed a smile as he turned and gazed upon the altar. Again the doors opened, again the clamor of the piazza intruded upon the silence, but this time Gabriel didn't bother to turn, because immediately he recognized the distinctive cadence of Ari Shamron's walk.

A moment later Shamron was at his side, looking up at the altarpiece. "What is this,

Gabriel?" he asked impatiently. Shamron had no capacity to appreciate art. He found beauty only in a perfectly conceived operation or the destruction of an enemy.

"These frescoes were painted, coincidentally, by Raphael. He rarely worked in fresco, only for popes and their close associates. A well-connected banker named Agostino Chigi owned this chapel, and when Raphael presented Chigi his bill for the frescoes, he was so outraged that he went to Michelangelo for a second opinion."

"What was Michelangelo's reaction?"

"He told Chigi he would have asked for more."

"I'm sure I would have sided with the banker. Let's take a walk. Catholic churches make me nervous." He managed a terse smile. "A remnant of my Polish childhood."

THEY WALKED ALONG THE EDGE OF THE PIAZZA, and the vigilant Rami shadowed them like Shamron's guilty conscience, hands in his pockets, eyes on the move. Shamron listened silently while Gabriel told him about the missing collection.

"Did she tell the police?"

"No."

"Why not?"

Gabriel told him what Anna had said when he asked her the same question.

"Why would the old man keep the paintings secret?"

"It's not unprecedented. Perhaps the nature of the collection didn't allow him to show it in public."

"Are you suggesting he was an art thief?"

"No, not an art thief, but sometimes things are a little more complicated than that. It's possible Rolfe's collection didn't have the most pristine provenance. We are talking about *Switzerland*, after all."

"Meaning?"

"The bank vaults and cellars of Switzerland are filled with history's booty, including art. It's possible those paintings didn't even belong to Rolfe. We can assume one thing: Whoever took them did it for a specific reason. They left behind a Raphael worth several million dollars."

"Can they be recovered?"

"I suppose it's possible. It depends on whether they've been sold yet."

"Can works like those be sold quickly on the black market?"

"Not without raising quite a racket. But then again, it might have been a commissioned theft."

"Meaning?"

"Someone paid someone else to pull off the job."

"Was the murder of Rolfe included in the fee?"

"Good question."

Shamron seemed suddenly tired. He sat on the edge of a fountain. "I don't travel as well as I used to," he said. "Tell me about Anna Rolfe."

"If we had a choice, we'd never be involved with her. She's unpredictable, volatile, and she smokes more than you do. But she plays the violin like no one else I've ever heard."

"You're good with people like that. Restore her." Shamron began to cough, a violent cough that shook his entire body. After a moment he said, "Does she have any idea why her father made contact with us?"

"She says she doesn't. They weren't exactly close."

This seemed to cause Shamron a moment of physical pain. His own daughter had moved to New Zealand. He telephoned her once a month, but she never returned his calls. His greatest fear was that she would not come home for his funeral or say *kaddish* for him. He took a long time lighting his next cigarette. "Do you have anything to go on?"

"One lead, yes."

"Worth pursuing?"

"I think so."

"What do you need?"

"The resources to mount a surveillance operation."

"Where?"

"In Paris."

"And the subject?"

14

*T*HE MINIATURE SUPERCARDIOID MICRO-
phone held by the man dressed as a
priest was no longer than an average fountain
pen. Manufactured by an electronics firm in
the Swiss industrial city of Zug, it allowed him
to monitor the conversation conducted by
the two men slowly circling the Piazza Navona.
A second man sitting in the café on the opposite side of the square was armed with an
identical piece of equipment. The man dressed
as a priest was confident that between them
they had recorded most of what was being said.

His assumptions were confirmed twenty
minutes later when, back in his hotel room,
he synchronized the two tapes in an audio playback deck and slipped on a pair of headphones. After a few minutes, he reached out
suddenly, pushed the stop button, then rewind,
then play.

"*Where?*"

"*In Paris.*"

"*And the subject?*"

"*An art dealer named Werner Müller.*"

STOP. REWIND. PLAY.

"*An art dealer named Werner Müller.*"

STOP.

He dialed a number in Zürich and relayed
the contents of the conversation to the man

at the other end of the line. When he had finished, he treated himself to a cigarette and a split of champagne from the minibar, the reward for a job well done. In the bathroom, he burned the pages of his notebook in the sink and washed the ashes down the drain.

15

*T*HE MÜLLER GALLERY STOOD AT THE bend of a small street between the rue Faubourg St. Honoré and the Avenue l'Opéra. On one side was a dealer of mobile telephones, on the other a boutique selling fine menswear that no man would wear. On the door was a sign, handwritten in neat blue script: BY APPOINTMENT ONLY. Behind the thick security glass of the window were two small decorative eighteenth-century works by minor French flower-painters. Gabriel did not like the French flower-painters. Three times he had agreed to restore a painting from the period. Each had been an exercise in exquisite tedium.

For his observation post Gabriel chose the Hôtel Laurens, a small hotel fifty yards north of the gallery on the opposite side of the street. He checked in under the name of Heinrich Kiever and was given a small garret that smelled of spilt cognac and stale cigarette smoke. He told the front-desk clerk that he was a German screenwriter. That he had come to Paris to rework a script for a film set in France during the war. That he would be working long hours in his room and wished not to be disturbed. He drank in the hotel bar and made boorish advances toward the waitress. He shouted at the chambermaids when they tried to clean his room. He screamed at the room service boys when they didn't bring his coffee quickly enough. Soon, the entire staff and most of the guests at the Hôtel Laurens knew about the crazy *Boche* writer in the attic.

On the way to Paris he had stopped at the airport in Nice, dropped off the rented Mercedes, and collected a Renault. The rental agent was a man called Henri, a Provençal Jew whose family had survived the French Holocaust. In the lexicon of the Office, Henri was a *sayan*, a volunteer helper. There were thousands of *sayanim* around the globe—bankers who could provide Office field agents with money, hotel clerks who could give them lodging, doctors who could quietly treat them if they were wounded or ill. In the case of Henri, he dispensed with the usual paperwork and issued the Renault to Gabriel in such a way that it could never be traced.

Shortly after his arrival in Paris, Gabriel reluctantly had made contact with the head of the local station, a man called Uzi Navot. Navot had strawberry-blond hair and the lumpy physique of a wrestler. He was one of Shamron's devoted acolytes and was jealous of the old

131

man's affections toward Gabriel. As a result he hated Gabriel, in the way a second son hates an elder brother, and he had buried a knife in Gabriel's back at every opportunity. Their meeting, on a bench next to the fountain in the Tuileries gardens, had the cold formality of two opposing generals negotiating a cease-fire. Navot made it clear that he believed the Paris station could handle a simple surveillance job without the help of the great Gabriel Allon. He also wasn't pleased that Shamron had kept him in the dark about why a Paris art dealer should warrant Office surveillance. Gabriel had remained stoically calm in the face of Navot's quiet tirade, tossing bits of baguette to the pigeons and nodding sympathetically from time to time. When Navot stormed off across a gravel footpath twenty minutes later, Gabriel had arranged for everything he needed: watchers, radios with secure frequencies, cars, bugging equipment, a 22-caliber Beretta pistol.

FOR TWO DAYS THEY WATCHED HIM. IT WAS NOT particularly difficult work; Müller, if he was a criminal, did not behave much like one. He arrived at the gallery each morning at nine forty-five, and by ten he was ready to receive customers. At one-thirty he would close the gallery and walk to the same restaurant on the rue de Rivoli, pausing once along the way to purchase newspapers from the same kiosk.

On the first day, a blunt-headed watcher called Oded followed him. On the second it was a reedy boy called Mordecai, who huddled outside at a freezing table on the sidewalk. After lunch he followed Müller back to the gallery, then came upstairs to Gabriel's hotel room for a debriefing.

"Tell me something, Mordecai," Gabriel said. "What did he have for lunch today?"

The watcher pulled his thin face into a disapproving frown. "Shellfish. An enormous platter. It was a massacre."

"And what did you eat, Mordecai?"

"Eggs and *pommes frites.*"

"How were they?"

"Not bad."

In the evenings, another predictable routine. Müller would remain at the gallery until six-thirty. Before leaving, he would place a dark-green plastic rubbish bag at the curbside for the overnight pickup, then would walk through the crowds along the Champs-Élysées to Fouquet's. On the first night it was Oded who collected the garbage and brought it to Gabriel's room and Mordecai who followed the art dealer to Fouquet's. On the second night, the two watchers reversed roles. As Müller sipped champagne with the film and literary crowd at Fouquet's, Gabriel performed the unenviable task of sifting through the rubbish. It was as ordinary as Müller's daily routine: discarded facsimiles in a half-dozen languages, unimportant mail, cigarette butts, soiled napkins, and coffee grounds.

After Fouquet's, Müller would stroll through the quiet side streets of the eighth arrondissement, have a light supper in a bistro, then head up to his apartment. After two nights of the same thing, Oded grew rebellious. "Maybe he's just a Swiss art dealer who doesn't deal much art. Perhaps you're wasting your time—*and ours.*"

But Gabriel was not deterred by the protestations of Oded and the rest of his small team. Shortly after midnight, he watched from the window of his room at the Hôtel Laurens as an unmarked van pulled to the curb outside the gallery. The next sequence unfolded with the fluidity of a choreographed dance. Two men emerged from the van. Twenty seconds later they had broken into the gallery and disarmed the alarm system. The work inside took less than a minute. Then the two men slipped out of the gallery and climbed back into the van. The headlights flashed twice and the van drove off.

Gabriel turned away from the window, picked up the telephone, and dialed the number for the gallery. After five rings, an answering machine picked up. Gabriel placed the receiver on the table next to the phone and turned up the volume on a small, hand-held radio. A few seconds later he could hear the recording on the answering machine, the voice of Werner Müller explaining that his gallery would reopen for business at ten o'clock the following morning. *Please telephone for an appointment.*

IN THE LEXICON OF THE OFFICE, THE BUG that had been planted in the Müller Gallery was known as a "glass." Concealed within the electronics of the telephone, it provided coverage of Müller's calls as well as conversations taking place inside the room. Because it drew its power from the telephone, it didn't require a battery and therefore could remain in place indefinitely.

The next morning, Müller received no prospective buyers and no telephone calls. He made two calls himself, one to Lyons to inquire about the availability of a painting and one to his landlord to complain about the plumbing in his apartment.

At noon, he listened to news on the radio. He ate lunch in the same restaurant, at the same time, and returned to the gallery late in the afternoon. At five o'clock, a telephone call: female, Scandinavian-accented English, looking for sketches by Picasso. Müller politely explained that his collection contained no Picasso sketches—or works by Picasso of any kind—and he was kind enough to give her the names and addresses of two competitors where she might have more luck.

At six o'clock, Gabriel decided to place a telephone call of his own. He dialed the gallery and in rapid, boisterous French, asked Herr Müller whether he had any floral still lifes by Cézanne.

Muller cleared his throat. "Unfortunately, *monsieur*, I don't have any paintings by Cézanne."

"That's strange. I was told by a reliable source that you had a number of works by Cézanne."

"Your reliable source was mistaken. *Bonsoir, monsieur.*"

The line went dead. Gabriel replaced the receiver and joined Oded in the window. A moment later, the art dealer stepped out into the gathering dusk and peered up and down the little street.

"Did you see that, Oded?"

"He's definitely got a serious case of the nerves."

"Still think he's just an art dealer who doesn't sell many pictures?"

"He looks dirty, but why set him on edge with a phone call like that?"

Gabriel smiled and said nothing. Shamron called it slipping a stone into a man's shoe. At first, it's just an irritant, but before long it produces an open wound. Leave the stone there long enough, and the man has a shoe full of blood.

Five minutes later, Werner Müller locked up his gallery for the night. Instead of leaving his garbage bag in its usual place, he dropped it next door, in front of the clothing boutique. As he started off toward Fouquet's, he looked several times over his shoulder. He did not notice the whisper-thin frame of Mordecai, trailing after him on the opposite side of the street. Werner Müller had a festering wound, thought Gabriel. Soon, he would have a shoe full of blood.

"Bring me his garbage, Oded."

MÜLLER'S WEEKEND WAS AS PREDICTABLE AS his workweek. He owned a dog that barked incessantly. Oded, who was monitoring the bug from a van parked around the corner, suffered from a chronic headache. He asked Gabriel if he could borrow a Beretta to shoot the dog and be done with it. And when Müller took the dog for a walk along the river, Oded begged for authorization to toss the beast over the embankment.

The monotony was broken Saturday evening by the arrival of a high-priced whore called Veronique. She slapped him. He cried and called her "Mama." The barking of the dog reached a feverish pitch. After two hours Oded, who considered himself something of a man of the world, had to leave the surveillance van for a bit of fresh air and a drink at the brasserie on the opposite side of the street. "A fuck for the ages," he told Gabriel afterward. "A clinic of depravity. It will be required listening for the boys in Psych Ops at King Saul Boulevard."

No one was more pleased than Oded when a gray and wet Monday dawned over Paris. Müller had one final quarrel with the dog before slamming the door of his apartment and heading into the street. Oded watched him

137

through the blacked-out glass of the surveillance van, an expression of pure loathing on his face. Then he raised the radio to his lips to check in with Gabriel at the Hôtel Laurens. "Looks like Romeo's heading to the gallery. He's your problem now."

And then the dog started up again, a few intermittent barks, like the crack of sniper fire, then an all-out artillery barrage. Oded removed his headphones and cradled his head in his hands.

16

HE ENGLISHMAN, LIKE GABRIEL ALLON, came to Paris by way of the Côte d'Azur, having made the night passage from Corsica to the mainland on the Calvi-to-Nice ferry. Coincidentally, he also rented a car in Nice—not at the airport but on the boulevard Victor-Hugo, a few blocks from the water. It was a Ford Fiesta that pulled badly to the right, and it made his drive more challenging than he would have preferred.

One hour from Paris, he pulled into a roadside café and gas station and entered the men's room. There he changed his clothing, trading his cotton trousers and woolen sweater for a sleek black suit. He used stage makeup to turn his sand-colored hair to platinum and slipped on a pair of rose-tinted eyeglasses. When he was finished, even he did not recognize the man in the mirror. He removed a Canadian passport from his bag and looked at the photograph: Claude Devereaux, two years until expiration. He slipped the passport into his jacket pocket and walked to the car.

It was late afternoon by the time he reached the outskirts of the city, the sky low and heavy, a half-hearted rain. He made his way to the fifth arrondissement, where he checked into a small hotel on the rue St-Jacques. He remained in his room throughout the early evening, had a brief nap, then went downstairs to the lobby, where he left his room key with the desk clerk and collected a stack of tourist maps and brochures. He smiled stupidly at the clerk—*My first time in Paris.*

Outside it was raining heavily. The Englishman dropped the maps and the brochures into a rubbish bin and made his way through the wet streets of the seventh to the Seine. And by nine o'clock he was sheltering beneath a dripping plane tree on the Quai d'Orleans, waiting for Pascal Debré.

A barge moved slowly past him, warm light glowing in the wheelhouse and the cabin. A short distance down the pier, three men were drinking wine from a bottle and night fishing by the light of a streetlamp. He pulled up the sleeve of his jacket and looked at the luminous face of his wristwatch. A few minutes past midnight. Where the hell was Debré? The rain picked up, slapping against the stone pier. He touched his hair. The platinum color was beginning to run.

Five minutes later he heard footsteps on the quay. He turned and saw a man walking toward him: polyester trousers, cheap boots, a waist-length leather jacket shiny with rain. He joined the Englishman beneath the tree and held out his hand. The last two fingers were missing.

"You picked a damned lousy spot to meet on a night like this, Pascal. What the hell took you so long?"

"I didn't select it for the view, my friend." He spoke *patois* with the accent of a southerner. With his two remaining fingers he pointed toward the three men drinking wine down the pier. "You see those boys? They work for me. And the barge that went past a moment ago? He works for me, too. We wanted to make sure you weren't being followed."

Debré shoved his hands into his pockets. The Englishman looked him over.

"Where's the package?"

"At the warehouse."

"You were supposed to bring it here."

"The Paris police have been running spot checks all night. Something about a bomb threat. One of the Arab groups. Algerian, I think. It wasn't safe to bring it with me now."

The Englishman hadn't seen any spot checks. "If there are spot checks, how am I going to get the package back into the city?"

"That's your problem, my friend."

"Where's the warehouse?"

"The docks, a few miles down the river." He cocked his head in the direction of the Latin Quarter. "I have a car."

The Englishman didn't like changes in plan, but he had no choice. He nodded and followed Debré up the stone steps, then across the Pont St-Louis. Above them Notre Dame burned with floodlight. Debré looked at the Englishman's hair and turned down his lips into a very Gallic look of disapproval. "You look ridiculous, but it's quite effective, I must say. I nearly didn't recognize you."

"That's the point."

"Nice clothes too. Very fashionable. You should be careful where you go dressed like that. Some of the boys might get the wrong idea about you."

"Where's the damned car?"

"Be patient, my friend."

It stood on the Quai de Montebello, engine running. A big man sat behind the wheel smoking a cigarette. Debré said, "Sit up front. You'll be more comfortable."

"Actually, I prefer the backseat, and if you ask me to sit in the front again, I'll be convinced that you're leading me into a trap. And the last thing you want is for me to feel trapped, Pascal."

"Suit yourself. Sit in the back if you like. I was just trying to be polite. *Jesus Christ!*"

THEY DROVE FOR TWENTY MINUTES, WIPERS working steadily against the rain, heater roaring. The lights of central Paris faded, and soon they were in a gloomy industrial quarter bathed in yellow sodium lamps. Debré sang along with the American music on the radio. The Englishman had a headache. He lowered his window and the damp air sawed at his cheek.

He wished Debré would shut up. The Englishman knew all about Pascal Debré. He was a man who had failed to live up to his own expectations of himself. He had wanted to be an assassin, like the Englishman, but he had botched an important hit on a member of a rival criminal group. The mistake cost him two fingers and seriously impacted the course of his career. He was exiled to the extortion side of the business, where he was known for his crude but effective pitch—*Give us money, or we will burn down your business. If you try to get the police involved, we'll rape your daughter and then cut her into a hundred pieces.*

They passed through a gate in a chain-link fence, then entered a soot-stained brick warehouse. The air was heavy with the stench of oil and the river. Debré led the way into a small office and switched on a light. A moment later he emerged, a large suitcase hanging from his good hand.

He swung the bag onto the hood of the car and popped the latches. "It's a simple device," Debré said, using his maimed hand as a pointer. "Here's the timer. You can set it for one minute, one hour, one week. Whatever you want. Here's the detonator, here's the small explosive charge. These canisters contain the

142

fuel. The bag is completely untraceable. Even if it happens to survive the fire—which is extremely unlikely—there's nothing about it that will lead the police to you or to us."

Debré closed the lid. The Englishman pulled out an envelope filled with francs and dropped it on the car next to the bag. He reached for the suitcase, but Debré put the two-fingered hand on his arm.

"I'm afraid the price has gone up, my friend."

"Why?"

"Blame it on an unforeseeable market fluctuation." Debré took out a gun and pointed it at the Englishman's chest. The driver moved into position behind him. The Englishman assumed he had drawn his weapon too.

Debré smiled. "You know how these things go, my friend."

"No, I don't, actually. Why don't you explain it to me?"

"After we spoke, I started to think."

"That must have been a new experience for you."

"Shut your fucking mouth!"

"Excuse me for interrupting, Pascal. Please continue."

"I asked myself a simple question. Why does a man like my friend need a device like this? He always kills with a knife. Sometimes a pistol but usually a knife. Then the answer came to me. He needs a device like this because his employers have requested it. If I raise my price, it will make no difference to him, because he will simply pass the cost on to his employer."

"How much do you want?"

"Two hundred."

"We had a deal at one hundred."

"The deal changed."

"And if I refuse?"

"You'll have to get your package somewhere else. If you do that, I might be tempted to call one of our friends on the police force, one of the ones we keep in wine and whores. I might tell this friend that you're in town working."

"Fine, I'll pay your new price, but after I use this device, I'm going to place an anonymous call to the Paris police and tell them who gave it to me. Thanks to your stupidity, I'll even be able to tell them where I got it. They'll raid the place, you'll be arrested, and your employers will take the rest of your fingers."

Debré was nervous now, eyes wide, licking his lips, the gun trembling in his left hand. He was used to people reacting with fear when he made threats. He didn't often deal with someone like the Englishman.

"All right, you win," said Debré. "We go back to the original price. One hundred thousand francs. Take the damned thing and get out of here."

The Englishman decided to push him some more. "How will I get back to Paris?"

"That's your problem."

"It's a long ride. The taxi fare will be expensive." He reached out and picked up the envelope. "Probably about one hundred thousand francs."

"What the hell do you think you're doing?"

"I'm taking the device and my money. If you try to stop me, I'll tell the police about your warehouse, and this time your boss in Marseilles certainly won't stop with your hand."

Debré raised the gun. The Englishman had let the game go on long enough. Time to end things. His training took over. He grabbed Debré's arm in a lightning-fast movement that caught the Frenchman off-guard. He twisted the arm violently, breaking it in several places. Debré screamed in agony, and the gun clattered to the warehouse floor.

Debré's partner made his move. The Englishman calculated he wouldn't fire his weapon because of Debré's proximity, which left only one option: to try to disable the Englishman with a blow to the back of the head. The Englishman ducked, and the punch sailed over his head. Then he grabbed Debré's gun and came up firing. Two shots struck the big man in the chest. He fell to the floor, blood pumping between his fingers. The Englishman fired two more rounds into his skull.

Debré was leaning against the hood of the car, clutching his arm, utterly defeated. "Take the damned money! Take the package! Just leave here!"

"You shouldn't have tried to cross me, Pascal."

"You're right. Just take everything and leave."

"You were right about one thing," the Englishman said as the heavy trench knife with the serrated blade slipped from his forearm sheath into his palm. A moment later

Pascal Debré was lying on the floor next to his partner, his face white as a sheet, his throat slashed nearly to the spine.

THE KEYS TO DEBRÉ'S CAR WERE STILL IN THE ignition. The Englishman used them to open the trunk. Inside was another suitcase. He lifted the lid. A second bomb, a duplicate of the one resting on the hood of the car. He supposed the Frenchman had scheduled another job later that night. The Englishman had probably saved someone's shop. He closed the lid of the suitcase, then softly lowered the trunk.

The floor was covered in blood. The Englishman walked around the corpses and stood over the hood of the car. He opened the suitcase and set the time for three minutes, then closed the lid and placed the case between the bodies.

He walked deliberately across the warehouse and opened the door. Then he went back to the car and climbed behind the wheel. When he turned the key, the engine coughed and died. *Dear God, no—Pascal's revenge.* He turned it a second time, and the engine roared into life.

He backed out, turned around in the drive, and sped through the gate in the chain-link fence. When the bomb went off, the flash in his rearview mirror was so bright that for a moment he was blinded. He followed the river road back toward Paris, purple spots floating in his vision.

Ten minutes later, he parked Debré's car in a tow zone near a Métro stop and got out. He removed the suitcase from the trunk and dropped the keys into a rubbish bin. Then he walked downstairs and boarded a train.

He thought about the old *signadora* back in his village on Corsica—her warning about the mysterious man whom he should avoid. He wondered if Pascal Debré had been that man.

He got out at the Luxembourg stop and walked through the wet streets of the fifth, back to his hotel on the rue St-Jacques. Upstairs in his room it occurred to him that he hadn't seen a single policeman during the trip home. Debré had definitely been lying about the checkpoints.

17

*G*ABRIEL DECIDED IT WAS TIME TO TALK TO Werner Müller. The next morning, he rang the gallery.

"Müller. *Bonjour.*"

"Do you speak German?"

"*Ja.*"

Gabriel switched from French to German.

"I saw a painting in the window of your gallery over the weekend that I'm interested in."

"Which one was that?"

"The flower arrangement by Jean-Georges Hirn."

"Yes, lovely, isn't it?"

"Indeed, it is. I was wondering if I might be able to see it sometime today."

"I'm afraid I'm rather busy today."

"Oh, really?"

Gabriel had been monitoring all calls to the gallery for seventy-two hours and was quite certain Müller could find time for an appointment.

"Just let me get my book and have a look at the schedule. Can you hold on a moment?"

"Of course."

"Yes, here it is. As it turns out, I've had an unexpected cancellation this afternoon."

"How fortunate."

"How quickly could you be here?"

"Actually, I'm in the neighborhood now. I could be there in ten or fifteen minutes."

"Splendid. And your name?"

"Ulbricht."

"I look forward to seeing you, Herr Ulbricht."

Gabriel severed the connection. He packed quickly, tucked the Beretta into the waistband of his trousers, then took one last look around the room to make certain he'd left no trace of himself behind. Before leaving, he walked to the window and peered down at the gallery. A man was ringing the bell: medium height, dark hair, an attaché case in his right hand. Perhaps Müller's appointment didn't cancel after all. Gabriel quickly dug out his camera and used up the roll taking photographs of the unexpected visitor. Then he removed the film, slipped it in his pocket, and placed the camera in his bag.

At the front counter, the desk manager expressed elaborate sorrow that Herr Kiever was leaving so soon. He asked whether the work had gone well and Gabriel said that he would know soon enough.

Outside, rain fell softly on his face. The Renault was parked on the street around the corner from the hotel, two tickets pinned to the windshield by the wiper blade. Gabriel stuffed them into his pocket and tossed the bag into the trunk.

He glanced at his watch. Twelve minutes had passed since he and Müller had spoken on the telephone. He should be a few minutes late— the German would expect that. He walked around the block twice to see if he was being followed, then went to the gallery and rang the bell. Müller opened the door to him.

"Good morning, Herr Ulbricht. I was beginning to worry about you."

"Actually, I had a bit of trouble finding the place again."

"You don't live in Paris?"

"I'm here on holiday, actually. I live in Düsseldorf."

"I see." Müller clapped his hands together theatrically. "So, you'd like to have a closer look at the Hirn. I don't blame you. It's an absolutely gorgeous painting. A fine addition to any collection. Let me remove it from the window. I'll just be a moment."

While Müller busied himself with the Hirn, Gabriel quickly looked around the room. Ordinary gallery, very ordinary paintings. At

149

the end of the room was Müller's desk, a hand-painted antique affair, and on the floor next to the desk was an attaché.

Müller lifted the painting from the display stand in the window. It was a small work, about eighteen inches by twelve, and Müller had no trouble handling the frame. He placed it on a felt-covered pedestal in the center of the room and switched on some additional lights.

As Gabriel moved into position to view the canvas, he glanced out the front window of the gallery. Something caught his eye in the café across the street. Something familiar, a flash, nothing more.

He turned his attention to the canvas and murmured a few kind words about the quality of the brushwork and the draftsmanship. "You seem to know something about art, Herr Ulbricht," Müller said.

"Just enough so that I spend all my money buying paintings I really can't afford," said Gabriel, and the two men shared a good-natured laugh.

Gabriel lifted his eyes from the Hirn and glanced out the window toward the café. There it was again, the sensation that he had seen something, or someone, before. He scanned the tables beneath the awning, and then he saw it. The man, folding his newspaper, standing up, walking away quickly. A man in a hurry, a man late for an important meeting. Gabriel had seen the man before.

The man who had just left the gallery...

Gabriel turned and glanced at the attaché. Then he looked out the window again, but the man had rounded a corner and was gone.

"Is there something wrong, Herr Ulbricht?"

Gabriel grabbed Müller's forearm. "You have to get out of the gallery! Now!"

The art dealer twisted his arm and broke Gabriel's grasp. He was surprisingly powerful.

"Get your hand off me, you madman!"

Gabriel grabbed Müller's arm again, but once again he pulled away.

"Get out of here, or I'm going to call the police."

Gabriel could have easily subdued Müller, but he guessed there wasn't time. He turned and walked quickly toward the door. By the time he arrived, Müller had released the security locks. Gabriel stepped into the street and started walking in the direction of the hotel.

And then the bomb exploded—a deafening thunderclap that knocked Gabriel to his hands and knees. He stood and started walking again as the sound of the blast echoed along the graceful facades of the surrounding streets. Then there was something that sounded like a tropical downpour but it was only the glass, raining onto the pavement from a thousand shattered windows. He raised his hands to shield his face but after a few seconds his fingers ran red with his own blood.

The shower of glass ended, the echo of the explosion receded into the distance. Gabriel resisted the impulse to look over his shoulder at the devastation. He had seen the results of a street bomb before and could imagine the scene behind him. Burning cars, blackened buildings, a devastated café, bodies, and blood, the stunned looks on the faces of the survivors. So he removed his hands from his face and hid them in the pockets of his jacket, and he kept walking, head down, ears ringing with the awful silence.

18

*P*ARIS HAD SUFFERED ITS UNFAIR SHARE OF terrorist bombings over the years, and the French police and security services had become quite efficient at dealing with the aftermath. Within two minutes of the explosion, the first units arrived. Within five minutes, the surrounding streets were sealed. Gabriel's car had been caught inside the cordon, so he had been forced to flee on foot. It was nearly dusk by the time he reached the sprawling rail yard on the southern edge of the city.

Now, sheltering in the loading bay of an abandoned factory, he took mental inventory of the things in the trunk. A suitcase, a few items of clothing, a camera, a tape recorder, the radio he had used to communicate with

the surveillance team. If the car was not collected soon, the police would impound it,
break open the trunk, and examine the contents. They would play the audiotape and
discover that Werner Müller's gallery and
telephones had been bugged. They would
develop exposed rolls of film and discover
photographs of the gallery's exterior. They
would calculate the angle of the photographs
and surmise that they had been taken from a
window of the Hôtel Laurens. They would question the staff at the hotel and discover that the
room in question had been occupied by a
rude German writer.

Gabriel's right hand began to throb. The
strain was catching up with him. He'd stayed
on the move after the bombing, ridden a
dozen Métro trains, walked countless miles
along the crowded boulevards. From a public
telephone near the Luxembourg Gardens, he
had made contact with Uzi Navot on the
emergency channel.

Gabriel looked up now and saw two cars
moving slowly along a narrow service road bor-
dered by a sagging chain-link fence. The
headlights were doused. The cars stopped
about fifty yards away. Gabriel jumped down
from the loading dock—the landing sent shock
waves of pain through his hands—and walked
toward them. The rear door of the first car flew
open. Navot was slumped in the backseat.
"Get in," he grumbled. Clearly, he had
watched too many American movies about the
Mafia.

Navot had brought a doctor, one of Ari Shamron's *sayanim*. He was sitting in the front passenger seat. He made an operating table of the center armrest, spreading a sterile cloth over it and switching on the dome light. The doctor cut away the dressing and examined the wound. He pulled his lips into a mild frown—*Not so bad. You bring me here for this?* "Something for the pain?" he asked, but Gabriel shook his head. Another frown, another tip of the head—*As you wish.*

The doctor flushed the wound with an antiseptic solution and went to work. Gabriel, the restorer, watched him intently. *Insert, pull, tug, snip.* Navot lit a cigarette and pretended to look out the window. When the doctor had finished the suturing, he dressed the wound carefully and nodded that he was done. Gabriel laid his right hand upon the sterile towel. As the doctor cut away the dirty dressing, he emitted a very French sigh of disapproval, as if Gabriel had ordered the wrong wine for fish with saffron butter sauce. "This one will take a few minutes, yes?" Navot waved his hand impatiently.

The doctor didn't care for Navot's attitude, and he took his time about it. This time he didn't bother to ask Gabriel whether he wanted anything for the pain. He simply prepared a syringe and injected an anesthetic into Gabriel's hand. He worked slowly and steadily for almost a half-hour. Then he looked up. "I did the best I could, under the circumstances." A hostile glance toward Navot—*I do this for free, boy. Shamron is going*

154

to hear about this. "You need proper surgery on that wound. The muscles, the tendons—" A pause, a shake of the head. "Not good. You're likely to experience some stiffness, and your range of motion will never be quite the same."

"Leave us," Navot said. "Go to the other car and wait there." Navot dismissed the driver too. When they were alone, he looked at Gabriel. "What the hell happened?"

"How many dead?" Gabriel asked, ignoring Navot's question.

"Three, so far. Four more in bad shape."

"Have you heard from the rest of the team?"

"They've left Paris. Shamron is bringing everyone home. This could get ugly."

"The car?"

"We've got a man watching it. So far, the police haven't made a move on it."

"Eventually, they will."

"What are they going to find when they do?"

Gabriel told him. Navot closed his eyes and swayed a bit, as though he had just been told of a death. "What about Müller's apartment?"

"There's a glass on his telephone."

"Shit."

"Any chance of getting inside and cleaning things up?"

Navot shook his head. "The police are already there. If they find your car and establish that Müller was under surveillance of some sort they'll tear apart his flat. It won't take them long to find the bug."

"Any friends on the force that might be able to help us?"

"Not for something like this."

"That bug is like a calling card."

"I know, Gabriel, but I wasn't the one who put it there."

Gabriel fished the roll of film from his pocket and handed it to Navot. "I got a picture of the man who left the bomb at the gallery. Get it to King Saul Boulevard tonight. Tell the troglodytes in Research to run it through the database. Maybe they can put a name to his face."

The film disappeared into Navot's big paw.

"Contact Shamron and tell him to get a security detail up to Anna Rolfe's villa right away." Gabriel opened the car door and put his foot on the ground. "Which car is mine?"

"Shamron wants you to come home."

"I can't find the man who planted that bomb if I'm sitting in Tel Aviv."

"You won't be able to find him if you're sitting in a French jail cell, either."

"Which car is mine, Uzi?"

"All right! Take this one. But you're on your own."

"Someday, I'll try to repay the favor."

"Have a good time, Gabriel. I'll stay here and clean up your fucking mess."

"Just get the film to Tel Aviv. Good dog."

ON THE COSTA DE PRATA, ANNA ROLFE lowered her violin and switched off the metronome. Her practice room was in shadow, the breeze from the open window cool and moist with the Atlantic. A professional-quality microphone hung over her stool from a chrome-colored stand. It was connected to a German-made tape deck. Today she had recorded much of her practice session. She played back the tape while she packed the Guarneri into its case and straightened her sheet music.

As always, she found it uncomfortable to listen to herself play, but she did it now for a very specific reason. She wanted to know exactly how she sounded; which passages of the piece were acceptable and which needed additional attention. She liked much of what she heard but picked out three or four sections in the second and third movements where the effects of her long layoff were apparent to her highly critical ear. Tonight, in her second practice session, she would focus exclusively on those passages. For now, she needed to clear her mind.

She went to her bedroom, removed a pale yellow sweater from her dresser drawer, and wrapped it around her shoulders. Then she went downstairs. A moment later, she slipped through the gate of her villa and set out along the winding track down toward the village. At the halfway point, she spotted a tiny Fiat station wagon coming up the track through the trees. Inside were four men. They were not Portuguese. Anna stepped to the side to the allow the car to pass, but it stopped instead, and the man seated in the front passenger seat got out.

"Miss Rolfe?"

"Who wants to know?"

"You are Miss *Anna* Rolfe, aren't you?"

She nodded.

"We're friends of Gabriel's."

IN MARSEILLE, THE ENGLISHMAN LEFT HIS car near the Abbaye St-Victor and walked through the darkened streets to the ferry terminal. As the vessel slipped over the calm waters of the harbor, he went downstairs to his private cabin. He lay on the narrow bed, listening to the news on Marseille radio. The bombing of the Müller Gallery in Paris was the lead item. Pascal Debré's bomb had caused innocent casualties, a fact which made him feel a good deal more like a terrorist than a professional. Tomorrow he would go see the old *signadora,* and she would chase away the *occhju* with her rituals and prayers and absolve him of his sins, the way she always did.

He switched off the radio. In spite of his fatigue, he wanted a woman. It was always that way after the completion of an assignment. He closed his eyes and Elizabeth appeared in his thoughts—Elizabeth Conlin, the pretty Catholic girl from the Ballymurphy housing estates, West Belfast, Northern Ireland. She'd had the instincts of a good professional. When it was safe for them to meet, she would hang a violet scarf in her bedroom window, and the Englishman would crawl through the window and into her bed. They would make love with excruciating slowness, so as not to wake the other members of her family. The Englishman would

158

cover her mouth with the palm of his hand to smother her cries. Once she bit down on the flesh of his thumb and drew blood. It stained the sheets of her bed. Afterward, he would lie next to her in the dark and let her tell him again how she wanted to get away from Belfast—away from the bombs and the British soldiers, the IRA gunmen and the Protestant paramilitaries. And when she thought he was sleeping, she would whisper a rosary, her penance for succumbing to the temptations of the Englishman's body. The Englishman never allowed himself to fall asleep in Elizabeth Conlin's bed.

One night when he crawled through her window, Elizabeth Conlin had been replaced by her father and two IRA enforcers. Somehow they knew the truth about the Englishman. He was driven to a remote farmhouse for what promised to be a lengthy and painful interrogation, followed by his own execution. Unlike most who had found themselves in a similar situation, the Englishman managed to leave the farmhouse alive. Four IRA men did not.

Within hours the Englishman was safely out of the province. Elizabeth Conlin did not fare so well. Her body was found the following morning in the Belfast city cemetery, her head shaved, her throat slashed, the punishment for sleeping with a British agent.

The Englishman had never been able to trust a woman since. Anton Orsati understood this. Once a week he brought a girl up to the Englishman's villa—not a Corsican girl, only French girls, specially flown in for the task of servicing the Englishman's particular needs. And he would wait with the old *paesanu* down the valley road until the Englishman had finished. The Englishman found the act of making love to Orsati's girls as cold and clinical as an assassination, but he endured it because he could not trust himself to choose a lover and was not yet prepared to live like a monastic hermit.

The assignment in Paris intruded on his thoughts. There was something that had been bothering him—the man who entered the gallery just before the bomb had exploded. The Englishman was the product of an elite unit and capable of spotting the influence in others: the light-footed gait; the subtle combination of absolute confidence and eternal vigilance. The man had been a soldier once—or perhaps something more complicated.

But there was something else. The Englishman had the nagging sensation he had seen the man somewhere before. And so he lay there for the next several hours, sorting through the countless faces stored in his memory, looking for him.

19

𝒯HE BOMBING OF THE MÜLLER GALLERY had done more than create a security problem for Gabriel in Paris. It had eliminated his only obvious lead in the case. Now he had to start over from the beginning, which is why, late the following morning, he was drifting across Mason's Yard toward Julian Isherwood's gallery through a gentle rain.

On the brick wall next to the door was a panel, and on the panel were two buttons and two corresponding names: LOCUS TRAVEL and ISHER OO FINE AR S. Gabriel pressed the second and waited. When the buzzer sounded, he pushed open the door and mounted the stairs: same threadbare brown carpet, same Rorschachesque stain on the third step where a hung-over Isherwood had spilled coffee the morning after Oliver Dimbleby's drunken birthday bash at the Mirabelle. At the top landing were two doors, one leading to the gallery, the other to a small travel agency where a plain woman sat behind a headmasterly desk, surrounded by posters promising boundless excitement in exotic locales. She glanced up at Gabriel, smiled sadly, and returned to her needlepoint.

Though Julian Isherwood clung unwisely to the paintings in his inventory, he did not do the same with the girls who answered his telephones and kept his appalling files. He hired and drove them away with seasonal regularity. So Gabriel was surprised to see Irina, a black-haired leopard of a girl whom Isherwood had taken on six months ago, still at her post behind the desk in the anteroom.

The door separating the anteroom and Isherwood's office stood slightly ajar. Isherwood was with a client. Gabriel could see a painting propped on the black, felt-covered viewing pedestal. Italian Old Master by the look of it; no one Gabriel recognized. Isherwood paced the carpet slowly behind it, hand on his chin, eyes on the floor, like a barrister awaiting an answer from a hostile witness.

"He'd like you to wait upstairs in the exhibition room," the girl purred. "I assume you know the way."

Gabriel entered the tiny lift and rode it upward. The exposition room was a place of shadows, quiet except for the rain pattering on the skylight. Large Old Master canvases hung on each of the walls: a Venus by Luini, a nativity by del Vaga, a baptism of Christ by Bordone, a luminous landscape by Claude. Gabriel left the lights off and sank heavily onto the velvet-covered divan. He loved this room. It had always been a sanctuary; an island of peace. He had once made love to his wife in this room. Years later, he had plotted the death of the man who had taken her away from him.

The door of the lift opened and Isherwood entered.

"My God, Gabriel, but you look like complete hell."

"Is that supposed to be a compliment?"

"What the hell's going on? Why aren't you in Zürich?"

"The owner of the painting you sent me to clean was a man named Augustus Rolfe. Ever heard of him?"

"Oh, good Lord—the one who was murdered last week?"

Gabriel closed his eyes and nodded. "I found his body."

Isherwood noticed the bandages. "What happened to your hands?"

"You heard about the explosion at the gallery in Paris yesterday?"

"Of course—this place is buzzing about it. Surely you weren't involved in that?"

"No, I just happened to be in the wrong place at the wrong time. I'll tell you everything, Julian, but first I need your help."

"What sort of help?" Isherwood asked cautiously.

"Nothing like the old days. I just need you to explain why an aging Swiss banker might have kept a very impressive collection of French Impressionist and Modern paintings hidden from the world in an underground vault."

Isherwood pressed the button on the intercom. "Irina, would you be a love and bring a pot of coffee up to the exposition room? And some of those biscuits too. The ones with the nuts. And hold all my calls, please. There's a good girl."

◆ ◆ ◆

GABRIEL KNEW THE BASICS ABOUT THE NAZI rape of Europe's art treasures during the Second World War. Adolf Hitler had dreamed of building a massive *Führermuseum* in his hometown of Linz and filling it with the world's finest collection of Old Master and Northern European art. In 1938, he initiated a secret operation codenamed *Sonderauftrag Linz*—Special Operation Linz—to acquire art for the *Führermuseum* by any means necessary. During the last months of peace, his agents secretly toured the museums, galleries, and private collections of Europe, selecting works for the future museum. When war broke out, Hitler's art thieves followed hard on the heels of the Wehrmacht. Hundreds of thousands of paintings, sculptures and *objets d'art* quickly vanished, many of them Jewish-owned. Thousands of works, valued at roughly $30 billion, were still missing.

Gabriel knew that Julian Isherwood could fill in the rest of the details for him. Isherwood was an above-average art dealer who'd had his fair share of triumphs, but when it came to the Nazi plunder of Europe he was something of an expert. He had written dozens of articles for newspapers and trade publications and five years earlier had co-authored a well-received book on the subject. Despite the pleas of his publisher, he had steadfastly refused to reveal his personal motivation for pursuing the topic.

164

Gabriel was among the handful of people who knew why: Julian Isherwood had lived through it.

"In 1940, London and New York didn't matter," Isherwood began. "Paris was the center of the art world, and the center of the Paris art scene was the rue de la Boétie in the eighth arrondissement. The famous Paul Rosenberg had his gallery at number twenty-one. Picasso lived across a courtyard at number twenty-three with his wife, the Russian dancer Olga Koklova. Across the street stood the gallery of Étienne Bignou. Georges Wildenstein had his gallery at number fifty-seven. Paul Guillaume and Josse Hessel were also there."

"And your father?"

"Isakowitz Fine Arts was next to Paul Rosenberg's. We lived in a flat above the main exposition rooms. Picasso was 'Uncle Pablo' to me. I spent hours at his flat. Sometimes, he'd let me watch him paint. Olga used to give me chocolate and cake until I was sick. It was an enchanted existence."

"And when the Germans came?"

"Well, it all came crashing down, didn't it? The invasion of the Low Countries started on May tenth. By June fourteenth, the Germans had entered Paris. Swastikas hung from the Eiffel Tower, and the German General Staff had set up shop at the Hôtel Crillon."

"When did the looting start?"

"Two days after Hitler's victory tour of Paris, he ordered all works of art owned by Jews to be transferred to German hands for so-called *safekeeping*. In reality, the plunder of France was on."

"If I remember correctly, Hitler set up an organization to oversee the looting of France."

"There were several, but the most important was a unit called the ERR: the *Einsatzstab Reichsleiter Rosenberg*. It was a formidable enterprise. It had its own intelligence service for hunting down works of art, a strike force for raids and seizures, and a staff of art historians and appraisers. My God, it even had its own carpenters for crating looted works for shipment to Germany."

"The rue de la Boétie must have been their first stop."

"The ERR went after the dealers *and* the collectors. The Rothschild collections were seized along with their residences. So were the collections of the Jewish banking magnate David David-Weill and Jacques Stern. All the Jewish-owned galleries on the rue de la Boétie were raided and their collections seized, including the inventory of Isakowitz Fine Arts."

"Did your father manage to protect any of his works?"

"Most dealers, my father included, tried to protect their most important pieces. They hid them in remote chateaux or bank vaults or shipped them out of the country. But the unprotected works were quickly snatched up by the Germans. Before the invasion, during the *drôle de guerre*, my father rented a villa in Bordeaux and moved his most important pieces there. We fled there as the Germans closed in on Paris. When France was divided into the Occupied Zone and the Unoccupied Zone, we ended up on the Vichy side of the line. But in the autumn of 1940, an ERR strike force with a French police escort broke down the door of the villa and seized my father's paintings."

"How did the Germans find his collection?"

"He'd made the mistake of telling a French dealer what he planned to do with his paintings. The Frenchman turned over the information to the ERR in exchange for a payoff of five percent of the value of my father's collection. *C'est la vie.*"

Gabriel knew what had happened next, and he had no intention of allowing Isherwood to tell it again. Shortly after the Germans moved into the Unoccupied Zone late in 1942, the SS and their allies in the Vichy government began rounding up Jews for internment and deportation to the death camps. Isherwood's father hired a pair of Basque smugglers to take young Julian over the Pyrenees into the sanctuary of Spain. His mother and father stayed behind in France. In 1943 they were arrested and sent to Sobibor, where they were immediately murdered.

Isherwood shivered once violently. "I'm afraid I feel a drink coming on. On your feet, Gabriel. Some fresh air will do us both some good."

THEY WALKED AROUND THE CORNER TO A wine bar in Jermyn Street and settled next to a hissing gas fire. Isherwood ordered a glass of Médoc. His eyes were on the flames, but his mind was still in wartime France. Like a child creeping into his parents' room, Gabriel gently intruded on his memories.

"What happened to the paintings once they were seized?"

"The ERR commandeered the Musée Jeu de Paume and used it as a storage facility and sorting house. A large staff worked night and day to catalogue and appraise the massive amount of art that was falling into German hands. Those works deemed suitable for the Führer's private collection, for the Linz project, or other German museums—mainly Old Masters and Northern European works— were crated and shipped off to the Fatherland."

"And the rest of it? The Impressionists and the Modern works?"

"The Nazis considered them degenerate, but they weren't about to let them get away without first extracting something in return. Most of the nineteenth- and twentieth-century works were sold off to raise cash or set aside to be used in exchanges."

"What sort of exchanges?"

"Take Hermann Göring, for example. He owned a large hunting lodge south of Berlin called Carinhall in honor of his dead wife, a

Swedish aristocrat named Carin von Fock. It contained one of the largest private collections in Europe, and Göring used his extraordinary power to enlarge it substantially during the war. He treated the storerooms of Jeu de Paume as though they were his private playground."

Isherwood drained his glass and ordered another.

"Göring was a greedy bastard—he grabbed more than six hundred paintings from the Jeu de Paume alone—but he went to great lengths to make it appear as though his acquisitions were, on paper at least, legal purchases rather than outright thefts. If Göring wanted a work, he had it specially appraised at a ludicrously low level by a handpicked fonctionnaire. Then he would immediately take possession and promise to send the money into a special ERR account. In reality, he paid nothing for the paintings he took from Paris."

"Did they end up in Carinhall?"

"Some, but not all. Göring shared Hitler's disdain for Modern and Impressionist paintings, but he knew they could be sold off or traded for pieces more to his taste. One deal was carried out by Göring's agents in Italy. In exchange for seven Italian Old Master works and several other *objets d'art*, Göring handed over nine paintings seized from the Jeu de Paume. Van Gogh, Degas, Cézanne, Renoir, and Monet, just to name a few—all stolen from Jewish collections and galleries. Göring carried out several other similar exchanges involving dealers in Switzerland."

"Tell me about the Swiss connection."

"Neutrality left the dealers and collectors of Switzerland in a unique position to capitalize on the rape of Paris. The Swiss were permitted to travel throughout much of Europe, and the Swiss franc was the world's only universally accepted currency. And don't forget that places like Zürich were awash in the profits of collaborating with Hitler. Paris was the place to buy looted art, but Zürich, Lucerne, and Geneva were the places to unload it."

"Or stash it?"

"But of course. The banking secrecy laws made Switzerland a natural dumping ground for looted art. So did the laws covering the receipt of stolen property."

"Explain the laws to me."

"They were brilliant, and thoroughly Swiss in subtlety. For example, if a person takes possession of an object in good faith, and that object happens to be stolen, it's rightfully his after five years."

"How convenient."

"Wait, there's more. If an art dealer finds himself in possession of a stolen work, it's the responsibility of the true owner to reimburse the *dealer* in order to reclaim his painting."

"So Swiss dealers and collectors could receive stolen works without any fear of the law or of losing money?"

"Exactly."

"What happened after the war?"

"The Allies dispatched an art expert named Douglas Cooper to Switzerland to try to find the truth. Cooper determined that hundreds, if not thousands, of stolen works had entered Switzerland during the war. He was convinced that many of them were hidden in bank vaults and bonded warehouses. Paul Rosenberg went to Switzerland to have a look round for himself. In a gallery in Zürich, he was offered a Matisse that had been looted from his very own collection."

"Remarkable," Gabriel said. "What did the Swiss government do with this information?"

"It promised the Allies that it would cooperate in a thorough inquiry. It promised to freeze all German assets that had entered the country during the war and to conduct a nationwide census of all such assets. It implemented neither measure. Douglas Cooper suggested suspending the licenses of any dealer who traded in looted art. The Swiss government refused. Then the Swiss Federation of Art Dealers told its members not to cooperate. In short, the Swiss government did what it always does. It shielded its business and its citizens from the eyes of foreigners."

"Did dealers like Paul Rosenberg try to reclaim their paintings in court?"

"A few tried, but the deck was stacked against them. The Swiss made it time-consuming and very expensive for a foreigner to try to reclaim property from a Swiss citizen. The Swiss usually took shelter behind a claim of good faith. And remember, most of the art in question was stolen by the Nazis in

1940. By 1945, under the five-year rule of Swiss law, the rightful owners no longer had a valid legal claim. Needless to say, most plaintiffs walked away empty-handed."

"Do you think any of it's still there?"

"In my opinion, Gabriel, most of it's still there. From the little bit you've told me, it sounds as though some of those paintings may have been in the hands of Augustus Rolfe."

"Not anymore."

Isherwood finished the last of his wine, and his gaze drifted back to the fire. "I think it's your turn to do the talking, Gabriel. Tell me everything. And no lies this time. I'm too old to be lied to anymore."

OUTSIDE IT WAS RAINING AGAIN. ON THE WAY back to the gallery they sheltered together beneath Isherwood's umbrella like mourners in a cortege. Gabriel had told Isherwood everything, beginning with the discovery of Rolfe's body and ending with the explosion at Werner Müller's gallery in Paris. Isherwood had drunk two more glasses of Médoc, and his haphazard gait showed the effects.

"*Shamron*," Isherwood said *sotto voce*, his voice dripping with scorn. "I should have known that bastard had something to do with this. I thought they'd finally put him out to pasture for good this time."

"They always find a reason to bring him back."

"They say she's quite the diva, Anna Rolfe."

"She has her moments."

"If I can give you one piece of advice, my dear boy, assume at all times that she knows more about her father and his collection than she's telling you. Daughters tend to be very protective of their fathers, even when they think their fathers are complete bastards."

"I'll try to keep that in mind."

"It may just be an ordinary art theft."

"They left a Raphael hanging on the wall of the parlor and blew up the art gallery belonging to the man who oversaw the collection. I don't think there's anything ordinary about what happened."

"Point taken," Isherwood said. "In fact, it sounds to me as if the only things you can trust in this whole wretched affair are the paintings themselves."

"I hate to be the one to break this to you, Julian, but paintings can't really talk. Besides, the collection is gone."

"The paintings can't talk, but their provenance *can*. Clearly, Augustus Rolfe took his collecting very seriously. Even if he acquired the paintings under less than perfect circumstances, he would have insisted on a provenance for each one of them. Provenance, after all, is everything."

"And if I can get the provenance?"

"Then I'll be able to tell you whether he was a legitimate collector or whether the old bastard was sitting atop a vault filled with looted art."

◆ ◆ ◆

GABRIEL HAD PLANNED TO LEAVE HIM IN DUKE Street, but Isherwood took him by the elbow and pulled him through the passageway into Mason's Yard. "Come with me. There's one more thing I need to show you."

As they entered the gallery, Irina recognized the telltale signs of a bottled lunch. She gave Isherwood a stack of telephone messages and went to work on a pot of coffee. Back in his office, Isherwood opened his private safe and withdrew two items, a sketch of a young boy and a photocopy of an old document several pages in length. He held up the sketch for Gabriel to see.

"Look familiar?"

"I can't say it does."

"The subject is me. The artist is Pablo Picasso. I carried it out of France with me."

"And the document?"

"I carried that as well. My father gave it to me right before I set out with the Basques. It's a detailed list of every painting in his private collection and professional inventory, written in his own hand. This is a copy, of course. The original's in terrible shape now."

He handed the list to Gabriel.

"I don't know how far you plan to take this thing, but if you happen to come across any of these, you'll let me know, won't you, petal?"

Gabriel slipped the list into the breast pocket of his jacket.

"Where are you off to now?" Isherwood asked.

174

"I'm not sure."

"There's a man you should talk to in Lyons. He helped me with a few things when I was researching the book. If Augustus Rolfe has any dirt under his fingernails, this man will know about it."

Isherwood flipped through the Rolodex and gave Gabriel the telephone numbers.

20

♦ *LONDON*

AROUND THE CORNER FROM ISHERWOOD Fine Arts, in Jermyn Street, a fair-haired man sat behind the wheel of a Rover sedan listening to the radio. For five days he had been watching the art dealer. He had followed him to his drunken lunches. Followed him home at night to his house in South Kensington. He'd even posed as a potential buyer in order to conceal a pair of tiny transmitters in the dealer's office. The transmitter broadcast a weak analog signal over an ordinary FM wavelength. The man was using the radio in the Rover to monitor the output. Ten minutes later, when the conversation inside ended, he picked up his cellular phone and dialed a number in Zürich.

"Our friend is on his way to Lyons to see the professor."

21

*P*ROFESSOR EMIL JACOBI WAS THE SELF-appointed guilty conscience of Switzerland. He believed that in order to save his country he first had to tear it down, and he had devoted his life to unearthing and exposing the unsavory elements of Swiss history. His explosive book, *The Myth*, had ignited a firestorm by detailing the extensive economic and trade links between Nazi Germany and Switzerland throughout the Second World War. Jacobi outlined the process by which Swiss banks accepted looted gold—and gold ripped from the teeth of Jews on the way to the gas chambers—and converted it into the hard currency Hitler used to buy the raw materials needed to keep his war machine running. Professor Jacobi's conclusion shocked the country and made him a national pariah: Switzerland and Nazi Germany were allies in everything but name, he wrote. Hitler could not have waged war without the help of Swiss bankers and arms makers. If not for Switzerland, the Wehrmacht would have ground to a halt in the autumn of 1944. Millions of lives would have been spared but for the greed of Swiss bankers.

Soon after publication of *The Myth*, life for Professor Jacobi in Switzerland became increasingly uncomfortable. He received death threats, his telephones were tapped, and officers of the Swiss security service monitored his movements. Fearing for his safety, he resigned his professorship in Lausanne and accepted a position in the history department of the University of Lyons.

It took Gabriel the better part of the next day to track him down.

He left two messages on Jacobi's answering machine at home and two more with his thoroughly unhelpful secretary at the university. At one-thirty in the afternoon, Jacobi called Gabriel on his cellular phone and agreed to a meeting. "Come by my flat at six this evening. We'll talk then." Then he rattled off the address and abruptly rang off. That left Gabriel several hours to kill. In a bookstore near the university he found a French-language copy of *The Myth* and spent the rest of the afternoon reading among the students in a café off the Place des Terreaux.

At six o'clock the professor was waiting in the foyer of his apartment building on the rue Lanterne. He wore a frayed tweed jacket, and his rimless spectacles were pushed up into a bird's nest of unruly gray hair. There were clips on the legs of his trousers to keep the cuffs from becoming entangled in the chain of his bicycle. "Welcome to exile," he said, leading Gabriel wearily up the staircase to his flat on the fourth floor. "We Swiss revere the right to free speech, but only if that speech refrains from criticism of Switzerland. I committed the mortal sin of a good Swiss, and so I find myself here, in the gilded cage of Lyons."

On the landing outside his door, the professor spent a long moment digging in his saddlebag through loose papers and battered notebooks, searching for the keys to his flat. When finally he found them, they were admitted into a small, sparsely furnished apartment. Every flat surface was piled with books, documents, and newspapers. Gabriel smiled. He had come to the right place.

Jacobi closed the door and hung his saddlebag over the latch. "So you wish to discuss the murder of Augustus Rolfe? As it turns out, I've been following that case quite carefully."

"I thought you might. I was wondering if we could compare notes."

"Are you a historian as well, Mr. Allon?"

"Actually, I'm an art restorer, but in this matter I'm working for the government of Israel."

"Well, this promises to be an interesting evening. Clear the things off that chair and sit down. I'll see to the coffee."

PROFESSOR JACOBI SPENT SEVERAL MINUTES DIGging through his towering stacks of paper for the file on Augustus Rolfe. It was very slender.

"Herr Rolfe was a private banker in the truest sense of the word, Mr. Allon. I'm afraid much of what I'm going to tell you is based on conjecture and rumor."

"I've often found that one can learn a great deal about a man by the rumors that swirl around him."

"When one is dealing with a Swiss banker, especially a private banker like Augustus Rolfe, rumor is sometimes the best one can hope for." The professor slipped on his glasses and opened the file. "There are very small private banks in Zürich, and there are extremely large ones. The giants like Union Bank of Switzerland and Credit Suisse both have private banking divisions, though they handle only very wealthy customers."

"How large?"

"Usually, a minimum deposit of approximately five million dollars. It's been reported that the intelligence agencies of your country utilized the private banking services of Credit Suisse." The professor glanced at Gabriel over the open file. "But then, I'm sure you know nothing of that."

Gabriel let the question sail by. "From what I know of Augustus Rolfe, he fell into the first category."

"That's right. The Rolfe bank was a small enterprise—Rolfe and a half-dozen employees, if that. If you wanted someone to hide your money or your belongings in Switzerland, Augustus Rolfe was your best friend. He was one of the most discreet and most influential bankers in Zürich. He had very powerful friends. That's what makes his murder so baffling to me."

"What else do you know about him?"

"He took over control of the family business from his father in the early thirties—not a good time for the banks of Switzerland. There was the worldwide depression, the German panic, a currency crisis in Austria that was sending shock waves through Zürich. Swiss banks were falling like dominoes. Many private banks were forced to merge with larger competitors to survive. Rolfe managed to hang on by his fingernails."

Jacobi licked the tip of his finger and turned a page.

"Then Hitler comes to power in Germany and starts making trouble for the Jews. Jewish money and valuables flow into the private banks of Zürich—including Rolfe's."

"You know this to be fact?"

"Absolutely. Augustus Rolfe opened more than two hundred numbered accounts for German Jews."

Jacobi turned over a few pages of the file.

"Here's where the facts end and the rumors begin. In the late thirties, agents of the Gestapo start coming to Zürich. They're looking for all the Jewish money that's been spirited out of Germany and deposited in Swiss banks. It's rumored that Rolfe cooperated with the Gestapo agents in violation of Swiss banking laws and revealed the existence of Jewish-held numbered accounts at his bank."

"Why would he do that?"

"Would you like my theory?"

"Sure."

"Because he knew that the money deposited

by a few Jews was nothing compared to the riches that awaited him if he cooperated with Nazi Germany."

"Is there evidence to suggest that he did?"

"Indeed," Jacobi said, his eyebrows shooting up over the rims of his spectacles. "It's a fact that Augustus Rolfe made frequent trips to Nazi Germany throughout the war."

"Who did he see there?"

"It's not known, but his travels raised enough eyebrows that Rolfe came under investigation after the war."

"What came of it?"

"Absolutely nothing. Rolfe melted back into the world of Zürich banking, never to be heard from again—until a week ago, of course, when someone walked into his villa on the Zürichberg and put a bullet in his head."

Jacobi closed the file and looked at Gabriel.

"Would you care to pick up the story, Mr. Allon?"

WHEN GABRIEL WAS FINISHED, PROFESSOR Jacobi spent a long time polishing his spectacles on the fat end of his tie. Then he shoved them back onto his forehead and poured himself another cup of coffee. "It sounds as though you've run up against the great conspiracy of silence."

"What do you mean by that?"

"When you're dealing with Switzerland, Mr. Allon, it's best to keep one thing in mind. Switzerland is not a real country. It's a business, and it's run like a business. It's a business that is constantly in a defensive posture. It's been that way for seven hundred years."

"What does that have to do with Rolfe's murder?"

"There are people in Switzerland who stand to lose a great deal if the sins of the past are exposed and the sewers of the Bahnhofstrasse are given the thorough flushing they so desperately need. These people are an invisible government, and are not to be taken lightly, which is why I live here instead of Lausanne. If you choose to pursue this matter, I suggest you watch your back."

Ten minutes later Gabriel was walking down the stairs with his copy of *The Myth* tucked beneath his arm. He paused in the foyer for a moment to open the cover and read the words the professor had scrawled on the title page.

Beware the gnomes of Zürich—Emil Jacobi.

THAT IMAGE OF GABRIEL WAS CAPTURED BY THE man with a long-range digital camera standing in the window of the apartment house on the opposite side of the street. One hour earlier he had also snapped a photograph of Gabriel's arrival. The pictures were not necessary, just a professional touch. Allon's entire conversation with Emil Jacobi had been picked up by the pair of sensitive transmitters the man had planted in the professor's apartment six

months earlier. As Allon walked away, the surveillance artist fired off several more photographs. Then he sat down in front of his
playback deck and listened to the tapes. After
thirty minutes of steady work, he had completed
a thorough transcript of the encounter. He spent
ten more minutes checking the transcription
for accuracy, then he encrypted the report and
sent it via secure e-mail to Zürich, along with
the photographs of Allon.

Thirty seconds after that, the information
appeared on the computer screen of Gerhardt Peterson, who immediately picked up
his telephone to request an urgent meeting with
Herr Gessler. Gerhardt Peterson did not like
Emil Jacobi, and neither did Herr Gessler.
Jacobi's one-man crusade against the financial oligarchy of Switzerland had become
tiresome and costly. Both men agreed that it
was time to deal with the meddlesome little
professor.

The following morning, before leaving his
flat for the office, Gerhardt Peterson made a
telephone call from the privacy of his study.
It lasted no more than two minutes. The fate
of Emil Jacobi, the guilty conscience of
Switzerland, had been sealed by a financial
transaction, the transfer of two hundred thousand dollars into a numbered account in
Geneva controlled by Anton Orsati. Gerhardt Peterson found that very fitting indeed.

22

*W*HEN GABRIEL ARRIVED AT ANNA ROLFE'S villa the following morning, he was pleased to see it being guarded by at least four men: one at the gate, a second at the base of the vineyards, a third on the tree line, and a fourth perched on the hilltop. Shamron had sent Rami, his taciturn personal bodyguard, to supervise the detail. He greeted Gabriel in the drive. When Gabriel asked how Anna was dealing with the team, Rami rolled his eyes— *You'll see soon enough.*

He entered the villa and followed the sound of Anna's violin up the staircase. Then he knocked on the door of her practice room and entered without waiting for permission. She spun round and berated him for interrupting her, then screamed at him for turning her home into an armed camp. As her tirade intensified, Gabriel looked down and fingered his bandages. A trickle of fresh blood had seeped through. Anna noticed this too. Immediately she fell silent and gently led him to her bedroom to change his dressings. He couldn't help but look at her while she attended to him. The skin at the base of her neck was damp; the violin strings had left tiny valleys in the fingertips of her left hand. She was more beautiful then he remembered.

"Nice job," he said, inspecting her work.

"I know something about bandaging hands, Mr. Allon. You have some things to tell me about my father, yes?"

"More questions than answers at this point. And please call me Gabriel."

She smiled. "I have an idea, *Gabriel*."

IN A NYLON RUCKSACK, ANNA PACKED A PICNIC lunch of bread and cheese and cold chicken. Last she added a chilled bottle of wine, which she wrapped in a woolen blanket before placing it in the bag. Rami gave Gabriel a Beretta and a pair of boyish-looking bodyguards. On the shaded footpaths of the pine grove, with Rami's chaperons in close attendance, Gabriel told Anna about Paris. He did not tell her about his conversations with Julian Isherwood and Emil Jacobi. That could wait.

The trees broke and the ruins appeared, perched on the face of a steep hillside. A wild goat hopped onto a granite boulder, bleated at them, then melted into the gorse. Gabriel shouldered the rucksack and followed Anna up the path.

He watched the muscles of her legs flexing with each stride, and thought of Leah. A hike on an autumn day like this, twenty-five years earlier—only then the hillside had been in the Golan and the ruins were Crusader. Leah had painted; Gabriel had just returned from Europe, and his desire to create had been chased away by the ghosts of the men he had

185

killed. He had left Leah at her easel and climbed to the top of the hill. Above him had stood the military fortifications along the Syrian border; below stretched the Upper Galilee and the rolling hills of southern Lebanon. Lost in thought, he had not heard Leah's approach. "They're still going to come, Gabriel. You can sit there for the rest of your life looking at them, but they're still going to come." And without looking at her Gabriel had said: "If I used to live there, in the Upper Galilee, and now I lived up there, in a camp in Lebanon, I'd come too."

The snap of Anna unfurling the picnic blanket shattered Gabriel's memory. She spread the blanket over a patch of sunlit grass, as Leah had done that day, while Gabriel ritually uncorked the wine. Rami's watchers took up their positions: one atop the ruins, one on the footpath below. As Anna pulled meat from the bones of the chicken, Gabriel showed her the photo of the man who had left the attaché-bomb at the gallery.

"Ever seen him before?"

She shook her head.

Gabriel put away the photo. "I need to know more about your father."

"Like what?"

"Anything that can help me find out who killed him and took his collection."

"My father was a Swiss banker, Gabriel. I know him as a man, but I know next to nothing about his work."

"So tell me about him."

"Where shall I start?"

"How about his age. You're thirty-eight?"

"Thirty-*seven*."

"Your father was eighty-nine. That's a rather large age difference."

"That's easy to explain. He was married to someone before my mother. She died of tuberculosis during the war. He and my mother met ten years later. She was quite a gifted pianist. She could have played professionally, but my father wouldn't hear of it. Musicians were one step above exhibitionists, in his opinion. Sometimes I wonder what brought them together in the first place."

"Were there children from the first marriage?"

Anna shook her head.

"And your mother's suicide?"

"I was the one who found her body." She hesitated for a moment, then said: "One never forgets something like that. Afterward, my father told us she'd had a history of depression. I loved my mother dearly, Gabriel. We were extremely close. My mother did not suffer from depression. She wasn't taking any medication, she wasn't under the care of a psychiatrist. She was moody, she was temperamental, but she was not the kind of woman who commits suicide for no reason. Something or someone *made* her take her own life. Only my father knew what it was, and he kept it secret from us."

"Did she leave a suicide note?"

"According to the inquest, there was no note. But I saw my father take something from her body that looked very much like a note.

187

He never showed it to me, and apparently he never showed it to the police either."

"And the death of your brother?"

"It happened a year later. My father wanted him to go to work in the bank and carry on the family tradition, but Max wanted to race bicycles. And that's exactly what he did—quite well, in fact. He was one of the best riders in Switzerland and a top European professional. He was killed in an accident during the Tour of Switzerland. My father was devastated, but at the same time, I think he felt a certain vindication. It was as if Max had been punished for daring to contradict his wishes."

"And you?"

"I was alone with him. The two people I loved most in the world were gone, and I was trapped with a man I loathed. I threw myself more deeply into violin. The arrangement seemed to suit both of us. As long as I was playing music, my father didn't have to pay any attention to me. He was free to do what he loved most."

"Which was?"

"Making money, of course. He thought his wealth absolved him of his sins. He was such a fool. From the beginning of my career, people thought I played with such fire. They didn't realize that fire was fueled by hatred and pain."

Gabriel broached the next subject cautiously. "What do you know about your father's activities during the war?"

"*Activities?* That's an interesting word. What are you trying to imply by that?"

"I meant nothing by it. I just need to know whether there was something in your father's past that might have led to his murder."

"My father was a banker in Switzerland during the Second World War." Her voice had turned suddenly cold. "That doesn't automatically make him a monster. But to be perfectly honest, I know virtually nothing about my father's *activities* during the war. It was not something he ever discussed with us."

Gabriel thought of information Emil Jacobi had given him in Lyons: Rolfe's frequent trips to Nazi Germany; the rumors of Rolfe's connection to important members of the Nazi hierarchy. Had Rolfe really managed to keep all these things secret from his daughter? Gabriel decided to push it a little further—gently.

"But you have your suspicions, don't you, Anna? You'd have never taken me to Zürich if you didn't have suspicions about your father's past."

"I only know one thing, Gabriel: My mother dug her own grave, climbed inside, and shot herself. It was a hateful, vengeful thing to do. And she did it for a reason."

"Was he dying?"

The bluntness of this final question seemed to take her by surprise, for she looked up suddenly, as though prodded by a sharp object. "My father?"

Gabriel nodded.

"As a matter of fact, Gabriel, yes, my father was dying."

◆ ◆ ◆

WHEN THE FOOD WAS GONE, GABRIEL POURED out the last of the wine and asked her about the provenance.

"They're locked in the desk of my father's study."

"I was afraid you were going to say that."

"Why do you want to see them?"

"I want to look at the chain of possession for each work. The provenance might tell us something about who took them and why your father was killed."

"Or it might tell you nothing at all. And remember one thing: My father purchased all those paintings legally. They belonged to him, no matter what quirk you might find in the provenance."

"I'd still like to see them."

"I'll show you where they are."

"No, you'll *tell* me where they are, and I'll get them and bring them back here. You can't come to Zürich now."

"Why not?"

"Because it's not safe. Which leads me to my next topic."

"What's that?"

"Your recital in Venice."

"I'm not canceling it."

"It's not safe for you to perform in public now."

"I don't have a choice. If I don't keep this engagement, my career is over."

"The people who killed your father have made it abundantly clear that they'll do anything to prevent us from finding their identity. That would include killing you too."

"Then you'll just have to make certain they don't succeed, but I'm going to perform next week, and there's nothing you can do to stop me."

COLUMNS OF GUNMETAL CLOUD HAD APPEARED over the sea and started their advance inland. A chill wind rose and moaned in the ruins. Anna shivered in the abrupt cold and folded her arms beneath her breasts, her eyes on the approaching weather. Gabriel packed up the remains of their lunch, and in the gathering darkness they ambled down the hill, shadowed by the two silent watchers. When they reached the foot-paths of the pine grove it began to rain heavily. "Too late," Anna shouted above the pounding. "We're caught." She took him by the arm and led him to the shelter of a towering pine. "We need to keep your bandages dry," she said, a note of concern creeping into her voice. She dug a wrinkled nylon anorak from the pocket of the rucksack and held it over their heads, and there they huddled for the next twenty minutes like a pair of refugees, Rami's watchers standing silently on either side of them like andirons. While they waited for the weather to break, Anna told Gabriel the security codes for the villa and the location of the provenance in her father's files. When finally the rain moved off, Anna bound Gabriel's hands in the anorak, and they proceeded carefully down the wet track to the villa. At the front gate, Gabriel relinquished her into the custody of Rami and climbed into his car. As he drove away, he took one last look over his shoulder and saw Anna Rolfe chasing Rami across the drive, shouting, "Bang, bang, Rami! You're dead!"

23

*M*OTZKIN LIKED IT IN LISBON. HE'D DONE the glamour postings. He'd done London. He'd done Paris and Brussels. He'd spent a nail-biting year in Cairo posing as a journalist from a newspaper in Ottawa. It was quiet in Lisbon these days, and that was fine with Motzkin. The odd surveillance job, a bit of liaison work. Just enough to keep him from going stir crazy. He had time for his books and his stamps and for long siestas with his girl in the Alfama.

He had just returned from her flat when the telephone on his desk rattled softly. Motzkin lifted the receiver and brought it cautiously to his ear. This was the time Ari Shamron usually chose to poke his head out of his foxhole and make life miserable for his *katsas*. But thankfully it wasn't Shamron—just the guard down in the lobby. It seemed there was a visitor, a man who knew Motzkin's name.

Motzkin rang off and punched up the lobby surveillance camera on his computer monitor. The station regularly fielded walk-ins of all shapes and sizes. Usually a quick once-over could determine whether the person should be seen or frog-marched to the gate.

As the image appeared on his screen, Motzkin murmured: "I'll be damned." Imagine, the living legend, walking into the embassy, looking like something the proverbial cat dragged in. Last Motzkin had heard, he was holed up in some English cottage with his paintings and his demons. "I'll be damned," he repeated as he clambered down the stairs. "Is it really you?"

IN THE COMMUNICATIONS ROOM, MOTZKIN established a secure link with Shamron's office at King Saul Boulevard in Tel Aviv. Then he closed the soundproof door and watched Gabriel through the glass. It was an unpleasant conversation; that much Motzkin could tell. But then there were few people inside the Office who hadn't crossed swords with the old man at one time or another, and the battles between Shamron and the great Gabriel Allon were the stuff of Office lore. Twenty minutes later, when Gabriel slammed down the telephone and stepped out of the room, his face was ashen.

"The old man is sending a report through in thirty minutes. I need a few things."

Motzkin took Gabriel upstairs to the station and allowed him to shower and change into clean clothing. Then he arranged airline tickets and a car and gave him two thousand dollars from the petty-cash box.

By the time they returned to the communications room, the report was sliding off the secure fax machine. It had been compiled by Research Section at King Saul Boulevard and was based on information shared through standing agreements with British and French intelligence.

The subject was a man named Christopher Keller.

Gabriel scooped the pages from the tray, sat down at the table, and started to read.

BORN IN LONDON, THE ONLY SON OF TWO successful Harley Street physicians, Christopher Keller made it clear at an early age that he had no intention of following in the footsteps of his parents. Obsessed with history, especially military history, he wanted to become a soldier. His parents forbade him to enter the military, and he acceded to their wishes, at least for a time. He entered Cambridge and began reading history and Oriental languages. He was a brilliant student, but in his second year he grew restless and one night vanished without a trace. A few days later he surfaced at his father's Kensington home, hair cut to the scalp, dressed in an olive-drab uniform. Keller had enlisted in the British army.

After basic training, he joined his infantry regiment, but his intellect, physical prowess, and lone-wolf attitude quickly set him apart from his peers. Soon a recruiter from the Special Air Service came knocking. He had seen Keller's file and spoken to his superiors. Keller was invited to the Regiment's head-quarters at Hereford to undergo the initial training course.

His performance was extraordinary. The instructors in the unarmed combat course wrote that they had never seen a man who possessed such an instinctual knack for the taking of human life. In the "killing house"— an infamous facility where recruits practice close-quarters combat, hostage rescue, and antiterrorist "room clearing" drills—Keller achieved the highest possible scores. On the final day of the course, he carried a fifty-five-pound rucksack and ten-pound assault rifle during a forty-mile march across the windswept moorland known as the Brecon Beacons, an endurance test that had left men dead. Keller completed the course thirty minutes faster than any man had ever done it before. He was accepted into the Regiment and assigned to a Sabre squadron specializing in mobile desert warfare.

Then the course of his career took an abrupt turn. Another man appeared on the scene, this time from military intelligence. He was looking for a unique brand of soldier capable of performing close observation and other special operations in Northern Ireland. He said he was impressed by Keller's linguistic skills and his ability to improvise and think on his feet. Was Keller interested? That night he packed his kit and moved from Hereford to a secret base in the Scottish Highlands.

During his training Keller displayed a remarkable gift. For years, British security and intelligence forces had struggled with the myriad of accents in Northern Ireland. In Ulster, the opposing communities could identify each other by the sound of a voice. The accent of Catholic West Belfast is different from that of Protestant West Belfast; the accent of the Upper Falls Road is different from that of the Lower Falls. The way a man uttered a few simple phrases could mean the difference between life and an appalling death. Keller developed the ability to mimic the intonations perfectly. He could even shift accents at a moment's notice—a Catholic from Armagh one minute, a Protestant from Belfast's Shankill Road the next, then a Catholic from the Ballymurphy housing estates. He operated in Belfast for more than a year, tracking members of the IRA, picking up bits of useful gossip from the surrounding community. He worked alone, with almost no supervision from his case officer at military intelligence.

His assignment in Northern Ireland came to an abrupt end one night when he was kidnapped in West Belfast and driven to a remote farmhouse in County Armagh. There, he was accused of being a British spy. Keller knew the situation was hopeless, so he decided to fight his way out. By the time he left the farmhouse, four hardened terrorists from the Provisional Irish Republican Army were dead. Two had been virtually cut to pieces.

Keller returned to Hereford for a long rest. He took punishing hikes on the Brecon Beacons and trained new recruits in the art of silent killing. But it was clear to the Regiment's commanders and psychologists that Belfast had changed Keller.

Then in August 1990, Saddam Hussein invaded Kuwait. Five months later, Keller and his unit were roaming the western desert of Iraq, searching out and destroying the Scud missile launchers that were raining terror on Tel Aviv. On the night of January 28, Keller and his team located a launcher in the desert one hundred miles northwest of Baghdad. He passed along the coordinates to his commanders in Saudi Arabia. Ninety minutes later, a formation of Coalition fighter-bombers streaked low over the desert, but in a disastrous case of friendly fire, they attacked the SAS squadron instead of the Scud site. British officials concluded that the entire unit was lost, though no conclusive remains were ever found.

What came next was essentially a theory— again based on intelligence reports. Some months after the disaster in the Iraqi desert, a new and highly professional killer was reported to be working in Europe. Police informants spoke of a man known only as "the Englishman." None could offer more than the vaguest descriptions of him. To date, the mysterious assassin was a suspect in at least twenty unsolved murders. British intelligence suspected that Christopher Keller and the Englishman were the same man.

The file concluded with two photographs. The first was the one Gabriel had taken of the man entering the gallery in Paris. The second showed a group of men on a deserted moorland. One of the faces was circled. Gabriel spent a long time comparing the two pictures. Then he picked up the telephone and called Shamron in Tel Aviv. "I have the strangest sensation I've actually met this man before," Gabriel told him. He had expected Shamron to be surprised by the remark. Instead, the old man told him to stay near the fax machine, and then he rang off.

IN 1988, GABRIEL ALLON CARRIED OUT ONE of the most celebrated operations in the history of Israeli intelligence: the assassination of the PLO's second-in-command, Abu Jihad. He had conducted a long and dangerous surveillance operation on the Palestinian's villa in Tunis, and he had trained the hit team at a mockup in the Negev desert. Then, one warm night in April, he led a team of Sayaret commandos into the house and shot Abu Jihad to death in front of his wife and children. Thinking about that night now, he could still see the look of pure hatred in their dark eyes.

Eighteen months after the assassination, a team of British intelligence and SAS officers involved in the fight against IRA terror came to Tel Aviv to study the tactics of the Israelis. Ari Shamron summoned Gabriel to the Academy and compelled him to deliver a luncheon lecture on the Tunis operation. One of the men attending the lecture was an SAS lieutenant.

The item that came across the fax machine was a photograph. It had been taken after the luncheon to commemorate the spirit of cooperation between the secret warriors of the two countries. Gabriel, eternally camera-shy, wore sunglasses and a sun hat to conceal his identity. The man next to him stared directly into the camera lens. Gabriel carefully examined the face.

It was Christopher Keller.

24

MÜNICH ♦ ZÜRICH

*T*HE COURIER WAS WAITING FOR GABRIEL at the gate in Münich. He had hair the color of caramel and carried a sign that said MR. KRAMER—HELLER ENTERPRISES. Gabriel followed him through the terminal and across the carpark through blowing snow until they came to a dark-blue Mercedes sedan.

"There's a Beretta in the glove box and some brisket on the back seat."

"You *bodlim* think of everything."

"We live to serve." He handed Gabriel the keys. "*Bon voyage.*"

Gabriel climbed behind the wheel and started the engine. Ten minutes later he was speeding along the E54 motorway back to Zürich.

THE SWISS ARE AN INSULAR AND TRIBAL PEOPLE, possessing an almost animal instinct to spot outsiders. Anything out of the ordinary is reported to the police, no matter how insignificant. Indeed, the Swiss citizenry is so vigilant that foreign intelligence agencies operating inside the country regard them as a second security service. With this fact in mind, Gabriel was careful to project an image of familiarity as he walked from his car to Augustus Rolfe's villa.

He thought of an Office operation a few years earlier. A team of agents had been sent to Switzerland to bug the flat of a suspected Arab terrorist living in a small town outside Bern. An old lady spotted the team outside the Arab's apartment house and telephoned the police to report a group of suspicious men in her neighborhood. A few minutes later the team was in custody, and the fiasco was reported around the world.

He climbed the slope of the Rosenbühlweg. The familiar silhouette of the Rolfe villa, with its turrets and its towering portico, rose above him. A car passed, leaving two ribbons of black in the fresh snow.

He punched in the code to the keyless entry system. The buzzer howled, the deadbolt snapped back. He pushed open the gate and climbed the steps. Two minutes later he was inside Rolfe's villa, padding across the dark entrance hall, a small flashlight in one hand, a Beretta in the other.

ON THE SECOND-FLOOR CORRIDOR, THE DARKNESS was absolute. Gabriel moved forward through the pencil-width beam of his flashlight. The study would be on his left, Anna had said—overlooking the street, first door past the bust. Gabriel turned the knob. Locked. *But of course.* He removed a pair of small metal tools from his coat pocket. God, how long had it been? The Academy, a hundred years earlier. He had been a green recruit, and Shamron had stood over him the entire time, shouting abuse in his ear. "You have fifteen seconds. Your teammates are dead unless you get that door open, Gabriel!"

He got down on one knee, slipped the tools into the lock, and went to work, flashlight between his teeth. A moment later, under Gabriel's diligent assault, the old lock gave up the fight. He got to his feet, stepped inside, and closed the door behind him.

The room smelled of woodsmoke and dog and faintly of tobacco. He lifted the flashlight and played it about the interior. Its tiny pool of light meant that he experienced the room a few square feet at a time. A sitting area furnished with eighteenth-century armchairs. A Flemish Renaissance oak writing table. Bookshelves stretching from a burnished wood floor to a molded ceiling.

Augustus Rolfe's desk.

Strange, but it didn't seem like the desk of a powerful man. There was an air of donnish clutter: a stack of files, a faded leather blotter, a teacup filled with paper clips, a pile of antique books. Gabriel lifted the cover with his index finger and was greeted by the scent of ancient paper and dust. He turned the light toward the first page. *Goethe.*

As he closed the volume, the light fell upon a large ashtray of cut glass. A dozen cigarette butts lay haphazardly, like spent cartridges, in a bed of ash. He examined the butts more carefully. Two different brands. Most were Benson & Hedges, but three were Silk Cuts. The old man probably had smoked the Benson & Hedges, but who had smoked the Silk Cuts? *Anna?* No, Anna always smoked Gitanes.

He turned his attention back to the provenance. Anna had said Rolfe kept them in the bottom right-hand desk drawer in a file labeled PERSONAL CORRESPONDENCE. The drawer, like the entrance to Rolfe's study, was locked. This time he had a key. He pulled it open and began leafing through the personal papers of Augustus Rolfe.

He came across a file labeled MAXIMILIAN. He took it between his thumb and forefinger, then hesitated. Did he have any right? It felt too much like voyeurism. Like peering through a lighted window during an evening walk through a city and seeing a couple quarreling. Or an old man sitting alone in front of a television. But what might the file reveal? What sort of things had this man saved about his son? What might Gabriel learn from it about this man Augustus Rolfe?

He pulled out the file, laid it across the open drawer, lifted the cover. Photographs, magazine clippings from the sporting pages of European newspapers, tributes from teammates, a long piece from the Zürich newspaper on the cycling accident in the Alps—*"He was a good man, and I was proud to call him my son," Augustus Rolfe, a prominent Zürich banker, said in a statement issued by his lawyer. "I will miss him more than any words could ever express."* Crisply folded, meticulously dated and labeled. August Rolfe may have disagreed with his son's chosen profession, Gabriel concluded, but he was a proud father.

Gabriel closed the file, slipped it back in its proper place, and resumed the search for personal correspondence. Another file caught his eye: ANNA. Again he hesitated, then drew out the file. Inside were childhood photographs of Anna playing the violin, invitations to recitals and concerts, newspaper clippings, reviews of her performances and recordings. He looked more carefully at the photographs. There were definitely two Annas—before the suicide of her mother, and after. The difference in her appearance was striking.

Gabriel closed the file and slipped it back into the drawer. Time to get back to the business at hand. He flipped through the files until he came to the one marked PERSONAL CORRESPONDENCE. He removed it, placed it on Rolfe's desk, and lifted the cover. Letters, some handwritten, some typed on professional stationery. German, French, Italian, English—the linguistic patchwork quilt that is Switzerland. Gabriel leafed through them quickly until he came to the end of the stack. Then he went back to the beginning and repeated the process more slowly. The result was the same.

The provenance were gone.

As Gabriel played his flashlight beam about the study, he thought of a training drill he had undergone at the Academy. An instructor had led him into a room decorated like a hotel suite, handed him a document, and given him a minute to find five suitable hiding places. Had he been given the test in Rolfe's study instead of an ersatz hotel room, he could have come up with a hundred places to hide a document. A false floorboard, a large book, beneath a carpet or floorboard, inside a piece of furniture, locked away in a concealed wall safe. And that was only in the study. There were thousands of places in the rambling villa for Rolfe to conceal a sheath of documents. This was a man who had built an underground bunker for his secret art collection.

204

If Rolfe wanted to hide something, the odds of Gabriel finding it were slim.

The thought of leaving Zürich empty-handed after so difficult and treacherous a journey was galling to Gabriel. There were two possible explanations for the missing documents. Number one: They had been removed, by Rolfe or someone like Werner Müller. Number two: Rolfe had somehow misplaced them. Surely it was possible. He was an old man. Old men make mistakes. Memories fade. File labels become harder to read.

Gabriel decided to search the desk thoroughly.

There were four file drawers, two on each side, and Gabriel started with the top left. He fell into a monotonous routine: remove a single file, carefully inspect the contents, replace it, move on to the next.

It took Gabriel thirty minutes to search all four drawers.

Nothing.

He pulled open the center drawer: pens, pencils, bits of scrap paper, a bottle of glue, a staple remover. A miniature tape recorder. Gabriel picked it up and inspected it with his flashlight. There was no tape inside. He searched the drawer carefully. A tape recorder, no tapes. *Odd.*

He closed the drawer, sat down in Rolfe's chair, and stared at the desk. The center drawer...something wasn't right. He pulled it open, looked inside, closed it again. Open, close. Open, *close....*

THE DRAWER ITSELF WAS ABOUT FOUR INCHES deep, but the storage space was shallower. Two inches, Gabriel calculated, perhaps even less. He tried to pull the drawer completely out of the desk, but a catch prevented it from coming out. He pulled harder. Same result.

He looked at his watch. He had been in the villa forty-five minutes, probably longer than was wise. Now, he had two choices: Walk away, or trust his instincts.

He stood up, grasped the drawer with both hands, and pulled as hard as he could. The catch gave way and the drawer tumbled onto the floor, spilling the contents.

Gabriel lifted the now-empty drawer and turned it over in his hands. Solid, well-crafted, abnormally heavy. He looked carefully at the base. It was quite thick—an inch perhaps.

Walk away, or trust your instincts?

There was no neat way to go about it, not if he was going to get his answer quickly. He leaned the drawer against the side of the desk and adjusted the angle. Then he raised his foot and slammed it down. Once, twice, a third time, until the wood began to splinter.

THE BASE OF THE DRAWER WAS CONSTRUCTED of not one piece of wood but two, identical in dimension, one laid atop the other. Between them was a large, rectangular envelope, yellow with age, the flap secured with a bit of frayed twine. *The provenance?* Seemed like an awfully elaborate scheme to conceal provenance. Gabriel separated the shattered bits of wood and held the envelope in his hand. A tremor shook his fingers as he unwound the twine and pried open the flap.

He removed the contents, a sheaf of ancient flimsies, and laid them on the desk. He sorted through them carefully, as though he feared they might crumble at his touch. *Kronin... pesetas...escudos...pounds.* The documents were copies of currency transactions and bank transfers carried out during the war. He looked at the dates. The first of the transactions, a transfer of several thousand Swiss francs to the Union Bank of Stockholm, had occurred in February 1942. The last, a transfer of funds to the Bank of Lisbon, had taken place in June 1944.

He set aside the flimsies. The next item was a single sheet of plain white paper with no letterhead. On the left side of the page was a list of names, all German. On the right side was a corresponding list of twelve-digit numbers. Gabriel read a few lines:

Karl Meyer: *551829651318*
Manfred König: *948628468948*
Josef Fritsch: *268349874625*

He gathered up the flimsies and lifted the flap of the envelope. He was about to slip the papers inside when he felt something caught in the bottom corner. He reached inside and drew the objects out.

A pair of photographs.

He looked at the first one: Augustus Rolfe, young, handsome, rich, sitting in a restaurant. Judging from the state of the table, a good deal of wine had been consumed. Seated next to him was a fleshy, decadent-looking man in civilian dress with dueling scars on his cheeks. Gabriel did not recognize him.

He turned his attention to the second photograph. The setting was a terrace in an Alpine home—Rolfe, standing at the balustrade, admiring the magnificent view, accompanied by two men in uniform. Gabriel recognized them both.

One was Heinrich Himmler. The other was Adolf Hitler.

GABRIEL SLIPPED THE PHOTOGRAPHS AND THE documents back into the envelope. It was legal-sized, too large to fit into a pocket, so he shoved it down the front of his trousers and secured it by zipping his leather jacket. He looked at the desk. Nothing to be done about the drawer; it was broken to bits. He pushed the fragments under the seating compartment with his foot and concealed them with Rolfe's chair. The Beretta was lying on Rolfe's leather blotter. He dropped it into his pocket and turned to leave.

He navigated by the beam of the weak penlight. Once again, he had the sensation of experiencing the room a fragment at a time, this time in reverse order. With each movement of the light, a new piece of information: the oak writing table, the eighteenth-century armchairs, a leather ottoman...

A man standing in the doorway, with a gun pointed at Gabriel's heart.

25

♦ *ZÜRICH*

*G*ABRIEL TOSSED THE FLASHLIGHT ACROSS the room, drew his Beretta, and dropped to the floor. The man in the doorway fired. The gun was silenced, but the muzzle flash was visible in the darkness. The shot ripped through the air over Gabriel's head and shattered the window behind Rolfe's desk. Before the man could shoot again, Gabriel rose onto one knee and fired in the direction of the muzzle flash. The shots struck their target—Gabriel knew this because he could hear the rounds tearing through tissue and shattering bone. He got to his feet and ran forward, firing as he went, the way he had been trained at the Academy. *The way he had done it so many times before.* When he was standing over the man, he reached down, placed the barrel into his ear, and fired one last time.

The body convulsed, then went still.

Gabriel knelt and searched the dead man's pockets: no billfold, no keys, no money. A Glock nine-millimeter lay on the floor a few feet from the body. Gabriel slipped it into his pocket and went into the corridor.

Next to the center stairwell was an alcove with a set of tall windows overlooking the street. Gabriel looked down and saw two men pounding up the front steps. He ran across the corridor to the windows overlooking the rear garden. Outside was another man, gun drawn, feet apart, talking on a hand-held radio.

As Gabriel descended the curving staircase, he ejected the spent cartridge from his Beretta and inserted the backup. He retraced the route Anna had taken the night she showed him the secret vault: through the great dining room, through the kitchen, down the back staircase, through the wine cellar, into the cutting room.

He came to a doorway with a window of paned glass that led into the garden. Gabriel pushed open the door a few inches and peered out. The man with the radio and the gun was prowling the snowy terrace. The other team had entered the house—Gabriel could hear the trample of feet on the first floor above him.

He stepped outside and trotted across the garden directly toward the man with the gun. In rapid German, he said: "You there! Did you see which way that jackass went?" The man looked at him in utter confusion. Gabriel kept moving forward. "What's wrong with you, man? Are you deaf? Answer me!"

When the man lifted his radio to his mouth, Gabriel's arm swung up, and he started firing. Five shots, the last into his chest from three feet away.

Gabriel looked up toward the house. He could see flashlight beams playing over the drawn curtains. Then the curtains parted and a face appeared. A shout. Hammering on glass.

Gabriel turned and sprinted across the garden until he came to a wall—seven feet in height, he guessed, with a row of wrought-iron spikes across the top. Glancing over his shoulder, he spotted the two men from the house. One was kneeling over the dead man, the other scanning the garden by the beam of a powerful flashlight.

Gabriel jumped up and grabbed hold of the metal spikes at the top of the wall. The beam of light fell on him, and someone shouted in German. He pulled himself up, flailing his feet against the wall. A shot struck the stucco, then another. Gabriel could feel sutures tearing in his hands.

He threw his leg over the top and tried to drop onto the other side, but his coat had become tangled on a spike, and he dangled there helplessly, his head exposed, blinded by the flashlight. He twisted his body violently until the spike released him, and he fell into the opposing garden.

The envelope slipped through his coat and dropped into the snow. Gabriel scooped it up, shoved it back into his trousers, and started running.

◆ ◆ ◆

A BURST OF HALOGEN LAMPLIGHT TURNED the night electric white. Somewhere an alarm screamed. Gabriel ran along the side of the villa until he reached another wall, this one shielding the villa from the street. He scaled it quickly and dropped onto the other side.

He found himself in a narrow street. Lights were coming on in the neighboring villas—the Swiss and their legendary vigilance. As he ran down the street, Ari Shamron's Eleventh Commandment played in his head: *Thou shalt not get caught!*

He came to Krähbühlstrasse, the wide boulevard where he had parked. He sprinted down the gentle curving slope of the street until he spotted his car. He skidded to a stop and came crashing to the pavement. Two men were peering into the interior with flashlights.

As he clambered to his feet, the men trained their flashlights on him. He turned in the opposite direction and headed back up the hill. *Thou shalt do anything to avoid being arrested!*

He drew the Glock he had taken from the man in the study and kept running. He was beginning to tire. The cold air was searing his lungs, and his mouth tasted of rust and blood. After a few steps, he saw headlights coming down the hill: a big Audi sedan, wheels spinning on the new snow.

He glanced over his shoulder down the hill. The two men were chasing him on foot. No side streets, no alleys—he was trapped. *Thou shalt shed innocent blood if necessary!*

The Audi was speeding directly toward him. He stopped running and leveled the Glock in his outstretched hands. When the car fishtailed and slid to a halt a few feet away, he took aim at the silhouette behind the wheel. Before he could fire, the passenger door flew open.

"Get in, Gabriel!" Anna Rolfe shouted. "Hurry."

SHE DROVE WITH THE SAME INTENSITY WITH which she played the violin—one hand on the steering wheel, the other gripping the stick shift. Down the Zürichberg, across Limmat, into the quiet streets of the city center. Gabriel took a long look over his shoulder.

"You can slow down now."

She eased off the gas.

"Where did you learn to handle a car like that?"

"I was a Zürich girl with a lot of money. When I wasn't practicing the violin, I was tearing around the Zürichsee in one of my father's cars. I'd wrecked three by the time I was twenty-one."

"Congratulations."

"Bitterness doesn't suit you, Gabriel. My cigarettes are in the console. Do me a favor and light one."

Gabriel opened the console and took out the

pack of Gitanes. He lit it with the dashboard lighter. The smoke caught at the back of his throat and he nearly choked.

Anna laughed at him. "Imagine, an Israeli who doesn't smoke."

"What the hell are you doing here?"

"That's all you have to say? If I hadn't shown up, you'd have been arrested."

"No, if you hadn't shown up, I'd be dead. But I still want to know what the hell you're doing here. Did Rami give you permission to leave the villa?"

"I suspect that by now he's probably discovered that I'm not there."

"How did you get away?"

"I went upstairs to my studio to practice. I rolled a tape on a particularly long piece. I suppose you can guess the rest."

"How did you get off the grounds?"

"Carlos told Rami that he was going into the village to do some marketing. I was in the back beneath a blanket."

"It's safe to assume several dozen members of my service are now engaged in a frantic and pointless search for you. That was a very stupid thing to do. How did you get to Zürich?"

"I flew here, of course."

"Directly from Lisbon?"

"Yes."

"How long have you been here?"

"About two hours."

"Did you go inside your father's house?"

She shook her head. "When I arrived I saw two men waiting outside in a parked car. At first I thought they might be private security. Then I realized something was wrong."

"What did you do?"

"I didn't feel safe waiting in the car, so I drove around the neighborhood, hoping to find you before you tried to go in. I missed you, of course. Then I heard the alarms going off."

"Did you tell anyone you were coming?"

"No."

"Are you sure?"

"Of course I'm sure. Why?"

"Because it explains a lot of things. It means that the villa is under constant watch. It means that they know we came back here. It means they followed me to Rome. They've been following me ever since."

"What happened inside my father's house?"

WHEN GABRIEL HAD FINISHED, ANNA SAID: "DID you get the provenance at least?"

"They were gone."

"That's not possible."

"Someone must have gotten to them first."

"Did you find anything else?"

I found a photograph of your father with Adolf Hitler and Heinrich Himmler, admiring the view from the Berghof at Berchtesgaden.

"No," Gabriel said. "I didn't find anything else."

"Are you sure about that? You didn't use the opportunity to rifle through any of my father's personal papers?"

Gabriel ignored her. "Did your father smoke?"

215

"Why does that matter now?"

"Just answer the question, please. Did your father smoke?"

"Yes, my father smoked!"

"What kind of cigarettes?"

"Benson & Hedges."

"Did he ever smoke Silk Cuts?"

"He was very set in his ways."

"What about someone else in the household?"

"Not that I know of. Why do you ask?"

"Because someone was smoking Silk Cuts in your father's study recently."

They came to the lake. Anna pulled to the side of the street. "Where are we going?"

"*You're* going back to Portugal."

"No, I'm not. We do this together, or not at all." She dropped the Audi into gear. "Where are we going?"

26

$\mathcal{S}$OME MEN MIGHT BE SQUEAMISH ABOUT installing a voice-activated taping system in their home. Professor Emil Jacobi was not one of them. His life was his work, and he had little time for anything else; certainly nothing that might cause him any embarrassment if it was captured on audiotape.

He received a steady stream of visitors to his

flat on the rue Lanterne: people with unpleasant memories of the past; stories they had heard about the war. Just last week, an old woman had told him about a train that had stopped outside her village in 1944. She and a group of friends were playing in the meadow next to the tracks when they heard moans and scratches coming from the cargo cars. When they moved closer, they saw that there were people on the train: miserable, wretched people, begging for food and water. The old woman realized now that the people were Jews—and that her country had allowed the Nazis to use its railways to ship human cargo to the death camps in the East.

If Jacobi had tried to document her story by taking hand-written notes, he would have failed to capture it all. If he had placed a tape-recorder in front of her, she might have become self-conscious. It had been Jacobi's experience that most elderly were nervous around tape recorders and video cameras. And so they had sat in the cluttered comfort of his flat like old friends, and the old woman had told her story without the distraction of a notebook or a visible tape recorder. Jacobi's secret system had caught every word of it.

The professor was listening to a tape now. As usual, the volume was set quite loud. He found it helped to focus his concentration by blocking out the noise from the street and the students who lived in the next flat. The voice emanating from his machine was not that of the old woman. It was the voice of a man: the man who had come the previous day. Gabriel Allon. An amazing story, this tale of Augustus Rolfe and his missing collection of paintings. Jacobi had promised the Israeli he would tell no one about their discussion, but when the story broke, as Jacobi knew it eventually would, he would be perfectly positioned to write about it. It would be yet another black eye for Jacobi's mortal enemies, the financial oligarchy of Zürich. His popularity in his native country would sink to new depths. This pleased him. Flushing sewers was dirty work.

Emil Jacobi was engrossed in the story now, as he had been the first time he had heard it; so engrossed that he failed to notice the figure who had slipped into his flat—until it was too late. Jacobi opened his mouth to call out for help, but the man smothered his cry with an iron grip. The professor spotted the glint of a knife blade arcing toward him, then felt a searing pain across the base of his throat. The last thing he saw was his killer, picking up the tape player and slipping it into his pocket as he walked out.

27

♦ *VIENNA*

ON THE WESTERN FRINGES OF VIENNA, Gabriel had to grip the wheel tightly to keep his hands from shaking. He had not been back to the city since the night of the bombing—since the night of fire and blood and a thousand lies. He heard a siren and was uncertain whether it was real or just memory until the blue lights of an ambulance flashed in his mirror. He pulled to the side of the road, his heart hammering against his ribs. He remembered riding with Leah in an ambulance and praying that she would be released from the pain of her burns, no matter what the price. He remembered sitting over the shattered body of his son while, in the next room, the chief of the Austrian security service screamed at Ari Shamron for turning central Vienna into a war zone.

He pulled back into the traffic. The discipline of driving helped to settle his turbulent emotions. Five minutes later, in the Stephansdom Quarter, he stopped outside a souvenir shop. Anna opened her eyes.

"Where are you going?"

"Wait here."

He went inside, and returned to the car two minutes later with a plastic shopping bag. He handed it to Anna. She removed both items: a pair of large sunglasses and a baseball hat with *Vienna!* stenciled across the crown.

"What am I supposed to do with these?"

"Do you remember what happened at the airport in Lisbon the night you showed me your father's missing collection?"

"It's been a long night, Gabriel. Refresh my memory."

"A woman stopped you and asked for your autograph."

"It happens all the time."

"My point exactly. Put them on."

She placed the sunglasses over her eyes and tucked her hair beneath the hat. She examined her own appearance in the vanity mirror for a moment, then turned to look at him.

"How do I look?"

"Like a famous person trying to hide behind a pair of large sunglasses and a stupid hat," he said wearily. "But it will have to do for now."

He drove to a hotel on the Weihburggasse called the Kaiserin Elisabeth and checked in under the name of Schmidt. They were given a room with floors the color of honey. Anna fell onto the bed, still wearing the hat and glasses.

Gabriel went into the bathroom and looked at his face for a long time in the mirror. He lifted his right hand to his nose, smelled gunpowder and fire, and saw the faces of the two men he had killed at the Rolfe villa in Zürich. He ran warm water into the basin, washed his hands and his neck. Suddenly the bathroom was filled with ghosts—pallid, lifeless men with bullet holes in their faces and their chests. He looked down and found that the basin was filled with their blood. He wiped his hands on a towel, but it was no good—the blood still was there. Then the room began to spin, and he fell to his knees over the toilet.

When he returned to the bedroom, Anna's eyes were closed. "Are you all right?" she murmured.

"I'm going out. Don't go anywhere. Don't open the door for anyone but me."

"You won't be long, will you?"

"Not too long."

"I'll wait up for you," she said, drifting closer toward sleep.

"Whatever you say."

And then she was asleep. Gabriel covered her with a blanket and went out.

DOWNSTAIRS IN THE LOBBY, GABRIEL TOLD THE officious Viennese desk clerk that Frau Schmidt was not to be disturbed. The clerk nodded briskly, as if to give the impression that he would lay down his life to prevent anyone from interrupting Frau Schmidt's rest. Gabriel pushed a few schilling across the counter and went out.

He walked in the Stephansplatz, checking his tail for surveillance, storing faces in his memory. Then he entered the cathedral and drifted through the tourists across the nave until he came to a side altar. He looked up at the altarpiece, a depiction of the martyrdom of Saint Stephen. Gabriel had completed a restoration of the painting the night Leah's car was bombed. His work had held up well. Only when he cocked his head to create the effect of raked lighting could he tell the difference between his inpainting and the original.

He turned and scanned the faces of the people standing behind him. He recognized none of them. But something else struck him.

Each one of them was transfixed by the beauty of the altarpiece. At least something good had come of his time in Vienna. He took one last look at the painting, then left the cathedral and headed for the Jewish Quarter.

ADOLF HITLER'S BARBAROUS DREAM OF RID-ding Vienna of its Jews had largely succeeded. Before the war some two hundred thousand had lived here, many of them in the warren of streets around the Judenplatz. Now there were but a few thousand left, mainly newer arrivals from the East, and the old Jewish Quarter had been transformed into a strip of boutiques, restaurants, and nightclubs. Among Viennese it was known as the Bermuda Triangle.

Gabriel walked past the shuttered bars along the Sterngasse, then turned into a winding walkway that ended in a staircase of stone. At the top of the stairs was a heavy studded door. Next to the door was a small brass plaque: WARTIME CLAIMS AND INQUIRIES—APPOINTMENTS ONLY. He pressed the bell.

"May I help you?"

"I'd like to see Mr. Lavon, please."

"Do you have an appointment?"

"No."

"Mr. Lavon doesn't accept unscheduled visitors."

"I'm afraid it's an emergency."

"May I have your name, please?"

"Tell him it's Gabriel Allon. He'll remember me."

♦ ♦ ♦

THE ROOM INTO WHICH GABRIEL WAS SHOWN
was classic Viennese in its proportions and furnishings: a high ceiling, a polished wood floor
catching the light streaming through the tall
windows, bookshelves sagging beneath the
weight of countless volumes and files. Lavon
seemed lost in it. But then, disappearing into
the background was Lavon's special gift.

At the moment, however, he was balanced
precariously atop a library ladder, flipping
through the contents of a bulging file and
muttering to himself. The light from the windows cast a greenish glow over him, and it was
then Gabriel realized that the glass was bul-
letproof. Lavon looked up suddenly, tipping
his head downward in order to see over the pair
of smudged half-moon reading glasses perched
at the end of his nose. Cigarette ash dropped
into the file. He seemed not to notice, because
he closed the file and slipped it back into its
slot on the shelf and smiled.

"Gabriel Allon! Shamron's avenging angel.
My God, what are you doing here?"

He climbed down the ladder like a man
with old pains. As always, he seemed to be
wearing all his clothing at once: a blue button-
down shirt, a beige rollneck sweater, a cardigan,
a floppy herringbone jacket that seemed a
size too large. He had shaved carelessly, and
wore socks but no shoes.

He held Gabriel's hands and kissed his

cheek. *How long had it been?* Twenty-five years, thought Gabriel. In the lexicon of the Wrath of God operation, Lavon had been an *ayin*, a tracker. An archaeologist by training, he had stalked members of Black September, learned their habits, and devised ways of killing them. He had been a brilliant watcher, a chameleon who could blend into any surroundings. The operation took a terrible physical and psychological toll on all of them, but Gabriel remembered that Lavon had suffered the most. Working alone in the field, exposed to his enemies for long periods of time, he had developed a chronic stomach disorder that stripped thirty pounds from his lean frame. When it was over, Lavon took an assistant professorship at Hebrew University and spent his weekends on digs in the West Bank. Soon he heard other voices. Like Gabriel, he was a child of Holocaust survivors. Searching for ancient relics seemed trivial when there was so much still to be unearthed about the immediate past. He settled in Vienna and put his formidable talents to work in another way: tracking down Nazis and their looted treasure.

"So, what brings you to Vienna? Business? Pleasure?"

"Augustus Rolfe."

"Rolfe? The banker?" Lavon lowered his head and glared at Gabriel over his glasses. "Gabriel, you weren't the one who—" He made a gun of his right hand.

Gabriel unzipped his jacket, removed the envelope he had taken from Rolfe's desk, and

224

handed it to Lavon. Carefully he pried open the flap, as if he were handling a fragment of ancient ceramic, and removed the contents. He glanced at the first photograph, then the second, his face revealing nothing. Then he looked up at Gabriel and smiled.

"Well, well, Herr Rolfe takes a lovely photograph. Where did you get these, Gabriel?"

"From the old man's desk in Zürich."

He held up the sheath of documents. "And these?"

"Same place."

Lavon looked at the photographs again. "Fantastic."

"What do they mean?"

"I need to pull a few files. I'll have the girls get you some coffee and something to eat. We're going to be a while."

THEY SAT ACROSS FROM EACH OTHER AT A rectangular conference table, a stack of files between them. Gabriel wondered about the people who had come before him: old men convinced the man in the flat next door was one of their tormentors at Buchenwald; children trying to pry open a numbered account in Switzerland where their father had hidden his life savings before being shipped east into the archipelago of death. Lavon picked up one of the photographs—Rolfe seated in a restaurant next to the man with dueling scars on his cheeks—and held it up for Gabriel to see.

"Do you recognize this man?"

225

"No."

"His name is Walter Schellenberg, Brigade-führer SS." Lavon took the top file from the stack and spread it on the table before him. "Walter Schellenberg was the head of Department Four of the Reich Security Main Office. Department Four handled foreign intelligence, which effectively made Schellenberg the international spymaster of the Nazi Party. He was involved in some of the most dramatic intelligence episodes of the war: the Venlo Incident, the attempt to kidnap the Duke of Windsor, and the Cicero operation. At Nuremberg he was convicted of being a member of the SS, but he received a light sentence of just six years in prison."

"Six years? Why?"

"Because during the last months of the war he arranged for the release of a few Jews from the death camps."

"How did he manage that?"

"He sold them."

"So why was the spymaster of the Nazi Party having dinner with Augustus Rolfe?"

"Intelligence services the world over have one thing in common: They all run on money. Even Shamron couldn't survive without money. But when Shamron needs money, he just lays a hand on the shoulder of a rich friend and tells him the story of how he captured Eichmann. Schellenberg had a special problem. His money was no good anywhere outside Germany. He needed a banker in a neutral country who could provide him with hard currency and then transfer that money through

226

a dummy company or some other front to his agents. Schellenberg needed a man like Augustus Rolfe."

Lavon picked up the documents Gabriel had taken from Rolfe's desk. "Take this transaction. Fifteen hundred pounds sterling, wired from the accounts of Pillar Enterprises Limited to the account of a Mr. Ivan Edberg, Enskilde Bank, Stockholm, the twenty-third of October, 1943."

Gabriel inspected the document, then slid it back across the table.

"Sweden was neutral, of course, and a hotbed of wartime intelligence," Lavon said. "Schellenberg surely had an agent there, if not an entire network. I suspect Mr. Edberg was one of those agents. Perhaps the leader and paymaster of the network."

Lavon slipped the transfer order back into the pile and removed another. He peered down at it through his reading glasses, squinting from the smoke of the cigarette between his lips.

"Another transfer order: one thousand pounds sterling from the account of Pillar Enterprises Limited to a Mr. Jose Suarez, care of the Bank of Lisbon." Lavon lowered the paper and looked up at Gabriel. "Portugal, like Sweden, was neutral, and Lisbon was an amusement park for spies. Schellenberg operated there himself during the Duke of Windsor affair."

"So Rolfe was Schellenberg's secret banker. But how does that explain the photograph of Rolfe at Berchtesgaden with Himmler and Hitler?"

Lavon prepared his next cup of coffee with the reverence of a true Viennese: a precise measure of heavy cream, just enough sugar to remove the bitter edge. Gabriel thought of Lavon in a safe flat in Paris, living on mineral water and weak tea because his ravaged stomach would tolerate nothing else.

"Everything changed inside Germany after Stalingrad. Even the true believers knew it was over. The Russians were coming from the east, the invasion from the west was inevitable. Anyone who'd accumulated wealth as a result of the war wanted desperately to hang onto that wealth. And where do you think they turned?"

"The bankers of Switzerland."

"And Augustus Rolfe would have been in a unique position to capitalize on the changing tide of the war. Based on these documents, it appears as though he was an important agent of Walter Schellenberg. I suspect the Nazi bigwigs would have held Herr Rolfe in very high esteem."

"Someone who could be trusted to look after their money?"

"Their money. Their stolen treasures. All of it."

"What about the list of names and the account numbers?"

"I think it's safe to assume that those are German clients. I'll run them through our database and see if they correspond with known members of the SS and the Nazi Party, but I suspect they're pseudonyms."

"Would there be any other record of the accounts in the banks files?"

Lavon shook his head. "Typically, the real identities of holders of numbered accounts are known by only the top officers of a bank. The more notorious the customer, the fewer people who know the name attached to the account number. If these accounts belonged to Nazis, I doubt whether anyone knew about them but Rolfe."

"If he kept the list after all these years, does it mean the accounts still exist?"

"I suppose it's possible. It depends a great deal on who owned them. If the holder was able to get out of Germany at the end of the war, then I would doubt the account is still active. But if the holder was arrested by the Allies—"

"—then it's possible his money and valuables are still in the vault of the Rolfe bank."

"Possible, but unlikely."

Lavon gathered up the documents and photographs and slipped them back into the envelope. Then he looked up at Gabriel and said, "I've answered all your questions. Now, it's time for you to answer some of mine."

"What do you want to know?"

"Just one thing, actually," Lavon said, holding the envelope aloft. "I'd like to know what the hell are you doing with the secret files of Augustus Rolfe."

LAVON LIKED NOTHING BETTER THAN A GOOD story. It had always been that way. During the Black September operation, he and Gabriel had shared a kinship of the sleepless: Lavon because

of his stomach, Gabriel because of his conscience. Gabriel thought of him now, an ema-
ciated figure sitting cross-legged on the floor,
asking Gabriel what it felt like to kill. And
Gabriel had told him—because he had needed
to tell someone. "There is no God," Lavon had
said. "There is only Shamron. Shamron decides
who shall live and who shall die. And he sends
boys like you to wreak his terrible vengeance."

Now, as then, Lavon did not look at Gabriel
as he told his story. He stared down at his hands
and turned over his cigarette lighter between his
nimble little fingers until Gabriel had finished.

"Do you have a list of the paintings that were
taken from the secret vault?"

"I do, but I'm not sure how accurate it is."

"There's a man in New York. He's dedicated
his life to the subject of Nazi art-looting. He
knows the contents of every stolen collection, every transaction, every piece that's
been recovered, every piece that's still missing.
If anyone knows anything about the collecting
habits of Augustus Rolfe, it's him."

"Quietly, Eli. Very quietly."

"My dear Gabriel, I know of no other way."

They pulled on their coats, and Lavon
walked him across the Judenplatz.

"Does the daughter know any of this?"

"Not yet."

"I don't envy you. I'll call you when I hear
something from my friend in New York. In the
meantime, go to your hotel and get some
rest. You don't look well."

"I can't remember the last time I slept."

Lavon shook his head and laid his small hand on Gabriel's shoulder. "You've killed again, Gabriel. I can see it in your face. It's the stain of death. Go to your room and wash your face."

"You be a good boy and watch your back."

"I used to watch yours."

"You were the best."

"I'll let you in on a little secret, Gabriel. I still am."

And with that Lavon turned and vanished into the crowd on the Judenplatz.

GABRIEL WALKED TO THE LITTLE TRATTORIA where he had eaten his last meal with his Leah and Dani. For the first time in ten years, he stood on the spot where the car had exploded. He looked up and saw the spire of Saint Stephen's, floating above the rooftops. A wind rose suddenly; Gabriel turned up the collar of his coat. What had he expected? Grief? Rage? Hatred? Much to his surprise, he felt nothing much at all. He turned and walked back to the hotel in the rain.

A COPY OF *DIE PRESSE* HAD BEEN SLIPPED under the door and lay on the floor in the alcove. Gabriel scooped it up and entered the bedroom. Anna was still asleep. At some point, she had removed her clothing, and in the dim light he could see the luminous skin of her shoulder glowing against the bedding. Gabriel dropped the newspaper on the bed next to her.

Exhaustion pounced on him. He needed to sleep. *But where?* On the bed? Next to Anna? Next to the daughter of Augustus Rolfe? How much did she know? What secrets did her father keep from her? What secrets had she kept from Gabriel?

He thought of the words Julian Isherwood had said to him in London: "Assume at all times that she knows more about her father and his collection than she's telling you. Daughters tend to be very protective of their fathers, even when they think their fathers are complete bastards." No, he thought—he would not be sleeping next to Anna Rolfe. In the closet he found an extra blanket and a spare pillow, and he made a crude bed for himself on the floor. It was like lying on a slab of cold marble. He reached up and blindly patted the duvet, searching for the newspaper. Quietly, so as not to wake her, he opened it. On the front page was a story about the murder in Lyons of the Swiss writer Emil Jacobi.

28

♦ *VIENNA*

*I*T WAS DUSK WHEN ELI LAVON TELE-phoned Gabriel's hotel room. Anna stirred, then drifted back into an uneasy sleep. During the afternoon, she had kicked away her blankets, and her body lay exposed to the cold air seeping through the half-open window. Gabriel covered her and went downstairs. Lavon was sitting in the parlor, drinking coffee. He poured some for Gabriel and handed him the cup.

"I saw your friend Emil Jacobi on the television today," Lavon said. "Seems someone walked into his apartment in Lyons and slashed his throat."

"I know. What did you hear from New York?"

"It's believed that between 1941 and 1944, Augustus Rolfe acquired a large number of Impressionist and Modern paintings from galleries in Lucerne and Zürich—paintings that a few years before had hung in Jewish-owned galleries and homes in Paris."

"What a surprise," Gabriel murmured. "A large number? How many?"

"Unclear."

"He purchased them?"

"Not exactly. It's thought that the paintings acquired by Rolfe were part of several large exchanges carried out in Switzerland by agents of Hermann Göring."

Gabriel remembered things Julian Isherwood had told him about the ravenous collecting habits of the Reichsmarschall. Göring had enjoyed unfettered access to the Jeu de Paume, where the confiscated art of France was stored. He had taken possession of hundreds of Modern works to use as barter for the Old Master works he preferred.

"It's rumored that Rolfe was allowed to purchase the paintings for only a nominal

233

sum," Lavon said. "Something far below their fair value."

"So if that were the case, the acquisitions would have been entirely legal under Swiss law. Rolfe could say that he purchased them in good faith. And even if the paintings were stolen property, he would be under no legal obligation to return them."

"So it would appear. The question we should be asking is this: Why was Augustus Rolfe allowed to buy paintings that passed through the hands of Hermann Göring at bargain-basement prices?"

"Does your friend in New York have an answer to that question?"

"No, but you do."

"What are you talking about, Eli?"

"The photographs and the bank documents you found in his desk. His relationship with Walter Schellenberg. The Rolfe family collected for generations. Rolfe was well connected. He knew what was going on across the border in France, and he wanted a piece of the action."

"And Walter Schellenberg needed some way to compensate his private banker in Zürich."

"Indeed," Lavon said. "Payment for services rendered."

Gabriel sat back in his chair and closed his eyes.

"What next, Gabriel?"

"It's time to have a conversation I've been dreading."

◆ ◆ ◆

WHEN GABRIEL WENT BACK UPSTAIRS TO THE room, Anna was beginning to awaken. He shook her shoulder gently, and she sat up with a start, like a child confused by strange surroundings. She asked for the time, and he told her it was early evening.

When she was fully conscious, he pulled a chair to the end of the bed and sat down. He left the lights off; he had no wish to see her face. She sat upright, her legs crossed, her shoulders wrapped in bedding. She was staring at him—even in the darkness, Gabriel could see her eyes locked on him.

He told her about the origins of her father's secret collection. He told her the things he had learned from Emil Jacobi and that the professor had been killed the previous night in his apartment in Lyons. Finally, he told her about the documents he had found in her father's desk—the documents linking him to Hitler's spymaster, Walter Schellenberg.

When he was finished, he laid the photographs on the bed and went into the bathroom to give her a moment of privacy. He heard the click of the bedside lamp and saw light seeping beneath the bathroom door. He ran water in the sink and counted slowly in his head. When an appropriate amount of time had passed, he went back into the bedroom. He found her coiled into a ball, her body silently convulsing, her hand clutching the photo-

235

graph of her father, admiring the view at Berchtesgaden with Adolf Hitler and Heinrich Himmler.

Gabriel pulled it from her grasp before she could destroy it. Then he placed his hand on her head and stroked her hair. Anna's weeping finally became audible. She choked and began to cough, a heavy smoker's cough that left her gasping for breath.

Finally, she looked up at Gabriel. "If my mother ever saw that *picture*—" She hesitated, her mouth open, tears streaming down her cheeks. "She would have—"

But Gabriel pressed the palm of his hand against her lips before she could utter the words. He didn't want her to say the rest. There was no need. If her mother had seen that picture, she would have killed herself, he thought. She would have dug her own grave, put a gun into her mouth, and killed herself.

THIS TIME IT WAS ANNA'S TURN TO RETREAT into the bathroom. When she returned she was calm, but her eyes were raw, and her skin was without color. She sat at the end of the bed with the photographs and documents in her hand. "What's this?"

"It looks like a list of numbered accounts."

"Whose numbered accounts?"

"The names are German. We can only guess at who they really are."

She studied the list carefully, brow furrowed.

"My mother was born on Christmas Day, 1933. Did I ever tell you that?"

"Your mother's birth date has never come up between us, Anna. Why is it relevant now?"

She handed him the list. "Look at the last name on the list."

Gabriel took it from her. His eyes settled on the final name and number: ALOIS RITTER 251233126.

He looked up. "So?"

"Isn't it interesting that a man with the same initials as my father has an account number in which the first six digits match my mother's birthday?"

Gabriel looked at the list again: ALOIS RITTER...AR...251233...Christmas Day, 1933...

He lowered the paper and looked at Anna. "What about the last three numbers? Do they mean anything to you?"

"I'm afraid they don't."

Gabriel looked at the numbers and closed his eyes. 126...Somewhere, at some point, he was certain he had seen them in connection with this case. He had been cursed with a flawless memory. He never forgot anything. The brushstrokes he had used to heal the painting of Saint Stephen in the cathedral. The tune that had been playing on the radio the night he had fled the Niederdorf after killing Ali Hamidi. The smell of olives on Leah's breath when he had kissed her goodbye for the last time.

Then, after a moment, the place where he had seen the number 126.

◆ ◆ ◆

ANNA CARRIED A PICTURE OF HER BROTHER always. It was the last photo ever taken of him— leading a stage of the Tour of Switzerland the afternoon of his death. Gabriel had seen the same photograph in the desk of Augustus Rolfe. He looked at the number attached to the frame of the bicycle and the back of his jersey: 126.

Anna said, "It looks like we're going back to Zürich."

"We have to do something about your passport. And your appearance."

"What's wrong with my passport?"

"It has your name in it."

"And my appearance?"

"Absolutely nothing. That's the problem."

He picked up the telephone and dialed.

THE GIRL CALLED HANNAH LANDAU CAME TO the hotel room at ten o'clock that night. She wore bangles on her wrists and smelled of jasmine. The case hanging from her arm was not unlike the one Gabriel used for his paint-brushes and pigments. She spoke to Gabriel for a moment, then drew Anna into the bath-room by the hand and closed the door.

One hour later, Anna emerged. Her shoulder-length blond hair had been cropped short and dyed black; her green eyes had been turned blue by cosmetic lenses. The transformation was truly remarkable. It was as though she were another woman.

"Do you approve?" Hannah Landau asked.

"Take the picture."

The Israeli girl snapped a half-dozen photographs of Anna with a Polaroid camera and laid the prints on the bed for Gabriel to see. When they had finished developing, Gabriel said, "That one."

Hannah shook her had. "No, I think that one."

She snatched up the picture without waiting for Gabriel's approval and returned to the bathroom. Anna sat down at the vanity and spent a long time examining her appearance in the mirror.

Twenty minutes later, Hannah came out. She showed her work to Gabriel, then walked across the room and dropped it on the vanity in front of Anna. "Congratulations, Miss Rolfe. You are now a citizen of Austria."

29

*H*ALFWAY BETWEEN THE HAUPTBAHNHOF and Zürichsee is the epicenter of Swiss banking, the Paradeplatz. The twin headquarters of Credit Suisse and the Union Bank of Switzerland glare at each other like prizefighters over the broad expanse of gray brick.

They are the two giants of Swiss banking and among the most powerful in the world. In their shadow, up and down the length of the Bahnhofstrasse, are other big banks and influential financial institutions, their locations clearly marked by bright signs and polished glass doors. But scattered in the quiet side streets and alleys between the Bahnhofstrasse and Sihl River are the banks few people notice. They are the private chapels of Swiss banking, places where men can worship or confess their sins in absolute secrecy. Swiss law forbids these banks from soliciting for deposits. They are free to call themselves banks if they wish, but they are not required to do so. Difficult to locate, easy to miss, they are tucked inside modern office blocks or in the rooms of centuries-old townhouses. Some employ several dozen workers; some only a handful. They are private banks in every sense of the word. This is where, the following morning, Gabriel and Anna Rolfe began their search.

She threaded her arm through Gabriel's and pulled him along the Bahnhofstrasse. This was her town; she was in charge now. Gabriel watched the passing faces for signs of recognition. If Anna was going to be noticed anywhere in the world, it would be here. No one gave her a second look. Hannah Landau's rapid makeover seemed to be working.

"Where do we start?" Gabriel asked.

"Like most Swiss bankers, my father maintained professional accounts in other Swiss banks."

"Correspondent accounts?"

"Exactly. We'll start with the ones where I know he'd done business in the past."

"What if the account isn't in Zürich? What if it's in Geneva?"

"My father was a Züricher through and through. He'd never even consider handing over his money or his possessions to a Frenchman in Geneva."

"Even if we find the account, there's no guarantee we're going to have access to it."

"That's true. The bankers make the accounts only as secret as the account-holder wants. We may be allowed access with just a number. We may need a password. We might be shown the door. But it's worth a try, isn't it? Let's start over there."

Without warning she changed direction, darting across the Bahnhofstrasse in front of a speeding tram, pulling Gabriel by the hand. Then she led him into a smaller street, the Bärengasse, and stopped before a simple doorway. Above the doorway was a security camera, and mounted on the stone wall next to it was a brass plaque, so small it was nearly unnoticeable: HOFFMAN & WECK, BÄRENGASSE 43.

She pressed the bell and waited to be admitted. Five minutes later, they were back on the street again, walking to the next bank on Anna's list. There the performance took slightly longer—seven minutes by Gabriel's estimate—but the result was the same: back on the street, empty-handed.

And on it went. Each performance was a slight variation of the same theme. After enduring a moment of scrutiny through the security camera, they would be admitted into a vestibule, where an officer of the bank would greet them cautiously. Anna did all the talking, conducting each encounter in brisk but polite *Züridütsch*. Finally, they would be escorted to the sacristy, the hallowed inner office where the secret records were kept, and seated in chairs before the banker's desk. After a few meaningless pleasantries, there would be a discreet clearing of the throat, a polite reminder that time was being wasted, and on the Bahnhofstrasse time was certainly money.

Then Anna would say: "I'd like access to the account of Herr Alois Ritter." A pause, a few taps on a computer keyboard, a long gaze into a glowing monitor. "I'm sorry, but it appears we have no account in the name of Alois Ritter."

"Are you certain?"

"Yes, quite certain."

"Thank you. I apologize for wasting your valuable time."

"Not at all. Take our card. Perhaps you'll require our services in the future."

"You're very kind."

After visiting eleven banks, they had coffee in a small restaurant called Café Brioche. Gabriel was getting nervous. They had been traipsing around the Bahnhofstrasse for nearly two hours. They could not go unnoticed for long.

The next stop was Becker & Puhl, where they were greeted by Herr Becker himself. He was starched and fussy and very bald. His office was drab and as sterile as an operating room. As he stared into his computer monitor, Gabriel could see the ghostly reflections of names and numbers scrolling across the polished lenses of his rimless spectacles.

After a moment of quiet contemplation, he looked up and said, "Account number, please."

Anna recited it from memory: *251233126.*

Becker tapped the keyboard. "Password?"

Gabriel felt his chest tighten. He looked up and noticed Herr Becker eyeing him over the computer terminal.

Anna cleared her throat gently and said: "Adagio."

"Follow me, please."

THE LITTLE BANKER ESCORTED THEM FROM HIS office to a high-ceilinged conference room with paneled walls and a rectangular smoked-glass table. "Your privacy can be better assured this way," he said. "Please, make yourself comfortable. I'll bring you the contents of the account in a few moments."

When Becker returned, he was carrying a metal safe-deposit box. "According to the covenant on the account, anyone who presents the proper account number and password is permitted access to the deposit boxes," Becker said as he slid the box onto the tabletop. "I possess all the keys."

"I understand," said Anna.

Becker whistled tunelessly as he removed a heavy ring of keys from his pocket and selected the appropriate one. When he found it, he held it aloft to check the engraving, then inserted it into the lock and lifted the lid. Instantly, the air smelled of decaying paper.

Becker stepped back to a respectful distance. "There *is* a second safe-deposit box. I'm afraid it's rather large. Do you wish to see that one as well?"

Gabriel and Anna looked at each other across the table and at the same time said: "Yes."

GABRIEL WAITED FOR BECKER TO LEAVE THE room before lifting the lid. There were sixteen in all, neatly rolled, shrouded in protective coverings: Monet, Picasso, Degas, van Gogh, Manet, Toulouse-Lautrec, Renoir, Bonnard, Cézanne, a stunning nude in repose by Vuillard. Even Gabriel, a man used to working with priceless art, was overwhelmed by the sheer volume of it. How many people had searched for these very pieces? How many years? How many tears had been shed over their loss? And here they were, locked in a safe-deposit box, in a vault beneath the Bahnhofstrasse. How fitting. How perfectly logical.

Anna resumed her search of the smaller box. She lifted the lid and began removing the contents. First came the cash—Swiss francs, French francs, dollars, pounds, marks—which she handled with the ease of someone used to

244

money. Next came an accordion file folder filled with documents, and finally a stack of letters, bound by a pale-blue elastic band.

She loosened the band, laid it on the table, and began flipping through the stack of envelopes with her long, agile fingers. *Forefinger, middle finger, forefinger, middle finger, pause.... Forefinger, middle finger, forefinger, middle finger, pause....* She pulled one envelope from the stack, turned it over in her hand, tested the flap to make certain it was still sealed, then held it up for Gabriel to see.

"You might be interested in this."

"What is it?"

"I don't know," she said. "But it's addressed to you."

IT WAS THE PERSONAL STATIONERY OF A MAN from another time: pale gray in color, A4 in size, AUGUSTUS ROLFE centered at the top, no other superfluous information such as a fax number or an e-mail address. Only a date: one day before Gabriel arrived in Zürich. The note was rendered in English, handwritten by a man no longer capable of producing legible handwriting. The result was that it might have been written in almost any language using any alphabet. With Anna looking over his shoulder, Gabriel managed to decipher the text.

Dear Gabriel,
I hope you do not find it presumptuous that

I have chosen to address you by your real name, but I have known your true identity for some time and have been an admirer of your work, both as an art restorer and as a guardian of your people. When one is a Swiss banker, one hears things.

If you are reading this note, it certainly means that I am dead. It also means that you have probably uncovered a great deal of information about my life—information that I had hoped to convey to you personally. I will attempt to do that now, posthumously.

As you know by now, you were not brought to my villa in Zürich to clean my Raphael. I made contact with your service for one reason: I wanted you to take possession of my second collection—the secret collection in the underground chamber of my villa which, I trust, you are aware of—and return the works to their rightful owners. If the rightful owners could not be located, it was my wish that the paintings be hung in museums in Israel. I turned to your service because I preferred that the matter be handled quietly, so as not to bring additional shame on my family or my country.

The paintings were acquired with a veneer of legality but quite unjustly. When I "purchased" them, I was aware that they had been confiscated from the collections of Jewish dealers and collectors in France. Gazing upon them has given me untold hours of pleasure over the years, but like a man who lies with a woman not his own, I have been left with the ache of guilt. It was my wish to return those paintings before my death—to atone for my misdeeds in this life before moving on to the next. Ironically, I found inspiration in the foundation of your religion. On Yom Kippur, it is not enough for one to feel sorry for the foul deeds one has done. To achieve forgiveness, one must go to the injured parties and make amends. I found particular relevance in Isaiah. A sinner asks God: "Why, when we fasted, did You not see? When we starved our bodies, did You pay no heed?" And God replies: "Because on your fast day you see to your business and oppress all your laborers! Because you fast in strife and contention, and you strike with a wicked fist!"

My greed during the war was as boundless as my guilt is now. There are sixteen paintings in this bank. They represent the rest of my secret collection. Please do not leave without them. There are people in Switzerland who want the past to remain exactly where it is—entombed in the bank vaults of the Bahnhofstrasse—and they will stop at nothing to achieve that end. They think of themselves as patriots, as guardians of the Swiss ideal of neutrality and fierce independence. They are intensely hostile to outsiders, especially those that they regard as a threat to their survival. Once, I considered these men my friends—another of my many mistakes. Unfortunately, they became aware of my plans to relinquish the collection. They sent a man from the security services to frighten me. It is because of his visit that I am writing this letter. It is because of his masters that I am now dead.

One final thing. If you are in contact with my daughter, Anna, please take care that no harm comes to her. She has suffered enough because of my folly.

Sincerely,
Augustus Rolfe

THE LITTLE BANKER WAS WAITING OUTSIDE IN the anteroom. Gabriel signaled him through the glass door, and he entered the viewing room. "May I help you?"

"When was the last time this account was accessed?"

"I'm sorry, sir, but that information is privileged."

Anna said, "We need to remove a few items. Would you happen to have a bag of any kind?"

"Regrettably, we do not. We're a bank, not a department store."

"May we have the box?"

"I'm afraid there will be a fee."

"That's fine."

"A rather *substantial* fee."

Anna pointed to the stack of cash on the tabletop.

"Do you have a currency preference?"

30

*I*N A BAKERY FIVE MILES NORTH OF ZÜRICH, Gabriel made a telephone call and bought a Dinkelbrot. When he returned to the car, he found Anna reading the letter her father had written the night before his murder. Her hands were shaking. Gabriel started the engine and pulled back onto the motorway. Anna folded the letter, slipped it back into the envelope, then placed the envelope in the safe-deposit box. The box containing the paintings lay on the back seat. Gabriel switched on the wipers. Anna leaned her head against the window and watched the water streaking across the glass.

"Who did you call?"

"We're going to need some help getting out of the country."

"Why? Who's going to stop us?"

"The same people who killed your father. *And* Müller. *And* Emil Jacobi."

"How will they find us?"

"You entered the country on your own passport last night. Then you rented this car in your own name. It's a small town. We should act on the assumption that they know we're in the country and that someone saw us on the Bahnhofstrasse, despite your new appearance."

"Who's *they*, Gabriel?"

249

He thought of Rolfe's letter. *There are people in Switzerland who want the past to remain exactly where it is—entombed in the bank vaults of the Bahnhofstrasse—and they will stop at nothing to achieve that end.*

What the hell was he trying to say? *People in Switzerland...* Rolfe knew exactly who they were, but even in death, the secretive old Swiss banker couldn't reveal too much. Still, the clues and the circumstantial evidence were there. Through the use of conjecture and educated guesses, Gabriel might be able to fill in the pieces the old man had left out.

Instinctively, he approached the problem as though it were a painting in need of restoration—a painting that, unfortunately, had suffered significant losses over the centuries. He thought of a Tintoretto he had once restored, a version of *The Baptism of Christ* that the Venetian master had painted for a private chapel. It was Gabriel's first job after the bombing in Vienna, and he had deliberately sought out something difficult in which to lose himself. The Tintoretto was just that. Vast portions of the original painting had been lost over the centuries. Indeed, there were more blank spots on the canvas than those covered with pigment. Gabriel effectively had to repaint the entire work, incorporating the small patches of the original. Perhaps he could do the same with this case: repaint the entire story around the few patches of fact that were known to him.

Perhaps it went something like this...

Augustus Rolfe, a prominent Zürich banker,

decides to give up his collection of Impressionist paintings, a collection he knows contains works confiscated from Jews in France. In keeping with his character, Rolfe wishes to conduct this transaction quietly, so he contacts Israeli intelligence and asks for a representative to be sent to Zürich. Shamron suggests Gabriel meet with Rolfe at his villa, using the restoration of the Raphael as cover for the visit.

Unfortunately, they became aware of my plans to relinquish the collection...

Somewhere along the line, Rolfe makes a mistake, and his plan to hand over the paintings to Israel is discovered by someone who wishes to stand in his way.

They think of themselves as patriots, as guardians of the Swiss ideal of neutrality and independence. They are intensely hostile to outsiders, especially those that they regard as threats to their survival. ...

Who would feel threatened by the prospect of a Swiss banker handing over an ill-gotten collection of paintings to Israel? *Other Swiss bankers with similar collections?* Gabriel tried to look at it from their perspective—the perspective of those "guardians of the Swiss ideal of neutrality and fierce independence." What would have happened if it became public knowledge that Augustus Rolfe possessed so many paintings thought to have been lost forever? The outcry would have been deafening. The world's Jewish organizations would have descended on the Bahnhofstrasse, demanding that the bank vaults be opened. Nothing short of a nationwide systematic search would have been acceptable. If you were one of these so-called guardians of the Swiss ideal, it might have been easier to kill a man and steal his collection than face uncomfortable new questions about the past.

They sent a man from the security services to frighten me. . . .

Gabriel thought of the Silk Cut cigarettes he had found in the ashtray on the desk in Rolfe's study.

. . .a man from the security services. . .

Gerhardt Peterson.

They meet in the quiet of Rolfe's Zürich study and discuss the situation like reasonable Swiss gentlemen, Rolfe smoking his Benson & Hedges, Peterson his Silk Cuts. "Why hand over the paintings now, Herr Rolfe? So many years have gone by. There's nothing that can be done now to change the past." But Rolfe doesn't budge, so Peterson arranges with Werner Müller to steal the paintings.

Rolfe knows that Gabriel is coming the next day, but he's concerned enough to write a letter and leave it in his secret account. He tries to throw off a false trail. Using a telephone he knows is tapped, he makes an appointment to be in Geneva the next morning. Then he makes arrangements for Gabriel to let himself into the villa and he waits.

But at 3:00 A.M., the security system at the villa suddenly goes down. Peterson's team enters the house. Rolfe is killed, the paintings are taken. Six hours later, Gabriel arrives at the villa and discovers Rolfe's body. During the interrogation, Peterson realizes how the old man planned to surrender his collection. He also realizes that Rolfe's plan had progressed further than he ever imagined. He releases Gabriel, warns him never to set foot on Swiss soil again, and puts him under surveillance. Perhaps he places Anna under surveillance too. When Gabriel begins his investigation, Peterson knows it. He launches a cleanup operation. Werner Müller is killed in Paris and his gallery destroyed. Gabriel is seen meeting with Emil Jacobi in Lyons, and three days later Jacobi is murdered.

Anna tore the end off the loaf of Dinkelbrot. "Who's 'they'?" she repeated.

Gabriel wondered how long he had been silent, how many miles he had driven.

"I'm not sure," he said. "But perhaps it went something like this."

"DO YOU REALLY THINK IT'S POSSIBLE, Gabriel?"

"Actually, it's the only *logical* explanation."

"My God, I think I'm going to be sick. I want to get out of this country."

"So do I."

"So if your theory is correct, there's still one more question to be answered."

"What's that?"

"Where are the paintings now?"

"The same place they've always been."

"Where, Gabriel?"

"Here in Switzerland."

253

31

*T*HREE MILES FROM THE GERMAN BORDER, at the end of a narrow valley dotted with logging villages, stands drab little Bargen, famous in Switzerland if for no other reason than that it is the northernmost town in the country. Just off the motorway is a gas station and a market with a gravel parking lot. Gabriel shut down the car engine, and there they waited in the steel afternoon light.

"How long before they get here?"

"I don't know."

"I have to pee."

"You have to hold it."

"I always wondered how I would react in a situation like this, and now I have my answer. Faced with danger, a life-and-death situation, I'm overcome by an uncontrollable need to urinate."

"You have incredible powers of concentration. Use them."

"Is that what you would do?"

"I never urinate."

She swatted his arm, gently, so as not to hurt his damaged hand.

"I heard you in the bathroom in Vienna. I heard you throwing up. You act as though nothing bothers you. But you're human after all, Gabriel Allon."

"Why don't you smoke a cigarette? Maybe that will help you think of something else."

"How did it feel to kill those men in my father's house?"

Gabriel thought of Eli Lavon. "I didn't have much time to consider the morality or the consequences of my actions. If I hadn't killed them, they would have killed me."

"I suppose it's possible they were the ones who killed my father."

"Yes, it's possible."

"Then I'm glad you killed them. Is that wrong for me to think that way?"

"No, it's perfectly natural."

She took his advice and lit a cigarette. "So now you know all the dirty secrets of my family. But today I realized that I really don't know a thing about you."

"You know more about me than most people do."

"I know a little about what you *do*—but nothing about *you*."

"That's as it should be."

"Oh, come on, Gabriel. Are you really as cold and distant as you pretend to be?"

"I've been told I have a problem with preoccupation."

"*Ah!* That's a start. Tell me something else."

"What do you want to know?"

"You wear a wedding ring. Are you married?"

"Yes."

"Do you live in Israel?"

"I live in England."

"Do you have children?"

"We had a son, but he was killed by a terrorist's bomb." He looked at her coldly. "Is there anything else you'd like to know about me, Anna?"

HE SUPPOSED HE DID OWE HER SOMETHING, after everything she had surrendered about herself and her father. But there was something else. He suddenly found that he actually *wanted* her to know. And so he told her about a night in Vienna, ten years earlier, when his enemy, a Palestinian terrorist named Tariq al-Hourani, planted a bomb beneath his car—a bomb that was meant to destroy his family because the Palestinian knew it would hurt Gabriel much more than killing him.

It had happened after dinner. Leah had been edgy throughout the meal, because the television above the bar was showing pictures of Scud missiles raining down on Tel Aviv. Leah was a good Israeli girl; she couldn't stand the thought of eating pasta in a pleasant little Italian restaurant in Vienna while her mother was sitting in her flat in Tel Aviv with packing tape on the windows and a gas mask over her face.

After dinner they walked through drifting snow to Gabriel's car. He strapped Dani into his safety seat, then kissed his wife and told her that he would be working late. It was a job for Shamron: an Iraqi intelligence officer who was plotting to kill Jews. This he didn't tell Anna Rolfe.

When he turned and walked away, the car engine tried to turn over and hesitated, because the bomb Tariq had placed there was drawing its power from the battery. He turned and shouted for Leah to stop, but she must not have heard him, because she turned the key a second time.

Some primeval instinct to protect the young made him rush to Dani first, but he was already dead, his body blown to pieces. So he went to Leah and pulled her from the flaming wreckage. She would survive, though it might have been better had she not. Now she lived in a psychiatric hospital in the south of England, afflicted with a combination of post-traumatic stress syndrome and psychotic depression. She had never spoken to Gabriel since that night in Vienna.

This he didn't tell Anna Rolfe.

"IT MUST HAVE BEEN DIFFICULT FOR YOU— being back in Vienna."

"It was the first time."

"Where did you meet her?"

"At school."

"Was she an artist too?"

"She was much better than I am."

"Was she beautiful?"

"She was very beautiful. Now she has scars."

"We all have scars, Gabriel."

"Not like Leah."

"Why did the Palestinian plant the bomb beneath the car?"

"Because I killed his brother."

Before she could ask another question, a Volvo truck pulled into the parking lot and flashed its lights. Gabriel started the car and followed it to the edge of a pine grove outside the town. The driver hopped down from the cab and quickly pulled open the rear door. Gabriel and Anna got out of their car, Anna holding the small safe-deposit box, Gabriel the one containing the paintings. He paused briefly to hurl the car keys deep into the trees.

The container of the truck was filled with office furniture: desks, chairs, bookshelves, file cabinets. The driver said, "Go to the front of the cabin, lie down on the floor, and cover yourself with those extra freight blankets."

Gabriel went first, clambering over the furniture, the deposit box in his arms. Anna followed. At the front of the cabin, there was just enough room for them to sit with their knees beneath their chins. When Anna was in place, Gabriel covered them both with the blanket. The darkness was absolute.

The truck teetered onto the road, and for several minutes they sped along the motorway. Gabriel could feel the tire spray on the undercarriage. Anna began to hum softly.

"What are you doing?"

"I always hum when I'm scared."

"I'm not going to let anything happen to you."

"You promise?"

"I promise," he said. "So what were you humming?"

"'The Swan' from *The Carnival of Animals* by Camille Saint-Saëns."

"Will you play it for me sometime?"

"No," she said.

"Why not?"

"Because I never play for my friends."

TEN MINUTES LATER: THE BORDER. THE TRUCK joined a queue of vehicles waiting to make the crossing into Germany. It crept forward a few inches at a time: accelerate, brake, accelerate, *brake*. Their heads rolled back and forth like a pair of children's toys. Each touch of the brake produced a deafening screech of protest; each press of the throttle another blast of poisonous diesel fumes. Anna leaned her cheek against his shoulder and whispered, "Now I think *I'm* going to be sick." Gabriel squeezed her hand.

ON THE OTHER SIDE OF THE BORDER ANOTHER car was waiting, a dark-blue Ford Fiesta with Münich registration. Ari Shamron's truck driver dropped them and continued on his synthetic journey to nowhere. Gabriel loaded the safe-deposit boxes into the trunk and started driving—the E41 to Stuttgart, the E52 to Karlsruhe, the E35 to Frankfurt. Once during the night he stopped to telephone Tel Aviv on an emergency line, and he spoke briefly with Shamron.

At 2:00 A.M. they arrived in the Dutch

market town of Delft, a few miles inland from the coast. Gabriel could drive no farther. His eyes burned, his ears were ringing with exhaustion. In eight hours, a ferry would leave from Hoek van Holland for the English port of Harwich, and Gabriel and Anna would be on it, but for now he needed a bed and a few hours of rest, so they drove through the streets of the old town looking for a hotel.

He found one, on the Vondelstraat, within sight of the spire of the Nieuwe Kerk. Anna handled the formalities at the front desk while Gabriel waited in the tiny parlor with the two safe-deposit boxes. A moment later, they were escorted up a narrow staircase to an overheated room with a peaked ceiling and a gabled window, which Gabriel immediately opened.

He placed the boxes in the closet; then he pulled off his shoes and stretched out on the bed. Anna slipped into the bathroom, and a moment later Gabriel heard the comforting sound of water splashing against enamel. The cold night air blew through the open window. Scented with the North Sea, it caressed his face. He permitted himself to close his eyes.

A few minutes later Anna came out of the bathroom. A burst of light announced her arrival; then she reached out and threw the wall switch, and the room was in darkness again, except for the weak glow of streetlamps seeping through the window.

"Are you awake?"

"No."

"Aren't you going to sleep on the floor, the way you did in Vienna?"

"I can't move."

She lifted the blanket and crawled into bed next to him.

Gabriel said, "How did you know the password was 'adagio'?"

"Albinoni's *Adagio* was one of the first pieces I learned to play. For some reason, it remained my father's favorite." Her lighter flared in the darkness. "My father wanted forgiveness for his sins. He wanted absolution. He was willing to turn to you for that but not to me. Why didn't my father ask me for forgiveness?"

"He probably didn't think you'd give it to him."

"It sounds as though you speak from experience. Has your wife ever forgiven you?"

"No, I don't think she has."

"And what about you? Have ever you forgiven yourself?"

"I wouldn't call it forgiveness."

"What would you call it?"

"Accommodation. I've reached accommodation with myself."

"My father died without absolution. He probably deserved that. But I want to finish what he set out to do. I want to get those paintings back and send them to Israel."

"So do I."

"How?"

"Go to sleep, Anna."

Which she did. Gabriel lay awake, waiting for the dawn, listening to the gulls on the

261

canal and the steady rhythm of Anna's breathing. No demons tonight, no nightmares—the guiltless sleep of a child. Gabriel did not join her. He wasn't ready to sleep yet. When the paintings were locked away in Julian Isherwood's vault—then he would sleep.

Part Three

32

*O*N THE EVE OF THE SECOND WORLD WAR, General Henri Guisan, the commander in chief of Switzerland's armed forces, announced a desperate plan to deal with an invasion by the overwhelmingly superior forces of Nazi Germany. If the Germans come, Guisan said, the Swiss Army would withdraw to the natural fortress of the Alpine Redoubt and blow up the tunnels. And there they would fight, in the deep valleys and on the high mountain ice fields, to the last man. It had not come to that, of course. Hitler realized early in the war that a neutral Switzerland would be more valuable to him than a Switzerland in chains and under occupation. Still, the general's heroic strategy for dealing with the threat of invasion lives on in the imagination of the Swiss.

Indeed, it was on Gerhardt Peterson's mind the following afternoon as he skirted Lucerne and the Alps loomed before him, shrouded in cloud. Peterson could feel his heart beat faster as he pressed the accelerator and his big Mercedes roared up the first mountain pass. Peterson came from Inner Switzerland, and he could trace his lineage back to the tribesmen of the Forest Cantons. He took a certain comfort in the knowledge that people with his blood had roamed these mountain valleys at the same time a young man called Jesus of Nazareth was stirring up trouble at the other end of the Roman Empire. He became uneasy whenever he ventured too far from the security of his Alpine Redoubt. He remembered an official visit to Russia he had made a few years earlier. The limitless quality of the countryside had played havoc with his senses. In his Moscow hotel room, he had suffered his first and only bout of insomnia. When he returned home, he went straight to his country house and spent a day hiking along the mountain trails above Lake Lucerne. That night he slept.

But his sudden trip into the Alps that afternoon had nothing to do with pleasure. It had been precipitated by two pieces of bad news. The first was the discovery of an abandoned Audi A8 on a road near the town of Bargen, a few miles from the German border. A check of the registration revealed that the car had been rented the previous evening in Zürich by Anna Rolfe. The second was a report from an informant on the Bahnhofstrasse. The affair was spinning out of control; Peterson could feel it slipping away.

It began to snow, big downy flakes that turned the afternoon to white. Peterson switched on his amber fog lamps and kept his foot down. One hour later, he was rolling through the town of Stans. By the time he reached the gates of the Gessler estate, three inches of new snow covered the ground.

As he slipped the car into park, a pair of Gessler's security men appeared, dressed in dark-blue ski jackets and woolen caps. A moment later, the formalities of identification and scrutiny behind him, Peterson was rolling up the drive toward Gessler's chateau. There, another man waited, tossing bits of raw meat to a ravenous Alsatian bitch.

ON THE SHORES OF LAKE LUCERNE, NOT FAR from Otto Gessler's mountain home, is the legendary birthplace of the Swiss Confederation. In 1291, the leaders of the three so-called Forest Cantons—Uri, Schwyz, and Unterwalden—are said to have gathered in the Rütli Meadow and formed a defensive alliance against anyone who "may plot evil against their persons or goods." The event is sacred to the Swiss. A mural of the Rütli Meadow adorns the wall of the Swiss National Council chamber, and each August the meeting on the meadow is remembered with a national day of celebration.

Seven hundred years later, a similar defensive alliance was formed by a group of the country's richest and most powerful private bankers and industrialists. In 1291, the enemy had been an outsider: the Holy Roman Emperor Rudolf I of the Hapsburg dynasty, who was trying to assert his feudal rights in Switzerland. Today, once again, the enemies were outsiders, but now they were scattered and more numerous. They were the Jews who were trying to pry open the bank vaults of Switzerland to look for money and whatever else they could lay their hands on. They were the governments demanding that Switzerland pay billions of dollars for accepting Nazi gold during the Second World War. And the journalists and historians who were trying to paint the Swiss as willing allies of Germany—Hitler's money men and arms suppliers who prolonged the war at the cost of millions of lives. And the reformers inside Switzerland who were demanding an end to the sacred laws of banking secrecy.

This new alliance took its inspiration from the fiercely independent forest dwellers who gathered along Lake Lucerne in 1291. Like their ancestors, they swore to fight anyone who "may plot evil against their persons or goods." They saw the events raging beyond their Alpine Redoubt as a gathering storm that could wipe away the institutions that had given Switzerland, a tiny, landlocked country with few natural resources, the second-highest standard of living in the world. They called themselves the Council of Rütli, and their leader was Otto Gessler.

PETERSON HAD EXPECTED TO BE SHOWN, AS usual, to Otto Gessler's makeshift television studio. Instead, the guard escorted him along a lamplit footpath to a single-level wing of the chateau. Passing through an unusually heavy set of French doors, Peterson was greeted by a sweltering tropical heat and an opaque cloud of vapor that reeked of chlorine. Ornate lamps glowed through the mist like storm lanterns, and turquoise water made wavelike patterns on the soaring open-beamed ceiling. The room was quiet except for the ripple of Otto Gessler's laborious crawl. Peterson removed his overcoat and scarf and waited for Gessler to complete his lap. The snow that had collected on his leather city loafers quickly melted, soaking his socks.

"Gerhardt?" A pause for air, another stroke. "Is that you?"

"Yes, Herr Gessler."

"I hope—the snow—didn't make—your drive—too difficult."

"Not at all, Herr Gessler."

Peterson hoped the old man would take a break; otherwise they were going to be at it all night. A bodyguard appeared at the edge of the pool, then receded behind a veil of mist.

"You wished to speak to me about the Rolfe case, Gerhardt?"

"Yes, Herr Gessler. I'm afraid we may have a problem."

"I'm listening."

For the next ten minutes, Peterson brought Gessler up to date on the case. Gessler swam while Peterson spoke. Splash, silence, splash, *silence...*

"What conclusion do you draw from these developments?"

"That they know more about what happened to Augustus Rolfe and the collection than we would wish."

"An obstinate people, don't you agree, Gerhardt?"

"The Jews?"

"Never can seem to leave well enough alone. Always looking for trouble. I won't be beaten by them, Gerhardt."

"No, of course not, Herr Gessler."

Through the curtain of mist, Peterson glimpsed Gessler rising slowly up the steps of the shallow end of the pool; a pale figure, shockingly frail. A bodyguard covered his shoulders in a toweling robe. Then the curtain of mist closed once more, and Gessler was gone.

"She needs to be eliminated," came the dry, disembodied voice. "So does the Israeli."

Peterson frowned. "There will be consequences. Anna Rolfe is a national treasure. If she is murdered so soon after her father, there are bound to be uncomfortable questions, especially in the press."

"You may rest assured that there will be no outpouring of national grief if Anna Rolfe is killed. She refuses even to live in Switzerland, and she's almost done herself in any number of times. And as for the press, they can ask all the questions they want. Without facts, their stories will read like conspiratorial gossip. I only care whether the authorities ask questions. And that's what we pay you for, Gerhardt—to make certain the authorities don't ask questions."

"I should also warn you that the Israeli secret service does not play by the usual rules.

If we target one of their agents for assassination, they'll come after us."

"I'm not afraid of the Jews, Gerhardt, and you shouldn't be, either. Contact Anton Orsati right away. I'll move some additional funds into your operational account, as well as something extra into your personal account. Consider it an incentive to make certain that this affair is resolved quickly and quietly."

"That's not necessary, Herr Gessler."

"I know it's not necessary, but you've earned it."

Peterson hastily changed the subject. He didn't like to think about the money too much. It made him feel like a whore. "I really should be getting back to Zürich, Herr Gessler. The weather."

"You're welcome to spend the night here."

"No, I really should be getting back."

"Suit yourself, Gerhardt."

"May I ask you a question, Herr Gessler?"

"Certainly."

"Did you know Herr Rolfe?"

"Yes, I knew him well. He and I were quite close once. In fact, I was there the morning his wife committed suicide. She dug her own grave and shot herself. It was young Anna who discovered the body. A terrible thing. Herr Rolfe's death was unfortunate but necessary. It wasn't personal, it was business. You do understand the difference, don't you, Gerhardt?"

33

*J*ULIAN ISHERWOOD WAS SEATED AT HIS desk, leafing through a stack of paper-work, when he heard the sound of a delivery truck rumbling across the bricks of Mason's Yard. He walked to his window and peered out. A man in blue coveralls was climbing out the front passenger side and making his way to the door. A moment later came the howl of the buzzer.

"Irina? Did you schedule any deliveries for today?"

"No, Mr. Isherwood."

Oh, Christ, thought Isherwood. *Not again.*

"Irina?"

"Yes, Mr. Isherwood?"

"I'm feeling a bit hungry, petal. Would you be a love and bring me a panini from that marvelous shop in Piccadilly?"

"I'd like nothing better, Mr. Isherwood. May I perform any other meaningless and degrading tasks for you?"

"No need to be snotty, Irina. Cuppa tea as well. And take your time."

THERE WAS SOMETHING ABOUT THE MAN IN blue coveralls that reminded Isherwood of the fellow who had searched his house for termites. He wore rubber-soled shoes and worked with the quiet efficiency of a night nurse. In one hand was a device about the size of a cigar box with meters and dials; in the other was a long wand, like a flyswatter. He began in the basement storerooms, then moved to Irina's office, then Isherwood's, then the exposition room. Lastly, he tore apart the telephones, the computers, and the fax machine. After forty-five minutes, he returned to Isherwood's office and laid two tiny objects on the desk.

"You had bugs," he said. "Now they're dead."

"Who in God's name put them in here?"

"That's not my job. I'm just the exterminator." He smiled. "There's someone downstairs who'd like a word with you."

Isherwood led the way through the cluttered storerooms to the loading bay. He opened the outer door, and the delivery truck pulled inside.

"Close the door," said the man in the blue coveralls.

Isherwood did as he was told. The man opened the back door of the truck and a cloud of dense smoke billowed forth. Crouched in the back, a picture of misery, was Ari Shamron.

THE MAN IN THE ROVER SEDAN HAD MOVED from Jermyn Street to King Street, which was still well within the one-mile range of the transmitters he had placed in the gallery, but it had been some time since he had heard any sound at all. Indeed, the last thing he had monitored was the art dealer asking his secretary to get him lunch. It had struck him as odd, since the dealer had eaten lunch out every day since the man had been watching him. So odd, in fact, that he had made a notation of the time in his logbook. Forty-five minutes after that, a burst of raw static came over his car radio. Someone had just found his transmitters. He swore softly and quickly started the car. As he drove away, he picked up his mobile phone and dialed Zürich.

THE HOEK VAN HOLLAND-TO-HARWICH FERRY was delayed several hours by heavy weather in the North Sea, and so it was late afternoon by the time Gabriel and Anna Rolfe pulled into Mason's Yard. Gabriel gave two short blasts of the horn, and the door of the loading bay slowly rose. Once inside, he shut down the engine and waited for it to close again before getting out of the car. He removed the large safe-deposit box from the back seat and led Anna through the storeroom to the lift. Isherwood was waiting there.

"You must be Anna Rolfe! It is an honor to meet you, truly. I had the distinct privilege of seeing you perform an evening of Mendelssohn once. It was a deeply moving experience."

"You're very kind."

"Won't you please come inside?"

"Thank you."

"Is he here yet?" Gabriel asked.

"Upstairs in the exposition room."

"Let's go."

"What's in the box?"

"In a minute, Julian."

Shamron stood in the center of the room, smoking his vile Turkish cigarettes, completely oblivious to the Old Master canvases surrounding him. Gabriel could see that the old man was wrestling with his memory. A year earlier, in this very room, they had set in motion the final stage of an operation that ended in the death of Tariq al-Hourani. When he saw Anna Rolfe enter the room, his face brightened, and he shook her hand warmly.

Gabriel placed the safe-deposit box on the floor and lifted the lid. Then he removed the first painting, unwrapped it, and laid it on the floor.

"My God," Isherwood whispered. "A Monet landscape."

Anna smiled. "Wait, it gets better."

Gabriel removed the next canvas, a van Gogh self-portrait, and laid it next to the Monet.

"Oh, good heavens," murmured Isherwood.

Then came the Degas, then the Bonnard, then the Cézanne and the Renoir, and on it went until the sixteen canvases stretched the length of the gallery. Isherwood sat down on the divan, pressed his palms against his temples, and wept.

Shamron said, "Well, that's quite an entrance. The floor is yours, Gabriel."

ANNA HAD HEARD IT ALL DURING THE DRIVE from Zürich to the German border, so she stepped away and consoled Isherwood while he gazed at the paintings. Gabriel covered everything he had learned about Augustus Rolfe and his collection, concluding with the letter Rolfe had left in the safe-deposit box in Zürich. Then he told Shamron his plan for recovering the rest of Rolfe's collection: the twenty works that were stolen from the vault at his villa in Zürich. When Gabriel finished, Shamron crushed out his cigarette and slowly shook his head.

"It's an interesting idea, Gabriel, but it has one fatal flaw. The prime minister will never approve it. In case you haven't noticed, we're in a virtual war with the Palestinians now. The prime minister will never approve an operation like this in order to recover a few paintings."

"It's more than a few paintings. Rolfe is hinting at the existence of an organization of Swiss bankers and businessmen who would do anything to protect the old order. And we certainly have the evidence to suggest they exist, including three dead bodies: Rolfe, Müller, and Emil Jacobi. And they tried to kill me."

"The situation is too explosive. Our fickle friends here in Europe are angry enough at us right now. We don't need to pour gasoline on the flames with this kind of operation. I'm sorry,

Gabriel, but I won't approve it, and I won't waste the prime minister's time by asking him."

Anna had left Isherwood's side in order to listen to the debate between Gabriel and Shamron. "I think there's a rather simple solution to the problem, Mr. Shamron," she said.

Shamron twisted his bald head around to look at Anna, amused that the Swiss violinist would dare to venture an opinion on the course of an Israeli intelligence operation.

"What's that?"

"Don't tell the prime minister."

Shamron threw back his head and laughed, and Gabriel joined him. When the laughter died away, there was a moment of silence, broken by Julian Isherwood.

"Dear God, I don't believe it!"

He was holding the Renoir, a portrait of a young girl with a bouquet of flowers. He was turning it over in his hands, looking at the painting, then the back of the canvas.

Gabriel said, "What is it, Julian?"

Isherwood held the Renoir so that Gabriel and the others could see the image. "The Germans were meticulous record-keepers. Every painting they took was sorted, catalogued and marked—swastika, serial number, initials of the collector or dealer from whom it was confiscated."

He turned the canvas over to reveal the back. "Someone tried to remove the markings from this one, but they didn't do a terribly good job of it. Look closely at the bottom left corner. There's the remnants of the swastika, there's the serial number, and there are the initials of the original owner: *SI*."

"Who's *SI?*" Anna asked.

"*SI* is Samuel Isakowitz, my father." Isherwood's voice choked with tears. "This painting was taken from my father's gallery on the rue de la Boétie in Paris by the Nazis in June of 1940."

"You're certain?" Anna asked.

"I'd stake my life on it."

"Then please accept it, along with the deepest apologies of the Rolfe family." Then she kissed his cheek and said, "I'm so sorry, Mr. Isherwood."

Shamron looked at Gabriel. "Why don't you walk me through it one more time."

THEY WENT DOWNSTAIRS TO ISHERWOOD'S office. Gabriel sat behind Isherwood's desk, but Shamron prowled the room as he listened to Gabriel's plan again.

"And what shall I tell the prime minister?"

"Listen to Anna. Tell him nothing."

"And if it blows up in my face?"

"It won't."

"Things like this always blow up in my face, Gabriel, and I have the scars to prove it. So do you. Tell me something. Is it my imagination, or is there a little more spring in your step tonight?"

"You want to ask me a question?"

"I don't wish to sound indelicate."

"That's never stopped you before."

"Are you and this woman more than just accomplices in the search for her father's killer?" When silence greeted his question, Shamron smiled and shook his head. "Do you remember what you said to me about Anna Rolfe on the Piazza Navona?"

"I told you that, given a choice, we would never use a woman like her."

"And now you want to involve her more deeply?"

"She can handle it."

"I have no doubts about *her*, but can *you* handle it, Gabriel?"

"I wouldn't suggest it if I felt otherwise."

"Two weeks ago, I had to beg you to look into Rolfe's death. Now you want to wage war against Switzerland."

"Rolfe wanted those paintings to come to us. Someone took them, and now I want them back."

"But your motivation goes beyond the paintings, Gabriel. I turned you into a killer, but in your heart, you're the restorer. I think you're doing this because you want to restore Anna Rolfe. If that's the case, then the next logical question is this: Why does he want to restore Anna Rolfe? And there's only one logical answer. He has feelings for the woman." Shamron hesitated. "And that's the best news I've heard in a very long time."

"I care for her."

"If you care for her, you'll convince her to cancel her appearance in Venice."

"She won't cancel."

"If that's the case, then perhaps we can use it to our advantage."

"How so?"

"I've always found deception and misdirection to be useful tactics in a situation like this. Let her give her concert. Just make certain your friend Keller doesn't make the recital a truly unforgettable experience."

"Now, that's the Ari Shamron I know and love. Use one of the world's finest musicians as a diversion."

"We play the cards we're dealt."

"I'm going to be with her in Venice. I want someone I can trust to handle the Zürich end of things."

"Who?"

"Eli Lavon."

"My God, a reunion of the Class of '72! If I were a few years younger, I'd join you."

"Let's not get carried away. Oded and Mordecai did well in Paris. I want them too."

"I see something of myself in Oded." Shamron held up his stubby bricklayer's hands. "He has a very powerful grip. If he gets hold of this man, he won't get away."

34

*E*VA HAD INSISTED ON THE EXPENSIVE FLAT overlooking the Zürichsee, despite the fact that it was beyond the reach of Gerhardt Peterson's government salary. For the first ten years of their marriage, they'd made up the shortfall by dipping into her inheritance. Now that money was gone, and it had fallen upon Gerhardt to keep her in the style to which she felt entitled.

The flat was dark when he finally arrived home. As Peterson stepped through the doorway, Eva's amiable Rottweiler charged him in the pitch dark and drove his rocklike head into Peterson's kneecap.

"Down, Schultzie! That's enough, boy. Down! Damn you, Schultzie!"

He fumbled along the wall and switched on the light. The dog was licking his suede shoe.

"All right, Schultzie. Go away, please. That's quite enough."

The dog trotted off, claws clicking on the marble. Peterson limped into the bedroom, rubbing his knee. Eva was sitting up in bed with a hardcover novel open on her lap. An American police drama played silently on the television. She wore a chiffon-colored dressing gown. Her hair was freshly coiffed, and there was a gold bracelet on her left wrist that

Peterson didn't recognize. The money Eva spent on the surface of the Bahnhofstrasse rivaled the funds buried beneath it.

"What's wrong with your knee?"

"Your dog attacked me."

"He didn't *attack* you. He adores you."

"He's too affectionate."

"He's a man, like you. He wants your approval. If you'd just give him a little attention now and again, he wouldn't be so exuberant when you come home."

"Is that what his therapist told you?"

"It's common sense, darling."

"I never wanted the damned dog. He's too big for this flat."

"He makes me feel safe when you're away."

"This place is like a fortress. No one can get in here. And the only person Schultzie ever attacks is me."

Eva licked the tip of her forefinger and turned the page of her novel, ending the discussion. On the television, the American detectives were breaking down the door of a flat in a poor tenement. As they burst into the room, a pair of suspects opened fire with automatic weapons. The policemen fired back, killing the suspects. Such violence, thought Peterson. He rarely carried a gun and had never fired one in the line of duty.

"How was Bern?"

Peterson had lied to her to cover up his visit to see Otto Gessler. He sat on the edge of the bed and removed his shoes.

"Bern was Bern."

"That's nice."

"What are you reading?"

"I don't know. A story about a man and a woman."

He wondered why she bothered. "How are the girls?"

"They're fine."

"And Stefan?"

"He made me promise that you would come into his room and kiss him goodnight."

"I don't want to wake him."

"You won't wake him. Just go in and kiss his head."

"If I don't wake him, what difference will it make? In the morning, I'll tell him that I kissed him while he was asleep, and he'll be none the wiser."

Eva closed her book and looked at him for the first time since he had entered the room. "You look terrible, Gerhardt. You must be famished. Go make yourself something to eat."

He padded into the kitchen. *Go make yourself something to eat.* He couldn't remember the last time Eva had offered to fix him a meal. He had expected that once the sexual intimacy was gone between them, other things would rise in its place, like the pleasure of sharing a home-cooked meal. But not with Eva. First she'd chained the door to her body; then to her affections. Peterson was an island in his own home.

He opened the refrigerator and picked through a desert of half-empty takeaway containers for something that hadn't spoiled or grown a beard of mold. In one grease-spotted carton, he struck gold: a little mound of noodle and bacon raclette. On the bottom shelf, hidden behind a container of green ricotta cheese, lay two eggs. He scrambled them and heated the raclette in the microwave. Then he poured himself a very large glass of red wine and walked back into the bedroom. Eva was buffing her toenails.

He divided his food carefully, so that with each bite of egg he would have an accompanying scoop of raclette. Eva found this habit annoying, which partially explained why he did it. On the television there was more mayhem. Friends of the slain criminals had now avenged their comrades' death by killing the police detectives. More evidence of Herr Gessler's theory of life's circular quality.

"Stephan has a soccer match tomorrow." She blew on her toes. "He'd like you to come."

"I can't. Something's come up at the office."

"He's going to be disappointed."

"I'm afraid it can't be helped."

"What's so important at the office that you can't go see your son's soccer game? Besides, nothing important ever happens in this country."

I have to arrange the murder of Anna Rolfe, he thought. He wondered how she would react if he said it aloud. He considered saying it, just to test her—to see whether she ever listened to a word he said.

Eva finished her toes and returned to her novel. Peterson placed his empty plate and cutlery on the night table and switched off the light. A moment later, Schultzie smashed head-first through the door and began lapping the bits of egg and grease from Eva's precious hand-painted china. Peterson closed his eyes. Eva licked the tip of her index finger and turned another page.

"How was Bern?" she asked.

35

♦ *CORSICA*

*N*EWS OF THE ENGLISHMAN'S DARK MOOD spread rapidly round the little valley. On market day he moved through the village square in silence, joylessly selecting his olives and his cheeses. Evenings he sat with the old ones, but he avoided conversation and refused to be baited into a game of boule, even when his honor was called into question. So pre-occupied was the Englishman that he seemed not to notice the boys on their skateboards.

His driving was dramatically worse. He was seen tearing along the valley road in his battered jeep at unprecedented speeds. Once, he was forced to swerve to avoid the wretched goat of Don Casabianca and ended up in a ditch at the side of the road. At that point Anton Orsati intervened. He told the Englishman about an infamous feud that had taken place between two rival clans over the accidental death of a hunting dog. Four people died before peace was finally made—two at the hands of Orsati *taddunaghiu*. It had happened a hundred years ago, but Orsati stressed that the lessons were still relevant today. His skilled use of Corsican history worked to perfection, as he knew it would. The next morning, the Englishman presented Casabianca with a large ham and apologized for frightening his goat. After that his driving was noticeably slower.

Still, something was clearly wrong. A few of the men from the square were so concerned that they paid a visit to the *signadora*. "He hasn't been here in some time. But when he does come, you can be sure I won't reveal his secrets to you jackasses. This house is like a confessional. Go, now!" And she chased them away with the business end of a stick broom.

Only Don Orsati knew the source of the Englishman's black mood. It was the assignment in Lyons; the Swiss professor called Emil Jacobi. Something about the killing had left a tear in the Englishman's conscience. Don Orsati offered to get the Englishman a girl—a lovely Italian girl he had met in San Remo—but the Englishman refused.

Three days after the Englishman's return from Lyons, Don Orsati invited him to dinner. They ate in a restaurant near the square and afterward walked arm in arm through the narrow streets of the dark town. Twice, villagers appeared out of the gloom, and twice

286

they quickly turned in the opposite direction. Everyone knew that when Don Orsati was speaking privately with the Englishman it was best to walk away. It was then that Don Orsati told him about the assignment in Venice.

"If you want me to send one of the other boys—"

"No," the Englishman said quickly. "I'll do it."

"You're sure?"

"Yes."

"I hoped you'd say that. None of the others are truly capable of a job like this. Besides, I think you'll enjoy the assignment. There's a long tradition of our work in Venice. I'm sure you'll find the setting rather inspiring."

"I'm sure you're right."

"There's a friend of mine there called Rossetti. He'll give you all the help you require."

"You have the dossiers?"

Only a man as powerful as Anton Orsati could leave the dossiers for two people he planned to murder on the front seat of a car, but such was the nature of life in the Corsican village. The Englishman read them by lamplight in the square. When he opened the second file, a look of recognition flashed through his eyes that even Orsati was able to detect.

"Is there something wrong?"

"I know this man—from another life."

"Is that a problem?"

He closed the file. "Not at all."

THE ENGLISHMAN STAYED UP LATE, LISTENING to the audiotape he had taken from the professor's apartment in Lyons. Then he read the stack of clippings and obituaries he had collected by trolling newspaper websites on the Internet, followed by the dossiers Anton Orsati had just given him. He slept for a few hours; then, before dawn the next morning, he placed a small overnight bag in the back of his jeep and drove into the village.

He parked in a narrow street near the church and walked to the house where the *signadora* lived. When he knocked softly on the door, she pushed open the shutters in the second-floor window and peered down at him like a gargoyle.

"I had a feeling it was you. The *scirocco* is blowing. It brings dust and evil spirits."

"Which one am I?"

"I can see the *occhju* from here. Wait there, my child. I'll just be a moment."

The Englishman smoked a cigarette while he waited for the old woman to dress and come downstairs. She answered the door in a widow's plain black frock and pulled him inside by the wrist, as though she feared there were wild animals about. They sat on opposite sides of the rough wooden table. He finished his cigarette while the old women tended to her oil and water.

"Three drops, though I'm certain I already know the answer."

He dipped his finger into the oil and allowed three drops to fall into the water. When the oil shattered, the old woman embarked on her familiar routine of blessings and prayers. When he repeated the test, the oil coalesced into a single ball, floating on the surface of the water. This pleased the old woman.

"That's a neat trick you've got there," said the Englishman.

"It's not a trick. You of all people should know that."

"I meant no disrespect."

"I know. Even though you are not a Corsican by birth, you have the soul of a Corsican. You are a true believer. Do you wish to have something to drink before you go? Some wine, perhaps?"

"It's six o'clock in the morning."

The old woman tilted her head, as if to say, *So what.*

"You should be at home in bed," she said. Then she added: "With a woman. And not the whores that Don Orsati brings you. A real woman who will give you children and see to your clothes."

"The women of Don Orsati are the only ones who will have me."

"You think a decent woman wouldn't have you because you are a *taddunaghiu*?"

The Englishman folded his arms.

"I want to tell you a story."

He opened his mouth to object, but the old woman was on her feet before he could utter a sound and shuffling into the kitchen for the wine. The bottle was dark green and had no label. Her hand shook as she poured out two glasses.

"My husband was very good with his hands," the *signadora* said. "He was a cobbler and a mason. He used to work sometimes for Don Tomasi in the next valley. Have you heard of the Tomasi clan?"

The Englishman nodded and sipped his wine. They were still notorious troublemakers.

"Don Tomasi hired my husband to build a new wall around his garden. It was a thing of beauty, I assure you, but Don Tomasi said it was flawed and refused to pay my husband for his work. They quarreled violently, and the don ordered a pair of his gunmen to drag my husband off his property. It's still there, by the way."

"The wall around the garden?"

"Indeed!" The old woman drank some wine and gathered herself for the rest of the story. "My husband was a good worker, but he was a gentle man. An *agnello*. Do you know this term?"

"A lamb."

The *signadora* nodded. "He was not the kind of man to fight with his fists or a knife. Word of his treatment at the hands of Don Tomasi spread through the village. My husband became a laughingstock. Two nights after the incident he was baited into a fight in the square. He suffered a stab wound in his abdomen and died."

Something flashed behind the old woman's eyes. Anger. Hatred.

"Clearly, blood vengeance was required," she said calmly. "But who? The oaf who murdered my husband in the square? He was not the one who was *truly* responsible for his death. It was Don Tomasi who had blood on his hands. But how was I supposed to kill Don Tomasi? He lived in a large house on the top of a hill, surrounded by vicious dogs and armed men. There was no way for me to kill him! So I went to see Anton Orsati's father, and I hired a *taddunaghiu* to do the deed for me. It cost me every bit of money I had, but it was worth it. The *taddunaghiu* slipped through Don Tomasi's defenses and slit his throat while he slept—killed him like the pig that he was. Justice was done."

He reached across the table and laid her palm on the back of his hand.

"Sometimes, Christopher, a *taddunaghiu* can do good things. Sometimes, he can right a terrible wrong. Sometimes, he can dispense justice as well as vengeance. Remember the things I've told you."

"I will," he said.

He gave her a thick roll of money. Without looking at it, the old woman said, "It's too much. It's always too much."

"You give me peace. Peace is priceless."

He stood up to leave, but she grabbed his wrist with surprising strength. "Sit with me while I drink my wine. I still miss my husband, you know. Even after all these years."

And so he sat there, watching the candlelight flickering in the creases of her face, while she finished the last of the wine. Then her eyes closed and her chin fell forward onto her chest.

The Englishman carried her upstairs and laid her gently in her bed. She awoke briefly. Her hand reached up, and she fingered the talisman hanging from his neck: the red coral hand. Then she touched his face and drifted back to sleep.

He went downstairs and climbed into his jeep, then drove to Calvi and boarded the first ferry for Marseille. There, he collected a car Orsati had left for him near the waterfront and set out for Venice.

36

♦ *VENICE*

*T*HE ITALIAN PRESS HAD COME ALIVE. There was an avalanche of speculation about which pieces Anna Rolfe would perform. Would she attempt her signature piece, Giuseppe Tartini's demonic sonata, "The Devil's Trill?" Surely, the music writers speculated, Miss Rolfe would not try such a difficult composition after being away from the stage for so long.

There were appeals to move the recital to a larger venue. It was scheduled to take place in the upper hall of the Scuola Grande di San Rocco, a room which seated only six hundred, and competition for tickets had deteriorated into something of a scrum among the Venetian well-to-do. Zaccaria Cordoni, the promoter, refused to consider moving the recital, though in an effort to preserve his good standing in Venice he adroitly laid blame at the feet of Anna Rolfe. Miss Rolfe had requested a small venue, he said, and he was a mere prisoner to the demands of the artist. A magazine with Socialist leanings printed a hysterical editorial arguing that once again music had been hijacked by the moneyed classes. It called for demonstrations outside the San Rocco on the night of the concert. Fiona Richardson, Anna Rolfe's agent and manager, released a statement in London promising that Miss Rolfe's considerable appearance fee would be donated to the preservation of the *scuola* and its magnificent artwork. All of Venice breathed a sigh of relief over the gesture, and the controversy receded as gently as the evening tide.

There was also speculation about where Anna Rolfe would stay in Venice. The *Gazzettino* reported that the Hotel Monaco, the Grand Canal, and the Gritti Palace were locked in a titanic struggle to attract her, while the *Nuova Venezia* suggested that Miss Rolfe would avoid the distractions of a hotel by accepting an invitation to stay at a privately owned palazzo. As it turned out, neither newspaper was correct, because at midday on a rainy Friday, the day before the performance, Anna and Gabriel arrived by water taxi at the private dock of the Luna Hotel Baglioni, a quiet establishment on the Calle dell'Ascencione, not far from the tourist mayhem of the Piazza San Marco.

Anna appeared briefly at the front desk and was greeted by the hotel's shining senior staff. She introduced Gabriel as Monsieur Michel Dumont, her friend and personal assistant. As if to reinforce this image, Gabriel made a point of carrying two violins into the lobby. In French-accented English, he reiterated Miss Rolfe's desire for complete privacy. The chief concierge, a polished man called Signore Brunetti, assured him that Miss Rolfe's presence in the hotel would be the most closely guarded secret in Venice. Gabriel thanked him warmly and signed the registry.

"Miss Rolfe will be staying in the Giorgione suite on the fifth floor. It's one of our finest rooms. Your room is right next door. I trust these arrangements are satisfactory?"

"Yes, thank you."

"Allow me to personally escort you and Miss Rolfe to your suite."

"That won't be necessary."

"Do you require help with your luggage, Monsieur Dumont?"

"No, I can manage, thank you."

"As you wish," said Signore Brunetti, and sadly the concierge surrendered the keys.

IN A QUIET BACKWATER OF THE *SESTIERI* OF Santa Marco stands the tiny establishment of Rossetti & Rossetti Fine Jewelry, specializing in antique and one-of-a-kind pieces. Like most Venetian shopkeepers, Signore Rossetti closes his business at one o'clock each afternoon for lunch and reopens at four in time for the evening trade. Well aware of this fact, the Englishman pressed the security buzzer at five minutes till one and waited for Rossetti to open the door.

It was a small shop, no larger than the kitchen in the Englishman's Corsican villa. Passing through the doorway, he was immediately confronted by a horseshoe-shaped glass display counter. When the door closed behind him and the deadbolt snapped into place, the Englishman had the sensation of being imprisoned in a crystal vault. He unbuttoned his macintosh and placed his briefcase on the scuffed wood floor.

Signore Aldo Rossetti stood motionless as a footman behind the counter, dressed in a neatly pressed double-breasted suit and a banker's somber tie. A pair of gold-rimmed reading glasses clung to the tip of his regal nose. Behind him was a tall case of deeply varnished wood with shallow drawers and small brass knobs. Judging from Rossetti's uncompromising stance, the case might have contained secret documents he was sworn to protect at all costs. The deep silence of the room was broken only by the ticking of an antique clock. Rossetti shook the Englishman's hand sadly, as though his visitor had come to confess unforgivable sins.

"I was about to leave for lunch," Rossetti said, and at that moment, as if to accentuate his point, the antique clock on the wall behind him tolled one o'clock.

"This won't take long. I'm here to collect the signet ring for Signore Bull."

"The signet?"

"Yes, that's right."

"For Signore Bull?"

"I believe he told you that I was coming."

Rossetti tilted his head backward and peered at the Englishman as though he were an item of questionable value and provenance. Satisfied, he lowered his head and came round from behind the counter to change the sign in the window from OPEN to CLOSED.

UPSTAIRS WAS A SMALL PRIVATE OFFICE. ROSsetti settled himself behind the desk and invited the Englishman to sit in the little armchair next to the window.

"I received a call a short time ago from a porter at the Luna Hotel Baglioni," Rossetti said. "The violinist and a friend have just checked in. Do you know the Baglioni?"

The Englishman shook his head.

Like most Venetians, Rossetti kept a map of the city within easy reach, if only to give assistance to a foreign tourist hopelessly lost in its labyrinthine alleys. Rossetti's looked as though it had been purchased during the rule of the last doge—a dog-eared, tattered affair, with Scotch tape along the splitting seams, so old it had lost all color. He spread it across his desk, smoothing it with both hands, as though it showed the location of buried treasure.

"The Luna Hotel Baglioni is here"—a tap on the map with the tip of his delicate forefinger—"on the Calle dell'Ascencione, a few steps from the San Marco *vaporetto* stop. The Calle dell'Ascencione is very narrow, no bigger than this street. There's a private dock in the Rio della Zecca. It will be impossible for you to watch the front and the back of the hotel on your own."

The Englishman leaned over the map for a closer look. "You have a suggestion?"

"Perhaps I can use my resources to keep watch on the violinist. If she moves, I can alert you."

"You have someone inside the hotel?"

Rossetti lifted an eyebrow and dipped his head, a neutral gesture, neither in the affirmative or the negative, which said he wished to discuss the matter no further.

"I assume there will be an additional fee for this service?"

"For Don Orsati? It will be my pleasure."

"Tell me how it would work."

"There are places you can wait around the hotel without drawing attention to yourself. The Piazza San Marco, of course. The cafés along the Calle Marzo. The Fontamenta delle Farine overlooking the canal." Rossetti noted each location with an amiable tap on the map. "I assume you have a mobile telephone?"

The Englishman tapped his coat pocket.

"Give me the number and stay close to the

hotel. When they move, someone will telephone you."

He was reluctant to enter into a partnership with Rossetti, but unfortunately the Italian was correct. There was no way he could watch the hotel on his own. He recited his telephone number, and Rossetti jotted it down.

"Of course, there is a chance the violinist will remain in her hotel until the performance at the San Rocco," said Rossetti. "If that's the case, you'll have no choice but to carry out your assignment then."

"You have a ticket?"

Rossetti removed the ticket from his top drawer and placed it carefully on the desktop. Then, using the thumb and forefinger of each hand, he slid it gently forward. The Englishman picked up the ticket and turned it over in his hands. Rossetti looked out his window while his customer inspected the merchandise, confident he would find it satisfactory.

"It's real? Not a forgery?"

"Oh, yes, quite real, I assure you. And quite difficult to come by. In fact, I was tempted to keep it for myself. You see, I've always been a fan of Miss Rolfe. Such passion. Such a pity she has to—" Rossetti cut himself off. "Do you know the San Rocco?"

The Englishman pocketed the ticket and shook his head. Rossetti turned his attention back to his map. "The Scuola Grande di San Rocco is located here, across the Grand Canal in the *sestieri* of San Polo and Santa Croce, just to the south of the Frari church. San Rocco was the patron saint of contagious diseases, and the *scuola* was originally built as a charitable institution for the sick. The construction was financed by donations from wealthy Venetians who believed they could avoid the Black Death by giving money to the *scuola*."

If the assassin found this piece of Venetian history the slightest bit interesting, he gave no sign of it. Undeterred, the little Italian jeweler made a church steeple of his fingers and carried on with his lecture.

"The *scuola* has two primary levels, the ground-floor hall and the upper hall. In 1564, Tintoretto was commissioned to decorate the walls and the ceilings of the buildings. It took him twenty-three years to complete his task." He paused for a moment to consider this fact, then added: "Can you imagine a man of such patience? I would hate to match wits with such a man."

"Where will the concert be? In the ground-floor hall or the upper hall?"

"The upper hall, of course. It's reached by a wide marble staircase designed and built by Scarpagnino. The walls there are decorated with paintings of the Black Death. It's quite moving."

"And if I'm forced to carry out the assignment inside the upper hall?"

Rossetti pressed his church steeple to his lips and whispered a silent petition. "If you have no other choice, then you will have no trouble making your way down the staircase and out the front entrance. From there you can vanish into the alleys of San Polo, and no one will find you." He paused a moment, then said: "But as a Venetian, I implore you to find some other way. It would be a tragedy if you damaged one of the Tintorettos."

"Tell me about the area around the San Rocco."

"The church and the *scuola* share a small square. Behind them is a canal, the Rio della Frescada, which gives access to both structures. There are only two ways for Miss Rolfe to reach the San Rocco on the night of the concert, on foot or by water taxi. If she walks, she will be exposed for long periods of time. She will also have to cross the Grand Canal at some point, either by *vaporetto* or *traghetto*."

"Could she cross by bridge?"

Rossetti considered this question carefully. "I suppose she could cross the Rialto Bridge or the Academia Bridge, but it would add a great deal of distance to her journey. If I were a gambling man, I would wager that Miss Rolfe will take a water taxi from the dock of the hotel directly to the San Rocco."

"And if she does?"

"The Rio della Frescada is a very narrow canal. There are four bridges between the entrance on the Grand Canal and the landing for the San Rocco. You will have ample opportunity there. As the Americans like to say, it will be like shooting fish in a barrel."

The Englishman cast the Italian a dismissive look that said no job could be so crudely described, especially when the target was under professional protection.

"Don Orsati said you would require weaponry. A handgun and perhaps something with a little more firepower in the event things don't go as planned."

Rossetti stood and shuffled across the floor toward an ancient strongbox. He worked the tumbler, then pulled open the heavy doors. He removed an attaché case, placed it on the desk, and sat down again. Opening the case, he removed two weapons, each bound in felt rags, and placed them on the desk. He unwrapped the first and handed it over: a Tanfolglio S Model nine-millimeter with a jet-black barrel and walnut grip. It smelled of clean gun oil. The assassin pulled the slide, felt the weight and balance of the weapon, and peered down the barrel through the sights.

"It has a fifteen-shot magazine, and the longer barrel makes it very accurate," Rossetti said. "Your seat for the concert is in the second-to-last row. I'm afraid it's the best I could do. But even from there, a man of your training should have no trouble making the shot with the Tanfolglio."

"I'll take it. And an extra magazine."

"Of course."

"And the second gun?"

Rossetti unwrapped it and handed it to the assassin. It was an Austrian-made tactical machine pistol. The Englishman picked up the weapon and looked it over carefully.

"I specifically asked for a Heckler and Koch MP-Five," the Englishman said.

"Yes, I know, but I couldn't secure one on

such short notice. I'm sure you'll find the Steyr-Mannlicher to your liking. It's lightweight and easy to conceal. Besides, it *is* a last resort."

"I suppose it will have to do."

"You have a special affection for the Heckler and Koch?"

The Englishman did. It was the weapon he had used when he was in the SAS, but he wasn't about to share that piece of information with Rossetti. He wrapped both weapons in their original cloth covers and placed them carefully in his briefcase, along with the extra magazines and boxes of ammunition.

"Will you require anything else?"

When the assassin shook his head, Rossetti took his pencil to a small scratch pad and began calculating the tab: weapons, tickets for the performance, personal services. Arriving at a total in lira, he slid it across the desk for the assassin to see. The assassin looked at the bill, then at Rossetti.

"Do you mind if I pay in dollars?"

Rossetti smiled and converted the lira sum into dollars, using that day's exchange rate. The Englishman counted out the sum in crisp fifty-dollar bills and added five hundred dollars in gratuity. Signore Rossetti shrugged his shoulder, as if to say a gratuity was not necessary, but the assassin insisted and Rossetti slipped the money discreetly into his pocket.

Downstairs, Rossetti and the Englishman walked out together, Rossetti locking the door behind them. A torrent of rain greeted them, great curtains of water that pounded the little alley and ran toward the storm drains like a swollen mountain stream. The Italian had pulled on a pair of knee-length rubber boots; the Englishman was reduced to hopping and skipping through the puddles in his suede loafers. This amused the Venetian jeweler.

"Your first time in Venice?"

"Yes, I'm afraid so."

"It's been like this every day for a week, and still the tourists come. We need them—God knows, I'd have no business without them—but sometimes even I tire of their presence."

At a *vaporetto* stop, they shook hands.

"I have to say that I find this a most distasteful business, but I suppose you must do what you are paid to do. A violinist"—he raised his hands in a thoroughly Italian gesture—"A violinist can be replaced. But the *Tintorettos*...the Tintorettos are irreplaceable. Please, I will never forgive myself if I played any role in their destruction."

"I assure you, Signore Rossetti, that I will make every effort to avoid damaging them."

The Italian smiled. "I trust that you will. Besides, can you imagine the curse that would befall a man who put a bullet hole through the Savior or the Virgin?"

The little jeweler made the sign of the cross, then turned and melted into the alley.

37

*G*ABRIEL'S TEAM GATHERED THAT AFTER-
noon in the sitting room of Anna Rolfe's
hotel suite. They had come to Venice by different routes, with the passports of different
countries and with different cover stories. In
keeping with Office doctrine, they all posed
as couples. The operation had been conceived and set into motion so hastily that it
had never been given a proper code name.
Anna's hotel room was called the Giorgione
Suite, and from that moment on Gabriel's
Venetian field unit took the name as their
own.

There were Shimon and Ilana. Playing the
parts of French newlyweds, they had driven
to Venice from the Cote d'Azur. They were
dark-eyed and olive-skinned, equal in height
and nearly equal in physical beauty. They
had trained together at the Academy, and
their relationship was strained when Ilana
bested Shimon on the shooting range and
broke his collarbone during a session on the
foam-rubber mats in the gymnasium.

There were Yitzhak and Moshe. In an accommodation to the realities of relationships in
the modern world, they posed as a gay couple from Notting Hill, even though both were
quite the other thing, Yitzhak aggressively so.

304

There was Deborah from the Ottawa station. Gabriel had worked with her on the Tariq operation and was so impressed with her performance that he had insisted she be a part of the Venice team. Shamron had balked at first, but when Gabriel refused to back down, he put her on the next plane from Ottawa and concocted a compelling lie for her section chief.

Seated next to her on the sofa, his leg hanging suggestively over the armrest, was Jonathan. Taciturn and bored, he had the air of a man kept waiting in a doctor's office for a routine physical he did not need. He was a younger version of Gabriel—Gabriel before Vienna perhaps. "He takes his killing seriously," Shamron had said. "But he's no gunslinger. He has a conscience, like you. When it's over, and everyone's safe, he'll find a nice quiet toilet where he can throw up his guts." Gabriel found this element of Jonathan's character reassuring, as Shamron knew he would.

The session lasted one hour and fifteen minutes, though why Gabriel made a note of this fact he did not know. He had chosen to conduct that day's run in Castello, the *sestiere* which lay just to the east of the Basilica San Marco and the Doge's Palace. He had lived in Castello when he was serving his apprenticeship and knew the tangled streets well. Using a hotel pencil as a pointer, he plotted his route and choreographed the movements of the team.

To cover the sound of his instructions, he played a recording of German dances by

305

Mozart. This seemed to darken Jonathan's mood. Jonathan reviled all things German. Indeed, the only people he hated more than the Germans were the Swiss. During the war, his grandfather had tried to preserve his money and heirlooms by entrusting them to a Swiss banker. Fifty years later, Jonathan had tried to gain access to the account but was told by an officious clerk that the bank first required proof that Jonathan's grandfather was indeed dead. Jonathan explained that his grandfather had been murdered at Treblinka—with gas manufactured by a Swiss chemical company, he had been tempted to say—and that the Nazis, while sticklers for paperwork, had not been thoughtful enough to provide a death certificate. Sorry, the clerk had said. No death certificate, no money.

When Gabriel finished his instructions, he opened a large stainless-steel suitcase and gave a secure cell phone and a nine-millimeter Beretta to each member of the team. When the guns were out of sight again, he walked upstairs, collected Anna from the bedroom, and brought her down to meet Team Giorgione for the first time. Shimon and Ilana stood and applauded quietly. Slipping into character, Yitzhak and Moshe commented on the cut of her fashionable leather boots. Deborah eyed her jealously. Only Jonathan seemed to have no interest in her, but Jonathan was to be forgiven, for by then he had eyes only for the assassin known as the Englishman.

◆ ◆ ◆

TEN MINUTES LATER, GABRIEL AND ANNA were walking along the Calle dell'Ascencione. The other members of the team had gone before them and taken up their positions— Jonathan to the San Marco *vaporetto* stop, Shimon and Ilana to look at shoes in the shop windows of the Calle Frezzeria, Yitzhak and Moshe to a table at Caffé Quadri in the Piazza San Marco. Deborah, the baby of the group, was given the unenviable assignment of feeding cracked corn to the pigeons in the shadow of the campanile tower. With admirable forbearance, she allowed the beasts to climb onto her shoulders and roost in her hair. She even found a handsome *carabiniere* to take her photograph with the disposable camera she'd purchased from a kiosk in the center of the square.

As Gabriel and Anna entered the piazza, a thin rain was falling, like mist from a room vaporizer. The forecast called for more heavy weather in the next two days, and there were fears of a severe *acqua alta*. Work crews were erecting a network of elevated duckboards, so that the tourist trade could continue when the lagoon tide turned San Marco into a shallow lake.

Anna wore a car-length quilted jacket, chunky enough to conceal the Kevlar vest beneath. Her hood was up, and she wore sunglasses in spite of the sunless afternoon sky.

307

Gabriel was vaguely aware of Jonathan at his heels, a tourist guidebook open in his palms, his eyes flickering about the square. He glanced to his left and saw Shimon and Ilana strolling beneath the arcade. Hundreds of café tables receded into the distance like the ranks of an army on parade. The basilica floated before them, the great domes etched against the leaden sky.

Anna threaded her arm through Gabriel's. It was a wholly spontaneous gesture, neither too intimate nor too detached. They might have been friends or professional colleagues; they might have just completed the act of love. No one would have been able to tell how she felt by the way she touched him. Only Gabriel could, and that was only because he could feel a slight tremor in her body and the powerful fingers of her left hand digging into the tendons of his arm.

They took a table at Caffè Florian beneath the shelter of the arcade. A quartet played Vivaldi rather poorly, which drove Anna to distraction. Shimon and Ilana had walked the length of the square and were pretending to gaze upon the lions in the Piazzetta dei Leoncini. Yitzhak and Moshe remained at their table on the opposite side of the piazza, while Deborah continued to be mauled by the pigeons. Jonathan sat down a few feet from Gabriel.

Anna ordered the coffees. Gabriel pulled out his telephone and checked in with each component of his team, beginning with Yitzhak and ending with a distraught Deborah. Then he pocketed the phone, caught Jonathan's eye, and shook his head once.

They remained in place while Anna finished her coffee. Then Gabriel asked for the check, a signal to the rest of the team that the second act was about to begin. Jonathan did the same. Even though he was on Shamron's expense account, his face revealed his disgust at the outrageous sum they were asking for a *cappuccino* and a bottle of mineral water.

Five minutes later, Team Giorgione was drifting in formation over the Ponte della Paglia into the *sestiere* of Castello—first Shimon and Ilana, then Yitzhak and Moshe, then Gabriel and Anna. Jonathan hovered a few feet from Gabriel's back, though by now he had put away his tourist guide and had his fingers wrapped tightly around the butt of his Beretta.

AND FORTY YARDS BEHIND THEM ALL WAS THE Englishman. Two questions played in his thoughts. Why was the girl who had been feeding the pigeons in San Marco now walking five paces behind Gabriel Allon? And why was the man who had been seated near Allon at Caffè Florian walking five paces ahead of her?

The Englishman was well-versed in the art of countersurveillance. Anna Rolfe was under the protection of a skilled and professional service. But then that's the way Allon would play it. The Englishman had studied at his feet; knew the way he thought. The Gabriel Allon that the Englishman met in Tel Aviv would never go out for a stroll without a purpose, and the purpose of this one was to expose the Englishman.

On the Riva degli Schiavoni, the Englishman bought a postcard from a tourist kiosk and watched Allon and Anna Rolfe disappear into the streets of Castello. Then he turned in the other direction and spent the next two hours walking slowly back to his hotel.

VENICE IS A CITY WHERE THE USUAL RULES OF street surveillance and countersurveillance do not apply. It is a virtuoso piece requiring a virtuoso's sure hand. There are no motor-cars, no buses or streetcars. There are few places to establish a worthwhile fixed post. There are streets that lead to nowhere—into a canal or an enclosed courtyard with no means of escape. It is a city where the man being pur-sued holds all the advantages.

They were very good, Team Giorgione. They had been trained by the surveillance artists of the Office, and they had honed their skills on the streets of Europe and the Middle East. They communicated silently, drifting in and out of Gabriel's orbit, appearing and reappearing from different directions. Only Jonathan remained constantly in the same position, five paces from Gabriel's back, like a satellite in stationary orbit.

They moved north through a series of church squares, until finally they settled in a small café on the edge of the broad Campo Santa Maria della Formosa. Gabriel and Anna took a table, while Jonathan remained standing at the bar with a group of men. Through the windows, Gabriel caught momentary glimpses of the team: Shimon and Ilana buying *gelato* from a vendor at the center of the square. Yitzhak and Moshe admiring the plain exterior of the church of the Santa Maria Formosa. And Deborah, in a flash of her old spirit, playing football with a group of Italian schoolboys.

This time it was Jonathan who checked in with the team members by secure cell phone. When he was finished, he turned toward Gabriel and mouthed two words: *She's clean.*

LATE THAT EVENING, WHEN TEAM GIORGIONE had finished its debriefing and its members had decamped back to their hotel rooms, Gabriel lingered in the half-light of the sitting room, staring at the photographs of Christopher Keller. Upstairs, in the bedroom, Anna's violin fell silent. Gabriel listened as she placed it back in its case and snapped the latches. A moment later, she descended the staircase. Gabriel gathered up the photographs and slipped them into a file folder. Anna sat down and lit a cigarette.

Gabriel said, "Are you going to try it?"

"'The Devil's Trill'?"

"Yes."

"I haven't decided yet."

"What will you do if you think you can't pull it off?"

"I'll substitute a series of unaccompanied sonatas by Bach. They're quite beautiful, but they're not the 'Trill.' The critics will wonder why I chose not to play it. They'll speculate that I returned too quickly. It will be great fun."

"Whatever you decide to play, it's going to be marvelous."

Her gaze fell upon the manila folder on the coffee table.

"Why did you do that?"

"Do what?"

"Why did you hide the photographs of him when I came into the room? Why don't you want me to see him?"

"You worry about 'The Devil's Trill,' and I'll worry about the man with the gun."

"Tell me about him."

"There are some things you don't need to know."

"He may very well try to kill me tomorrow night. I have a right to know something about him."

Gabriel could not argue with this, and so he told her everything he knew.

"Is he really out there?"

"We have to assume he is."

"Rather interesting, don't you think?"

"What's that?"

"He can change his voice and appearance at will and he vanished amid fire and blood in the desert of Iraq. He sounds like the Devil to me."

"He is a devil."

"So, I'll play his sonata for him. Then you can send him back to Hell."

38

*L*ATE THE FOLLOWING AFTERNOON, THE Englishman drifted along Calle della Passion, the soaring Gothic campanile of the Frari church rising ahead of him. He sliced through a knot of tourists, adroitly shifting the position of his head to avoid their umbrellas, which bobbed like jellyfish adrift on the tide. In the square was a café. He ordered coffee and spread his guidebooks and maps over the little table. If anyone was watching, they would assume he was just another tourist, which was fine with the Englishman.

He had been working since early that morning. Shortly after breakfast, he had set out from his hotel in Santa Croce, maps and guidebooks in hand, and spent several hours wandering San Marco and San Polo, memorizing their streets and bridges and squares— the way he'd done before, in another lifetime, in West Belfast. He'd paid particular attention to the streets and canals around the Frari church and the Scuola Grande di San Rocco— had played a game with himself, wandering in circles in San Polo until, quite intentionally, he would find himself lost. Then he would navigate his way back to the Frari church, testing himself on the street names as he went. Inside the *scuola*, he spent a few minutes in the ground-floor hall, pretending to gaze upon the massive Tintorettos, but in reality he was more interested in the relationship of the main entrance to the staircase. Then he went upstairs and stood in the upper hall, locating the approximate position on the floor where he expected to find himself seated during the recital. Rossetti had been right; even from the back of the room, it would be no problem for a professional to kill the violinist with the Tanfolglio.

He looked at his watch: a few minutes after five o'clock. The recital was scheduled to begin at eight-thirty. He had one final piece of business to conduct before then. He paid his check and walked through the gathering darkness toward the Grand Canal. Along the way he stopped in a men's shop and purchased a new jacket, a quilted black nylon coat with a corduroy collar. The style was quite fashionable in Venice that season; he had seen dozens of coats just like it during the day.

He crossed the Grand Canal by *traghetto* and made his way to Signore Rossetti's store in San Marco. The little jeweler was standing behind his counter, preparing to close up shop for the night. Once again the Englishman followed him up the groaning staircase to his office.

"I need a boat."

"That will be no problem. When would you like it?"

"Right away."

The jeweler stroked the side of his cheek. "There's a young man I know. His name is Angelo. He owns a water taxi. Very careful, very dependable."

"He's not the kind to ask uncomfortable questions?"

"Not at all. He's performed jobs like this before."

"Can you reach him on short notice?"

"I think so, yes. What sort of arrangement do you require?"

"I'd like him to be waiting on the Rio di San Polo, near the Museo Goldoni."

"I see. That should not be a problem, though there *will* be an extra charge for night service. It's customary in Venice. One moment, please. Let me see if I can reach him."

Rossetti found the man's name in his telephone book and dialed his number. After a brief conversation, the deal was done. Angelo would be at the Museo Goldoni in fifteen minutes and he would wait there.

"Perhaps it would be easier if you paid me," Rossetti said. "I'll look after the boy's interests."

Once again the transaction was carried out in dollars after Rossetti worked out the sum on his pad of scratch paper. The Englishman saw himself out and walked to a restaurant on the Calle della Verona, where he dined simply on vegetable soup and fettuccine with cream and mushrooms. It was not the happy din of the little restaurant that filled his ears during the meal, but the memory of the conversation he had heard on the tape he had taken from Emil Jacobi—the conversation between the Swiss professor and Gabriel Allon about the sins of a man named Augustus Rolfe. The father of the woman he had been hired to kill.

A few moments later, when ordering his espresso, he asked the waiter for a piece of paper. He wrote a few words on it, then slipped it into his pocket. After supper he walked to the Grand Canal and boarded a *traghetto* that would take him to the San Rocco.

THE EXPLOSION OF LIGHTNING SHATTERED the studied calm of the lobby of the Luna Hotel Baglioni. The lights dimmed, braced themselves, then flickered back to life. Signore Brunetti, the head concierge, clasped his hands and murmured a prayer of thanks.

Gabriel led Anna across the lobby to the dock. Jonathan walked a step ahead of them. Deborah was a step behind, the Guarneri in one hand, the Stradivarius in the other. Signore Brunetti lifted his hand in farewell and wished her the very best of luck. The rest of the staff broke into circumspect applause. Anna smiled and pulled her hood over her head.

Three water taxis waited at the dock, engines idling, dark varnished prows shimmering in the rain and lights. Jonathan went first, followed by Gabriel. Looking to his right, he saw Moshe and Yitzhak standing atop the footbridge at the entrance of the Grand Canal. Moshe was looking in the other direction, eyes fastened on the crowd at the San Marco *vaporetto* stop.

Gabriel turned and motioned for Anna to step outside. He handed her off to the driver of the second water taxi, then followed her into the cabin. Jonathan and Deborah climbed aboard the first taxi. Moshe and Yitzhak stayed on the bridge until the taxis passed beneath it. Then they descended the steps and boarded the final boat.

Gabriel glanced at his watch: seven-thirty.

THE GRAND CANAL CURVES LAZILY THROUGH the heart of Venice, like a child's reversed S, in the bed of an ancient river. On Gabriel's instruction, the taxis kept to the center, following its long, gentle sweep around the edge of San Marco.

Gabriel stayed inside the cabin with Anna, the curtains drawn, the lights doused. In the first taxi, Jonathan stood at the prow next to the driver, eyes on the move. In the third, Yitzhak and Moshe did the same thing. All three were thoroughly soaked ten minutes later when the taxis turned into the Rio della Frescada.

This was the portion of the journey that worried Gabriel the most. The narrow canal would force the taxis to slow dramatically, and there were four bridges between the Grand Canal and the San Rocco. It was the perfect spot for an assassination.

Gabriel pulled out his telephone and dialed Jonathan. Anna squeezed his hand.

ZACCARIA CORDONI WAS PACING THE GROUND-floor hall of the Scuola Grande di San Rocco, dressed in a black suit and his trademark maroon silk scarf, an unlit cigarette between his fingers. Fiona Richardson, Anna's manager, was at his side.

"Where is she?" Cordoni asked.

"She's on her way."

"You're sure?"

"She called me before she left the hotel."

"She's not going to back out, is she, Fiona?"

"She's coming."

"Because if she backs out on me, I'll see to it that she never performs in Italy again."

"She'll be here, Zaccaria."

Just then Anna entered the room, surrounded by Gabriel's team.

"Anna! Darling!" breathed Cordoni. "You look absolutely delicious this evening. Is there anything else we can do for you to make tonight a smashing success?"

"I'd like to see the upper hall before the audience arrives."

Cordoni held out his hand gallantly.

"Right this way."

◆ ◆ ◆

ANNA HAD PERFORMED AT THE SAN ROCCO twice before, but in keeping with her pre-performance ritual she slowly toured the venue to make certain everything was to her liking—the placement of the stage and the piano, the arrangement of the seats, the lighting. Gabriel did the same, but for a very different reason.

When the inspection was complete, Cordoni led her through a doorway behind the stage into a large gallery with dark wood floors and tapestries on the walls. Adjacent to that room was a small parlor that would serve as Anna's dressing room. A security man from the *scuola* stood guard at the door. He wore a burgundy-colored blazer.

"I've printed two programs for this evening's performance," Cordoni said carefully. "One with 'The Devil's Trill' and one without it. The doors will be opening in five minutes."

Anna looked at Gabriel, then at Fiona Richardson. "I'm not sure an evening in Venice would be complete without Tartini. Hand out the program with 'The Devil's Trill.'"

"You're sure, Anna?" asked Fiona.

"Positive."

"As you wish," said Zaccaria Cordoni.

WHEN CORDONI AND FIONA RICHARDSON were gone, Anna removed her coat and opened the case containing the Guarneri. When

Gabriel sat down, Anna looked at him, hands on her hips.

"What do you think you're doing?"

"I'm going to stay here with you."

"No, you're not. I need to be alone before a performance. I can't have you here distracting me."

"I'm afraid you're going to have to make an exception tonight."

"Tell me something, Gabriel. If you were restoring one of those Tintorettos out there, would you like me standing over your shoulder watching?"

"I see your point."

"Good—now get out of here."

ANNA HAD BEEN GIVEN A GIFT: THE ABILITY TO block out all distraction; the strength to create an impenetrable bubble of silence around herself, to enclose herself in a cocoon. She had discovered this gift the morning of her mother's suicide. A simple scale—G Minor played over two octaves, the ascent, the descent—was enough to send her through a mystical porthole to another time and place. Unfortunately, her ability to create this perfectly ordered place of silence did not extend beyond the violin, and God knows almost everything else in her life had been chaos.

She had known musicians who had come to loathe their instruments. Anna had never done that. Her violin was the anchor which prevented her from drifting into the rocks—a lifeline which pulled her to safety each time she was in danger of drowning. When she was holding her violin, only good things happened. It was when she let go that things spun out of control.

It did not come automatically, this mystical bubble. It had to be summoned. She hung her coat over the back of a baroque chair and crushed out her cigarette. She removed her wristwatch and dropped it into her handbag. She had no need for time now—she would create her own moment in time, a moment that would exist only once and would never be duplicated.

She had decided to use the Guarneri tonight. It seemed only fitting, since the instrument had probably been assembled two hundred years earlier in a workshop not far from where she was sitting now. She opened the case and ran her forefinger down the length of the instrument: the head, the fingerboard, the bridge, the body. She was a lady, this Guarneri of Anna's. Dignified and graceful, no flaws or failings, no scars.

She removed the violin from its case and placed it against her neck, so that the button pressed against the familiar spot a few inches above the base of her shoulder. Her dress was strapless; she didn't like anything between her body and her instrument. At first the violin felt cool against her skin, but soon the heat of her body suffused its wood. She placed the bow on the G string and pulled. The violin responded with a thick, resonant tone.

Her tone. Anna Rolfe's tone. The door to her mystical place was now open.

She permitted herself to look once at her hand. The scars were so ugly. She wished there was something she could do to hide them. Then she pushed the thought from her mind. Her hand did not play the violin; it was her head that played. Her fingers would obey her brain.

She switched off the lights and closed her eyes, then laid the bow across the strings and pulled slowly, coaxing sound from the violin. She executed no scales, performed no exercises, played no portion of the compositions she would perform that evening. There was nothing she could do now to prepare further. The pieces were so imbedded in her cells that she would play them not from memory but from *instinct*. Now she simply drew sound from the violin and allowed the sound to flow through her body. *It's just you and me, fiddle*, she thought. *Just you and me*.

She could hear the murmur of a conversation beyond her closed door. She threw a switch in her mind, and it was gone. Through the walls seeped the low din of the upper hall beginning to fill with members of the audience. She threw the switch, and it too was gone.

It's just you and me, fiddle. Just you and me. ...

She thought of the man in Gabriel's photographs, the assassin known as the Englishman. It had been a long time since she had been able to put her trust in a man. She supposed her father's betrayal—the lies he had told her about the reasons for her mother's suicide—had spoiled her for all men. But tonight she would place her life in the hands of Gabriel Allon. Her father had set in motion a plan to try to atone for terrible sins he had committed. He was murdered before he was able to finish what he started. Gabriel would have to finish it for him. And Anna would help him the only way she knew how—by playing her violin. Beautifully.

The bubble began to close around her, to enfold her. There was no assassin, no photograph of her father with Adolf Hitler, no Gabriel Allon. Just her and the violin.

There was a faint tapping at the door. Instantly, Anna's bow stopped.

"Five minutes, Miss Rolfe."

"Thank you."

The bow slid along the string once more. The sound flowed through her body. The violin turned to fire against her skin. The bubble closed around her. She was lost. Soon the door was open and she was floating toward the upper hall. As she entered the room she assumed there was applause—she knew this only from experience, not from any information she was receiving from her senses. She could not see the audience, nor could she hear it.

She dipped her head and waited an instant before lifting the violin above her shoulder and pressing it to her neck. Then she laid the bow on the strings, hesitated, and began to play.

GABRIEL ESTABLISHED HIS WATCH POST beneath Tintoretto's *Temptation of Christ.* Slowly, his eyes swept the room. Person by person, face by face, he searched the chamber for the man in the photograph. If the assassin was there, Gabriel did not see him.

He checked the disposition of his team. Yitzhak stood directly across the hall from Gabriel. A few feet away, at the top of the staircase, stood Moshe. Shimon and Ilana roamed the back of the hall, and a few feet to Gabriel's right was Jonathan, arms folded, chin on his chest, his dark gaze up.

For a moment he allowed himself to look at Anna. She performed "The Devil's Trill" unaccompanied, as Tartini had intended. The first movement was spellbinding—the floating and distant snatches of simple melody, the hints of Baroque ornamentation; the repeated intrusion of the unsettling double-stop of E-flat and G. The Devil's chord.

Anna played with her eyes closed, her body swaying slightly, as if she were physically drawing sound from her instrument. She was no more than ten feet away from him, but for now Gabriel knew she was lost to him. She belonged to the music now, and whatever bond that had existed between them was broken.

He watched her now as an admirer—and vaguely, he thought, as a restorer. He had helped her to discover the truth about her father and to come to terms with her family's past. The damage was still there, he thought, but it was concealed, invisible to the naked eye, like in a perfect restoration.

She executed the treacherous chromatic descent at the end of the first movement. Pausing for a moment, she began the second movement. Mischievous and faster-paced, it was full of demanding string crossings that required her hand to move repeatedly from the first position to the fifth and from the E string to the G. Eighteen minutes later, when the third movement dissolved into a final arpeggiated G-minor chord, the audience exploded into applause.

Anna lowered the violin and drew several deep breaths. Only then did she open her eyes. She acknowledged the applause with a slight bow. If she ever looked at Gabriel, he did not know it, because by then he had turned his back to her and was scanning the room, looking for a man with a gun.

39

♦ *VENICE*

A STEADY RAIN WAS FALLING ON THE Campo San Rocco. The miserable weather did nothing to dampen the spirits of the large crowd that lingered there after the recital, hoping for one last glimpse of Anna

Rolfe. The atmosphere was electrically charged. After performing "The Devil's Trill," Anna had been joined onstage by her longtime accompanist, Nadine Rosenberg, for Brahms's *Sonata No. 1 for Violin and Piano in D Minor* and Pablo Sarasate's *Zigeunerweisen*. The evening's final piece, Paganini's demonic solo *Caprice No. 24*, had brought the audience to its feet.

Anna Rolfe was unaware of the crowd outside. At that moment she was standing in the gallery behind the stage with Zaccaria Cordoni and Fiona Richardson. Fiona was conducting an animated conversation in German on her mobile telephone. Anna was smoking a much-deserved Gitane, trying to come down off the high of the performance. She was still holding the violin. The old Guarneri had been good to her tonight. She wanted it near her a little longer.

Gabriel was standing a few feet away, watching her carefully. Anna caught his eye briefly and smiled. She mouthed the words *thank you* and discreetly blew him a kiss. Fiona ended her conversation and slipped the telephone into her pocketbook.

"Word travels fast, my dear. You're going to have a busy winter. Paris, Brussels, Stockholm, and Berlin. And that's just the first week."

"I'm not sure I'm really ready to get back on the merry-go-round again, Fiona."

Zaccaria Cordoni laid a hand on her shoulder. "If I may be presumptuous, you are definitely ready. Your performance tonight was inspired. You played like a woman possessed."

"Maybe I am possessed," she said mischievously.

Fiona smiled and glanced toward Gabriel. "You want to tell us about your mysterious Frenchman—the handsome Monsieur Dumont?"

"Actually, what I'd like to do is spend a few minutes alone."

She walked across the room and took Gabriel's hand. Fiona and Cordoni watched them walk down the corridor to the dressing room. Fiona frowned.

"Whoever Monsieur Dumont is, I hope he doesn't break her heart like the others. She's like fine crystal: beautiful but easily broken. And if that bastard breaks her, I'll kill him."

ANNA CLOSED THE DOOR OF HER DRESSING room and collapsed into Gabriel's arms.

"You were amazing tonight."

"I couldn't have done it without you."

"I just watched over you to make sure nothing happened. You're the one who made magic."

"I wish we could celebrate."

"You're getting on a plane out of here. And I have a job to do."

"Was he here tonight?"

"The assassin?"

She nodded, her head pressed against his chest.

"I don't know, Anna."

She sat down, suddenly exhausted. On the

coffee table in front of her was the case for the Guarneri. She undid the latches and lifted the lid. Inside was a single sheet of paper, folded in half, with *Anna* written on it.

She looked up at Gabriel. "Did you leave this for me?"

"Leave what?"

"This note in my violin case. It wasn't here when I left the room to go onstage."

She reached into the case and picked it up. When she did, an object slipped out. It was a narrow length of leather, and hanging from the end of it was a piece of red coral, shaped like a hand.

GABRIEL REACHED INTO THE CASE AND REMOVED the pendant, his heart pounding against his ribs. "What does the note say?"

"'You need this more than I do. Tell Gabriel he owes me one. With compliments.'"

Drawing his Beretta, he opened the door to the dressing room and looked out. Zaccaria Cordoni spotted him and hurried down the corridor to see what was the matter. Gabriel slipped the Beretta back into his pocket.

"Where's the man who was outside this door before the recital?"

"What man?"

"The security guard in the burgundy-colored jacket. Where is he now?"

"I have no idea. Why?"

"Because someone came into this room while Anna was onstage."

"Was any harm done?"

"He left a note." Gabriel held up the coral charm. "And this."

"May I see that?"

Gabriel handed the necklace to Cordoni, who turned it over in his hand and smiled.

"You know what that is?"

"Yes, I think I do. It's harmless."

"What is it?"

"A long time ago, we Cordonis used to be Corsicans. My great-grandfather came to Italy and started the Venetian branch of the family, but I still have distant relatives living in a valley on the southern end of the island."

"What does that have to do with the pendant?"

"It's a talisman, a Corsican good-luck charm. Corsican men wear them. They believe it wards off the evil eye—the *occhju*, as Corsicans refer to it." Cordoni handed it back to Gabriel. "Like I said, it's harmless. Someone was just giving Miss Rolfe a gift."

"I wish it was that simple." Gabriel slipped the talisman into his pocket next to the Beretta, then looked at Cordoni. "Where's the man who was standing outside this door?"

The Englishman spotted the water taxi bobbing in the Rio di San Polo beneath the shelter of a footbridge. Rossetti's man sat behind the wheel wearing a hooded anorak. The Englishman boarded the taxi and ducked into the cabin.

Rossetti's man opened the throttle. The boat grumbled and shuddered, then got underway. A moment later, they were cruising along the Grand Canal at speed. The Englishman rubbed a clear spot in the condensation and looked out at the passing scenery for a few moments. Then he drew the curtains.

He pulled off the black quilted jacket, then removed the burgundy blazer and rolled it into a ball. Ten minutes later, he opened the cabin window and cast the blazer upon the black water of the lagoon.

He stretched out on the bench seat, thinking of the story he would concoct for Anton Orsati. He reached up to his throat for his talisman. He felt naked without it. In the morning, when he was back on Corsica, he would visit the old *signadora* and she would give him a new one.

40

GERHARDT PETERSON'S OFFICE WAS IN darkness except for the small halogen lamp that cast a disk of light over his desk. He had stayed late because he had been expecting a telephone call. He was not sure who would place the call—perhaps the Venice municipal police; perhaps the *carabiniere*—but he had been quite certain it would come. *Sorry to bother you so late, Herr Peterson, but I'm afraid there's been a terrible tragedy in Venice tonight concerning the violinist Anna Rolfe....*

Peterson looked up from his files. Across the room, a television flickered silently. The late national newscast was nearly over. The important stories from Bern and Zürich had been covered, and the program had deteriorated into the mindless features and lighter fare that Peterson usually ignored. Tonight, though, he turned up the volume. As expected, there was a story about Anna Rolfe's triumphant return to the stage that evening in Venice.

When it was over, Peterson switched off the television and locked his files away in his personal safe. Perhaps Anton Orsati's assassin had been unable to carry out his assignment because Anna Rolfe was too heavily protected. Perhaps he'd gotten cold feet. Or perhaps they were dead and the bodies simply hadn't been discovered yet. His instincts told him that this was not the case; that something had gone wrong in Venice. In the morning, he would contact Orsati through the usual channels and find out what had happened.

He slipped some papers into his briefcase, extinguished the desk lamp, and went out. Peterson's seniority permitted him to park his Mercedes in the cobblestone courtyard instead of the distant staff lot adjacent to the rail yard. He had instructed the security staff to keep a special watch on his car. He had not told them why.

He drove south along the Sihl River. The streets were nearly deserted: here a lone taxi; here a trio of guest workers waiting for a streetcar to take them back to their crowded flats in Aussersihl or the Industrie-Quartier. It was the responsibility of Peterson's staff to make certain they didn't make trouble there. No plots against the despot back home. No protests against the Swiss government. Just do your job, collect your check, and keep your mouth shut. Peterson considered the guest workers a necessary evil. The economy couldn't survive without them, but it sometimes seemed the Swiss were outnumbered in Zürich by the damned Portuguese and Pakistanis.

He glanced again into his rearview mirror. It seemed he was not being tailed, though he could not be certain. He knew how to follow a man, but his training in the detection and evasion of surveillance had been rudimentary.

He drove through the streets of Wiedikon for twenty minutes, then over to the Zürichsee to the garage of his apartment house. After passing through the metal security gate, he waited just on the other side to make certain no one came after him on foot. Down the twisting passage he drove to his reserved parking space. His flat number, 6C, was stenciled onto the wall. He pulled into the space and shut down the lights, then the motor. And there he sat for a long moment, hands choking the wheel, heart beating a little too quickly for a man of his age. A very large drink was in order.

He walked slowly across the garage, suddenly bone-weary. He passed through a doorway and entered the vestibule where a lift would carry him up to his flat. Standing before the closed stainless-steel doors, head craning to watch the progress of the glowing floor numbers, was a woman.

She pressed the call button several times and cursed loudly. Then, taking note of Peterson's presence, she turned and smiled apologetically. "I'm sorry, but I've been waiting for the damned lift for five minutes. I think there must be something wrong with the fucking thing."

Perfect *Züridütsch*, thought Peterson. She was no foreigner. Peterson quickly assessed her with his practiced eye. She was dark-haired and pale-skinned, a combination that he had always found terribly attractive. She wore a pair of blue jeans that accentuated her long legs. Beneath her leather jacket was a black blouse, unbuttoned just enough to reveal the lace of her brassiere. Attractive, fine-boned, but not the kind of beauty that would turn heads on the Bahnhofstrasse. Young but not inappropriately so. Early thirties. Thirty-five at the outside.

She seemed to sense Peterson's careful appraisal, because she held his gaze with a pair of mischievous gray eyes. It had been six months since his last affair, and it was time for another. His last mistress had been the wife of a distant colleague, a man from the fraud division. Peterson had managed it well. It had been rewarding and pleasant for a time, and when it was time for it to end, it dissolved without rancor or remorse.

He managed a smile in spite of his fatigue. "I'm sure it'll be along in a moment."

"I don't think so. I think we're going to be trapped here all night."

The suggestiveness of her remark could not be missed. Peterson decided to play along to see how far it would go. "Do you live in this building?"

"Boyfriend."

"Surely your boyfriend will send help eventually, don't you think?"

"He's in Geneva tonight. I'm just staying at his flat."

He wondered who her boyfriend was and which flat she was staying in. He allowed himself to picture a brief and all-too-hurried sexual encounter. Then his fatigue crept up on him and chased away all thoughts of conquest. This time it was Peterson who pressed the call button and Peterson who muttered a curse.

"It's never going to come." She pulled a pack of cigarettes from her coat pocket. Removing one, she placed it between her lips and flicked her lighter. When no flame appeared, she flicked it several more times, then said, "Shit. I guess this isn't my night."

"Here, let me." Peterson's lighter expelled a tongue of blue and yellow flame. He held it in place and allowed the woman to take it as she saw fit. As she inserted the end of her cigarette into the fire, her fingers lightly caressed the back of his hand. It was a deliberately intimate gesture, one that sent a charge of current up the length of his arm.

So powerful was the effect of her touch that Peterson failed to notice that she had raised her cigarette lighter very close to his face. Then she squeezed the hammer, and a cloud of sweet-smelling chemical filled his lungs. His head snapped back and he stared at the woman, eyes wide, barely comprehending. She tossed her cigarette to the floor and pulled a gun from her handbag.

The gun wasn't necessary, because the chemical had its intended effect. Peterson's legs turned to water, the room started to spin, and he could feel the floor rushing up to embrace him. He feared he was going to strike his head, but before his legs buckled completely, a man appeared in the vestibule and Peterson folded into his arms.

Peterson had a glimpse of his savior's face as he was dragged from the vestibule and hurled into the back of a paneled van. It was rabbinical and studious and strangely gentle. Peterson tried to thank him, but when he opened his mouth to speak he blacked out.

41

𝒢ERHARDT PETERSON FELT AS THOUGH he were rising from the depths of an Alpine lake. Upward he came, through layers of consciousness, pockets of warm water and cold, until his face broke the surface and he filled his lungs with air.

He found himself not in the Alpine lake of his dreams but in a cold cellar with a terra-cotta floor and rough whitewashed stucco walls. Above his head was a small window, set in an alcove at ground level, and through it streamed a weak sienna light. For a moment he struggled to orient himself in time and space. Then he remembered the dark-haired woman at the elevator; the ruse with the cigarette; her hand touching his as she sprayed a sedative into his face. He felt suddenly embarrassed. How could he have been so weak? So vulnerable? What signals had he given off that made them come after him with a woman?

The throbbing pain in Peterson's head was uncharted territory, something between trauma and a torrential hangover. His mouth seemed filled with sand, and he was violently thirsty. He was stripped to his briefs, bound by packing tape at the ankles and wrists, his bare back propped against the wall. The fragile appearance of his own body shocked him. His pale

336

hairless legs stretched before him, toes pointed inward, like the legs of a dying man. A layer of flab hung over the waistband of his briefs. He was painfully cold.

They had permitted him to retain his watch, but the crystal was smashed and it no longer kept time. He studied the light leaking through his window and decided it was the light of sunset. He worked out the time, though even this simple problem caused his head to pound. They had taken him shortly before midnight. He guessed it was now five or six in the afternoon of the following day. *Eighteen hours.* Had he been unconscious for eighteen hours? That would explain his thirst and the unbearable stiffness in his back and joints.

He wondered where they had taken him. The quality of light and air was no longer Swiss. For a moment he feared they had spirited him to Israel. No, he'd be in a proper cell in Israel, not a cellar. He was still close to Switzerland. France, maybe. Perhaps Italy. The Jews liked the south of Europe. They blended in well.

There was another scent that took him a few moments to place: incense and sandalwood, a woman's fragrance. And then he remembered: outside the elevator in Zürich; the hand of the woman who had sedated him. But why was her scent on him? He looked down at the skin covering his ribcage and saw four red lines: scratches. His underwear was stained, and there was a cracking stickiness at his crotch. What had they done to him? *Eighteen hours, powerful drugs…*

337

Peterson fell sideways and his cheek struck the cold terra-cotta floor. He retched. Nothing came up, but his nausea was intense. He was sickened by his own weakness. He felt suddenly like a rich man who gets into trouble in a poor neighborhood. All his money, all his culture and superiority—his *Swissness*—meant nothing now. He was beyond the protective walls of his Alpine Redoubt. He was in the hands of people who played the game by very different rules.

He heard footsteps on the staircase. A man entered, small and dark, with a quickness that suggested hidden strength. He seemed annoyed that Peterson had regained consciousness. In his hand was a silver pail. He lifted it with both hands and showered Peterson with ice-cold water.

The pain was intense, and Peterson screamed in spite of himself. The little man knelt beside him and rammed a hypodermic needle into Peterson's thigh, so deep it seemed to strike bone, and once more Peterson slid benevolently below the surface of his lake.

WHEN GERHARDT PETERSON WAS A BOY, HE HAD heard a story about some Jews who had come to his family's village during the war. Now, in his drug-induced coma, he dreamed of the Jews again. According to the story, a family of Jews, two adults and three children, had crossed into Switzerland from unoccupied France. A farmer took pity on them and gave them shelter in a tiny outbuilding on his property. An officer from the cantonal police learned there were Jews hiding in the village but agreed to keep their presence a secret. But someone in the village contacted the federal police, who descended on the farm the next day and took the Jews into custody. It was the policy of the government to expel illegal immigrants back into the country from which they had made their unlawful border crossing. These Jews had crossed into Switzerland from the unoccupied south of France, but they were taken to the border of occupied France and driven into the waiting arms of a German patrol. The Jews were arrested, placed on a train to Auschwitz, and gassed.

At first, Gerhardt Peterson had refused to believe the story. In school he had been taught that Switzerland, a neutral country during the war, had opened its borders to refugees and to wounded soldiers—that it been Europe's Sister of Mercy, a motherly bosom in the heart of a continent in turmoil. He went to his father and asked him whether the story about the Jews was true. At first his father refused to discuss it. But when young Gerhardt persisted, his father relented. Yes, he said, the story was true.

"Why does no one talk about it?"

"Why should we talk about it? It's in the past. Nothing can be done to change it."

"But they were killed. They died because of someone in this village."

"They were *here* illegally. They came without permission. And besides, Gerhardt, we didn't kill them. It was the Nazis who murdered them. Not us!"

"But Papa—"

"Enough, Gerhardt! You asked me if it was true, and I gave you an answer. You are never to discuss it again."

"Why, Papa?"

His father did not answer him. But even then Gerhardt Peterson knew the answer. He was not to discuss the matter further because in Switzerland, one doesn't discuss unpleasant matters from the past.

PETERSON AWOKE TO ANOTHER PAIL OF ICY water. He opened his eyes and was immediately blinded by a searing white light. Squinting, he saw two figures standing over him, the little troll-like man with the bucket, and the kinder-looking soul who had carried him to the van in Zürich after he had been drugged by the woman.

"Wake up!"

The troll threw more freezing water onto Peterson. His neck jerked violently, and he cracked his head against the wall. He lay on the floor, drenched, shivering.

The troll tromped up the stairs. The meeker one squatted on his haunches and looked at him sadly. Peterson, slipping back into unconsciousness, confused reality with his dreams. To Peterson the little man was the Jew from his village whose family had been expelled to France.

"I'm sorry," groaned Peterson, his jaw trembling with cold.

"Yes, I know," said the man. "I know you're sorry."

Peterson began to cough, a retching cough that filled his mouth with phlegm and fluid.

"You're going to see the big man now, Gerhardt. This will only hurt a little, but it will clear your head." Another injection; this time in the arm, delivered with clinical precision. "You mustn't have a foggy head when you talk to the big man, Gerhardt. Are you feeling better? Are the cobwebs beginning to clear?"

"Yes, I think so."

"That's good. You mustn't have cobwebs in your head when you talk to the big man. He wants to know everything that you know. He needs you sharp as a tack."

"I'm thirsty."

"I don't doubt it. You've been a very busy boy the past few days. A very naughty boy too. I'm sure the big man will give you something to drink if you cooperate with him. If you don't"—he shrugged his shoulder and stuck out his lower lip—"then it's back down here, and this time my friend will use more than a little bit of water."

"I'm cold."

"I can imagine."

"I'm sorry."

"Yes, I know you're sorry. If you apologize to the big man and tell him everything you know, then he'll get you something to drink and some warm clothes."

"I want to talk to him."

"Who do you want to talk to?"

"I want to talk to the big man."

"Should we go upstairs and find him?"

"I'm sorry. I want to talk to the big man."

"Let's go, Gerhardt. Come, take my hand. Let me help you."

42

*G*ABRIEL WORE NEATLY PRESSED KHAKI trousers and a soft beige sweater that fit him smartly through the waist and shoulders. Everything about his appearance said comfort and satisfaction, the precise image he wished to convey. Eli Lavon shepherded Peterson into the room and pushed him into a hard, straight-backed chair. Peterson sat like a man before a firing squad, his gaze fixed on the wall.

Lavon showed himself out. Gabriel remained seated, eyes down. He was never one to celebrate victories. He knew better than most that in the business of intelligence, victories are often transitory. Occasionally, with time, they didn't seem like victories at all. Still, he took a moment to relish the fine circular quality of the affair. Not long ago, Gabriel had been the one in custody and Peterson had been asking the questions—Peterson of the fitted gray suit and polished Swiss arrogance. Now he sat before Gabriel shivering in his underwear.

A white Formica table separated them, bare except for a manila file folder and Gabriel's mug of steaming coffee. Like Peterson's cell in the basement, the room had terra-cotta floors and stucco walls. The blinds were drawn. Windblown rain beat a meddlesome rhythm against the glass. Gabriel regarded Peterson with an expression of distaste and fell into a speculative silence.

"You won't get away with this."

It was Peterson who broke the silence. He had spoken in English but Gabriel immediately switched to German; the carefully pronounced and grammatically correct High German of his mother. He wished to point out the laxity of Peterson's *Schwyzerdütch*. To emphasize Peterson's *Swissness*. To isolate him.

"Get away with what, Gerhardt?"

"Kidnapping me, you fucking bastard!"

"But we already did get away with it."

"There were security cameras in the garage of my apartment house. That trick with your whore was recorded on videotape. The Zürich police probably have it already."

Gabriel smiled calmly. "We took care of the security cameras, just like you took care of the security cameras at Rolfe's villa the night you murdered him and stole his paintings."

"What are you ranting about?"

"The paintings in Rolfe's secret collection. The paintings he received during the war for services rendered to the SS. The paintings he wanted to return."

"I don't know what you're talking about. I don't know anything about a secret collection, and I certainly had nothing to do with the murder of Augustus Rolfe! No one would ever believe I had anything to do with his death."

"You killed Augustus Rolfe. Then you killed Werner Müller in Paris. Then Emil Jacobi in Lyons. You tried to kill me in Zürich. You sent a man to kill Anna Rolfe in Venice. That makes me angry, Gerhardt."

"You're deranged!"

Gabriel could see that Peterson's manufactured defiance was slowly beginning to weaken.

"You've been away from work for a long time. Your superiors would like to talk to you too. They can't find you either. Needless to say, your wife would like to know where the hell you are too. She's worried sick."

"My God, what have you done? What on *earth* have you done?"

Peterson seemed incapable of sitting still now. He was rocking in his chair and shivering. Gabriel sipped his coffee and pulled a face as though it were too hot. Then he lifted the cover on the manila file and began removing photographs. He took them out one at a time and had a brief look for himself before sliding them across the tabletop so Peterson could see.

"She takes a nice picture, don't you think, Gerhardt? My, my, you seem to be enjoying yourself there. And look at this one. I'd hate to have to explain that one to Mrs. Peterson. *And* the press. *And* your minister in Bern."

"You're nothing but a blackmailer! No one will believe those photographs are real. They'll see them for what they are: a cheap smear by a cheap blackmailer. But then blackmail and murder are the currency of your service, aren't they? It's what you're good at."

Gabriel left the photographs on the table in plain sight. Peterson made a valiant effort not to look at them.

"So that's the story you tell your wife and your superiors? That you're an innocent victim of blackmail? That you were kidnapped by Israeli intelligence and drugged? Do you know what your superiors will ask you? They'll say: 'Why would Israeli intelligence single you out for such treatment, Gerhardt? What have you done that would make them act like this?' And you'll have to come up with an answer."

"That won't be a problem."

"Are you certain about that? It may not be so easy, given the fact that some of the most reputable news organizations in the world will be uncovering interesting bits and pieces of the story on a daily basis. It will be like water torture, pardon the comparison. You may survive it, but your career will be ruined. Your dreams of becoming chief of the Federal Police will remain just that: a dream. Politics will be closed off to you. Business as well. Do you think your friends in the banks will come

345

to your assistance? No, I doubt it, since you'll have nothing to offer them. Imagine, no job, no pension, no financial support from your friends."

Gabriel paused in order to lift the cover on the file folder and remove a half-dozen more photographs: surveillance shots of Peterson's wife and children. Deliberately he placed them next to the pictures of Peterson and the girl.

"Who will take care of your wife? Who will take care of your children? Who will pay the rent on that nice flat of yours on the Zürichsee? Who will make the payments on that big Mercedes? It's not a very pleasant picture, but it doesn't have to be that way. I don't like murderers, Gerhardt, especially when they kill for a bank, but I'm offering you a way out. I suggest that you take it before it's too late."

"What do you want from me?"

"You're going to work for me now."

"That's impossible!"

"You're going to help me get Rolfe's paintings back." Gabriel hesitated, waiting for Peterson to deny knowledge of any paintings, but this time he said nothing. "We'll handle it quietly, the *Swiss* way. Then you're going to help me get back other things. You're going to help me clean up the mess of Swiss history. Together, Gerhardt, we can move mountains."

"And if I refuse?"

"You can go back downstairs with my friend and think about it for a while. Then we'll talk again."

"Take those damned pictures away!"

"Give me an answer and I'll take them away."

"What you don't understand is that either way I'll be destroyed. It's just a question of which poison I choose to drink." Peterson's chin fell to his chest, his eyes closed. "I'm thirsty."

"Answer my questions, and I'll get you something to drink."

IN THE CORRIDOR OUTSIDE THE ROOM, ELI Lavon sat on the cold floor, his back to the wall, his eyes closed. Only his right hand betrayed his emotions. It was squeezing his cigarette lighter. Though he lived in Vienna, the sound of German shouted in anger still made the back of his neck burn.

The fissures had appeared, but Peterson had not yet cracked. Lavon could tell he was close. The drugs, the water, the pictures with the girl. The fear of what waited around the next bend in the road. It was building in him. Eli Lavon hoped it happened soon.

He had never seen Gabriel like this. Never seen him angry. Never heard him raise his voice. Something about the affair had torn open all the old wounds. Leah. Tariq. Shamron. Even his parents. Gabriel was a man on a very short fuse.

Let it go, Herr Peterson, thought Lavon. *Tell him everything he wants to know. Do exactly what he says. Because if you don't, I fear my good friend*

Gabriel is going to take you into the mountains and start shooting. And that's not going to be good for anybody. Not you. And especially not Gabriel. Lavon didn't care about Peterson. It was Gabriel he loved. He didn't want more blood on the hands of Gabriel Allon.

So no one was more relieved than Lavon when the shouting finally stopped. Then came the thumping—Gabriel pounding on the wall with one of his wounded hands. Still seated on the floor, Lavon reached up and opened the door a few inches. Gabriel spoke to him in Hebrew. The language had never sounded so sweet to Lavon, though he was quite sure it had the opposite effect on Gerhardt Peterson. "Bring him some clothes, Eli. And some food. Herr Peterson is cold and hungry. Herr Peterson would like to tell us a few things."

THE BLUE TRACK SUIT WAS A FASHION TRAGEDY, intentionally so. The top was too large, the legs of the trousers too short. Gerhardt Peterson looked like a man in the clutches of a midlife crisis who digs out a pair of ancient togs for a life-threatening jog in the park. The food was not much better: a lump of coarse bread, a bowl of clear soup. Oded brought a pitcher of ice water. He made a point of spilling a few drops on Peterson's hand, a reminder of what lay ahead if Peterson didn't start talking. Gabriel ate nothing. He had no intention of sharing a meal with Gerhardt Peterson. The Swiss ate steadily but slowly, as though he wished to

348

postpone the inevitable. Gabriel let him take his time. Peterson finished the soup and polished the bowl with the heel of his bread.

"Where are we, by the way?"

"Tibet."

"This is my first trip to Tibet." Peterson managed a wounded smile. When Gabriel refused to play along, the smile quickly faded. "I'd like a cigarette."

"You can't have one."

"Why not?"

"I don't like smoke."

Peterson pushed away his empty soup bowl.

HAD GABRIEL ALLON NOT BECOME AN ASSASSIN, he would have made a perfect interrogator. He was a natural listener: a man who spoke only when necessary; who had no need to hear the sound of his own voice. Like a deerstalker, he was also graced with an unnatural stillness. He never touched his hair or his face, never gestured with his hands or shifted in his chair. It was this very stillness, coupled with his silence and immutable patience, which made him such a frightening opponent over a bare table. Though even Gabriel was surprised at Gerhardt Peterson's sudden willingness to talk.

"How did I know about Rolfe's collection?" Peterson asked, repeating Gabriel's first question. "There is precious little that takes place in Zürich that I don't know about. Zürich is the largest city in Switzerland, but it is still a small place. We have our hooks in deep: banking, business, the foreign workers, the media."

Gabriel didn't want Peterson to build confidence by rambling on about his professional achievements, so he quickly cut him off. "That's all very interesting, but how did you find out about Rolfe?"

"Rolfe was a sick old man—everybody on the Bahnhofstrasse and the Paradeplatz knew that. Everyone knew he didn't have long to live. Then the rumors start to fly. Rolfe is losing his mind. Rolfe wants to set things right before he meets the big banker in the sky. Rolfe wants to talk. Augustus Rolfe was a banker in Zürich for a very long time. When a man like him wants to talk, it can only come to no good."

"So you put him under surveillance."

Peterson nodded.

"Since when is it a crime in Switzerland to talk?"

"It's not a crime, but it's definitely frowned upon—especially if it exposes less-than-flattering elements of our past to the rest of the world. We Swiss don't like to discuss unpleasant family matters in front of foreigners."

"Did your superiors know you'd placed Rolfe under watch? Did your minister in Bern?"

"The Rolfe affair really wasn't an official matter."

And then Gabriel remembered Rolfe's letter: *There are people in Switzerland who want the past to remain exactly where it is—entombed in the bank vaults of the Bahnhofstrasse—and they will stop at nothing to achieve that end.*

"If it wasn't an official matter, then on whose behalf were you following Rolfe?"

Peterson hesitated for a moment; Gabriel feared he might stop talking. Then he said: "They call themselves the Council of Rütli."

"Tell me about them."

"Get me more of that vile soup, and I'll tell you anything you want to know."

Gabriel decided to allow him this one victory. He raised his hand and beat his palm on the wall three times. Oded poked his head in the door as if he smelled smoke. Gabriel murmured a few words to him in Hebrew. Oded reacted by pulling his lips into a remorseful frown.

"And bread," said Peterson as Oded was leaving. "I'd like some more of that bread with my soup."

Oded looked to Gabriel for instruction.

"Bring him some fucking bread."

THIS TIME THEY TOOK NO BREAK FOR FOOD, so Peterson was forced to deliver his lecture on the Council of Rütli with a spoon in one hand and a lump of bread in the other. He spoke for ten minutes without interruption, pausing only to slurp his soup or tear off another mouthful of bread. The history of the Council, its goals and objectives, the power of its membership—all of these topics he covered in

351

substantial detail. When he had finished, Gabriel asked: "Are you a member?"

This question seemed to amuse him. "Me? A schoolteacher's son from Bernese Oberland"—he touched his bread to his breast for emphasis—"a member of the Council of Rütli? No, I'm not a member of the Council, I'm just one of their faithful servants. That's what all of us are in Switzerland—servants. Servants to the foreigners who come here to deposit their money in our banks. Servants to the ruling oligarchy. Servants."

"What service do you provide?"

"Security and intelligence."

"And what do you receive in return?"

"Money and career support."

"So you told the Council about the things you'd heard about Rolfe?"

"That's right. And the Council told me the kinds of things he was hiding."

"A collection of paintings that he'd been given by the Nazis for banking services rendered during the war."

Peterson inclined his head a fraction of an inch. "Herr Rolfe was concealing valuable objects and a controversial story, a terrible set of circumstances from the Council's point of view."

"So what does the Council instruct you to do?"

"To tighten the watch around him. To make certain Herr Rolfe doesn't do anything rash in his final days. But there are disturbing signs. A visitor to Rolfe's bank—a man from an international Jewish agency who is active in the question of the dormant Holocaust accounts."

The casualness with which Peterson made this reference set Gabriel's teeth on edge.

"Then we intercept a series of faxes. It seems that Rolfe is making arrangements to hire an art restorer. I ask myself a simple question: Why is a dying man wasting time restoring his paintings? It's been my experience that the dying usually leave details like that to their survivors."

"You suspect Rolfe is planning to hand over the paintings?"

"Or worse."

"What could be worse?"

"A public confession of his dealings with high-ranking Nazis and officers of German intelligence. Can you imagine the spectacle such an admission would create? It would sweep the country like a storm. It would make the controversy of the dormant accounts look like a mild dustup."

"Is that all the Council was afraid of?"

"Isn't that enough?"

But Gabriel was listening not to Gerhardt Peterson but to Augustus Rolfe: *Once, I considered these men my friends—another of my many mistakes.*

"They were afraid that Augustus Rolfe was going to reveal the existence of the Council. He knew about the Council, because he was a member, wasn't he?"

"Rolfe? He wasn't just a member of the Council. He was a charter member."

"So you went to see him?"

"I tell him that I've heard things—nothing specific, mind you, very subtle. Rolfe is old, but he still has an agile mind, and he knows exactly what I'm trying to tell him. He's a Swiss banker, for Christ's sake. He knows how to have two conversations at the same time. When I leave, I'm convinced the Council has big problems."

"So what do you do?"

"Resort to Plan B."

"And that is?"

"Steal the fucking paintings. No paintings, no story."

PETERSON REFUSED TO CONTINUE WITHOUT A cigarette, and reluctantly Gabriel agreed. Once more he beat his palm against the wall, and once more Oded jutted his head through the open door. He gave Peterson a cigarette from his own pack. When he struck the hammer of his lighter, Peterson flinched so violently he nearly fell from his chair. Oded laughed helplessly all the way to the door. Peterson drew at the cigarette gingerly, as though he feared it might explode, and every few seconds Gabriel lifted his arm to bat away the smoke.

"Tell me about Werner Müller," Gabriel said.

"He was the key to everything. If we were going to get at Rolfe's secret collection, we needed Müller's help. Müller was the one who designed the security system. So I had my men dig up as much dirt on Müller as we could find. Müller didn't have clean hands, either. None of us really does, do we?" When Gabriel said nothing, Peterson continued. "I went to Paris to have a chat with Müller. Needless to say, he agreed to work for our cause."

Peterson smoked the cigarette nearly to the filter, then morosely crushed it out in his empty soup bowl.

"The job was set for the next night. Rolfe was planning to go to Geneva and spend the night at his apartment there. The art restorer was scheduled to arrive the next morning. The team broke into the villa, and Müller guided them down to the viewing chamber."

"Were you part of the team?"

"No, my job was to make sure the Zürich police didn't show up in the middle of it, nothing more."

"Go on."

"Müller disarms the security system and shuts down the cameras. Then they go inside the vault, and guess what they find?"

"Augustus Rolfe."

"In the flesh. Three o'clock in the morning, and the old man is sitting there with his fucking paintings. Müller panics. The burglars are strangers to Rolfe, but the old man and Müller are in business together. If the old man goes to the police, it's Müller who'll take the fall. He grabs a gun from one of the Council's men, marches the old man upstairs to the drawing room, and puts a bullet in his brain."

"Six hours later, I show up."

Peterson nodded. "Rolfe's body gave us an opportunity to test the veracity of the art restorer. If the art restorer discovers the body and telephones the police, chances are he's just an art restorer. If he finds the body and tries to leave town—"

Peterson held up his hands as if to say no other explanation was necessary.

"So you arrange to have me arrested."

"That's right."

"What about the first detective who interrogated me?"

"Baer? Baer knew nothing. To Baer you were just a suspect in the murder of a Swiss banker."

"Why bother to arrest me? Why not just let me go?"

"I wanted to scare the shit out of you and make you think twice about ever coming back."

"But it didn't stop there."

Peterson shook his head. "No, unfortunately, it was just the beginning."

GABRIEL KNEW MOST OF THE REST, BECAUSE he had lived through it. Peterson's rapid-fire account served only to reinforce his existing beliefs or to fill in gaps.

Just as Peterson suspected, Anna Rolfe does not report the theft of her father's secret collection. Peterson immediately places her under surveillance. The job is handled by assets connected to the Council of Rütli and

Swiss security-service officers loyal to Peterson. Peterson knew that Gabriel went to Portugal a week after Rolfe's funeral to see Anna Rolfe, and he knew that they traveled to Zürich together and visited the Rolfe villa.

From that moment on, Gabriel is under surveillance: Rome, Paris, London, Lyons. The Council retains the services of a professional assassin. In Paris, he kills Müller and destroys his gallery. In Lyons, he kills Emil Jacobi.

"Who were the men waiting for me that night at Rolfe's villa?" Gabriel asked.

"They worked for the Council. We hired a professional to handle things outside our borders." Peterson paused. "You killed them both, by the way. It was a very impressive performance. And then we lost track of you for thirty-six hours."

Vienna, thought Gabriel. His meeting with Lavon. His confrontation with Anna about her father's past. Just as Gabriel had suspected, Peterson picks up their trail the next day on the Bahnhofstrasse. After discovering Anna Rolfe's car abandoned at the German border, the Council presses the panic button. Gabriel Allon and Anna Rolfe are to be hunted down and murdered by the professional at the first opportunity. It was supposed to happen in Venice....

PETERSON'S HEAD SLUMPED TOWARD THE tabletop as the effects of the stimulants subsided. Peterson needed sleep—natural sleep, not the kind that came from a syringe. Gabriel had only one question left, and he needed an answer before Peterson could be carried off and handcuffed to a bed. By the time he asked it, Peterson had made a pillow of his hands and was resting, face down, on the table. "The paintings," Gabriel repeated softly. "Where are the paintings?" Peterson managed only two words before he slid into unconsciousness. *Otto Gessler.*

43

ONLY GERHARDT PETERSON SLEPT THAT night. Eli Lavon awakened his girl in Vienna and dispatched her on a two A.M. run to his office in the Jewish Quarter to scour his dusty archives. One hour later, the results of her search rattled off the fax machine, so meager they could have been written on the back of a Viennese postcard. Research Section in Tel Aviv contributed its own slender and thoroughly unhelpful volume, while Oded roamed the dubious corners of the Internet in a search for cybergossip.

Otto Gessler was a ghost. A rumor. Finding the truth about him, said Lavon, was like trying to catch fog in a bottle. His age was anyone's guess. His date of birth was unknown, as was the place. There were no photographs.

He lived nowhere and everywhere, had no parents and no children. "He'll probably never die," Lavon said, rubbing his eyes with bewilderment. "One day, when his time comes, he's just going to disappear."

Of Gessler's business affairs, little was known and much was suspected. He was thought to have a controlling interest in a number of private banks, trust companies, and industrial concerns. Which private banks, which trust companies, and which industrial concerns no one knew, because Otto Gessler operated only through front companies and corporate cutouts. When Otto Gessler did a deal, he left no physical evidence—no fingerprints, no footprints, no DNA—and his books were sealed tighter than a sarcophagus.

Over the years, his name had cropped up in connection with a number of money-laundering and trading scandals. He was rumored to have cornered commodities markets, sold guns and butter to dictators in violation of international sanctions, turned drug profits into respectable real-estate holdings. But the leather glove of law enforcement had never touched Otto Gessler. Thanks to a legion of lawyers spread from New York to London to Zürich, Otto Gessler had paid not one centime in fines and served not one day in jail.

Oded *did* discover one interesting anecdote buried in a highly speculative American magazine profile. Several years after the war, Gessler acquired a company which had manufactured

arms for the Wehrmacht. In a warehouse outside Lucerne, he had discovered five thousand
artillery pieces that had been stranded in
Switzerland after the collapse of the Third
Reich. Unwilling to allow unsold inventory to
remain on his books, Gessler went in search of
a buyer. He found one in a rebellious corner of
Asia. The Nazi artillery pieces helped topple a
colonial ruler, and Gessler earned twice the
profit the guns would have fetched in Berlin.

As the sun rose over the row of cypress
trees bordering the garden, Lavon unearthed
one redeeming trait about Otto Gessler. It was
suspected that each year Gessler gave millions
of dollars to fund medical research.

"Which disease?" asked Gabriel.

"Greed?" suggested Oded, but Lavon shook
his head in wonder. "It doesn't say. The old
bastard gives away millions of dollars a year,
and he conceals even that. Otto Gessler is a
secret. Otto Gessler is Switzerland incar-
nate."

GERHARDT PETERSON SLEPT UNTIL TEN
o'clock. Gabriel permitted him to bathe and
groom at his leisure and to dress in the clothes
he had been wearing at the time of his dis-
appearance, now cleaned and pressed by Eli
Lavon. Gabriel thought the cold mountain air
would be good for Peterson's appearance, so
after breakfast they walked the grounds. The
Swiss was a head taller and better dressed
than his companions, which made him appear

360

as though he was a landowner issuing instructions to a group of day laborers.

Peterson tried to fill in some of the bare canvas of their portrait of Otto Gessler, though it quickly became clear he knew little more than they did. He gave them the precise location of his mountain villa, the details of the security, and the circumstances of their conversations.

"So you've never actually seen his face?" asked Oded.

Peterson shook his head and looked away. He had never forgiven Oded for the ice-water showers in the cellar and refused to look at him now.

"You're going to take me to him," Gabriel said. "You're going to help me get the paintings back."

Peterson smiled; the cold, bloodless smile Gabriel had seen in the holding cell in Zürich after his arrest. "Otto Gessler's villa is like a fortress. You can't walk in there and threaten him."

"I'm not planning to threaten."

"What do you have in mind?"

"I want to offer him a business deal. It's the only language he speaks. Gessler will return the paintings in exchange for a substantial finder's fee and an assurance from me that his role in this affair will never come to light."

"Otto Gessler makes a habit of only dealing from a position of strength. He can't be bullied, and the last thing he needs is more money. If you try this, you'll walk out of there empty-handed, if you walk out at all."

"Either way, I'll walk out."

"I wouldn't be so sure of that."

"I'll walk out because it's *your* responsibility to make sure nothing happens to me. We know where you live, we know where your children go to school, and we always know where to find you."

Again, Peterson's arrogant smile flashed across his lips.

"I wouldn't think a man with your past would threaten another man's family. But I suppose desperate times call for desperate measures. Isn't that how the saying goes? Let's get this over with, shall we? I want to get out of this fucking place."

Peterson turned and started up the hill toward the villa, Oded silently at his heels. Eli Lavon laid a small hand on Gabriel's shoulder. "Maybe he's right. Maybe you shouldn't go in."

"He'll get me out. Besides, at this point, Gessler gains nothing from killing me."

"Like the man says: Desperate times call for desperate measures. Let's go home."

"I don't want them to win, Eli."

"People like Otto Gessler always win. Besides, where the hell are you planning on getting the money to buy back the paintings from him? Shamron? I can't wait to see the look on the old man's face when you file your expense report for this one!"

"I'm not getting the money from Shamron. I'm getting it from the man who stole the paintings in the first place."

"Augustus Rolfe?"

"Of course."

"Atonement, yes?"

"Sometimes, Eli, forgiveness comes at a heavy price."

IT WAS MIDDAY BEFORE THEY LEFT. PETERSON seemed annoyed to find his Mercedes parked in the gravel forecourt next to the Volkswagen van they'd thrown him into after his kidnapping. He climbed into the front passenger seat and reluctantly allowed Oded to cuff his wrist to the armrest on the door. Gabriel got behind the wheel and gunned the engine a little too aggressively for Peterson's taste. Oded sprawled in the back seat, his feet on the tan leather and a Beretta on his lap.

The Swiss border lay only fifteen miles from the villa. Gabriel led the way in the Mercedes, followed by Eli Lavon in the van. It was a quiet crossing; the wearied border guard waved them across after a cursory inspection of their passports. Gabriel had briefly removed Peterson's handcuffs, but a mile past the border he pulled off the road and chained him to the door again.

From there it was northwest to Davos; then up to Reichenau; then west, into the heart of Inner Switzerland. In the Grimselpass it began to snow. Gabriel eased off the throttle so Lavon could keep pace in his clunky Volkswagen van.

Peterson grew more restless as they drove farther north. He gave Gabriel directions as though he were leading him to a buried body. When he asked for the handcuffs to be removed, Gabriel refused.

"You're lovers?" Peterson asked.

"Oded? He's cute, but I'm afraid he's not my type."

"I meant Anna Rolfe."

"I know what you meant. I thought a touch of humor might help to defuse the situation. Otherwise, I might be tempted to strike you very hard in the face."

"Of course you're lovers. Why else would you be involved in this affair? She's had many lovers. I'm certain you won't be the last. If you'd like to see her file, I'd be happy to show it to you—as a professional courtesy, of course."

"Do you do anything for principle, Gerhardt, or do you do things only for money? For example, why do you work for the Council of Rütli? Do you do it only for the money, or do you do it because you believe in what they're doing?"

"Both."

"Oh, really. Which principle compels you to work for Otto Gessler?"

"I work for Otto Gessler because I'm sick of watching my country being dragged through the mud by a bunch of damned foreigners over something that happened before I was born."

"Your country turned looted Nazi gold into hard currency. It turned the dental gold and wedding rings of the Jewish people into hard currency. Thousands of terrified Jews

364

placed their life savings in your banks on the way to the death chambers of Auschwitz and Sobibor, and then those same banks kept the money instead of handing it over to their rightful heirs."

"What does this have to do with me? Sixty years! This happened sixty years ago! Why can't we move on from this? Why must you turn my country into an international pariah over the actions of a few greedy bankers six decades ago?"

"Because you have to admit wrongdoing. And then you have to make amends."

"Money? Yes? You want money? You criticize the Swiss for our supposed greed, but all you want from us is money, as if a few dollars will help right all the wrongs of the past."

"It's not *your* money. It helped to turn this landlocked little amusement park of a country into one of the richest in world, but it's not *your* money."

In the heat of the argument, Gabriel had been driving too fast, and Lavon had fallen several hundred yards behind. Gabriel slowed down so Lavon could close the gap. He was angry with himself. The last thing he wanted now was to debate the morality of Swiss history with Gerhardt Peterson.

"There's one more thing I need to know before we talk to Gessler."

"You want to know how I knew about your connection to the Hamidi assassination."

"Yes."

"A few years ago—eight or nine, I can't remember exactly—a Palestinian with a questionable past wished to acquire a residence visa that would allow him to live temporarily in Geneva. In exchange for the visa, and a guarantee from us that his presence in Switzerland would not be revealed to the State of Israel, this Palestinian offered to tell us the name of the Israeli who killed Hamidi."

"What was the Palestinian's name?" Gabriel asked, though he didn't need to wait for Peterson's answer. He knew. He suppose he'd known it all along.

"His name was Tariq al-Hourani. He's the one who placed the bomb under your wife's car in Vienna, yes? He's the one who destroyed your family."

FIVE MILES FROM OTTO GESSLER'S VILLA, AT the edge of a dense pine forest, Gabriel pulled to the side of the road and got out. It was late afternoon, light fading fast, temperature somewhere around twenty degrees. A mountain peak loomed above them, wearing a beard of cloud. Which was it? The Eiger? The Jungfrau? The Mönch? He didn't really care. He simply wanted to get this over with and get out of this country and never set foot in it again. As he stalked around the car, through six inches of wet snow, an image appeared in his mind: Tariq telling Peterson about the bombing in Vienna. It was all he could do not to pull Peterson from the car and beat him senseless. At that moment, he wasn't sure who he hated more—Tariq or Peterson.

Gabriel unlocked the handcuffs and made Peterson crawl over the shifter to get behind the wheel. Oded got out and joined Eli Lavon in the van. Gabriel took Peterson's spot in the front passenger seat and, with a jab of the Beretta to the ribs, spurred him into motion.

Darkness descended over the valley. Peterson drove with both hands on the wheel, and Gabriel kept the Beretta in plain sight. Two miles from Gessler's villa, Lavon slowed and pulled to the side of the road. Gabriel twisted round and looked through the rear window as the headlights died. They were alone now.

"Tell me one more time," Gabriel said, breaking the silence.

"We've gone over this a dozen times," Peterson objected.

"I don't care. I want to hear you say it one more time."

"Your name is Herr Meyer."

"What do I do?"

"You work with me—in the Division of Analysis and Protection."

"Why are you bringing me to the villa?"

"Because you have important information about the activities of the meddlesome Jew named Gabriel Allon. I wanted Herr Gessler to hear this news directly from the source."

"And what am I going to do if you deviate from the script in any way?"

"I'm not going to say it again."

"Say it!"

"Fuck you."

Gabriel wagged the Beretta at him before

slipping it into the waistband of his trousers. "I'll put a bullet in your brain. And the guard's. That's what I'll do."

"I'm sure you will," Peterson said. "It's the one thing I know you're good at."

A mile farther on was an unmarked private road. Peterson downshifted and took the turn expertly at considerable speed, the centrifugal force pressing Gabriel against the door. For an instant he feared Peterson was up to something, but then they slowed and glided along the narrow road, trees sweeping past Gabriel's window.

At the end of the road was a gate of iron and stone that looked as though it could withstand an assault by an armored personnel carrier. As they approached, a security man stepped into the lights and waved his arms for them to stop. He wore a bulky blue coat that failed to conceal the fact that he was well armed. There was snow in his cap.

Peterson lowered his window. "My name is Gerhardt Peterson. I'm here to see Herr Gessler. I'm afraid it's an emergency."

"Gerhardt Peterson?"

"Yes, that's right."

"And who is that man?"

"He's a colleague of mine. His name is Herr Meyer. I can vouch for him."

The guard murmured a few inaudible words into the mouthpiece. A moment later the gate opened, and he stepped out of their path and waved them through.

Peterson drove at a jogging pace. Gabriel looked out his window: arc lights in the trees, another blue-coated guard, this one being yanked through the forest by an Alsatian on a lead. *My God*, he thought. The place looks like the *Führerbunker*. Add some razor wire and a minefield, and the picture would be complete.

Ahead of them, the trees broke and the lights of the villa appeared, softened by a bridal veil of the drifting snow. Another guard stepped into their path. This one made no attempt to hide the compact submachine gun hanging from his shoulder. Once again Peterson lowered the window, and the guard put his big face inside the car.

"Good evening, Herr Peterson. Herr Gessler is making his way to the pool house now. He'll see you there."

"Fine."

"Are you armed, Herr Peterson?"

Peterson shook his head. The guard looked at Gabriel. "And what about you, Herr Meyer. Are you carrying a gun this evening?"

"*Nein.*"

"Come with me."

A STRING OF TINY LAMPS, MOUNTED ON POSTS no higher than a man's knee, marked the course of the footpath. The snow was deeper here than on the valley floor—a foot or more had fallen—and every fourth lamp or so was buried beneath a tiny drift.

Peterson walked at Gabriel's side. The guard who had met them at the top of the drive now led the way. At some point another had come up behind them. Gabriel could feel the warm breath of an Alsatian on the back of his knee. When the dog nuzzled his hand, the guard jerked the lead. The animal growled in response; a low, deep-throated growl that made the air around it vibrate. *Nice dog,* thought Gabriel. *Let's not do anything to upset the fucking dog.*

The pool house appeared before them, long and low, ornate globe lamps glowing through the rising mist. There were guards inside; Gabriel could just make them out through the fogged windows. One of them appeared to be leading a tiny robed figure.

And then Gabriel felt a searing pain in his right kidney. His back arched, his face tilted upward, and for an instant he saw the stiletto tips of the pine trees stretching toward the heavens, and in his agony the heavens were a van Gogh riot of color and motion and light. Then the second blow fell, this one at the back of his head. The heavens turned to black, and he collapsed, face down, in the snow.

44

NIDWALDEN, ♦ SWITZERLAND

*G*ABRIEL OPENED ONE EYE; THEN, SLOWLY, the other. He might as well have kept them closed, because the darkness was perfect. *Absolute black,* he thought. *Theoretical black.*

It was bitterly cold, the floor rough concrete, the air heavy with sulphur and damp. His hands were cuffed behind him with his palms pointed out, so that the muscles of his shoulders burned with lactic acid. He tried to imagine the contorted position of his body and limbs: right cheek and right shoulder pressed against the concrete; left shoulder in the air; pelvis twisted; legs knotted. He thought of art school—the way the teachers used to twist the limbs of the models to expose muscle and sinew and form. Perhaps he was just a model for some Swiss Expressionist painting. *Man in a Torture Chamber*—artist unknown.

He closed his eyes and tried to right himself, but the slightest contraction of his back muscles set his right kidney on fire. Grunting, he fought through the pain, and managed to set himself upright. He leaned his head against the wall and winced. The second blow had left a knot the size of an egg at the back of his head.

He dragged his fingertips over the wall: bare rock; granite, he supposed. Wet and slick with moss. A cave? A grotto of some sort? Or just another vault? The Swiss and their damned vaults. He wondered if they would leave him here forever, like a gold bar or a Burgundian armchair.

The silence, like the darkness, was complete. Nothing from above or below. No voices, no barking dogs, no wind or weather; just a silence which sang in his ear like a tuning fork.

He wondered how Peterson had done it. How had he signaled the guard that Gabriel was an intruder? A code word at the gate? A missing password? And what of Oded and Eli Lavon? Were they still sitting in the front seat of the Volkswagen van, or were they in the same position as Gabriel—or worse? He thought of Lavon's warning in the garden of the villa in Italy: *People like Otto Gessler always win.*

Somewhere the seal of a tightly closed door was broken, and Gabriel could hear the footsteps of several people. A pair of flashlights burst on, and the beams played about until they found his face. Gabriel squeezed his eyes shut and tried to turn his head from the light, but the twisting of his neck caused his head wound to pound.

"Put him on his feet."

Peterson's voice: firm, authoritative, Peterson in his element.

Two pairs of hands grabbed his arms and pulled. The pain was intense—Gabriel feared his shoulder joints were about to pop out of their sockets. Peterson drew back his fist and buried it in Gabriel's abdomen. His knees buckled, and he doubled over. Then Peterson's knee rose into his face. The guards released him, and he collapsed into the same contorted position in which he'd awakened.

Man in a Torture Chamber by Otto Gessler.

THEY WORKED AS A TEAM, ONE TO HOLD HIM, the other to hit him. They worked efficiently and steadily but without joy and without enthusiasm. They had been given a job—to leave every muscle in his body bruised and every spot on his face bleeding—and they carried out their assignment in a thoroughly professional and bureaucratic manner. Every few minutes they would leave to smoke. Gabriel knew this because he could smell the fresh tobacco on them when they came back. He tried to hate them, these blue-coated warriors for the Bank of Gessler, but could not. It was Peterson whom he hated.

After an hour or so Peterson returned.

"Where are the paintings you took from Rolfe's safe-deposit box in Zürich?"

"What paintings?"

"Where is Anna Rolfe?"

"Who?"

"Hit him some more. See if that helps his memory."

And on it went, for how long Gabriel did not know. He didn't know whether it was night or day—whether he had been here an hour or a week. He kept time by the rhythm of their punches and the clocklike regularity of Peterson's appearances.

"Where are the paintings you took from Rolfe's safe-deposit box in Zürich?"

"What paintings?"

"Where is Anna Rolfe?"

"Who?"

"All right, see if he can handle a little more. Don't kill him."

Another beating. It seemed shorter in duration, though Gabriel could not be sure, because he was in and out of consciousness.

"Where are the paintings?"

"What...paintings?"

"Where is Anna Rolfe?"

"Who?"

"Keep going."

Another knifelike blow to his right kidney. Another iron fist to his face. Another boot to his groin.

"Where are the paintings?"

Silence...

"Where is Anna Rolfe?"

Silence...

"He's done for now. Let him lie there."

HE SEARCHED THE ROOMS OF HIS MEMORY for a quiet place to rest. Behind too many doors he discovered blood and fire and could find no peace. He held his son, he made love to his wife. The room where he found her nude body was their bedroom in Vienna, and the encounter he relived was their last. He wandered through paintings he had restored—through oil and pigment and deserts of bare canvas—until he arrived on a terrace, a terrace above a sea of gold leaf and apricot, bathed in the sienna light of sunset and the liquid music of a violin.

TWO GUARDS CAME IN. GABRIEL ASSUMED IT was time for another beating. Instead, they carefully unlocked the handcuffs and spent the next ten minutes cleaning and bandaging his wounds. They worked with the tenderness of morticians dressing a dead man. Through swollen eyes, Gabriel watched the water in the basin turn pink, then crimson, with his blood.

"Swallow these pills."

"Cyanide?"

"For the pain. You'll feel a little better. Trust us."

Gabriel did as he was told, swallowing the tablets with some difficulty. They allowed him to sit for a few minutes. Before long the throbbing in his head and limbs began to subside. He knew it was not gone—only a short postponement.

"Ready to get on your feet?"

"That depends on where you're taking me."

"Come on, let us help you."

They each grasped him gingerly by an arm and lifted.

"Can you stand up? Can you walk?"

He put his right foot forward, but the deep contusions in his thigh muscles made his leg collapse. They managed to catch him before he could hit the floor again and for some reason found great humor in this.

"Take it slowly. Little steps for a little man."

"Where are we going?"

"It's a surprise. It won't hurt, though. We promise."

They led him through the door. Outside, a corridor stretched before him like a tunnel, long and white, with a marble floor and an arched ceiling. The air smelled of chlorine. They must have been close to Gessler's swimming pool.

They started walking. For the first few yards Gabriel needed every bit of their support, but gradually, as the drugs circulated through his body and he became used to being vertical, he was able to move at a laborious shuffle without aid—a patient taking a first postoperative stroll through a hospital ward.

At the end of the corridor was a double door, and beyond the doorway a circular room, about twenty feet across, with a high-domed ceiling. Standing in the center of the room was a small, elderly man dressed in a white robe, his face concealed by a pair of very large sunglasses. He held out a spindly, purple-veined hand as Gabriel approached. Gabriel left it hovering there.

"Hello, Mr. Allon. I'm so glad we could finally meet. I'm Otto Gessler. Come with me, please. There are a few things that I think you might enjoy seeing."

Behind him, another double doorway opened, slowly and silently, as though on well-oiled automatic hinges. As Gabriel started forward, Gessler reached out and laid his bony hand on Gabriel's forearm.

It was then that Gabriel realized Otto Gessler was blind.

45

*B*EFORE THEM LAY A CAVERNOUS STATUARY hall with an arched ceiling reminiscent of the Musée d'Orsay. The light streaming through the overhead glass was man-made. On each side of the hall were a dozen passageways leading to rooms hung with countless paintings. There were no labels, but Gabriel's trained eye discerned that each had its own mission: fifteenth-century Italian; seventeenth-century Dutch and Flemish; nineteenth-century French. And on it went, gallery after gallery, a private museum filled with Europe's lost masters. The effect was overwhelming, though obviously not to Gessler—Gessler could see none of it.

"I'm sorry about the treatment you had to endure at the hands of my men, but I'm afraid you have only yourself to blame. You were very foolish to come here."

He had a reedy voice, dry and thin as parchment. The hand on Gabriel's forearm was weightless, like a breath of warm air.

"Now I know why you were so anxious to silence Augustus Rolfe. How many do you have?"

"To be honest, even I don't know any more."

They passed the door to another room: fifteenth-century Spanish. A blue-coated security man paced lazily back and forth, like a museum guard.

"And you can't see any of it?"

"No, I'm afraid I can't."

"Why keep them?"

"I think of myself rather like an impotent man. Just because I am unable to lie with my wife does not mean that I am willing to give her body to others."

"So you're married?"

"An admirable attempt, Mr. Allon, but in Switzerland the right to privacy is very sacred. You might say that I've taken it somewhat to the extreme, but it's how I've chosen to live my life."

"Have you always been blind?"

"You ask too many questions."

"I came to offer you a proposition for ending this affair, but I can see now that you would never agree to it. You are the Hermann Göring of the twenty-first century. Your greed knows no bounds."

"Yes, but unlike Herr Göring, whom I knew well, I am not guilty of looting."

"What would you call this?"

"I'm a collector. It's a very special collection, a very private one, but a collection nonetheless."

"I'm not the only one who knows about this. Anna Rolfe knows, and so does my service. You can kill me, but eventually, someone is going to find out what you have buried up here."

Gessler laughed, a dry, humorless laugh.

"Mr. Allon, no one is ever going to find out what's in this room. We Swiss take our privacy rights very seriously. No one will ever be able to open these doors without my consent. But just to make certain of that fact, I've taken an additional step. Using a little-known loophole in Swiss law, I declared this entire property a private bank. These rooms are part of that bank—vaults, if you will. The property contained in them is therefore covered by the banking secrecy laws of Switzerland, and under no circumstance can I ever be forced to open them or reveal their contents."

"And this pleases you?"

"Indeed," he said without reservation. "Even if I was forced to open these rooms, I could be prosecuted for no wrongdoing. You see, each of these objects was acquired legally under Swiss law, and morally under the laws of God and nature. Even if someone could prove beyond a shadow of a doubt that a work in my collection had been stolen from their ancestor by the Germans, they would have to reimburse me at fair market value. Obviously, the cost of repatriation would be astonishing. You and your friends in Tel Aviv can screech as much as you like, but I will never be forced to open the steel doors that lead to these rooms."

"You're a son of a bitch, Gessler."

"Ah, now you resort to curses and foul language. You blame the Swiss for this situation, but we are not to blame. The Germans started the war. We had the good sense to stay on the sidelines, and for this you wish to punish us."

"You didn't sit on the sidelines. You collaborated with Adolf Hitler! You gave him guns and you gave him money. You were his servants. You're all just servants."

"Yes, we did reap a financial reward for our neutrality, but why do you raise this now? After the war, we settled with the Allies and all was forgiven, because the West needed our money to help rebuild Europe. Then came the Cold War, and the West needed us again. Now, the Cold War is over, and everyone from both sides of the Iron Curtain is beating down the Swiss door with their cap in hand. Everyone wants an apology. Everyone wants money. But someday, you're going to need us again. It's always been that way. The German princes and the French kings, the Arab sheiks and the American tax evaders, the drug lords and the arms merchants. My God, even your intelligence agency utilizes our services when it needs them. You yourself have been a frequent client of Credit Suisse over the years. So please, Mr. Allon—please climb down off your moral high horse for a moment and be reasonable."

"You're a thief, Gessler. A common criminal."

"A *thief?* No, Mr. Allon, I've stolen nothing. I've acquired, through smart business tactics, a magnificent private collection of art along with staggering personal wealth. But I am not a thief. And what about you and your people? You bleat about the supposed crimes of the Swiss, but you founded your state on land stolen from others. Paintings, furniture, jewelry—these are just objects, which are easily replaced. Land, however, is an entirely different matter. Land is forever. No, Mr. Allon, I'm not a thief. I'm a winner, just like you and your people."

"Go to hell, Gessler."

"I am a Calvinist, Mr. Allon. We Calvinists believe that wealth on earth is granted to those who will be admitted to the Kingdom of Heaven. If the wealth in these rooms is any clue, I will be going in the opposite direction of Hell. The nature of your next life, I'm afraid, is somewhat less certain. You can make your remaining time on earth less unpleasant if you answer one simple question. Where are the paintings you removed from Augustus Rolfe's safe-deposit box?"

"What paintings?"

"Those paintings belong to me. I can produce a document that declares Rolfe turned them over to me shortly before his death. I am the rightful owner of those paintings, and I want them back."

"May I see the document, please?"

"Where are those paintings!"

"I don't know what you're talking about."

Gessler released Gabriel's arm. "Someone take him, please."

46

$\mathcal{T}$HE DRUGS WORE OFF, AS GABRIEL KNEW they would, and the pain returned stronger than before, as if it had used the respite to gather itself for a final assault. Every nerve in his body seemed to be transmitting charges of pain simultaneously. It overwhelmed his brain and he began to shiver—a violent, uncontrollable shiver that made his body hurt even more. He needed to be sick but prayed he wouldn't. He knew the contraction of vomiting would inflict a new round of exquisite suffering.

Once again he searched for a safe place for his thoughts to alight, but now the memory of Otto Gessler and his collection kept intruding. Gessler in his robe and sunglasses; room after room filled with pillaged Nazi art. He wondered whether it had really been true or just a side effect of the drugs they had made him take. No, he thought. It is true. It was all there, gathered in one place, just beyond his reach. Just beyond the world's reach.

The door opened and his body tensed. Who was it? Gessler's henchmen come to kill him? Gessler himself, come to show him another room filled with lost masters? But as his chamber filled with light, he realized it was neither Gessler or his thugs.

It was Gerhardt Peterson.

◆ ◆ ◆

"CAN YOU STAND UP?"

"No."

Peterson crouched before him. He lit a cigarette, took a long time looking at Gabriel's face. He seemed saddened by what he saw there.

"It's important that you try to stand up."

"Why?"

"Because they're coming to kill you soon."

"What are they waiting for?"

"Darkness."

"Why do they need darkness?"

"They're going to take your body up to the glacier field and drop it down a crevasse."

"That's comforting. I thought they'd just stuff me into a strongbox and deposit me in one of Gessler's numbered accounts."

"They considered that." A mirthless chuckle. "I told you not to come here. You can't beat him, I told you. You should've listened to me."

"You're always right, Gerhardt. You were right about everything."

"No, not everything."

He reached into his coat pocket and produced Gabriel's Beretta. He placed it in the palm of his hand and held it toward Gabriel like offertory.

"What's that for?"

"Take it." He wagged the gun a little. "Go on, take it."

"Why?"

"Because you're going to need it. Without it you have absolutely no chance of getting out of this place alive. With it, given your condition, I rate your chances at only one in three. Worth a try, though, don't you agree? Take the gun, Gabriel."

The gun was warm from Peterson's hand. The walnut grip, the trigger, the barrel—it was the first comforting object he had touched since he'd come to this place.

"I'm sorry you were beaten. It wasn't my choice. Sometimes, an agent in place must do regrettable things to prove his *bona fides* to the people he's deceiving."

"If memory serves, the first two blows were yours."

"I've never struck another man before. It probably hurt me more than it hurt you. Besides, I needed time."

"Time for what?"

"To make the arrangements to get you out of here."

Gabriel released the magazine into his palm and made certain the gun was loaded and not just another of Peterson's deceptions.

"I understand Gessler has quite a collection," said Peterson.

"You've never seen it?"

"No, I've never been invited."

"Is it true? Is this place really a bank? No one can ever get inside?"

"Gabriel, this entire country is a bank." Again Peterson reached into his pocket, and this time he produced a half-dozen tablets. "Here, take these. Something for the pain and a stimulant. You're going to need it."

Gabriel swallowed the pills in one gulp, then rammed the magazine into the butt. "What kind of arrangements have you made?"

"I found your two friends. They were holed up in a guest house in the village. They'll be waiting at the bottom of the mountain, at the edge of Gessler's property, near the spot where we left them yesterday."

Yesterday? Had it only been one day? It seemed more like a year. A lifetime.

"There's a single guard outside this door. You'll have to take care of him first. Quietly. Can you manage that? Are you strong enough?"

"I'll be fine."

"Follow the corridor to the right. At the end you'll find a flight of stairs and at the top of the stairs a doorway. That will put you outside, on the grounds. From there you just have to make your way down the slope of the mountain to your friends."

Through the guards and the Alsatians, thought Gabriel.

"Leave Switzerland the way we came in yesterday. I'll make sure the crossing is clear."

"What will happen to you?"

"I'll tell them that I came to see you one last time to try to convince you to tell me where the paintings were hidden. I'll tell them that you overpowered me and escaped."

"Will they believe you?"

"They might, or then again they may drop me into that crevasse that they'd reserved for you."

"Come with me."

"My wife, my children." Then he added: "My country."

"Why are you doing this? Why not let them kill me and be done with it?"

And then Peterson told him the story of what had happened in his village during the war—the story of the Jews who had crossed into Switzerland from France in search of refuge only to be expelled across the border into the arms of the Gestapo.

"After my father's death, I was going through some of the papers in his study, trying to put his affairs in order. I found a letter. It was from the federal police. A commendation. Do you know what the commendation was for? It was my father who had reported the presence of the Jews in our village. It was because of my father that they were sent back to the Germans and murdered. I don't want any more Jewish blood on the hands of this family. I want you to leave this place alive."

"When the storm hits, it might be unpleasant for you."

"Storms have a way of punching themselves out against the mountain ranges of this country. They say that up on the Jungfrau the wind blows two hundred miles per hour. But the storms never seem to have much strength left when they reach Bern and Zürich. Here, let me help you up."

Peterson pulled him to his feet.

"One in three?"

"If you're lucky."

Gabriel stood just inside the door. Peterson beat his fist on it twice. A moment later the bolts slid away, the door opened, and the guard entered the room. Gabriel stepped in front of him and, using every last bit of strength he could summon, rammed the barrel of the Beretta through the guard's left temple.

PETERSON FELT THE NECK FOR A PULSE. "VERY impressive, Gabriel. Take his coat."

"It has blood on it."

"Do as I say. It will make them hesitate before shooting you, and you'll need it for protection against the cold. Take his submachine gun too— just in case you need something more powerful than your Beretta."

Peterson helped Gabriel remove the dead man's jacket. He wiped the excess blood onto the floor and pulled it on. He hung the machine gun over his shoulder. The Beretta he kept in his right hand.

"Now me," said Peterson. "Something convincing but not quite as irrevocable."

Before Peterson could brace himself for the pain, Gabriel struck him with the butt of the Berretta high on the cheekbone, splitting flesh. Peterson momentarily lost his balance but stayed upright. He touched the wound with his fingertips, then looked at the blood.

"The blood of atonement, yes?"

"Something like that."

"Go."

47

*T*HE COLD THAT GREETED GABRIEL AS HE stepped through the doorway at the top of the stairs was like another blow to the face. It was late afternoon, nightfall fast approaching, wind singing in the pines. His hands began to burn with the cold. He should have taken the dead man's gloves.

He looked up and picked out the peak of the Jungfrau. A few brushstrokes of pale pink light lay high on its face, but the rest of the massif was blue and gray and entirely forbidding. "*They say that up on the Jungfrau the wind blows two hundred miles per hour.*"

The doorway was concrete and steel, like the entrance to a secret military bunker. Gabriel wondered how many were scattered around Gessler's estate, and what other wonders could be discovered by someone with access to them. He pushed those thoughts from his mind for now and concentrated on orienting himself. He was not fifty yards from the pool house, on the back side, a few yards from the trees.

"*...make your way down the slope of the mountain...*"

He walked across the open ground, through knee-deep snow, and entered the trees. Somewhere a dog began to bark. The hounds of

Gessler. He wondered how long it would be before another guard came to the cell and discovered the body. And how long Peterson could keep up the ruse that he'd been assaulted by a man who'd been beaten half to death.

It was dark in the trees, and as he groped his way forward, he thought of the night he'd crept through Rolfe's villa in Zürich and discovered the photographs hidden in the false desk drawer.

Herr Hitler, I'd like you to meet Herr Rolfe. Herr Rolfe has agreed to do a few favors for us. Herr Rolfe is a collector, like you, mein Führer.

There was one advantage to the cold: after a few moments he could no longer feel his face. Here the snow was a few inches less deep, but each step was a new adventure: an outcropping of rock; a fallen tree limb; a hole left by some burrowing animal. Four times he lost his balance and fell, and each time it was harder to get up than the last. But he did get up, and he kept walking, down the fall line of the slope, down to the spot where Oded and Eli waited.

Gabriel came upon a small clearing where a guard stood watch. The guard was twenty yards away, his back slightly turned, so that Gabriel saw him in semi-profile. He didn't trust himself to make the shot from that distance— not with his concussions and his swollen eyes and frozen hands—so he kept moving forward, hoping the dark would conceal his ragged appearance just long enough.

He managed a few steps before one of his footfalls snapped a tree limb. The guard pivoted and looked at Gabriel, uncertain what to do next. Gabriel kept moving forward, calmly and steadily, as though he were the next shift coming on duty. When he was three feet away he pulled the Beretta from his pocket and pointed it at the guard's chest. The round exited the man's back in a cloud of blood and tissue and polyester gossamer.

The gunshot echoed up the mountainside. Immediately a dog began to bark; then another; then a third. Lights came on up at the villa. Beyond the clearing was a narrow track, just wide enough for a small vehicle. Gabriel tried to run but could not. His muscles had neither the strength nor the coordination required to run down the slope of a snow-covered mountain. So he walked and barely managed that.

Ahead of him he sensed that the contour of the land was beginning to flatten out, as if Gessler's mountain was meeting the valley floor. And then he saw the lights of the Volkswagen and two figures—mere shadows, Lavon and Oded, stomping their feet against the cold.

Keep moving! Walk!

From behind, he heard a dog bark, followed by the voice of a man. "Halt, you! Halt before I shoot!"

Judging from the volume, they were very close; thirty yards, no more. He looked down the mountain. Oded and Lavon had heard it too, because they were now scrambling up the road to meet him.

Gabriel kept walking.

"Halt, I say! Halt now, or I'll shoot!"

He heard a rumble and turned around in time to see the Alsatian, released from the restraint of its lead, charging toward him like an avalanche. Behind the dog was the guard, a submachine gun in his hands.

Gabriel hesitated a fraction of a second. *Who first? Dog or man?* Man had a gun, dog had jaws that could break his back. As the dog leapt through the air toward him, he raised the Beretta one-handed and fired past the beast toward his master. The shot struck him in the center of his chest and he collapsed onto the track.

Then the dog drove his head into Gabriel's chest and knocked him to the ground. As he hit the frozen track, his right hand slammed to the ground and the Beretta fell from his grasp.

The dog went immediately for Gabriel's throat. He raised his left arm over his face, and it took that instead. Gabriel screamed as the teeth tore through the protective layer of the jacket and imbedded themselves in the flesh of his forearm. The dog was snarling, thrashing his giant head about, trying to move his arm away so it could be rewarded with the soft flesh of his throat. Frantically, he beat the snowy ground with his right hand, searching for the lost Beretta.

The dog bit down harder, breaking bone.

Gabriel screamed in agony. The pain was more intense than anything Gessler's thugs had inflicted on him. One last time he swept the ground with his hand. This time he found the grip of the Beretta.

With a vicious twist of its massive neck, the dog forced Gabriel's arm to the side and lunged for his throat. Gabriel pressed the barrel of the gun against the dog's ribs and fired three shots into its heart.

Gabriel pushed the dog away and got to his feet. There were shouts coming from the direction of villa, and Gessler's dogs were baying. He started walking. The left sleeve of his jacket was in tatters and blood was streaming over his hand. After a moment he saw Eli Lavon running up the track to him, and he collapsed in his arms.

"Keep walking, Gabriel. Can you walk?"

"I can walk."

"Oded, get ahold of him. My God, what have they done to you, Gabriel? What have they done?"

"I can walk, Eli. Let me walk."

Part Four

THREE MONTHS LATER

48

𝒯HE COTTAGE STOOD ABOVE A NARROW tidal creek, low and stout and solid as a ship, with a fine double door and white shuttered windows. Gabriel returned on a Monday. The painting, a fourteenth-century Netherlandish altarpiece, care of Isherwood Fine Arts, St. James's, London, came on the Wednesday. It was entombed in a shipping crate of reinforced pine and borne up the narrow staircase to Gabriel's studio by a pair of thick boys who smelled of their lunchtime beer. Gabriel chased away the smell by opening a window and a flask of pungent arcosolve.

He took his time uncrating the painting. Because of its age and fragile state, it had been shipped in not one crate but two—an inner crate that secured the painting structurally and an outer crate that cradled it in a stable environment. Finally, he removed the cushion of foam padding and the shroud of protective silicone paper and placed the piece on his easel.

It was the centerpiece of a triptych, approximately three feet in height and two feet in width, oil on three adjoining oak panels with vertical grain—almost certainly Baltic oak, the preferred wood of the Flemish masters. He made diagnostic notes on a small pad: severe convex warp, separation of the second and third panels, extensive losses and scarring.

And if it had been his body on the easel instead of the altarpiece? Fractured jaw, cracked right cheekbone, fractured left eye socket, chipped vertebrae, broken left radius caused by severe dog bite requiring prophylactic treatment of rabies shots. A hundred sutures to repair more than twenty cuts and severe lacerations of the face, residual swelling and disfigurement.

He wished he could do for his face what he was about to do for the painting. The doctors who had treated him in Tel Aviv had said only time could restore his natural appearance. Three months had passed, and he still could barely summon the courage to look at his face in the mirror. Besides, he knew that time was not the most loyal friend of a fifty-year-old face.

FOR THE NEXT WEEK AND A HALF HE DID nothing but read. His personal collection contained several excellent volumes on Rogier, and Julian had been good enough to send along two splendid books of his own, both of which happened to be in German. He spread them across his worktable and perched atop a tall hard stool, his back hunched like a cyclist, his fists pressed to his temples. Occasionally he would lift his eyes and contemplate the piece mounted on his easel—or look up to watch the rain running in rivulets over the skylight. Then he would lower his gaze and resume his reading.

He read Martin Davies and Lorne Campbell. He read Panofsky, and Winkler, and Hulin, and Dijkstra. And of course he read the second volume of Friedländer's monstrous work on early Netherlandish painting. How could he restore a work even remotely linked to Rogier without first consulting the learned Friedländer?

As he worked, the newspaper clippings rattled off his fax machine—one a day at least, sometimes two or three. At first it became known as "the Rolfe affair," then, inevitably, Rolfegate. The first piece appeared in the *Neue Züricher Zeitung*, then the Bern and Lucerne papers got in on the act, and then Geneva. Before long, the story spread to France and Germany. The first English-language account appeared in London, followed two days later by another in a prominent American weekly. The facts were tenuous, the stories speculative; good reading but not exactly good journalism. There were suggestions that Rolfe had kept a secret art collection, suggestions that he had been murdered for it. There were tentative links made to the secretive Swiss financier Otto Gessler, though Gessler's spokesman dismissed it all as malicious lies and gossip. When his lawyers began issuing not-so-subtle warnings about pending lawsuits, the stories quickly died.

The Swiss left demanded a parliamentary inquiry and a full-fledged government investigation. For a time it appeared as though Bern might be forced to dig deeper than the topsoil. Names would be named! Reputations would be ruined! But soon the scandal blew itself out. *Whitewash!* screamed the Swiss left. *Shame on Switzerland!* cried the Jewish organizations. Another scandal swept into the sewers of the Bahnhofstrasse. The Alps had absorbed the brunt of the storm. Bern and Zürich were spared.

A short time later, there was an odd post-script to the story. The body of Gerhardt Peterson, a high-ranking federal security officer, was found in a crevasse in the Bernese Oberland, the victim of an apparent hiking mishap. But Gabriel, alone in his Cornish studio, knew Peterson's death was no accident. Gerhardt Peterson was just another deposit in the Bank of Gessler.

ANNA ROLFE MANAGED TO REMAIN ALOOF from the scandal swirling about her dead father. After her triumphant appearance in Venice, she embarked on an extensive European tour, consisting of solo recitals and appearances with major Continental orchestras. The critics declared that her playing matched the fire and brilliance of her work before the accident, though some of the journalists moaned about her refusal to sit down for interviews. At the new questions surrounding her father's death, she released a paper statement referring all questions to a lawyer in

Zürich. The lawyer in Zürich steadfastly refused to discuss the matter, citing privacy and continuing inquiries. And on it went, until interest in the story spun itself out.

GABRIEL LIFTED HIS HEAD AND PEERED through the skylight. He hadn't noticed until now, but the rain had finally stopped. He listened to the weather forecast on Radio Cornwall while he straightened up the studio: no rain until evening, periods of sun, reasonable temperatures for the Cornish coast in February. His arm was only recently healed, but he decided a few hours on the water would do him good.

He pulled on a yellow oilskin coat, and in the kitchen he made sandwiches and filled a thermos flask with coffee. A few moments later, he was untying the ketch and guiding it under power away from the quay and down the Port Navas Creek to the Helford River. A steady wind blew from the northwest, bright sunlight sparkled on the wavelets and the green hillsides rising above the Helford Passage. Gabriel locked down the wheel, pulled up the mainsail and the jib. Then he shut down the engine and allowed the boat to be taken by the wind.

And soon it left him. He knew it was only temporary—it would last only until he closed his eyes or allowed his mind to lie fallow for too long—but for now he was able to concentrate on the boat rising and falling beneath him and not the beatings he had suffered or the things he had seen. Some nights, as he lay alone in his beastly single bed, he wondered how he would be able to live with such knowledge—the knowledge that Otto Gessler had so cruelly given him. In his weaker moments he considered going before the world's press himself, telling his story, writing a book, but he knew that Gessler would just hide behind his banking-secrecy laws. Gabriel would end up looking like yet another refugee of the secret world, peddling a half-baked conspiracy theory.

As he neared August Rock, he looked toward the west and saw something he didn't like in the towering cloud formation. He slipped down the companionway and switched on his marine radio. A storm was approaching: heavy rain, seas six to eight. He went back to the wheel, brought the boat about, then laid on the aft sail. The ketch immediately increased speed.

By the time he reached the mouth of the Helford it was raining heavily. Gabriel pulled up the hood of his oilskin and went to work on the sails, taking down the aft sail first, followed by the jib and the mainsheet. He switched on the motor and guided the boat upriver. A squadron of gulls gathered overhead, begging for food. Gabriel tore his second sandwich to bits and tossed it onto the water.

He passed the old oyster bed, rounded the point, and headed into the quiet of the tidal creek. The trees broke, and the roof of the cottage floated into view. As he drew nearer, he could see a figure standing on the quay, hands in pockets, collar up against the rain. Gabriel ducked down the companionway and grabbed a pair of Zeiss binoculars hanging from a hook next to the galley. He raised the glasses and focused them on the man's face, then quickly lowered them. He did not need to further authenticate the image.

ARI SHAMRON SAT DOWN AT THE SMALL TABLE in the kitchen while Gabriel made fresh coffee.

"You're actually starting to look like your old self again."

"You used to be a good liar."

"Eventually the swelling will go down. Do you remember Baruch? The terrible beating he took from the Hezbollah before we pulled him out? After a few months, he almost looked like himself again."

"Baruch was ugly to begin with."

"This is true. You were beautiful once. Me, I could do with a beating. It might actually improve my looks."

"I'm sure I could find several eager volunteers."

Shamron's face set into an iron grimace. For a moment, he seemed a little less like a weary old man and more like the Sabra warrior who had pulled Gabriel from the womb of the Betsal'el School of Art thirty years earlier.

"They'd look worse than you when I was finished with them."

Gabriel sat down and poured coffee for them both.

"Did we manage to keep it all a secret?"

"There were some rumors at King Saul Boulevard—rumors about unexplained movement of personnel and strange expenses incurred in Venice and Zürich. Somehow, these rumors reached the prime minister's office."

"Does he know?"

"He suspects, and he's pleased. He says that if it's true, he doesn't want to know."

"And the paintings?"

"We've been working quietly with a few art-restitution agencies and the American Department of Justice. Of the sixteen paintings you discovered in Rolfe's safe-deposit box, nine have been returned to the heirs of their rightful owners, including the one that belonged to Julian's father."

"And the rest?"

"They'll reside in the Israel Museum, just as Rolfe wished, until their owners can be located. If they can't be found, they'll hang there forever."

"How's Anna?"

"We still have a team with her. Rami is about to lose his mind. He says he'll do anything to get off her detail. He's ready to volunteer for patrol duty in Gaza."

"Any threats?"

"None yet."

"How long should we keep her under protection?"

"As long as you want. It was your operation. I'll leave that decision to you."

"At least a year."

"Agreed."

Shamron refilled his cup and lit one of his evil Turkish cigarettes. "She's coming to England next week, you know. The Albert Hall. It's the last stop on her tour."

"I know, Ari. I can read the papers too."

"She asked me to give you this." He slid a small envelope across the tabletop. "It's a ticket to the performance. She asked that you come backstage after the show to say hello."

"I'm in the middle of a restoration right now."

"You or a painting?"

"A painting."

"Take a break."

"I can't take the time to go to London right now."

"The Prince of Wales is going to make time to attend, but *you're* too busy."

"Yes."

"I'll never understand why you insist on allowing beautiful, talented women to slip through your fingers."

"Who said I was going to do that?"

"You think she's going to wait forever?"

"No, just until the swelling goes down."

Shamron gave a dismissive wave of his thick hand. "You're using your face as a convenient excuse not to see her. But I know the real reason. Life is for the living, Gabriel, and this pleasant little prison you've made for yourself is no life. It's time for you to stop blaming yourself for what happened in Vienna. If you have to blame someone, blame me."

"I'm not going to London looking like this."

"If you won't go to London, will you permit me to make another suggestion?"

Gabriel let out a long, exasperated breath. He had lost the will to resist him any longer.

"I'm listening," he said.

49

♦ *CORSICA*

HAT SAME AFTERNOON, THE ENGLISHMAN invited Anton Orsati up to his villa for lunch. It was gusty and cold—too cold to be outside on the terrace—so they ate at the kitchen table and discussed some mildly pressing matters concerning the company. Don Orsati had just won a contract to supply oil to a chain of two dozen bistros stretching from Nice to Normandy. Now an American import-export company wanted to introduce the oil to specialty shops in the United States. Demand was beginning to outpace supply. Orsati needed more land and more trees. But would the fruit stand up to his exacting standards? Would quality suffer with expansion? That was the question they debated throughout the meal.

After lunch, they settled next to the fire in the living room and drank red wine from an earthen pitcher. It was then that the English-man confessed that he had acted with dis-honor during the Rolfe affair.

Orsati poured himself some more of the wine and smiled. "When the signadora told me you came home from Venice without your talisman, I knew something out of the ordi-nary had taken place. What happened to it, by the way?"

"I gave it to Anna Rolfe."

"How?"

The Englishman told him.

Orsati was impressed. "I'd say you won that confrontation on points. How did you get the blazer?"

"I borrowed it from a security guard at the *scuola*."

"What happened to him?"

The Englishman looked into the fire.

Orsati murmured, "Poor devil."

"I asked nicely once."

"The question is, why? Why did you betray me, Christopher? Haven't I been good to you?"

The Englishman played the tape he'd taken from Emil Jacobi in Lyons. Then he gave Orsati the dossier he had prepared based on his own investigation and went into the kitchen to clean up the dishes from lunch. The Cor-sican was a notoriously slow reader.

When he returned, Orsati was finishing the dossier. He closed the file, and his dark gaze settled on the Englishman. "Professor Jacobi was a very good man, but we are paid to kill people. If we spent all our time wrestling with questions of right and wrong, no work would ever get done."

"Is that the way your father conducted his business? And his father? And his?"

Orsati pointed his thick forefinger like a gun at the Englishman's face. "My family is none of your affair, Christopher. You work *for* me. Don't ever forget that."

It was the first time Orsati had spoken to him in anger.

"I meant no disrespect, Don Orsati."

The Corsican lowered his finger. "None taken."

"Do you know the story of the *signadora* and what happened to her husband?"

"You know much about the history of this place, but not everything. How do you think the *signadora* keeps a roof over her head? Do you think she survives on the money she makes chasing away evil spirits with her magic oil and holy water?"

"You take care of her?"

Orsati gave a slow nod.

"She told me that sometimes a *taddunaghiu* can dispense justice as well as vengeance."

"This is true. Don Tomasi certainly deserved to die."

"I know a man who deserves to die."

"The man in your dossier?"

"Yes."

"It sounds as though he's very well protected."

"I'm better than any of them."

Orsati held his glass up to the fire and watched the light dancing in the ruby-colored wine. "You're very good, but killing a man like that will not be easy. You'll need my help."

"*You?*"

Orsati swallowed the last of his wine. "Who do you think climbed Don Tomasi's mountain and slit his evil throat?"

50

COSTA DE PRATA, ♦ PORTUGAL

*C*ARLOS THE VINEYARD KEEPER WAS THE first to see him arrive. He looked up from his work as the car pulled into the gravel drive and watched as the art restorer named Gabriel was greeted by the one called Rami. They exchanged a few words; Rami touched the scars on the art restorer's face. This Carlos could see from his post at the base of the vineyard. He was not a military man, but Carlos recognized a changing of the guard when he saw one. Rami was leaving, and not soon enough. Rami had tired of Our Lady's antics, as Carlos knew he would. Our Lady needed a man of unending patience to watch over her. Our Lady needed the restorer.

He watched as Gabriel crossed the drive and disappeared into the villa. Our Lady was upstairs in her room, practicing. Surely the restorer did not intend to interrupt her. For a moment Carlos considered running up the terrace to intervene, but then he thought better of it. The restorer needed to learn a lesson, and some lessons are best learned the hard way.

So he laid down his pruning shears and found the flask of bagaço in his pocket. Then he crouched amid his vines and lit a cigarette, watching the sun diving toward the sea, waiting for the show to begin.

THE SOUND OF HER VIOLIN FILLED THE VILLA as Gabriel climbed the stairs to her room. He entered without knocking. She played a few more notes, then stopped suddenly. Without turning around she shouted: "God damn you, Rami! How many fucking times have I told you—"

And then she turned and saw him. Her mouth fell open, and for an instant she released her grip on the Guarneri. Gabriel lunged forward and snatched it out of the air before it could hit the floor. Anna seized him in her arms.

"I never thought I'd see you again, Gabriel. What are you doing here?"

"I've been assigned to your security detail."

"Thank God! Rami and I are going to kill each other."

"So I've heard."

"How many people on the new team?"

"I thought I'd leave that decision in your hands."

"I think one man would be enough, if that's all right with you."

"That would be fine," he said. "That would be perfect."

51

NIDWALDEN, ♦ *SWITZERLAND*

*O*TTO GESSLER PROPELLED HIMSELF through silken water, gliding forward in perpetual darkness. He had swum well that day, two lengths more than usual—one hundred and fifty meters in all, quite an accomplishment for a man of his age. Blindness required him to carefully count each stroke, so that he did not crash headlong into the side of the pool. Not long ago he could devour each length with twenty-two powerful strokes. Now it required forty.

He was nearing the end of the last length: *thirty-seven... thirty-eight... thirty-nine...* He stretched out his hand, expecting the glass-like smoothness of Italian marble. Instead, something seized his arm and lifted him out of the water. He hung there for a moment, help-lessly, like a fish on a line, his abdomen exposed, his ribcage splayed.

And then the knife plunged into his heart. He felt a searing pain. Then, for the briefest instant, he could see. It was a flash of brilliant white light, somewhere in the distance. Then the hand released him, and back into his silken water he fell. Back into the perpetual darkness.

AFTERWORD

*D*URING THE OCCUPATION OF FRANCE, the forces of Nazi Germany seized hundreds of thousands of paintings, sculptures, tapestries, and other *objets d'art*. Tens of thousands of pieces remain unaccounted for to this day. In 1996, the Swiss federal assembly created the so-called Independent Commission of Experts and ordered it to investigate the actions of Switzerland during the Second World War. In its final report, released in August 2001, the commission acknowledged that Switzerland was a "trade center" for looted art, and that substantial numbers of paintings had entered the country during the war. How many of those works remain hidden in the vaults of Switzerland's banks and in the homes of its citizens no one knows.

ACKNOWLEDGMENTS

*T*HIS IS THE SECOND NOVEL FEATURING THE character Gabriel Allon and, like its predecessor, it could not have been written without the help and support of David Bull. Unlike the fictitious Gabriel, David Bull truly is one of the world's greatest art restorers, and I am privileged to call him a friend. His knowledge of the restoration process, the history of Nazi art-looting, and the pleasures of Venice were both invaluable and inspirational.

I am indebted to Sadie deWall, the assistant principal violist of the Charleston Symphony Orchestra, who introduced me to Tartini's wondrous sonata and helped me better understand the soul of a truly gifted musician. She answered all my questions, no matter how silly, and gave generously of her time.

Dr. Benjamin Shaffer, one of Washington's top orthopedists, described for me the intricate problem of treating crush injuries to the hand. A special thanks to the Swiss officials who helped demystify the country's police and security services and who, for obvious reasons, cannot be named. Thanks also to the officers of the Central Intelligence Agency who offered me guidance. It goes without saying that the expertise is theirs, the mistakes and dramatic license all mine.

Of the dozens of nonfiction works I consulted while writing this book, several proved invaluable, including Lynn Nicholas's seminal work on Nazi art-looting, *The Rape of Europa*; Hector Feliciano's *The Lost Museum*; and *The Lost Masters* by Peter Harclerode and Brendan Pittaway. Nicholas Faith's telling history of Swiss banking, *Safety in Numbers*, was a valuable resource. Jean Ziegler's courageous work, *The Swiss, the Gold, and the Dead*, inspired me.

The staffs of the Dolder Grand Hotel in Zürich and the Luna Hotel Baglioni in Venice made our research trips seem more like pleasure and less like work. My dear friend Louis Toscano twice read my manuscript, and it was made better by his sure hand. Greg Craig gave me the shirt off his back, literally. The friendship and support of my literary agent, Esther Newberg of International Creative Management, never meant more to me than during the writing of this book.

All writers should be so lucky as to have editors like Neil Nyren and Stacy Creamer. They gave me brilliant notes and strong shoulders to lean on. Indeed, sometimes it seemed they understood the characters and the story better than I did. A very heartfelt thanks to Stuart Calderwood, whose meticulous copyediting saved me much embarrassment.

Finally, I wish to express my profound gratitude to Phyllis Grann. There is, quite simply, none better.